A Glance at My Other

A Glance at My Other

Bruce Randal Wilkerson

Winchester, UK
Washington, USA

First published by Roundfire Books, 2017
Roundfire Books is an imprint of John Hunt Publishing Ltd., Laurel House, Station Approach, Alresford, Hants, SO24 9JH, UK
office1@jhpbooks.net
www.johnhuntpublishing.com
www.roundfire-books.com

For distributor details and how to order please visit the 'Ordering' section on our website.

ISBN: 978 1 78535 416 8
978 1 78535 417 5 (ebook)
Library of Congress Control Number: 2016951867

A CIP catalogue record for this book is available from the British Library.

Design: Stuart Davies
Cover Image: Bruce Randal Wilkerson

Printed and bound by CPI Group (UK) Ltd, Croydon, CR0 4YY, UK

Prologue

> *Autrui est secret parce qu'il est autre.* "Others are secret because they are other."
>
> —Jacques Derrida

I was getting used to being ignored. Even the waiters refused to speak to me after they heard my poor French. A group of students were laughing at the other side of the café and the two girls having coffee pretended I didn't exist. A lot of good it did me to hang around the Latin Quarter! Lying bored on the couch back home in the States would have been just as cheerful.

With an hour commute still ahead, I motioned the waiter over to pay the exorbitant three euros for an espresso. Most of the other American students lived with a family in Paris whereas I had drawn Bagnolet, a suburb with a reputation for being artistic, but which was in reality as sleazy as the family that put me up. Dinner was at eight and the mother did what she was paid for, a few minutes of morose conversation, while the twenty-one-year-old son scowled.

The waiter looked at me with a raised eyebrow, counted the change and grumbled an "au revoir" as I trudged out into the drizzly Paris weather. Boulevard Saint-Germain was one big traffic jam, with streams of people pushing their way down the sidewalks. Then, while I stood at a stoplight, two girls looked in my direction and giggled. Even if I was an ugly American, I didn't like being the butt of a joke so I quickly crossed the street toward the metro entrance between the stopped cars.

Buzzing and yelling made me look up—a motor scooter had almost run into me—what was he doing speeding around like that? Did he have a death wish? The kid began yelling and making hand signs which were easy to interpret so I turned my back and hurried away.

I was soon hidden in the mob of commuters rushing through the metro's tunnels and onto the jam-packed commuter-train cars. The blank faces were so depressing that I stared at the grimy windows, at the reflections flickering against the sooty walls speeding by outside, at the ghost of my bulky frame fluttering insubstantially behind the head of a young businessman. Why had I been born a fat klutz? The two workouts a week at the pool hadn't made me lose an ounce and coming to France wasn't going to help. I grabbed a seat next to an African lady and took out some required reading.

The apartment was a five-minute walk from the metro station, past greasy-spoon Arab sandwich shops and honking cars, after which I had to step around a homeless guy that slept in our entranceway before I climbed the two flights of creaky stairs. This wasn't at all what I had bargained for, so I began humming "My Way" and hoped that I could hold out for the last two months until Christmas and my return to the States.

My voice cracked—I wasn't Big Blue Eyes—in fact, it was generally wise for me to shut up and play the piano. Not that playing piano ever did me any good! It just classified me as someone popular kids avoided. Maybe if I had played death rock or hip-hop, I could have changed my reputation, but I refused to give up Vivaldi and Broadway just to fit in.

I was a loser and had to get used it. The last girl to have kissed me was my mother, whereas my grandmother just pinched my cheek. I couldn't even call myself a nerd because I didn't have the straight As to justify such a pretension. Out of spite, I blared one last "my way" before I opened the heavy green door to the apartment.

The son slammed his way out of his room with his hand down his pants while he sputtered and snorted like a puffed-up rooster chanting rap. I called him Human Beatbox because he always seemed to be making guttural hip-hop mouth noises.

"Eh, espèce de nul," he barked from his chest while his stare

dared me to move. *"Tu peux pas la fermer?"*[1]

I hadn't understood a word so I stared back and replied, "Is your mother here?" Maybe she could calm her pit bull of a son.

The wiry boy moved up closer to me with his chest stuck out. "Non, she no here," he answered with a glare and pushed me back. *"Maintenant casse-toi."*[2]

His gist was clear even if his French was lost on me and I cursed myself for being a wimp as the door slammed in my face. He had never been polite, but this was the first time he had been aggressive. The Institute for American Students would hear about this, I vowed, and threw my bag next to the door after having taken out a textbook. As a history major, I always had required reading—"History lines every street in France," my teacher had said as encouragement before I came to this decrepit country—he didn't mention that I'd be spending my time alone in cafés after being thrown out of my living space.

I sullenly made my way down the old stairway, stepped around the homeless guy and walked back out onto the drizzly street. Seeing as the mother wanted my money, she would talk some sense into her hooligan son when she got off of work. Until then, other than getting into a fight, my only option was to head back to another café.

Most of the people I passed on the main street were of North African origin and I had to wonder where the cliché of the Frenchman with his accordion ever came from. At the third intersection, I turned north toward the Canal de l'Ourque and a small bistro that looked out over the water. This wasn't the first time I had been there to get away from the family.

The grubby old waiter nodded his head and came over as soon as I had taken a table by the window. "So Monsieur Josh Cohn, you make *progrès.*" I don't know how he had learned my name, but he greeted me with it every time I came.

"Pas assez progrès (Not enough progress)," I stammered in my pidgin French.

He gave a big laugh and trumpeted, *"Un panaché, comme d'habitude?* (beer with soda as usual?)."

I stammered, *"Oui, merci,"* choking on the French *R* and sounding like a strangled cat.

The waiter went to clear a table near the door with a chuckle and my eyes turned toward the girl in the opposite corner. I had already noticed her in here once before—or rather I hadn't been able to ignore her—as she looked like an Arabian princess with a delicate oval face and long wavy black hair. Her dark eyes turned toward me; there was a hypnotic intensity in them . . . and I was staring like some sort of lecher. I looked down at my history book embarrassed at how rude I had been.

I could feel the girl was observing me while I stared at the pictures of French revolutionaries and hoped she wasn't irritated that I had been ogling her. After what seemed like an eternity, and before I got a cramp in my neck, I found the courage to glance up. Her eyes met mine and a tentative smile began spreading across her red lips only to falter while her brow wrinkled in sorrow. She looked away before I did.

The image wrenched my heart and I had to wonder how such a beautiful girl could be so unhappy. I peeked over my textbook to see her talking to the waiter, who looked at me, said something to the girl and then headed to my table. She had taken out her smartphone and was texting.

"Vous avez fait une touche,"[3] the waiter said, with a wink.

I wasn't sure what he said, or why he was winking, so after a second of stuttering I pulled out a five-euro bill to pay and hope he hadn't noticed how clueless I was. He handed me the change without saying another word and shuffled back to the bar.

A chilly wind blew across the room and a handsome man in his thirties stepped in through the door. He stood for a second near the entrance as if he expected everyone to look at him and then went to sit down next to the girl who was drying her eyes. I might have thought he was her boyfriend if a frown hadn't tightened her lips.

He gave a chuckle, seemingly enjoying her discomfort, and reached out to touch her hand before she jerked it back.

They spoke for a few minutes, the girl glowering and the man smiling, until she glanced at her phone, looked around, and tied a pink scarf over her long hair. The man then began joking with the owner while she hurried out of the bistro with her book bag. I watched her jogging away through the window and had this fantasy that she might sit down at my table one day. Was it wrong to dream of getting to know her?

I sat there lamely staring at the textbook for a few more minutes but I just couldn't get interested in the French Revolution with its Reign of Terror because my mind kept wandering back to the girl. I finally decided a stroll along the dark canal would be better than sitting here dreaming of things that could never be or trying to appear intelligent.

I stood up and said *"au revoir"* to the waiter, choking again on the French *R*, to which he nodded goodbye with his crooked smile. A white van rumbled past me as I walked out the door, slowed down, then sped away down the small street that ran along the canal with an angry roar of the engine. It seemed I didn't even have to open my mouth for people to know I didn't belong here. My parents back in the States would probably be preparing lunch and my little brother would be at school. The drizzle had stopped but the air smelled of mold. I sat down on a wet bench and stared at the black water while the cold seeped up around my butt.

Concentrating on my breathing, I tried to calm my nerves and appreciate the view. The street lamps, which flickered off the surface of the canal like ghosts in the wan evening light, gave the scene a romantic beauty with the footbridge, the flow of water, the somber pink cloth drifting in the current like . . . I had to look again—a person face down in the water!

I began yelling, "Help, call rescue," until I realized that nobody was around to hear me and my thoughts got so tangled looking for a solution that I simply jumped into the water. The cold was suffocating. My lungs exploded. My head came up and I did a breaststroke. If I didn't get out of the cold soon, I'd end up drowning as well.

The pink spot was just off to my left so, without putting my head back under water, I sprinted toward it. I was about to stop and get my bearings when my hand hit what must have been the person's foot. I grabbed it, tugged, and began doing a sidestroke toward the shore. It was a lot more difficult pulling the body through the water than I had imagined, like dragging a sack of cement, and my muscles were burning when I reached the bank.

I let out a sigh of relief and started hauling the body toward me only to realize that the stones were too slippery and steep to get out. I gave a few sputtering yells before I grabbed the girl—it was clearly a girl—around the chest and continued swimming downstream.

It seemed like forever before my hand hit a ladder. I locked my legs around it and began lifting her until I saw her face—it was the girl from the café!—and paused a second embarrassed about having my arms around her breasts. Then the thought that she might be dead gave me a shot of adrenaline and I continued pulling.

I was thankful she was so thin as I hoisted her out, backward, one rung at a time, all the while hollering until she was on dry ground. Then I heard somebody running up behind me. "Call an ambulance," I shouted, while I turned her head to the side to let the water drain out, pinched her nose, opened her jaw and—*thud*.

Sickening pain clenched my gut. I was face down in a puddle, wasn't I? . . . *thud*.

Blackness turned to light that sucked me up through the wind while I let myself float in the ebb. Why had I been worried? Warmth caressed my back and fog swirled around me before a hand seized my foot. Although I could have resisted, a lack of energy numbed my will as the hand began dragging me through the current just like I had done with the girl, pulling, until the scene came into focus: my body lying in a puddle of blood with its head caved in. I considered being frightened but a beam of light, the girl from the café, streamed in front of the vision. She was more beautiful than ever although the only thing I could focus on was the sorrow in the intensity of her eyes. The girl said something but no sound could be heard.

A spiral of wind then opened and would have carried me away if the girl hadn't held my hand firmly. She was shaking and pointing to the other spiral, the one going into her prone body, next to which a man in a gray hooded sweatshirt was stooping. Suddenly he stood up and fled.

I looked back at the girl whose face was screwed up in misery. I wanted to comfort her, to hold her and tell her it would be all right, but her other hand seized my arm.

"*Je suis désolée* (I'm sorry)," she mouthed, gripping me tightly.

I didn't have time to ask what she meant because, with a flick of her wrist, she whisked me like a blowball into the descending spiral.

* * *

1 "Hey loser, why don't you shut up?"

2 "Now, get lost."

3 "You've made a score."

Part 1

La pire souffrance est dans la solitude qui l'accompagne. "The worst agony is the solitude that accompanies it."

—André Malraux

Chapter 1

I was choking, coughing, heaving for air, and my eyes opened to a man bent over me. I wanted to say something but retched. No time to roll over, it covered my face and stomach. I felt it in my hair too, plastered to my face. That wasn't normal. The man held me while my abdomen contracted again. When I tried again to say something, I couldn't make a sound.

The man said in French—I was surprised that I understood—*"Don't tire yourself, honey, you've made it. The ambulance is coming."*[1]

Why did he say *"ma petite"*? I wasn't a girl! His eyes were soft albeit pained and there was a sweatband around his balding head. I tried to ask questions but the sounds weren't correct.

"Rest," [2] was all he replied.

A bustle of people and blinking blue lights then forced the man with the sweatband to move away and I was left staring at a young woman with a blue cap. While somebody put a mask over my face, raindrops tickled my forehead making me blink. I shut my eyes and hot pads were laid on my chest.

A male voice sighed, *"This man's dead."* [3]

I had this impression they were talking about me, yet I was lying here smelling of vomit, and when I tried to ask questions, they were all too preoccupied with loading me on to a gurney and rolling me off toward the flashing lights. This was a mistake; it was the girl who needed to be saved. I tried to speak again but only high-pitched mumbles escaped the mask—and I was crying—I hadn't done that since I was a baby.

I willed myself to imagine that no one could be dead while a tinfoil cover was wrapped around me and I felt the gurney being lifted and loaded into an ambulance. I had to wonder whether this was a nightmare as the siren sounded and I looked up into the eyes of the girl in the blue cap.

"What's your name?"[4] she asked.

I understood the French, she wanted to know my name, but such a simple question appeared very complex—especially since I knew I shouldn't understand French. "Jœsh," I slurred through the mask.

"Repeat that, honey. Your name is Jœsh? Is that your first or family name?" [5]

She was looking at me strangely. Why was I unable to pronounce my name correctly and why did it sound like I had a French accent? I tried to ask, "What happened," and made some slurred sounds while she went about wiping the vomit off my face.

"Don't tire yourself, you'll be alright,"[6] she said, just before the ambulance came to a halt. In a matter of seconds, I was rolled out of the back and through glass doors into a hall with people standing around. I wished they wouldn't stare. An intern then appeared with a flashlight in front of my eyes, disappeared, and I was rolled into a cubicle with white walls smelling of bleach. I turned my head to look at the different valves and bandages while more people appeared beside me to take my vital signs and stare at my face.

A nurse's face appeared in my line of vision. *"We need to get you cleaned up and changed or you'll catch cold. But first, we're going to put a few stitches in that cut on your arm."* She touched my face in several painful places. *"Somebody really worked you over,"*[7] she commented, before putting a cold liquid on my arm.

It was clear that I'd been hurt, I felt the pain, yet that wasn't possible. I was on the verge of panicking so I stared at the ceiling and its awful whiteness while the nurse continued to rub the painful place on my arm. The intern then came back, looked at me, said a few words before—the needle went in and I heard myself scream, shrill, foreign. Words were said again and when strong hands clamped my arm down, I opened my eyes to see it was the nurse. How could she be so much stronger than me?

Something commanding was said, letting me guess what was about to happen, so I clenched my teeth as the needle went in again, and again.

The nurse stoked my forehead. *"You were wonderful. Now, we're going to see if you can stand."*[8] She put her hand under my shoulder and I wanted to oblige so I sat up but I felt so light and supple that I hesitated. The nurse held my arm firmly, very firmly for a woman, and made more encouraging sounds.

I put my feet on the floor while the nurse held my shoulders—and I had to look up at her! The nurse was smiling reassuringly but I began to tremble, my legs to shake, and the nurse held me as if I weighed nothing.

"We'll have you sit,"[9] she stated.

My eyes stayed clenched shut while she coaxed me to into a wheelchair.

"The doctor said you can shower and change. It will make you feel better."[10]

I didn't want to understand. I wasn't French. The wheelchair moved while she continued speaking but I forced myself to not listen. The wheelchair stopped and my eyes opened to a tiled room with a shower pummel on the back wall.

"Here, I'll help you,"[11] the nurse said, while she grabbed my wet shirt and pulled it over my head. Even if it was embarrassing to be undressed by a woman, why couldn't I stop trembling?

"Are you cold?"[12] she asked, and threw a shirt that wasn't mine on the ground.

I shook my head, not at her question, but at everything happening. She then touched an elastic around my chest, removed a bra—and I jumped up to look in the mirror over the sink.

"Hey, easy!"[13] she shouted.

I paid no attention. My eyes were on the face of the girl in the café, the girl that I should have saved. I had only wished to speak to her, or maybe—but not this! This was worse than rape. My knees buckled.

The nurse bent down beside me. *"Everything will be fine,"* she kept repeating. *"Here, why don't you get under the shower?"*[14]

I had no fight left. The nurse finished undressing me, guided me to the water and held the pummel while water ran between the breasts and thighs that weren't mine. To my chagrin, the nurse said, *"Look how pretty you are."*[15]

She wasn't talking to me, I knew she couldn't have been talking about me, so my eyes closed tightly. I could feel the girl's thin arms around my chest, touching my back and squeezing those soft bulges on my . . . no, on her chest.

The nurse made a sound and I opened my eyes to see her handing me a bottle of liquid soap, but then a slender-fingered hand reached out to take it. Although I felt the bottle's weight, those fingers weren't mine. I, Josh, had thick fingers with hair on them. Was I a ghost? Was the girl's ghost watching and judging me while I invaded everything that should have remained private?

"Allez-y (Go ahead)," the nurse said encouragingly, while she mimed rubbing the soap on her body.

It took all of my will-power to rub my hands over the girl's skin which was soft, sensitive and immoral to touch. The nurse then squirted some soap into that long hair falling round those thin shoulders and helped me rub it in. The girl's hair was so long it fell down to the middle of her back.

"You have magnificent hair,"[16] the nurse cooed.

I wished I could have reacted and denied that it was mine, but a lethargic numbness was settling in. I was handed a sheet that I stared at dumbly until the nurse told me to use it as a towel. It felt rough against my skin. No, this wasn't my skin, it was hers, so I began to rub harder hoping I could strip it off.

"Not so hard, dear,"[17] the nurse said, and put her hand over mine.

I stopped for a second to stare into the nurse's blue eyes. They were beautiful, just the sort that I should have liked, and I was standing there nude in front of her. Why did she leave me indifferent? I pulled the sheet around myself afraid that I might become aroused.

"Here, put on this instead," the nurse chuckled and held out a hospital gown. I took it but waited for her to turn her back before I slipped it on. When she turned to look at me, there was an amused twist to her lip. *"Put your hair up on your head, it will be easier,"*[18] she suggested.

I stared at her blankly wondering how to go about that. She shook her head, made me sit back down in the wheelchair and her hands began to stroke the long mass of hair that was tickling my shoulders and falling across my eyes. In a few twists, she had it on top of my head. *"Voilà* (There you go)," she said, with a smile.

"Merci," I uttered, as she opened the door.

The nurse's eyes lit up at the sound of my voice and she patted my cheek. *"Let's go see the doctor,"*[19] she replied. It then dawned on me that I had pronounced the French *R* perfectly.

* * *

The nurse left me on a paper-covered bed and my eyes stayed riveted to the ceiling because at every breath I felt the girl's breasts tickle against the loose hospital gown. If they were hers, they were beautiful. She had been magnificent. I couldn't stand the thought that she had died because I hadn't resisted her hand on my arm while she threw me into the spiral.

The curtain was pulled aside and a lean young man with glasses stepped in. He was businesslike, no words, only interested in the file. Then his eyes turned to me, a smile lifted the corners of his mouth, and I couldn't help noticing how sensuous they were. I turned my head away so I didn't have to look at him.

His fingers touched my chin and gently turned my head in his direction. Another finger brushed a painful place on my cheek.

"Would you please open your eyes?"[20]

I stared into his brown eyes but got so embarrassed at the fluttering in my belly that I closed them again.

"Hello, I'm Dr. Lafarge," he said. *"Do you mind if I examine you? And would you please keep your eyes open."*[21]

I opened them again but didn't dare move while he flashed his penlight in my eyes and he had me follow his finger. I felt a tingle at his every touch.

"So what's your name, mademoiselle?" [22]

I heard the words, and then suddenly the meaning was lost. I knew I couldn't speak French—I wasn't her—and I shouldn't be having these emotions that were hers!

"Do you speak French?" [23] he asked, looking me carefully in the eyes.

Although I understood, I willed the words to be foreign. Then, when I started to answer, no words would come to mind, so I shook my head.

"Do you speak English?" he asked.

Of course I spoke English, I began to answer, but stuttered. I no longer knew what to say or how to say it. My head shook. "I don't know," I finally stammered, with a French accent.

"Is your name, Jœsh?" the doctor asked. His English accent was much better than mine. Then he repeated in French, *"Est-ce que tu t'appelles Jœsh?"* [24]

I was too confused to utter anything coherent, or think of a logical answer, because even though he thought that I was a young girl, he would see through this sham in no time. Embarrassed, I looked down at my hands—no, her hands, and saw the shine of nail polish. "I don't know . . . I'm not . . ." I squeaked, with a shake of my head.

"Can you remember your name?" he asked. *"Vous vous rappelez votre nom?"* he repeated in French.

I didn't dare answer. "I don't know," I repeated for safety.

"Who beat you? Who cut your arm?" he asked, and again translated into French, *"Qui vous a battue? Qui vous a entaillé le bras?"*

So the girl had been beaten before she fell into the canal. I touched a sore spot on my face. *"Je ne me rappelle pas* (I don't remember)," my mouth said, although it was a lie. I then realized that I had spoken French but couldn't fathom how the French sentence came to me. I didn't know why I was crying either, I never cried, and I felt all the more embarrassed because I couldn't stop.

"Were you abused sexually? *Avez-vous été victime d'un abus sexuel?"*

I looked at him open-mouthed. How could I have been? Then I remembered the girl—they thought I was the girl—my face turned red and I shook my head not wanting an answer.

"And you don't know how you fell into the water?" he said, more as a statement than a question. "Do you understand English or French better? *Vous comprenez mieux l'anglais ou le français?"*

"English," the girl's mouth answered—or was that me, Josh, speaking?

"Curieux (Intriguing)," he said to himself. He turned back to me. "We are going to keep you here under observation." A smile broke back through his professional attitude—I wasn't used to people smiling at me, especially not a tender smile which made my breath catch in my throat and which made me . . . her, blush. I turned my head away. I didn't want to look at the doctor ever again. I wasn't like that.

His hand touched my shoulder. It felt large and powerful. *"Ça va aller, vous allez voir,"* he said and translated, "Everything will be fine."

* * *

About half an hour later a gynecologist came to do some exams.

If I had had any doubts before about my present sex, they were quickly abandoned. When another woman came with a camera and took some pictures, I tried not to think about who I had become.

A man finally arrived with a wheelchair, and although I was sure I could walk, he carefully helped me into it. Did the medical team not want me walking because I had been hit on the head? Had they diagnosed me as crazy? I was still wearing nothing but the hospital gown so I wrapped the sheet they had given me around myself while I was wheeled through the corridors and into the elevator. It felt like everyone was staring at me and I wanted to hide, to be elsewhere. Why hadn't I died?

It was disturbingly quiet on the second floor while the nurse on duty took my file from the man and said something softly. The words slipped past me and I began to ask her to repeat but my mind went blank. She smiled, patted me on the shoulder and pushed me down the hall to the sixth door on the right. After she had switched on the lights, I saw that there was another bed occupied by an elderly black woman lying on her back.

The nurse blocked the wheels before she helped me carefully out of the wheelchair. I was sure I could have done it myself—the girl was quite fit—but no, she was dead. I choked back a sob that the nurse didn't seem to notice while she had me lie down on the bed. It was all business to her and my pulse and blood pressure had to be taken. She then woke the black woman to take her vital signs. The woman sighed, looked at me, shook her head then glanced back at me just before the lights were switched off.

I lay there with my eyes wide open wondering at the rays of light filtering in through the blinds. Where had the girl's soul gone? I had never been one for the metaphysical and was utterly confused as to how I could find myself in this body. Yet the girl hadn't completely disappeared, something of her remained, because she had been the one who had made me feel strange things for the doctor. That wasn't me. Was her ghost watching me right now?

"I'm sorry," I murmured to the dark with a very clear French accent before I hesitated and looked for my words. "I did not want you do this."

I waited a while hoping that some sort of answer would come. Maybe I should try speaking in French because it was absurd for me to speak English when I stumbled over the words. Yet English was my mother tongue, French was hers, and I was still Josh! I refused to let her change who I was, to make me want those unnatural things, to control my action, and yet—

"—I wanted save you," I continued in a whisper. "This is your life. Can't you take back it?"

"And you should get some sleep, miss?" The answer didn't come from anything unearthly, but from the black woman.

Fear suddenly made my chest seize up. If that woman had understood me, she might guess that I was a sham, that I was impersonating a girl. I closed my mouth but the tears couldn't be stopped.

The woman must have heard my crying. "I'm sorry miss, I didn't mean to frighten you," she whispered.

Her accent was African but her English was clearly better than mine. I looked over at her and could see she had turned on her side and was watching me. "No, I'm sorry. I should not be here," I admitted. "I should be dead."

She was observing me through the dark as if she could see my soul. "You mustn't be reproaching yourself with things you can't prevent."

"I'm a . . ." I had to search for the word "a fake" and it came out with an uncontrolled sob.

"No, miss, you are no fake. You are you." Her eyes seemed to glow while she spoke.

"Who are you?" I asked bewildered.

"I'm just an old woman who's had a stroke and who's talking to a pretty young girl."

My chagrin made my tongue slip and I admitted, "What if I am not the young girl you think?"

Her smile glinted in the spots of light that shone up from the street and, for a second, it seemed I was looking at a healthy young girl with beautiful white teeth. "Who you are is in your heart," she said, with her singing African accent, "and I can see you've got a good heart."

"But what if I did something horrible?" I stopped myself before I said more. For some reason I felt like confiding in her.

"We've all made errors. What is to be done about the pain we bring on others?" She looked around while her eyes shone in the half-light and she seemed to see things I had always ignored. "Was the spirit you were just talking to close to your heart?"

What could I answer? "We have . . ." The words didn't come to me immediately and just before I was about to give up, they popped into my mind. "We have become close," I mumbled.

"The spirit's not angry so you should sleep. You are tired and tomorrow, or after, one day you will feel better. On that, you must trust me. Now, this old woman needs her rest too if she is to stay in this world."

I don't know if she saw me smile. "Thank you," I whispered.

1 "Ne vous fatiguez pas, ma petite, vous vous en êtes sortie. Les pompiers, ils arrivent."

2 "Reposez-vous"

3 "Celui-ci est mort."

4 "Tu t'appelles comment?"

5 "Répète ça chérie, tu t'appelles Jœsh? C'est ton nom ou ton prénom?"

6 "Ne vous fatiguez pas, ça va aller,"

7 "Faut qu'on vous nettoie et on vous change ou vous allez attraper la crève. Mais d'abord, on va recoudre cette plaie sur ton bras. Quelqu'un vous a bien arrangée."

8 "Vous étiez formidable. Maintenant, on va voir si vous

pouvez vous lever."

9 "On va vous faire asseoir."

10 "Le médecin a dit que vous pouvez vous doucher et vous changer? Cela vous fera du bien."

11 "Tenez, je vous aide."

12 "Vous avez froid?"

13 "Holà, doucement!"

14 "Allez, ça va aller. Tenez, si vous vous mettiez sous la douche?"

15 "Regardez que vous êtes toute belle."

16 "Vous avez des cheveux magnifiques."

17 "Pas si fort, chérie."

18 "Tenez, mettez plutôt ça. Mettez vos cheveux sur la tête, ce sera plus facile."

19 "Allons voir le médecin."

20 "Voulez-vous ouvrir les yeux, s'il vous plait?"

21 "Bonjour, je suis le docteur Lafarge. Puis-je vous examiner? Et garder vos yeux ouverts, s'il vous plait."

22 "Donc, quel est votre nom, mademoiselle?"

23 "Est-ce que vous parlez français?"

24 "Is your name Jœsh?"

Chapter 2

I was playing the piano in the dark, the first nocturne by Chopin, and my right hand caressed the melody while my left ran through the arpeggios effortlessly. I had never been able to play this well, or with such expression, and as I listened to the notes falling like rain in the evening, I realized that I couldn't see the musical score. I began to wonder how I could play if I didn't have the music in front of me to read and my brain got flustered, my hands fumbled.

Irritated that I had to stop playing, I stood up to turn on the light, but the girl from the café was standing in front of me with her finger in front of her lips shushing me. Did she want me to stop playing the piano or not to speak? Before I had time to ask, she was waving me toward the door.

I expected us to exit onto the residential street in Evanston where I lived, but instead found myself surrounded by Middle-Eastern men who were eying me as if I were a beast to be sold on the market. One of them poked me and when I tried to yell, no sound would come out of my mouth. Then another grabbed hold of me from behind and before I could struggle loose, lights lit in front of my eyes and—

—a nurse was standing over me with a glass of water and a pill for me to take. Next to me, the elderly African lady lay on her back with her mouth open while she made grunting sounds from her throat. I looked at the pill in my hand while the nurse prepared to take my vital signs and wondered what sort of medicine it was.

The nurse crossed her arms over her chest and stared at me until I swallowed it and then proceeded to take my pulse, blood pressure and temperature. Then, while she woke the African lady, a medical aide arrived with a breakfast tray and helped me raise the back of the bed.

The medical aide was quite talkative, and even though I understood her prattle, I didn't say a word or answer any of her questions out of fear that I might slip up. She finally shook her head with a tender smile and closed the door on her way out.

"Good morning," the African lady said to me.

"Good morning," I answered, even if it was the girl's voice that spoke. "You sleep well?" The sounds I made were so high pitched it was embarrassing, but the woman took no notice.

"Yes, thank you," she answered, while she frowned at the breakfast plate. "We don't get proper food here. Everything's so bland."

She glanced in my direction as if I should say something, then began buttering the small bun we had been given. I watched her wondering why she intrigued me—there was something familiar about her even if I couldn't place it. "How learned you . . . ?" I began to ask, but stuttered. "How have you learned English?"

"Many people speak English in Cameroon," she laughed. "Where did you learn English?"

I felt the blood drain from my face and my heart speed up. If I answered truthfully, she would think I was crazy.

"You're right to be careful about what you say to others," she enunciated, looking me straight in the eye.

I nodded at her advice and then turned my head away as soon as I could. "Have you a family?" I asked to be polite and to change the subject.

She smiled when I glanced back at her. "Oh yes. I have four children and ten grandchildren. None of them speak a word of English. They teach it in school here, you see." She gave a chuckle. "They just don't like doing what they're told."

I was about to tell her that I hadn't liked school either because I had been teased and called a fatty, but then I noticed the girl's slim arm holding the butter knife with painted fingernails. It started shaking.

"Things change," I whispered.

"Don't you fret, miss. When I arrived in France all those years ago, I had nothing to my name. My husband and I had just our hands." She could see mine was trembling. "We both worked them raw to have a family. I know my grandkids don't think about this. They think everything comes to them. You be a good person and you'll find happiness."

My head shook because I didn't deserve happiness after having taken the girl's life. I should have been in a grave, not her! And how would I get by with no home or money? Could I contact my family? Would they even take my call?

"You stop worrying about what you can't control," she said, as her eyes turned toward the door. "And you be careful until we meet again. My family is going to send me to a place where they put old folks that they don't know what to do with, *Maison de Retraite Médicalisée Saint Jean* in Pantin. They seem to think that I've lost my wits."

I started to protest and tell her that she seemed as sharp, if not sharper, than most people in their twenties but she shushed me. "Just remember my name, Espérance, and that the name of the retirement home is *Maison de Retraite Médicalisée Saint Jean* in Pantin. Maybe you will want to come see me one day."

Before I could ask her what she meant, there came a knock and a man from the medical staff strode in with a wheelchair. While he blocked the wheels Espérance reclined back in bed and stared at the ceiling. The man took no notice of her and when he came to stand beside me, my hand automatically reached out to take his with a very feminine movement of the wrist. Why had I done that? I pulled it away quickly and wrapped the extra blanket around myself before I got up on my own to sit in the chair.

He wheeled me to the MRI section where I was stuck in a sort of submarine for twenty minutes. The noises made me jump and it took all my willpower to not scramble my way back out. I was shaking like a leaf when they put me in the public area for another half hour with people gazing in my direction.

There was a young man with black hair waiting on the other side of the room who kept looking over at me. It struck me that he was quite handsome and again my hand moved without my thinking to brush back my hair while he smiled at me. When I realized what I'd done, I turned my head quickly away. Was it the boy or the fact that I had to go to the toilet that made my thighs contract?

The hospital aide finally came back to take me upstairs and I got the courage to peek over at the boy who gave me a last smile that made my stomach flutter. Was the girl going to control my feelings, too? I shut my eyes tightly until we reached my room where I insisted on getting out of the wheelchair without the aide touching my hand or shoulder.

I sat on the bed to gaze at the white and sterile walls. Espérance had left while I was downstairs and, alone in the room, the minutes ticked by slowly. I finally stood back up on my own, feeling strangely slender and subtle rather than heavy and lumbering like I had always been. The girl's body moved gracefully as if it had its own memory and when I didn't concentrate, she would control my gestures. Her hand played with a strand of hair in a way that I had often seen girls do while her legs twisted around each other into the most improbable position.

While I sat there with my legs crossed, I realized it helped me ignore what was becoming urgent. Was it immoral for me to take care of the girl's necessities? I had been afraid to ask the medical aide for fear he would take me to the girls' room but now it was becoming clear that I wouldn't hold out much longer. My lower belly almost burst when I stood up to scurry into the toilet.

The job proved easier than expected and I was feeling much better until my eyes came across the mirror. The girl I had saved was staring at me and, though her dark eyes lacked the same fire, she was so beautifully slender with her milky-brown skin that Josh should have been aroused. Why wasn't I? My head turned away and I hurried out of the bathroom embarrassed that I had ogled at her in the mirror.

A knock came on the door and a woman in her fifties tramped into the room followed by two young men. All three were wearing white coats.

"Bonjour," the lady began. "I'm Dr. Clerc. I've heard you don't understand French well. Is that true?" [1]

The words were clear yet I shook my head in denial. "Not well," I answered in English.

"You speak English more better than French?" she asked, with a heavy accent.

"Yes, it is true," I lied, while she raised an eyebrow.

"Did you understand her name and what she said?" One of the young men asked.

I nodded "yes" knowing I was getting myself into trouble. They turned away from me and spoke together in low tones as if I weren't there. When they turned back, they wore expressions as if they were addressing a child.

"You had a very traumatic experience yesterday," the man began. He looked me in the eye for a response so I nodded that I had understood. "We have not found any injuries to your brain, however." I tried to smile because he had meant that to reassure me. "Do you remember your name today?" he asked.

I knew he was asking for the girl's name, which I still didn't know, so I just shook my head.

"We know your name is Neïla Saadallah. Your family lives in Bagnolet."

He raised an eyebrow as if I should say something, but I rather felt like screaming that my family lived in the USA—that my name was Josh, not Neïla!—but my head began turning while things went blurry. Then, when hands were holding me and easing me back into bed, I realized I had been hyperventilating like a wimp. The little black dots in front of my vision slowly cleared away and the doctor's face came back into focus.

"Neïla, we want you to rest. We're keeping you under observation.

Your family will come to visit." The young doctor hesitated and looked at the older woman. She nodded. *"You should know, however, that they do not speak English."*[2]

"What do you tell them?" I asked in English, before it dawned on me that he had just spoken French.

He turned and spoke to the older doctor. She said something quietly and he turned back to me. "What would you have us say to them?"

"What word have you put on my . . ." I couldn't find the English pronunciation for diagnosis ". . . on my *diagnostic*?"

"We say you have amnesia accompanied by a peculiar form of aphasia," he answered, after some hesitation.

I almost contradicted him—I remembered everything!—but when I looked back at their serious faces, I closed my mouth. What could I say to convince them otherwise? "Know they this?" I whispered in a fluty voice.

"Yes, we have told them that you don't remember your name." He then seemed to feel the need to justify himself. "You understand that you are a minor?"

I shook my head. "How old have . . . am I?"

"Sixteen. It's your mother who is your legal guardian."

"When must I see them?" I asked fearfully. I couldn't imagine facing the mother of the person I had just let die.

"They have been waiting here since this morning," he answered. "We will speak to them for a few minutes and then send them in."

I laid my head back wishing there was a way to escape the confrontation because I could never tell Neïla's mother that I wasn't her daughter. Would she even believe me? The doctors were probably about to send me off to the funny farm already, so imagine if I started telling them the whole story!

There was a knock on the door and a woman in her early fifties, wearing long robes and a scarf over her head and hair, came to stand in front of me, look me over with a straight face before she took me in a long embrace. I returned her hug not knowing what else to do. When she let go and backed off I noticed another person, tall and bearded with a long robe, enter the room. His eyes seemed to move continuously. *"My sister, how are you?"*[3] He asked in barking French and tight lips, after he had squared himself in front of the door.

How am I? I shook my head not knowing what to answer while the mother pushed back Neïla's uncombed hair from in front of my eyes.

"Is it true that you don't speak French any longer?" [4] He asked as though he were spitting.

I didn't want to answer so I stared at Neïla's slim stockinged feet.

"You speak English little, doctor say." His voice lacked intonation and it scared me. "No remember, he say."

It felt like a trap; if I admitted to speaking English, he might guess that I wasn't his sister Neïla, but if I spoke French, he might trick me into admitting the truth. Suddenly Neïla's mother felt like a safety net and I held on to her. *"Look, you've made her cry,"* [5] the mother said flatly.

His eyes went up and down Neïla's body. *"The young doctor saw her like that?"* [6] He pointed at me and I knew I had done something wrong. "Not decent!" he barked at me.

Although I had understood his words, I stared at him and shrugged because I hadn't caught his gist.

His scowl screwed up into an angry mask while his finger did circles in my direction. "You must dress decent. Not like bitch."

I wanted to respond and show him my mettle—I hadn't chosen to be in this body, let alone this hospital gown—but then his elusive eyes met mine and they were squinting as if he might strike out. He was dangerous. I looked back down at the floor.

His form came and stood over me, but I dared not lift my eyes. "You my sister. You obey."

The mother began running her fingers through Neïla's long

mane of hair, it was long and full of knots, while I tried to hold back tears that I should not normally have shed. What options did I have? I was now a minor with no place to go and I doubted the authorities would help me if I decided not to follow his orders. They would just say I was nuts and send me to a funny farm.

"I'll go get Hadja," [7] he hissed triumphantly before striding out the door.

"Pourquoi? (Why?)," I asked Neïla's mother in French before I realized what I was saying.

She raised an eyebrow and stared at me for a long moment. *"The doctor's a man,"* [8] she finally answered with a snort.

"So am I," I wanted to scream but held myself back. Was this what it was to be a girl? Could I not even be seen by a doctor? Mother sighed, and holding my head, looked me in the eyes. *"You're a Muslim, a Muslim."* [9]

I stopped myself from telling her I didn't believe in God and that my father was the sort of Jew that ate pizza on Passover. As for my mother's grandparents, I had never cared enough to ask which confession of Protestant they were supposed to be. Most of what I knew about religion came from vampire movies.

"You must cover your head and breasts." She showed me her head scarf. *"You must wear the hijab."* [10]

I would have to wear a hijab, an Islamic scarf? Maybe my lack of faith should have been shaken by the fact that I had died and come back in another body, but I still was outraged.

"Calm down. We've already had that discussion." She patted my hand. *"It's for your own good."* [11]

I wished I could argue with her and tell her what I thought about the enslavement of women—they had as many rights as the men, especially since I was the one being ordered to cover myself in a curtain!—but the situation was too perilous for me to speak out. Instead, I turned my back on her.

"Hadja is coming with your things," she said, as if nothing were

wrong. *"I only want what's good for you."* [12]

I sat there sulking, feeling more and more like an ass. What right did I have to step into her daughter's body and cause her this pain? Tears were rolling down Neïla's cheeks—my cheeks—and I realized I had to do my best to make this woman happy since I had stolen her daughter's life. Her hand touched my shoulder and I turned around and nodded.

Mother's lips pulled back into a tight smile just before the door opened and a young woman who was clearly related to Neïla trooped in wearing the hijab and a harassed expression. She dropped the bag she was carrying, rushed over to hug me tightly and then took my face in her hands to inspect me thoroughly.

"You were really worked over," [13] she said clicking her tongue. "True, you no speak French?" Her face screwed up and something told me I shouldn't answer so I looked away.

"The Jew *Américain,*" she said, with a snarl, "he do something to you?" I could see with my peripheral vision that her eyes were probing me for an answer. Everything was going to hell and I was sure this woman was about to see through my disguise. *"Come on, Neïla, stop it. I was joking,"* [14] she laughed sharply.

I still had the feeling that the hatred in her voice was genuine, so I couldn't control my trembling while she sat beside me.

"Do you want me to comb your hair?" [15] The woman mimicked combing her hair. "Hair, horrible," she laughed, and began petting me as you would a feral animal.

I didn't respond so the woman took out a comb and started tugging at that huge mass of hair. Josh had never really needed to do much with his thinning hair, but Neïla's was long, thick and so terribly tangled that it was going to take quite a bit of effort to bring back under control. The woman took her time, chuckling "pardon" each time she pulled too hard and I winced. After a nearly twenty minutes of this torture, she smoothed it out along my back and twisted it into a bun. *"Isn't she pretty?"* [16] she cooed.

The word "pretty" rang strangely.

"You need to be dressed too," [17] Mother added, although her eyes didn't move or give me a hint as to what to do next. Luckily the young woman tut-tutted and began helping me out of the hospital gown while I sat there like a zombie. She then stood back for a second to look at Neïla's nude body. I felt horribly exposed and my arms lifted to cover Neïla's breasts.

"Go ahead, put on your bra," the woman said, holding out a brassiere. I took it mechanically but was at a loss as to how to put it on. *"You don't even know how to get dressed any longer?"* she chided. *"Here, put it on like this,"* [18] she sighed before helping me place it in front while I squirmed at this stranger touching Neïla's body and brassiere.

When the cups were in place, the woman stepped back and indicated that I should clip it in the back myself. I had never been able to touch my toes, let alone scratch the middle of my back, so the feat seemed impossible. They both sat looking at me stoically while I held the cups in place, trembling, until I realized there was no way out of it. Slowly I reached my arms around to my back with surprising ease, found the little clip and attached it.

"You see you can do it," [19] the woman commented with an ironic laugh.

I knew Neïla was blushing with shame so I refused any further help with the panties, blouse or trousers and turned my back on them while they continued chatting. I didn't want to listen, or have them staring at my back.

There came a knock on the door and a nurse walked into the room, put a band around my arm to take my pulse and blood pressure—it was 10 over 6—before she turned to whisper something to Mother who in turn whispered in the woman's ear. The woman pulled back and humphed, but Mother's stare didn't budge. After a few seconds of this standoff, the woman took a scarf and headband out of the bag, handed them to me and grunted that I should put them on. I simply stared at her.

"You dress yourself but you refuse to put on your hijab, is that it?"[20] she barked.

I didn't want to wear it but did I have a say in the matter? Might this woman become violent if I refused? I turned the headband over a few times wondering how it went on.

"Give me a break!" [21] she huffed and pulled it out of my hands. In a few twists the headband was around my forehead and the scarf over my hair. I felt confined, lost and anonymous.

There was a knock on the door. The young woman stomped over to open it and then out between two men who were waiting in the hall, while Mother seemed completely disinterested. The first man was in his thirties, the other looked to be fifty, but I could tell from the cynical look in their eyes that they were policemen.

"You don't speak French, is that it?" [22] The younger policeman asked me straight out, with a scowl.

I felt Neïla's mother watching me and could hear her breathing. The hiss under her breath gave me the feeling that I had to be careful so I replied with an accent that was heavier than I liked, "I prefer English." I just hoped that they didn't speak it too well and that Mother didn't speak it at all.

The older policeman simply nodded while the younger one huffed, "We must to know what remember you from yesterday."

His English was rather poor, even Neïla could hear that, but it was a dangerous question. Should I tell him what Neïla would have remembered or what Josh remembered?

"Why?" I asked timidly, after a long pause.

"Do you"—his accent was really horrible—"did you wish to suicide?"

"Suicide?" Was it possible that Neïla had wanted to die when she threw me into this body? "I don't know," I replied with a shake of the head.

He looked at some notes and then back at me. "We must know; did you try to suicide you?"

"I don't know what happened," I whispered.

"Was there other person present?" His English was so bad I lost my embarrassment at how poor Neïla's was. "You remember other person?" he repeated.

"A man saved me," I said, after I found my words. "I remember him." The policeman nodded but lifted an eyebrow. He turned and spoke in a hushed voice to his colleague for a minute.

"What you remember of the man?" The younger policeman asked, with a knotted forehead.

"He saved me from the water, did he not?" That seemed safe enough for me to say.

"Yes, that is correct." The policeman's voice went up a tone on the last syllable, as if he expected me to continue.

"What happened to him?" I asked, even though I knew the answer.

"He is died," the younger policeman answered perfunctorily, and I could see he was observing my reactions carefully.

"When will he be . . . ?" I couldn't remember the word *buried* but it seemed like Neïla should pay Josh her respects. "Will it be possible that I go to the memorial service?"

"I don't know," he mumbled and stared me in the eyes. "You know how he is died?" The policeman was steering the conversation back to the crime. I shook my head not wanting to go in that direction. "He was murdered." The policeman paused and repeated in French, *"Il a été tué, un meurtre* (He was killed, a murder)."

I tried to show surprise but failed miserably. How could I get out of this?

"You commit suicide or you attacked?" he asked me, after another long pause. *"You were attacked too, weren't you?"* [23]

I sputtered a second then shook my head because I had no idea what had happened to Neïla. Mother then put her hand on my shoulder and although it felt solid and unforgiving, I still gripped it for reassurance.

This time the older one spoke. "We are not sure you tried suicide."

I immediately realized that his English was excellent, much better than Neïla's, which made me start to tremble again.

"Possibly you were attacked by the same person who killed the man," the older policeman said, after he was sure I was listening again. "What do you remember? You must tell us. You maybe are in danger."

My mouth opened and closed a few times. I had seen a man leaning over my body but I had already been killed. "Maybe a man with a gray . . . sweatshirt and a . . ." I made gestures indicating he had a hood over his face. When their eyes squinted, I immediately regretted having spoken.

"Did he look like the robber in Algeria?"

"What robber?" I asked confused.

The policeman shook his head, looked at his colleague, then back at me. "You sure his sweatshirt was gray?"

"I don't know. I am not sure." In death everything changes so who could really say what color it was? "I don't know—" Neïla's voice broke into a sob in spite of my efforts to stay calm.

The face of the older policeman softened. "We want you to be careful," he said. He then motioned Neïla's mother to the corner and spoke in French for a minute. She shook his hand with the tips of her gloved fingers and they nodded "au revoir" to me.

I was then left alone with the woman who thought she was my mother, the woman whose daughter's life I had stolen, but was I crying for her or for the mother who had lost her son?

"Je suis en danger (Am I in danger)?" I asked.

Mother looked at me sharply but didn't answer.

1 "Je suis le docteur Clerc. On m'a dit que vous ne comprenez pas le français, est-ce vrai?"

2 "Neïla, on veut que vous vous reposiez. On va vous garder

en observation. Votre famille viendra vous rendre visite. Cependant vous devez savoir qu'ils ne parlent pas anglais."

3 "Ma sœur, comment vas tu?"

4 "Est-ce que c'est vrai que tu ne sais plus parler français?"

5 "Regarde que tu la fais pleurer."

6 "Le jeune docteur l'a vue comme ça?"

7 "Je vais chercher Hadja."

8 "Le docteur est un homme."

9 "Tu es musulmane, musulmane."

10 "Tu dois couvrir tes cheveux et tes seins. Tu dois porter le hijab."

11 "Calme-toi. Nous avons déjà eu cette discussion. C'est pour ton bien."

12 "Hadja va arriver avec tes affaires. Je ne veux que ton bien."

13 "On t'a salement amochée,"

14 "Va, Neïla. Arrête. Je plaisantais."

15 "Veux-tu que je te coiffe?"

16 "Mais que tu es belle!"

17 "Il faut t'habiller aussi."

18 "Vas y, mets ton soutien-gorge. Tu sais même plus t'habiller? Tiens, mets le comme ça."

19 "Tu vois que tu peux le faire."

20 "Tu t'habilles mais tu refuses de mettre ton hijab, c'est ça?"

21 "C'est pas vrai!"

22 "Vous parlez français, c'est ça?"

23 "Vous avez été attaquée aussi, non?"

Chapter 3

The next day at the hospital dragged on with the monotony of a college lecture. The young woman who had helped me dress was Hadja, Neïla's eldest sister, and she spent her time punching at her smartphone as if I weren't there. Only when I got up to move did her eyes turn toward me. I suppose I wasn't very good company seeing as I had decided not to speak; the doctors said I had aphasia so I made it almost total.

Hadja did ask once what had happened to my smartphone and I shrugged because as far as I knew, it had been lost in the water. What good would it have done me anyway when I knew none of Neïla's friends? Hadja's eyes widened with surprise at my indifference and I could tell that she really thought I was nuts.

When I wanted to take a walk around the ward, I was chaperoned and had to wear the head scarf. I couldn't get used to the stares I got and the people who would look me up and down before averting their eyes. Hadja seemed to take a certain pride in this, whereas I was simply mortified and therefore spent most of my time in the room.

Mother relieved Hadja in the afternoon and she was patient enough to show me how to help her with her sewing. I quickly realized that Neïla wasn't new to it because her fingers proved to be quite adept even if Mother stopped me from time to time to point out that something was wrong.

What other memories had Neïla's body retained? It was upsetting to have her inside me ready to take control of my movements as if she weren't completely dead, as if she might return soon to take back her life. The thought both frightened and gave me resolve; I had to keep her body alive and in good health.

Neïla's mother was asked to leave in the early evening and after she had kissed me on either cheek, a medical aide set the dinner tray in front of me. Even though Josh would have gobbled the food up, the sparse hospital meal turned my stomach. Was it the stress that made me lose my appetite? I forced myself to eat the yogurt for fear that Neïla would fall ill.

I had no television or reading although one of the nurses had been kind enough to bring me a few magazines through which I thumbed. The troubles of starlets and princesses depressed me even more, so I took off the Muslim attire and sat at the side of the bed. A lady came to pick up the tray and tut-tutted at how little I ate. When I tried to smile and answer her, I got confused as to which language to speak, so I turned my head away. If I ever went back home, would they say my French accent was cute? That would make me feel even worse.

The hospital vents whirred while I lay back on the stiff sheet stretched over the plastic mattress. Neïla had too much energy for me to stay confined here all the time in this tiny room. I strayed to the window, and then to the bathroom, trying to ignore the mirror but Neïla's face caught my attention; she was so lovely with her hair pulled up into a loose bun while a few locks lay in a halo around her oval cheeks that I almost cried. The ugly bruise on her light-brown skin below the right cheekbone made her look so martyred and innocent that I turned my head away embarrassed at having observed her.

This whole situation seemed more and more absurd and cruel. Why should I be here while she was in that deathly void? I had only wanted to speak to her, not be her! Anger at what had been done to Neïla boiled up from my gut and I felt like shouting or screaming while the walls seemed to push in around me. What right did they have to force Neïla to wear a headscarf? I slipped on her pink sneakers and went to the door. At least I could try to gain her a little freedom.

I glanced down the hall, and since nobody was about, started walking toward the elevators. A nurse suddenly stepped out of one of the rooms and did a double take before she smiled.

"On se promène?" she asked. I preferred not to speak so I just nodded. "Going for a walk?" she then translated into English thinking I hadn't understood.

"Yes, can I?" I whispered.

"Yes but . . . ," she hesitated. "No leave floor. You do not must leave *service*." She shook her finger at me so I nodded obediently. "And you must to be back at nine hours for your *médicaments*." She pointed at her watch and repeated, "nine hours."

I should have said "merci" or something similar but the nurse was already headed off to another room. I watched her disappear and turned to go to the elevators. My sneakers were squeaking against the tile floor as I walked, however, another set of footsteps could be heard following. I looked in all directions but there was only the nurse who crossed the hall farther down. I tried to calm my breathing and punched the down button. My heart wouldn't stop pounding so I stood against the wall out of sight. The bell sounded, the door opened and I jumped in as fast as possible. Josh had never been this paranoid.

When the door opened on ground level, I hurried around a corner and waited for a few seconds. Nothing could be heard save the beating of my heart. Had I been imagining that someone was following me? My breathing began to slow to normal so I peeked around the corner. This hospital was huge.

I had no idea where the exit was so I meandered through the halls until I heard the whispering of voices and realized I had come to the main entrance. People were scattered here and there, although most looked like patients, so I walked as nonchalantly as possible past their stares toward the doors without anybody confronting me. I then rushed out into the evening chill.

Patients sat chatting on the front plaza and a gangly man with his intravenous beside him lit a cigarette. A whiff of his smoke blew past my nose, my hands quivered and I realized Neïla wanted a cigarette. Hesitating, I watched the other smokers inhaling the fumes and chided her for having such a nasty habit.

"So, do you want a cigarette?"[1]

I turned around and saw a tall, wiry young Arab man with a large smile behind me. Although I couldn't place it, something about him was familiar. He held out a package of cigarettes, which I almost accepted, but then his smile twitched slightly so I shook my head and forced my hand away. "No, thank you," I replied in English.

"What are you doing in front of the hospital?"[2] the man asked. His smile was too large for comfort and he had used the informal "tu"—I wasn't his friend or a child—but then I remembered that people thought I was Neïla and realized he was making a pass at her.

"I don't speak French," I replied, hoping that would calm his advances.

"You not speak French," he laughed. "Where you from?"

A gut feeling told me I had made an error. Josh was from Evanston, Illinois, but I needed to be careful. "Canada," I lied looking him in the eyes. They were dark just like Neïla's.

"You from Canada?" He broke out laughing and did a Michael Jackson-like spin. "And what's your name, mademoiselle?"

I felt my stomach knot up; he knew something. I looked back at his eyes and mouth, which were similar to Neïla's, and stammered, "no name," before I backed away with my eyes darting around for a way to escape.

"Isn't your name Neïla?" he said, approaching me with his smile. *"Don't you know who I am?"* [3]

Doors clanged shut—I scarcely heard his words—Neïla's family had put out a guard in case I should try to escape. I wanted to call for help, but my mouth flapped without making a sound so I began to walk, then run away.

A powerful hand clamped down on my shoulder and held me in place while another hand took my arm and spun me around. There was no use even trying to break free; I was helpless and weak while his smile beat down on me.

"Who are you?"[4] I screamed in a high-pitched treble.

Heads turned to look at us and he announced with a laugh to the onlookers, *"Don't worry, I'm her brother."* He then held me tighter and looked me in the eyes. *"Je suis ton frère chéri*—your brother—Mokhtar. You not know me?"[5]

I hated understanding his French words, English was my language, and I wanted nothing to do with him. I just wanted to get away. "I don't know you. I never met you!"

He bowed without letting go of my arm. "My name Mokhtar, your most loved brother." He put his other hand on my shoulder as if he were trying to be nice, but his fingers dug into my deltoid muscles. *"You're trembling, are you cold?"* His hand rubbed my arm to warm it. *"You mustn't go out like that."*[6]

"Can I know what's happening?" A large black man wearing a security guard's uniform approached with heavy steps. *"Is he bothering you?"*[7] the guard asked me, without taking his eyes off of Mokhtar.

"I'm her brother,"[8] Mokhtar responded in a light tone and let go of my shoulder.

The guard's dark eyes turned to me. *"Is it true that he's your brother?"*[9]

I wanted to deny it, but the guy just might be telling the truth. *"Je ne sais pas* (I don't know)," I murmured in French, with no accent.

The guard looked at me with a squint and then turned back to Mokhtar who was motioning to him. They spoke in hushed voices for a moment while Mokhtar pointed at a window on the third floor. I looked at my feet and those girly pink sneakers. He was pointing at my window.

The guard indicated for us to go back inside and I followed obediently even though I felt like fleeing. After a minute on the phone, the guard came back to stand beside me. *"The nurse is coming,"*[10] he stated flatly.

I sat down in a chair and turned my head so that I didn't have to look at the man who claimed to be my brother, while all the smokers were all watching me and gossiping. My eyes shut because I couldn't keep back the tears.

"What are you doing here?"[11] I recognized the nurse's irritated voice and opened my eyes to see her worried, compassionate expression. "Why you downstairs? You not have the right to come, I said you." She was shaking her finger at me and I knew I deserved it because I had put her in a bind.

"Don't cry, I'm really your brother,"[12] Mokhtar called, while the nurse led me upstairs. Since yesterday it seemed like I was crying all the time. Everything was out of control. The nurse's arm was around my shoulder and she whispered comforting sounds.

"He's Neïla's brother, not mine,"[13] I heard myself sob.

A pause interrupted the nurse's comforting. *"But you are Neïla,"*[14] she answered.

* * *

My thoughts got so snarled while I lay in bed that I lost all hope of getting to sleep. Dim light filtered through the crack under the door from the hall and I couldn't ignore the whir of the ventilation as hard as I tried. My breathing came heavy and I realized I was a man again, cumbersome with large hands, so I got up from bed telling myself it was a relief to be back to reality.

My feet flattened under my weight against the linoleum-tile floor as I walked to the door of the room. Unfortunately, I was wearing nothing but underwear. What else was there to put on? I would never fit into Neïla's clothes.

I peeked out the door and heard an old woman snoring in one of the other rooms. I was about to close it when I saw her, Neïla, at the opposite end of the hall beckoning toward the elevators. I tried to say something, but the only sound that came from my mouth was the whirring of the ventilation. She pointed to the down button and I pushed it.

The elevator tinged open and she hurried me in. I wanted to point out to her that I wasn't dressed, but she only stared into the emptiness until the elevator door opened and she motioned me down the same hallway I had taken earlier that evening. We were creeping cautiously when suddenly she looked panicked and began running. I tried to follow but Josh, with his awkward bulk, quickly fell behind.

My lungs were gasping for air, I was going to give up and collapse, but then I suddenly felt lighter and faster and sprinted toward the front doors as quick as a cat. It was locked. I tried a second door and it didn't open either. The third door was—

—somebody caught me and held me tightly by the shoulders. Neïla screamed, it was her voice wailing, while powerful hands held me as if I were a child. *"Calm down, mademoiselle,"*[15] the guard moaned—maybe that woke me up—he was so tall and Neïla was so tiny in his big hands that I broke down trembling and crying. He then began to apologize and lifted me into a chair. The night-shift nurse eventually came to fetch me back upstairs and accompany me to my room. When she left, I wanted the lights left on.

1 "Alors, tu veux une cigarette?"
2 "Qu'est-ce que tu fais ici devant l'hôpital?"
3 "Tu t'appelles pas Neïla? Tu sais pas qui je suis?"
4 "Qui es-tu?"
5 "Ne vous inquiétez pas, je suis son frère."
6 "Mais tu trembles, tu as froid? Faut pas que tu sortes comme ça."
7 "Je peux savoir ce qui se passe? Il vous embête?"
8 "Je suis son frère."
9 "Est-ce que c'est vrai qu'il est votre frère?"
10 "L'infirmière arrive."
11 "Mais qu'est-ce que vous faites ici?"
12 "Ne pleure pas, je suis vraiment ton frère."

13 “C’est le frère de Neïla, pas le mien.”

14 “Mais c’est toi Neïla.”

15 “Calmez-vous, mademoiselle.”

Chapter 4

After breakfast, I feigned not understanding when a nurse indicated I should gather my belongings. She simply raised an eyebrow and proceeded to put Neïla's clothes in a bag before she had me follow her out the door.

I was taken up a floor and all the way down to the end of a hall where there was a large double door with a keypad. The nurse punched a code, the doors slid open and she turned to invite me to enter with a smile on her lips. I stayed where I was and shook my head.

The nurse then nodded to a man who stepped into the hallway while her red lips stretched from ear to ear in determination. I glanced from the elevators to the man and then back at the nurse who had to cut off my retreat. She put her hand firmly on my shoulder and pushed me into the ward after which the doors slid closed behind me.

I was led me down the hall past the haunted eyes of the other people occupying this ward and I could see they were all missing a few nuts or bolts. I stopped where I was and when the nurse reached out to take my hand, I held it behind my back. I was not going to be led into a mental ward like a lamb to slaughter!

The nurse's lips simply stretched into a smile again. *"Don't worry. We just don't want you running away. We'll take care of you."*[1]

I ignored her smiling lips and looked into her frowning eyes. "I am not crazy," I stated and crossed my arms over my chest.

Neither her lips nor her eyes seemed to register what I had said. "Of course," she uttered with a nod, "please, your room is here."

The man was watching us from down the hall so when her hand came to rest on my shoulder again, I shuffled obediently to the new room and hunched down on the bed scowling. I certainly hadn't been the first one to gripe about being sent here and she took it all in stride with her hypocritical smile.

"Here's a towel if you wish to shower,"[2] she said, and laid it on the small table in front of a mirror.

I hissed at her as she left and sat there in a funk until I couldn't stand it any longer. Angry at myself and at this whole hospital, I grabbed the towel, the bag of clothing and went in search of the shower. With my eyes on the floor, I slipped past the crazy people haunting the hall and slammed the door to the shower room hoping to stay locked in there until the medical staff forgot me. Unfortunately, there was no lock.

It was unnerving to undress and wash Neïla's body when somebody might walk in at any second. Running my hands over intimate places was even worse so I tried explaining to her ghost that I had no choice, but then I began to really feel like a basket case.

I shut up and went to drying her skin. It was soft and hairless and I had to go easy with the towel whereas Josh could rub his carcass down like a packhorse. I then tried wrapping her long mane of hair in the towel like the nurse had done but failed miserably. In the end I simply let it hang down my back.

I opened the bag to see what clothes she had; the underwear were black or pink with lace. I felt shameless but for some reason I didn't want to wear the black ones and I even put on the pink bra. As for clothing, there wasn't much choice, blue jeans and a short black dress. No shirts. I sighed and put the dress over the jeans but didn't look in the mirror to see what it looked like.

I walked back to the room keeping my eyes down and trying not to make a sound. I then sat in a chair with my back to the mirror and began to tease the knots out of her hair with the comb Hadja had left me. It might have been easier if I had watched what I was doing but I was still unable to look at Neïla's face without the pain of what I'd done to her welling up inside me.

There came a knock and a young brown-haired woman with a ponytail entered. "Bonjour, Mademoiselle Saadallah," she stated, with a thoughtful smile before she glanced at the mirror in back of me. "I'm Dr. Moulin."[3] She extended her hand for me to shake.

I sat where I was and frowned.

"Can we speak a little?"[4] she asked in a level, controlled voice.

I didn't feel like having to deal with a psychiatrist, especially in French, so I decided to see if I could shake her by speaking English. "Yes, why not?" I replied. She sat facing me and seemed to wait for me to speak. A half-smile remained on her lips but frown lines appeared between her eyebrows. "You're a psychiatrist, are you not?" I stated, although the word *psychiatrist* came out with a funny sound.

She nodded to the question but kept her smile level. "Yes, I am."

"So you think I am crazy?"

She shook her head. "I think you had a trauma." Her English was excellent which made me even more uneasy. "Do you not understand French or do you not want to speak it?" she asked.

"I don't know" —I caught myself—"I have no confident . . . confidence in French."

"But your English is fine," she commented with a smile, which let me know that the trap was closing—I should have just shut up!—but now she was on to the fact that I wasn't Neïla. I looked away rather than respond. "Does that bother you?" she asked to my turned head.

"It doesn't bother me," I denied, looking back at her. Her gaze didn't move and I knew I had to say more or she would know she was right. "You think I should speak French?"

"And why 'should' you speak French?"

"Because she . . . *je veux dire* . . . I should . . ." I had screwed up. The psychiatrist raised an eyebrow when I decided to simply shake my head and keep my mouth shut.

"Who is 'she'? *Qui est-elle*?" the psychiatrist asked when it had become clear I wouldn't say more. "Are you speaking of yourself or of Neïla?"

I had been caught. My breathing got shallow, my head started spinning. "What will you tell her" —Damn! Slipped again— "my family?"

Her eyes had become twice as intense but her smile hadn't changed. "No, this is strictly private. Are you afraid of them?"

"No!" I denied before stumbling. "I just don't know . . . since the accident . . ."

"You think the accident changed you," she stated, and I had no choice but to nod. "Your speaking English is one of the changes, isn't it?" I shook my head but she didn't fall for my denial. "And are you afraid of what they might think of that? *De quoi avez-vous peur?* What are you afraid of?"

It was hard to say what I feared exactly but I was sure there was a danger somewhere. "I think it is very important they not know what has happened to me," I replied.

"They have the right to know certain things but our conversation is private." She took a long breath before continuing. "Why do you refer to yourself as 'she'?"

I wanted to deny everything again. My head shook but I couldn't stop the tears from blurring my vision.

"Why do you think you aren't the same person? *Pourquoi vous pensez que vous n'êtes pas la même personne?"*

"Parce que je suis pas," The words blurted out before I could stop them. "Because I'm not," I repeated in English. "I mean . . ." I didn't know what I meant. Why couldn't I just shut up?

"Who are you then?" she asked very calmly, but I refused to answer even though I could feel her eyes on my back. She would wait there until she had the answer. "Do you think you have become something different? Does this have anything to do with you speaking English?"

I wiped my sleeve across my eyes and turned to look her. "Yes!" I screamed in anger at her prying.

"What do you know about the man who saved you?" she asked calmly.

"The police say he's dead," I sighed, suddenly drained of all anger.

She nodded. "And what else?"

"The police did not say more," I replied.

"Do you know his origins?" she asked slowly, with an eyebrow raised.

"Nobody told me." Again she waited for me to say more so I decided to turn the question back on her. "What should I have to know?"

"It probably doesn't matter," she replied nonchalantly. She then looked at me carefully and said, "He was American." I simply nodded because I had of course known this. "Does that surprise you?" she asked.

I was trapped again, it should have been a surprise, and I was at a loss for words stuttering, "no . . . *je veux* . . . I mean yes."

"I'm not here to judge you, Miss Saadallah, I just want to help you. You did know he was American, didn't you?"

I felt horrible, like a loser, and I looked at my feet. The toenails were still painted red even though the polish had chipped. Maybe I was crazy. "Yes," I whispered. "His name was Josh, was it not?"

"I believe it was," she answered, and for some strange reason that made me feel better. I had proof that I wasn't totally psychotic; his name had been Josh. "You know you aren't at all responsible for his death?" she added, in a sympathetic tone of voice.

"Yes," I said, but my voice quivered. That was only half true. Neïla wasn't responsible for his death, but I was for hers.

"I would like to come back and speak to you again," she said, as she got up. "I want you to think about yourself and not about him, okay?"

I smiled just to make her happy. "One question," I said, before she turned to leave, "is it possible that I know about his funeral or memorial service? I should like to go."

She nodded. "I will think about it and we'll talk the next time I stop by. Is that okay? In the meantime, I will prescribe you something that will help calm your nerves."

"Thank you," I answered, while she walked to the door. When the door shut behind her I didn't know if I should feel better or worse.

1 "Ne vous inquiétez pas, on veut juste que vous ne vous enfuyez plus. On va s'occuper de vous."
2 "Voici une serviette si vous voulez prendre une douche."
3 "I'm Dr. Moulin."
4 "Est-ce qu'on peut parler un petit peu?"

Part 2

L'enfer c'est les autres. "Hell is the others."

—Jean-Paul Sartre

Chapter 5

The psychiatrist's prescription calmed my nerves, as she had promised; I spent the next two days laying on the bed like a vegetable. Mother came to watch me while I was sprawled there and Othmane, the bearded brother, also dropped by to make a stink about me not having the hijab with male doctors about. I let Mother do my hair up and put the scarf over it without complaining. I was beyond caring. The psychiatrist came back regularly, but I don't remember what I told her. The drugs muddled my thoughts too much for me to stay on my guard.

The doses must have been reduced on the third day because I didn't fall back asleep after breakfast. The psychiatrist stopped by and asked me general questions that I tried to elude, even though her silences were daunting.

Mother arrived in the middle of the afternoon wearing an uncommon smile. Then, when she began packing Neïla's personal items and humming some Arabic tune, I knew something was up. Even with the reduced dose, I was in too much of a trance to help so I just sat on the bed watching her fold the clothing and close the suitcase. Once she had finished, she rearranged my hijab and had me stand up.

We shuffled down the long hall, past all those psychotic eyes, to the sliding doors where a nurse told me goodbye. When I ignored her, she punched the code and the doors slid open. Mother then pulled me out into the hall where Othmane was standing beside an empty chair. Maybe it was his beard, but he seemed to scowl constantly. Mother had me stand in front of him so that he could inspect my headscarf and after a nod, he took off with us following behind his long strides. He certainly wasn't one to show effusions of joy.

As we crossed the front entrance area, I nearly had to jog to keep up and we got all sorts of stares, few amiable, so I pulled the scarf over my face to hide Neïla from all those accusatory eyes. The streets were rainy outside with few people about and I kept my eyes on Othmane's sandals splashing against the wet sidewalk. He stopped beside an old Renault and turned the key in the driver's seat latch. Mother popped the trunk to stow Neïla's bag and opened the door for me. My heart began to beat faster and I would have run away if she hadn't put her arm on my shoulder.

Othmane's car smelled so stale and decayed that I was surprised it even started. Mother sat in the front passenger seat and looked over at her son with an unreadable expression. She spoke from time to time to Othmane but with the rumbling of the engine, I couldn't hear a thing.

I had never gotten used to Parisian drivers so when we reached the *"périférique"* ("ring road"), I opened the window and closed my eyes to keep from panicking. When the car slowed down, I dared a glance at my surrounding and recognized the suburb where I had boarded with the greasy smell of the Arab sandwich shops drifting through the open window. I shut my eyes again as soon as the car darted forward into traffic while ghosts formed in my memory; Josh had strolled down this street just before he was murdered.

We arrived a few minutes later in front of a five-story gray apartment structure with washing hung from the windows next to satellite antennae. Elderly women watched the parking lot from behind shutters whose green paint had mostly chipped away and young boys sitting on the corner eyed us as we drove by.

Mother opened my door and grabbed my hand to pull me out after Othmane had parked on the other side of the street. We strode past a group of teenage boys, mostly of North African origin, who greeted Othmane with deference. Some of the boys said hello to me but I had no idea who they were so I bowed my head wishing I could go back to the hospital where nobody knew

Neïla. Mother put her arm firmly around my shoulders and led me into a graffiti-covered entryway where a young man was leaning against the wall. We hadn't passed any girls.

Rather than taking the elevator, Othmane opened the door to a stairwell that smelled of body odors and headed up with us huffing behind. My legs felt like rubber so I was relieved when Othmane held the door on the fourth floor to let us to step out into a hallway that had only one working light. Noises of people talking or yelling reverberated off the concrete and the odor of spicy cooking wafted out from the apartments. Was this Neïla's home?

I stopped where I was in the dimly lit hallway—I could never come here and take Neïla's place!—and what would I do if the murderer was behind one of these doors? Everything was foreign, frightening and the noises and shouts made my heart beat like a drum. I opened my mouth to protest but my voice wouldn't go above a whisper while I looked back for a way to escape. Then I felt Othmane's large hand take my arm.

While he pulled me another ten feet down the hall, Mother turned a key in the lock of the third door on the left and pushed it open. There came a howl and suddenly I had a young boy hugging me.

I screamed in fright.

"Leave her alone,"[1] Mother barked.

The boy stared up at me with wide black eyes and the gleam of tears while his left arm curled up oddly to his side. He didn't look dangerous so I knelt down in front of him, wishing I could remember who he was. My hand reached out and brushed a lock of dark hair from his face and his forehead creased with sorrow. Suddenly I was hugging him.

"Don't cry," he whispered in my ear, *"I didn't want to frighten you."*[2] That made Neïla cry even harder because I was the one who should have been apologizing.

Then Othmane had me take off Neïla's pink sneakers while

Mother chased the boy away. I kept my eyes on those tiny feet of hers while I was led into a living room with red and green drapery, a muted television on the right wall and people sitting everywhere on pillows and rugs. All their eyes were staring at me. I wished I could flee.

"Go ahead,"[3] Mother whispered.

I pulled the veil over my face and sat down on a pillow against the wall but nobody moved, as if I were supposed to make a speech. I felt certain I couldn't say a word in French, and that I would be stoned should I try, so I turned to face the wall in the hope that they wouldn't force me. Then a strong hard hand touched my shoulder and I recoiled while my heart raced like a captive bird's.

"Want you a cigarette?"[4] a man chuckled behind me.

I had already heard that laugh, so I opened my eyes onto the smile of the guy who had claimed to be my brother. He was holding out a package of cigarettes for me.

My head shook but I kept him in my line of sight.

"Oh right, I forgot, you don't smoke,"[5] he said with a laugh, and went over to sit beside another woman.

A teenage girl with a clear resemblance to Neïla, albeit a few pounds heavier, came and knelt in front of me with an ironic twist to her lip. *"You can take off your hijab in the* family," she said and began to remove my veil. I was about to refuse, this time I would have preferred to keep it on, but my hands trembled too badly. When the girl had finished, she stroked my hair and pushed a strand out of my face. *"You see, that's better, isn't it?"*[6]

My eyes darted around the room at the people—it seemed that the whole family had gathered to greet me—and an odor of meat, spices and pastry wafted in from the kitchen. They had organized a reception for me and I was ruining it. Then the smile of the young boy, bright although slightly crooked, caught my attention. I looked back at his left hand, which was still curled up against his side, and then at his left leg that was shorter than the other. He was handicapped.

Tears filmed his eyes, my hand reached out for him as if by reflex and he rushed toward me almost falling with his bad leg. We held each other like siblings needing comfort while the others began conversing and chatting. His name was Mustapha and he spoke to me in slurred words while the meal was served on a low table in the living room and I nodded or shook my head. For once, I was glad the doctors said I had aphasia.

1 "Laisse-la, laisse-la."
2 "Pleure pas, je voulais pas te faire peur."
3 "Vas-y"
4 "Tu veux une cigarette?"
5 "Ah oui, j'ai oublié, tu fumes pas."
6 "Tu peux enlever ton hijab en famille. Tu vois, ça va mieux, non?"

Chapter 6

Mustapha showed me his video games and I'm ashamed to admit that I enjoyed spending the afternoon chasing virtual *"bonbons."* It was certainly safer than listening to Neïla's family discussing religion and politics when I knew that I would have strongly contested their points of view.

In the middle of the afternoon, all of the women stood up and went into a bedroom where Djahida, the young girl who looked like Neïla, pointed in the direction of the window. All lifted their hands and recited, "Allahou Akbar." I looked at them dumbly while they mumbled prayers, crossed their hands over their chests and bent at the waists. Djahida gave me an irritated look but dropped to her knees and prostrated herself with her nose against the rug. She sat back on her knees with one foot curled under her and repeated the whole three times.

When everyone had finished, she came to me, looked me in the eyes and said, "Allahou Akbar, *répète.*" There was no choice but to obey, so I mumbled the words after her as she took me through the prayer step by step and had me repeat things that I didn't understand. This went on for about half an hour until finally Djahida smiled and took me back to the living room. I got the feeling I'd have to get used to praying.

* * *

It seemed I had to give everyone a kiss on both cheeks before they left. Djahida, Neïla's younger sister, then led me to a room that had clearly been decorated by girls and began pulling off her robes to expose her blue underwear. I turned away embarrassed and almost covered my eyes. Would I have to sleep in the same room as her?

"You're not going to just sit there! Put on your nightgown,"[1] she

barked.

I did as I was told. Then Djahida had me sit in front of the mirror while she combed out Neïla's long hair and I closed my eyes so as not to see Neïla's sad face. Afterward, I did my best to help her with hers but she got irritated at my incompetence and pushed me away.

While I sat on the bed observing her, I realized how much she looked like Neïla with those same dark eyes that turned up in the corners. Djahida would have been a real knockout if only she lost those little bulges on her hips and tummy. Why didn't I react to her at all? Although she was rather young, Josh should have gotten excited watching her groom herself in only a transparent nightgown. I curled up with my back to her feeling like a pervert.

After putting on the alarm, Djahida said goodnight and turned out her bedside lamp. Mother had insisted I continue taking the drugs so the darkness swirled in foggy patterns that muddled my thoughts and slowly Neïla's lean body, so tiny under the covers, was lifted by the eddy. The fog then swooshed away and I was sitting facing myself, Josh, who was staring at me and smiling. Only then did I realize that I was Neïla, not Josh, and that her body felt a tingling warmth every time that funny American smiled. He wasn't very handsome but she—or was it I?—liked his timid manners. This was impossible; Neïla had never spoken to Josh, had she?

The dream was ludicrous so I decided that I should wake up but the swirl of fog snatched me back and Neïla was sitting across the table from me shaking her head. I tried to grab her to pull her back into her body but my arm was too short to reach across the table and I only managed to spill the *panache*. The man with brown hair entered, looked at Josh, then at me with his winning smile and I wanted to slap him but—I was under water suffocating, screamed and sat upright in the bed.

"What's the matter?"[2] Djahida cawed, half asleep.

I said nothing and soon she was breathing loudly through her nose again while I lay awake looking at the shadows on the ceiling. Even though I would have loved to, I had never spoken to Neïla in the bar. Was it possible I really was Neïla and that I was crazy? I felt my existence turning in foggy circles—

—the alarm rang and I was curled up in a ball under the covers. I, Josh, had never slept like that. I had always slept on my back . . . if I really was Josh. I began shaking, curled back into the ball. I wasn't crazy. I knew who I was!

The lights switched on, blinding me, and Mother's voice stated in a level voice, *"Wake up, Djahida."*[3]

Was it worse to get up or to stay in bed? Djahida groaned letting me know that I was really still in the apartment and that it was no use wishing I could go back to another life. I had to face the facts, so I rolled over to put Neïla's tiny feet on the soft throw rug next to her bed, slipped on the pink robe that Djahida had given me, stood up, stepped into the hall and—

—Mustapha grabbed me in a tight giggling hug.

I screamed, Mustapha hugged even tighter, Djahida bellowed, and I couldn't help but smile. He then dragged me to the kitchen where Mother served green mint tea, bread and jam.

"Eat,"[4] Mother said, and sat facing me while I sipped the overly sweet beverage. I wanted to say something but was unable to muster the courage to ask if I could have it with less sugar.

Djahida came shuffling in a minute later. She didn't need to be told to eat and finished off three pieces of bread with oil and jam before she went to pack her book bag and help Mustapha get ready. From his anxiousness, I guessed they must have been late but that didn't bother Djahida. Just before I thought Mustapha might go into a fit of panic, she took his hand and led him out the door.

We were alone in the apartment and Mother began humming an Oriental tune while she went about clearing the table. I watched her until she had finished and sat down to do her sewing. Shouldn't Neïla have been going to school too? I was too afraid to ask the question so, with nothing better to do, I padded into the living room. The cushions were still set around where the people had sat last night and the smell of the spicy cooking lingered.

This cramped apartment already felt like a cage. Othmane and Mustapha shared a bedroom whereas Mokhtar, the brother with the smile, had gone to live on his own. I couldn't blame him. The last of the three bedrooms was for Mother and I had no idea if the father was still alive. I returned to the girls' bedroom.

A four-drawer dresser, a desk and an obsolete computer cramped this small room. The wallpaper was pink and blue with a poster of hip-hop singer pinned over Djahida's bed while Neïla had put several little pictures of cats over hers. It was strange because I had always liked cats, too. When I had been little, my best friend and I had made believe that we were cats but then I had grown up to be lumbering Josh. I sat on Neïla's bed wishing again that I were a cat and could slip out of the apartment unseen.

I had learned which of the drawers were Neïla's and that the closet was shared by both. I started looking through the dresser to see what sort of clothing Neïla had worn because, although it was embarrassing, I had to get used to sorting through her brassieres and panties. I closed the drawer and told myself I'd come back later.

I was more comfortable with the bookcase and desk on which Neïla had left some of her school material. Would I be able to cope with all the classes in French? I sat back in the chair and looked at the computer hoping I still knew my passwords, because if I didn't, this was all delirium.

The old thing took what seemed like a week to boot up. Then, when the desktop appeared, it was so girlish that I was about to change it but my hand hesitated; the more I looked at the picture of the three kittens, the more I warmed to them. After all, they were cute, weren't they? Suddenly it hit me that I actually liked the picture and I was so embarrassed that I had to sit back to gather my wits. Was Neïla controlling my emotions again? She was inside me, somewhere, as if her body retained memories and feelings that she was now handing on to me.

I looked back at her desktop picture defeated, unable to delete the picture, and with a sigh opened Facebook. Neither Neïla nor Djahida had memorized their passwords which meant that I wasn't going to be able to get into their accounts. However, when I entered my e-mail, the password appeared automatically. I clicked on "show password" and my mother's birthday appeared—how had Neïla learned it?

This was so unreal my head started spinning again and I remembered my dream; had Neïla known Josh? I hit enter, my breathing accelerated and while the hourglass was turning, my stomach knotted up. When my face appeared, I wasn't sure whether I should be relieved or not.

I stared at my picture wondering what had happened to me. Josh looked like a different person, nothing like I remembered, with a pleasant smile and intelligent eyes. Even though I had never really cultivated FB relations, the page was filled with condolences from all of my friends and then some. I felt like answering everybody and saying that I was fine—but was I? It all seemed like some horrible joke.

I had to sit back, my eyes staring blankly at the page, because I really was dead. On the latest post, there was written in English and French the date of a memorial service: tomorrow at a synagogue in Paris near Bagnolet. But I wasn't Jewish! My mother had never converted in spite of the pressure from my grandparents. Had they organized this so that they could cry for their goy grandson?

Neïla's body was trembling again but my mind was set; she had pay her respects, no matter what, and she should also write something. To do that, however, I had to change identities so I typed "Neïla Saadallah" in the research friends box and her face appeared, smiling so beautifully that my heart stopped.

Then I looked more closely and I realized that she had already asked to friend me. Had she really known me just like in my dream? Was I really Neïla—crazy, psychotic Neïla? If so, how had I known my e-mail? Or how had Neïla learned it and put it on the computer? I was sure I had never spoken to her, yet she had certainly known about me.

I had to slow my breathing before I clicked "yes" to accept her as a friend and go to her page. It was filled with rap videos that didn't interest me but I discovered that she was a high school student in "première L", that's to say literature, and that she was not in a relationship. The latter came as a relief although I began to dread the idea that I would have to take her place in French class.

If I wanted to write on Josh's wall, however, I needed to find her password. The first place I looked was in her drawers and, embarrassing as it was, I rummaged through all the underwear and blouses. Except for a few trinkets, there was nothing of interest. I then wondered if she had a diary, but nothing was under the pillows or mattress.

As a last resort, I started going through her school notebooks page by page. Most was just class work but from time to time I came across a little poem or joke. Her handwriting was pretty, quite the contrary to mine, and she liked fuchsia ink, flowers, cats, girly things, and I hated the fact that I was warming to it.

My hand suddenly pushed the page away—was I that girl who liked cats and flowers?—but then Neïla's hand picked up a pen to write her name. It trembled so much that the letters were all wobbly and yet there could be no confusion; the handwriting was hers. My head was spinning and though I didn't want to believe it, here was proof I was crazy. Why wouldn't she just take back her body and continue drawing those tacky little flowers? They suddenly looked so beautiful that tears ran down my cheeks.

The front door slammed and somebody started speaking in a low rumbling voice. I jumped up, suddenly fearful, and was about to hide in the corner until I heard Mother call Neïla's name. Gathering my courage, I went to the living room and saw Othmane sitting on a pillow studying a book in Arabic with French translations. Mother then came in with three plates that she set on the table and I realized she had been preparing lunch so I rushed into the kitchen to lend a hand. She gave me what must have been a smile before pointing to the tableware. I took the glasses and silverware and set them around the table while Mother arrived behind me with a spicy vegetable and grain dish. She served Othmane first who began eating before she served me and herself.

Othmane set his fork down and looked me in the eye. *"I'm happy that you have finally decided to act like a respectable woman."*[5]

I decided I should take offense and confront him, but his eyes didn't seem to focus on anything so I stared back down at my hands while Mother observed me expressionlessly. Had Neïla always been as much of a wimp as I was? I lost my appetite.

The meal ended with me hardly touching my food and when Mother began clearing the table, I stood up to help. Othmane barely glanced at us and lay down on a mat and pillows. I wanted to ask Mother if he had come back from work and what type of job he had but I remained silent while she washed the dishes and I dried them.

When I walked back out of the kitchen, Othmane was awake and motioned for me to sit in front of him. I dared not disobey. *"I've heard you wish to go to that funeral. I don't want you to go,"*[6] his voice commanded.

I wasn't sure I had understood so I raised my eyebrows.

"His name was Cohn. He was Jewish," he stated flatly. *"It's going to take place in a synagogue."*[7]

I shrugged. Although my name might be Cohn, I had never been accepted by my most orthodox relatives. It was my father who was Jewish, not my mother, and I didn't care if it took place in a Buddhist temple; I had to go.

He shook his head with finality. *"I won't put up with you shaming our family. It would be better that you die rather than dirtying our name."*[8]

I began to tremble with anger. Why would setting a foot in a synagogue be shameful? He ignored me and went back to his reading while I bored my eyes into him. Mother finally came and put her hand on my shoulder and pulled me away. I felt like turning against her, then like crying on her shoulder. I ended up running back to Neïla's room and sobbing into a pillow just like a wimp.

1 "Mais tu vas pas rester comme ça! Mets ta chemise de nuit."
2 "Qu'est-ce qui se passe?"
3 "Réveille-toi."
4 "Mange."
5 "Je suis content que tu te sois décidée finalement de te conduire en femme respectable."
6 "J'ai entendu que tu souhaites aller à certaines funérailles. Je ne veux pas que tu y ailles."
7 "Il s'appelait Cohn. Il était juif. Cela va se passer dans une synagogue."
8 "Je ne supporterai pas que tu fasses honte à ta famille. Il vaudrait mieux que tu meures plutôt que de salir notre nom."

Chapter 7

I was still huddled into the corner behind Neïla's bed when Mother opened the door wearing a cleaning lady's clothing and a scarf around her hair. Her eyes observed me a second before she motioned for me to follow her into the kitchen where she began her list of instructions for dinner. She said she would be at work until late, that everything was cooked and that I simply had to put it in the microwave. I nodded at every instruction until she kissed my cheek and headed out the door. I didn't have any choice but to obey.

Othmane was still reading and reciting things from his book, so I went back to Neïla's bedroom and took out her assigned book, *Germinal* by Zola. Even though I was afraid of the French, I still made it through the first chapter without the use of a dictionary. As a history major, I found it fascinating.

I then opened her history notes and saw she was studying the outset of the First World War. I already had a fairly good command of that topic but read through what the teacher had said anyway. At some point, Othmane came to check on me but when I ignored him, he went back to his Islamic studies. Did he have a job or was he a theological student? I didn't dare ask.

Neïla's two siblings came back from school at about six. Mustapha hugged me as hard as he could and I enjoyed watching his eyes sparkle while he told me all about his day. My new sister, however, barely spoke to me before she rushed into our bedroom to occupy the computer and pretend to do her homework. I stayed in the kitchen with Mustapha who had taken out his homework and was learning to conjugate the English verb *be* in the present. When he made an error, I corrected him out loud and his eyes opened so wide that I wondered if I should have kept quiet. Then he gave me a large smile so I continued helping him while I took care of the chores that Mother had given me.

We had dinner about eight and then sat watching an American police series, dubbed into French, about a psychopathic murderer. My heart began to accelerate when the forensic surgeon dissected the corpse of a young girl and then Djahida let out a wail of laughter. Neïla's body began to shake uncontrollably and I went back to the corner behind Neïla's bed until Djahida came to fetch me for evening prayer. She watched my every movement and finally nodded that I could go to bed.

Rain beat against the shutters but I felt warm curled up under the covers with Neïla's thin arms wrapped around her chest. It was strange because I had always slept on my back although it was soothing being able to curl up into a ball and pretend I was safe back at home. While I tried to forget the memorial service, I whispered to the night, to Neïla's ghost, begging for her to help me find a way out of this prison.

My eyes opened to the kaleidoscope patterns in the darkness. What time was it? The swirling black shapes suddenly coalesced into a beautiful but haggard human figure, Neïla, who was standing at the edge of my bed. She motioned for me to get up and I obeyed even though my heart began beating like a drum while I slid out of bed.

Neïla floated to the closet expecting me to follow but I first glanced at Djahida, who was fast asleep, before I tiptoed over. At the back were clothes like any teenage girl would wear, jeans and a blouse, that she had me put on. Her smile reassured me she was happy with what she saw, but then she frowned and motioned for me to put a scarf around my hair and to take a jacket.

I was surprised at how quickly I put the hijab on, it was as if Neïla were guiding my hand, although I kept looking over at Djahida for fear she might awake. Neïla then waved me into the living room, out the front door and into the stairwell before she had me put on her pink sneakers. There was no one about at this hour and so we slipped unnoticed down the stairs and out onto the street. The rain had turned to a drizzle that moistened the scarf over my hair and cooled my face while I walked between the cars. When I looked at Neïla's ghost's diaphanous eyes, they were so sad that I wanted to say something but she didn't, or couldn't, speak.

A group of boys were huddled in the entryway of a building across the parking lot but I don't think they saw us as I ducked behind a van and rushed down a small one-way street toward the Rue de Paris. Then suddenly Neïla glanced back in fright at something behind me; there was a gray hooded figure following us. I began running but the sound of the person's feet followed as if I had awakened from a dream to a nightmare. I turned a corner—

—a car slammed on its breaks, a man began yelling, I banged on the window. Words, French words, came spilling from my mouth begging the man to let me into the car. He stared at me, the latch clicked and I jumped into the passenger seat.

The man stared at me silently until a voice, Neïla's voice, yelled, "*Partez ou on est mort* (Go or we'll be dead)." I don't think he believed me but he sped away while the hooded figure stepped into an entranceway. It was like seeing the angel of death.

Although he was not very handsome, middle-aged and had a paunch, the man's eyes kept turning in my direction and he didn't try to hide the fact that he found me attractive. Josh hadn't been very handsome either, so I looked away feeling ashamed that I judged him harshly.

"*What's up with you?*"[1] he asked.

Maybe I should have told him everything but suddenly I couldn't come up with a single word in French and while he waited patiently, my heart beat faster and faster. I shook my head. He didn't seem satisfied. "*Was somebody chasing you?*" he asked. I nodded. "*Who?*"[2]

I shook my head. I didn't have a clue except I was sure it was the person who had killed me and now he wanted to kill Neïla.

The only person I could think of who might want to do that was Othmane who had said he would prefer to see Neïla dead than to shame the family. Just thinking of him made me tremble and my fear must have shown on my face.

"I'm taking you to see the police."[3] The man stated.

Now I shook my head violently. The police would never let me go to the memorial service and, what's more, they would take me back to that family. I was sure I never wanted to return.

"Come on, you can't just do nothing?"[4] he insisted.

I suddenly didn't trust the man. He looked away when he stopped at a light and I was out the door and running again. I don't think he tried following me, but I didn't look back or stop running until I was about to drop. The people who saw me probably thought they just saw a ghost.

Tired and thirsty, I dropped exhausted in an entranceway out of the drizzle where I curled up wondering if I should hide there until morning. The thirst, however, became unbearable, in spite of the water falling from the sky, so I began to walk toward a kebab snack bar that was still open.

The French words squeaked out of Neïla's parched throat while a Turkish man at the counter eyed me. *"May I have some water, please?"* The man looked at me as if he were trying to solve a riddle. *"I don't have any money but I'm very thirsty,"*[5] Neïla's voice squeaked. The man shook his head and went to fetch a cup of water, then refilled it when I had gulped it down.

"What are you doing out so late, honey?" he asked, using the form "tu" as if I were a friend or a child. I tried to smile but failed miserably. *"Have you got problems?"*[6]

I wasn't going to lie, so I nodded, but then I became afraid he might feel obliged to help me so I shook my head and said, "*ça va* (I'm fine)."

"Where is your family?" he asked very seriously. *"Are you hungry? Do you want something to eat?"*[7]

He seemed so worried that I felt terrible having to refuse. "*No,*

I was just thirsty."[8] Neïla's voice whispered.

"You can't go out like that alone." He reached for a telephone. *"I must call somebody."*[9]

"Non," I cried. *"Il faut pas* (You mustn't)." He looked at me and shook his head. *"Can I have another glass of water?"*[10] I asked to distract him.

I handed him my plastic cup and while he had his back turned, I ran out like a thief. I hated myself for acting disgracefully but knew he would have had me returned to the family. Even though Mother deserved to have her daughter back, and Mustapha his sister, Othmane frightened me too much.

1 "Qu'est-ce qui vous arrive?"

2 "On vous poursuivait? . . . Qui?"

3 "Je vous amène voir la police."

4 "Allons, vous ne pouvez pas restez comme ça sans rien faire?"

5 "Je peux avoir de l'eau, s'il vous plait? Je n'ai pas d'argent mais j'ai très soif."

6 "Qu'est-ce que tu fais dehors à une heure pareille, petite? Tu as des problèmes?"

7 "Où est ta famille? . . . Est-ce que tu as faim? Tu veux quelque chose à manger?"

8 "Non, J'avais juste soif."

9 "Tu ne peux pas aller dehors seule comme ça . . . Il faut que j'appelle quelqu'un."

10 "Je peux avoir un autre verre d'eau?"

Chapter 8

I couldn't run any longer so I started walking again. Few people were out at this hour, and fewer took notice of me, although I came across a few hookers who looked me up and down. The clients did too. One even looked ready to make me an offer but I didn't stop to listen.

I remembered the synagogue was in the 19th arrondissement and even though I didn't know Paris very well, it seemed like I had to cross the *périférique* and head north. It would have been easier if I could have taken the metro, but I didn't have the money and I was too scared of being stopped by the police to jump the barriers. I began to count my steps and at two thousand, I realized I was counting in French and stumbled. My legs felt like lead. A dim light began to show in the sky and—was I imagining things?—the synagogue was in front of me.

Across the street a bakery was opening and even though my mouth was dry, I didn't dare go in to ask for a glass of water. Since the ceremony wasn't until ten, I found a doorway that gave me shelter from the drizzle, curled up, tried to forget my fatigue and thirst—and awoke to street noises with people passing me, glancing at me, or just ignoring me. Did they think I was homeless? Was I homeless? I stood up and stretched.

In front of the synagogue a crowd had gathered and although some were clearly Jewish with their kippahs, others were from the Institute for American Students. I almost cried out to them, but my throat was too parched although a few glanced in my direction. Neïla must have looked scary after having slept outside under a doorway so I went to look in a store window mirror. Her eyes were red, her skin chalky and her hair was hidden under the scarf but she was still so beautiful I had to turn away.

A number of the boys watched me as I approached and even

if I knew them, their gazes made me nervous. A tall boy, I think his name was Jeff, stepped up to me catching me by surprise. He had hardly ever spoken to me when I in my own body but now he was all smiles. "*Puis-je vous aidez, mademoiselle* (Can I help you, mademoiselle)?" he asked with a grin.

His American accent was so hilarious that I smiled, until I realized that not only had I heard it as a French speaker would, but that I barely understood the garbled sounds the other Americans were making. Embarrassed, I decided to respond in French. "*Est-ce que la cérémonie pour Josh est ici* (Is the service for Josh here)?"

He looked at me confused. "Pardon?"

Another boy, I think his name was Ron, interrupted with a snort. "She's asking about Josh, knucklehead."

"Oh Josh, I'm sorry, he's dead," Jeff blurted. "Oh, but maybe you already know."

"I know he has passed," I replied with a shudder; somehow the word *dead* made me feel deceitful. "I wanted just make sure that here was his memorial service." The words all came out funny and with a laughable French accent, but the people who had gathered around seemed impressed.

"Did you know him?" Kim from medieval history class asked me with tears in her eyes.

Of course I knew Josh, I almost answered, but shook my head instead. Although it seemed ridiculous for me to pay my respects to myself, I was here for Neïla. She had to say something to my family. "No, not really," I answered, "but I would have liked to."

She sniffed and looked at me with her green eyes. "I can't believe he's dead like that. He was the nicest guy I've ever met. He was just so quiet . . . reserved."

I was supposed to say something, but it was as if Kim were describing somebody else so my thoughts muddled up. I glanced at the others who were nodding in agreement but my eyes were drawn to Quincy. He, rather than me, was the nicest guy around.

Even though he was a math major, he liked art, fencing and the Renaissance—we'd had a couple of great discussions over coffee after class. Yet I had never noticed how good-looking he was.

Quincy's eyes widened, stared back, and I was intrigued at how blue they were while I tried to think of something intelligent, witty, or just anything to say. How could I be looking at old Quince like that? I had always been straight, but now Neïla was taking control while I stammered idiotically, "Know you how he died?"

Quincy turned, rubbed his hand through his untrimmed brown hair while I wished myself to breathe normally and hoped he didn't think me too stupid. "I just know he was murdered," he mumbled. "They don't seem to know why but some of the people here say it was because he was Jewish. He apparently gave his life for some Ara—"

He looked back at me realizing his gaff. I felt awful, searched for something nice to say, and then realized everybody was staring at me as if I were winged cow. My heart began beating too fast to smile.

"What do they . . . ?" My voice cracked and faltered.

Quincy's eyes turned back to me so full of compassion that I wished I could hold him—but I couldn't hope to do that with my pal Quincy! Suddenly the fatigue, while thirst made my legs wobble and I felt very confused.

Kim, put her arm around me. "It's alright, you don't need to cry. He didn't mean anything by it," she whispered, and shot Quincy a glare.

"I know. It's not Quincy," I replied.

There were mumbles and stares; now I had made the gaff.

"You know his name?" Kim asked, perplexed. She stepped back to look me up and down. When I glanced over at Quincy, I saw his mouth was hanging open.

"I heard it," I lied. "I am sorry if—" There were no longer any doubts that Neïla was an emotional catastrophe because I broke down crying again and Kim took me back into her arms while Quincy tried apologizing for anything and everything.

The doors then opened and the crowd started moving. "Here," Kim said, guiding me inside, "let's get you washed up a bit before the service." She stepped over and asked the man at the door where the *"toilettes"* were. His eyes turned toward me and then squinted at the headscarf.

"Do you know the deceased?"[1] he asked, with downturned lips and a flared nose.

I was about to answer "of course" but what came out was more of a stammer.

"We want no . . ." he spat in English, while he waved his hand in circles. "No strangers."

I understood what he meant: no Arabs. I began to reply but then wavered between despair and anger at being refused entry when I had been in synagogues so many times before. His eyes showed triumph, my hopes sagged, but then Kim's arm pulled me in tight to her side. "This girl has more right to be here than you. Did you know Josh?"

"No but . . ." the man mumbled and pointed at my Arabic scarf.

"Her what?" Kim hissed, while her eyes flashed with such menace that the man's lips puckered up.

The man examined me angrily and after a moment hesitation, he sighed, "they are down," indicating stairs with a nod and a scowl.

Kim led me down the stairs while she whispered swear words that made Neïla's face blush scarlet. I had always found her outgoing, sort of a party girl, but had never thought that she could be so persuasive and I admired her all the more for her spirit.

At the bottom of the stairs, Kim took a right toward the girls' room and I pulled to a stop. Wasn't it was lewd for me to go in there? She looked at me with a raised eyebrow then took my hand firmly and pulled me inside.

A woman came out of one of the stalls and examined me with wide eyes, so I quickly ducked into the next stall to try and compose myself. I was beginning to regret having come. My eyes stayed on the little pink sneaker while I implored Neïla in whispers to come take her life back because I wasn't up to the task.

There came a knock on the door. "Are you alright?" Kim's voice chimed.

"Yes," I called back in a parched, nasal voice. I wiped my sleeve across my face to dry the tears dripping around my nostrils and opened the door to find myself face-to-face with Kim's worried expression. I began to apologize for having left her like that but she just tut-tutted and led me to the sink by the shoulders.

"Here, why don't you wash up a bit," she suggested softly.

The grime and dirt from last night must have been embarrassingly apparent so I began washing my hands, then my face and without thinking went to guzzling water at the faucet.

"Are you sure you're okay?" Kim asked with gravity when I looked up.

I replied, "yes," so weakly she clearly didn't believe it.

"You're the girl, aren't you?" she said, and stroked the bruise on my cheek.

"Yes," I nodded guiltily, knowing it was a lie.

"Why are you here alone, I mean your family must . . ." her words died off. She looked at me long and hard. "You're afraid," she stated.

I would have denied it, but I wasn't doing a very good job of lying so I nodded again.

"Nobody here will blame you. You mustn't be afraid of—"

"—It is not that," I said, with a shake of the head but didn't continue. It was better she not get involved.

"The newspaper said you don't remember anything. Is that

true?"

"Few things. What happened to her . . . me." I was making errors and had to be more careful.

"You must know that this isn't your fault, okay?" She took my face gently in her hands. "Now I don't want you going back upstairs looking like this, especially with Quincy saving us two seats." She gave me a wink that made my belly flutter with anticipation and guilt because as much as I knew it wrong, the idea of sitting next to Quincy excited me . . . or rather excited Neïla. I could tell I was blushing.

"First," she began, "let's take off this scarf."

"The family doesn't want . . ." I saw Neïla's head shake in the mirror and looked away. I wasn't planning on ever going back to that family. "No, it's okay." I reached up and took off the scarf myself.

"Your hair is so beautiful!" Kim exclaimed. "Here let me help you comb it out." She set about fixing up my hair before she applied some eyeliner, lipstick and blush on my face, and makeup on the bruise. After a minute or two she pointed to the mirror and I turned around to face the desire and despair in Neïla eyes. It was more than I could bear.

"Don't cry," she laughed, "or you'll make the eyeliner run."

Kim was so much nicer and caring than I had imagined and when I turned to stare at her blue eyes, Neïla's instincts suddenly took over and I was hugging her and giving her a kiss on both cheeks. Her smile was so sweet I almost cried again, but then got embarrassed at how girlish Neïla was making me act.

Kim glowed with pleasure, however, as she took my hand. Shouldn't I have felt some excitement or a tingle? When Josh had stared at Kim's legs and low-cut blouse in history class, the thought of holding her hand would have made me drop to my knees. How was it possible that Quincy made me go wobbly while this pretty blonde left me indifferent?

"Let's go. We don't want to keep Quincy waiting, do we?" she said with a giggle, while she dragged me out the door.

When we walked arm in arm into a churchlike room, a number of heads turned to watch us. I had been to enough Jewish memorial services to know that there would be no flowers and that I wouldn't see my body, Josh's body, in a wake. At a pulpit, there stood a rabbi but my eyes were drawn to my family—my parents, my brother, my grandparents, an uncle, my cousins. They were all here with tears in their eyes. I felt like running to them and telling them not to cry, but then my knees began to wobble. I was helpless.

Kim held me firmly and guided me to a place next to Quincy. The murmur of voices died away and the rabbi began to speak in French, then in broken English, before he went into a long sermon in Hebrew that I didn't understand. My thoughts wandered, my eyes shut, and ghosts seemed to hover in the air. Where was Neïla now?

My paternal grandfather's voice brought me out of my trance. He was giving a eulogy that was so full of praise I felt embarrassed. When he finished, there was a gleam of tears in his eyes that made me let out a sob. Had I just imagined that he didn't like me, that I was the goy grandson that disappointed him?

One of the teachers then shuffled up and gave a short eulogy so full of platitudes that I was more embarrassed for him than for what he said. I glanced at Quincy who had been in that class to see what he thought and our eyes met. Why did he blush? Was it the eulogy . . . or was he looking at Neïla and finding her attractive? I turned away wishing I could contain the flush of excitement washing through me, but my heart refused to slow down. Those were Neïla's emotions, not mine, yet it had become clear that I could never see Quincy as just a friend again.

"It's strange, it really seems like we've met before," Quincy whispered, as the service was ending.

I didn't have any idea what to answer as I glanced up at those blue eyes and hated myself for wanting him to hold me. My instincts told me to flee, to run away, but I was glued to my seat as if Neïla had taken control. Then her voice chimed, "Maybe we can meet again."

"I'd love to," he stuttered, while I blushed at what had come out of my mouth. "Have you got a telephone number or an e-mail?"

I almost gave Josh's cell phone, then shut up and shook my head. What was I thinking about? I had never learned either Neïla's address or number, and even if I had, I wasn't planning on ever going back. "No, I haven't got any of those," I answered sullenly.

He looked surprised, maybe thinking I was giving him the jilt, because Neïla was surely the first girl he had ever met who didn't have a smartphone. I felt a tear form in the corner of my eye so I turned away.

"Have you got a name?" he asked softly, and put a hand on my shoulder that made tremors run through my whole body.

"Neïla," I answered in a trembling whisper, while I turned back to face him and forced myself to smile.

"Here," he said, after a second's hesitation, and began jotting down information on a scrap of paper. "I'll give you mine. You tell me when you are free and I'll make sure I'm free." He then handed it to me. Our hands touched, lingered together, until I heard Kim cough. I jerked my hand away scared at how light-headed he made me feel.

When I turned back to him, he had a disappointed-looking smile that made me feel terrible. Had I insulted him? Would he never want to speak to me again? I was about to fall over myself with apologies when he stood up, moved into the aisle and he held out his hand for me. My hand moved toward his, touched his warm fingers, and even though I knew it was wrong to lust after my pal, didn't let go.

Kim was waiting for us in the aisle with her telephone and as soon as I had moved out from the seats, she grabbed me around the shoulder while Quincy wrapped his arm around my waist. Kim lifted her phone, three faces appeared on the screen with Neïla's in the middle, and she flashed a picture.

We stayed huddled together while she flashed a few more for good measure. I knew I should have been excited by Kim's breasts against my side but it was Quincy that sent warm waves all the way down to my stomach. His shoulders felt so strong, his hand so reassuring, that I gave in and let myself linger at his side. For an instant, I didn't care who I was or what I should do while I followed his steps and listened to each of his breaths.

My eyes opened back up as we stepped out into the wane Parisian sun—and I was standing right in front of my dad! I almost yelled, "Daddy," then got embarrassed that he would see me next to Quincy and pulled away. Why was he looking over my head and not recognizing me? I wanted just to hug him like we did every time I came back from college and began to step forward but Quincy put his arm on my shoulder. Then it all came back to me; Daddy didn't know me.

Quincy gently removed his hand from my shoulder and extended it to my father. They shook hands and exchanged a few words. Then I found myself alone in front of daddy. I tried to control my emotions, not to cry, but it was too much to look at him and not have him know who I was. When he noticed my tears, he gave me one of his typical facial expressions, the one with the rounded lips and raised eyebrows that he made anytime I was sad, and the tears came out twice as hard. I grabbed him around his chest in a big hug as if I were a kid needing comfort.

He held me gingerly until I stepped away. "Do we know each other?" he asked with his eyebrows still raised.

I had made a faux pas, I knew it. So I shook Neïla's head while her hair tickled my cheek. Daddy looked over at Quincy who shrugged.

"But you knew Josh." He said as a statement, and I nodded. "It's hard to believe he's gone like that." His voice cracked slightly on the last word.

"Maybe his spirit still is with you," I whispered, and looked up at him.

"I wish I could believe you. I did this ceremony for his mother and grandmother mostly. I never believed in anything supernatural." He shook his head sadly and I wanted to hold my daddy again, to tell him it wasn't as bad as he thought. "Did you know Josh from school?" he asked.

"No, I was . . . I mean, he . . ." Could I say he saved me? In reality it was Neïla who had saved me.

As I stuttered, recognition registered in my father's eyes. "It was you who—" He stopped speaking mid-sentence.

I nodded and lied. "He saved me. I had to see you and m . . . his mother." I glanced over at my mom. She was standing next to Kim who was holding her telephone up and nodding at me encouragingly. "Can I see her?" I felt lame having to ask to see my mom.

"Yes, of course," he replied and called, "Sharon, can you come over?"

Mom didn't look at me, but instead at something behind me, and I was about to turn around to see what it was, when a vicelike grip clamped down on my arm and a blow whipped my head sideways. My vision blanked out, then Othmane's voice was barking in my ear.

I couldn't fight back. His second slap hurt so much that spasms ran all the way down to my gut while he held me on my feet. The men in kippahs, those who were supposed to be keeping order, all stepped back leaving Quincy alone to face Neïla's brother. He held his head high, his chest out like some sort of knight or musketeer, and I found him so handsome that I quivered with fear. Othmane was dangerous, his hard jihadist scowl showed no compassion, and so I shook my head at Quincy. I couldn't bear the thought that anything might happen to him.

Luckily, one of his friends put a hand on Quincy's shoulder

and he stayed where he was while Othmane dragged me through the crowd. I caught a glimpse of Mom's flabbergasted face, standing beside Kim who had her telephone held above her head, and wished I could have said goodbye.

Othmane pulled me across the street without paying attention to the cars speeding by and pushed me up against his old jalopy. I glanced around hoping I could flee, but Othmane lifted his hand as if he were about to slap me again. I cringed, trembling, because his last slap still burned against my cheek. With a smile, he simply wrapped a scarf around my head before he threw me into the back of his car.

1 "Vous connaissez le défunt?"

Chapter 9

Mother shooed Mustapha and Djahida to their rooms before Othmane led me into the living room by the shoulders where Karim, Hadja's husband, was sitting on a cushion against the back wall. Hadja went over to sit beside him, but Mother glared at her and declared she should help with the cooking, "in the kitchen."

The blow to my stomach came unexpectedly and I found myself lying on my side unable to breathe. A hand then grabbed my hair, lifted me and while another slapped—everything went black as if I were in the void between death and life. It was then that I heard Neïla crying, her voice so shrill and pained that I wished I could comfort her, but I was being shaken, and then shaken again.

A face with a beard appeared. *"You disobeyed me,"*[1] Othmane was spitting in my face. Another blow hit me in the—I was doubled over about to retch until Othmane pulled me up again by Neïla's long mane of hair. He looked like a demon, my head was spinning and my vision was blinking on and off.

Karim had his hand on Othmane's shoulder. *"That's enough,"* he said. *"She's been punished."*[2]

For a second, I was sure Othmane would attack Karim as well, but then he dropped me and I cowered with my hands over my face. I didn't know what else to do. I thought about how Neïla had drowned, and that somebody had beaten her just like that, and that I was about to be thrown back into—

"—who was that boy?" Othmane was standing over me with his legs spread. He wanted to know about Quincy, but it would be dangerous to give his name, so I shook my head as if I didn't understand. Othmane raised his hand ready to strike me. *"Don't pretend you don't understand. Who was he?"*[3]

I knew I shouldn't speak, it would only get me in worse

trouble, but the fear muddled my brain and *"j'sais pas* (I don't know)" came out of my mouth.

"You spoke to him?"[4]

A slap caught me across my ear when I began to deny it and burning pain dizzied me. "Yes," I replied.

Othmane's eyebrow lifted with menace. *"Did you give him your number?"*[5]

"No, I don't know it,"[6] Neïla's voice whined.

He nodded, but his eyes became glaring slits. *"So he gave you his."*[7] That was a statement, not a question.

The blows had hurt so much that I nodded before letting out a gasp of tears. He held out his hand, I recoiled in fright, but then his hand lifted to strike me again so I quickly fumbled in my pocket for the scrap of paper. He ripped it from my hand and examined it carefully before putting it in his pocket. I was incapable of moving.

His eyes turned back to me as he sat on a cushion and his glare remained in my direction for what seemed like an hour. Hadja then came back in and started texting while I trembled uncontrollably. Finally Othmane stood up, strode out the door, and Karim let out a long breath.

A hand came to rest on my shoulder and Neïla's body quivered back against the wall. Hadja sat down beside me, clucked her tongue and I burst into tears against her shoulder not caring that she had driven the car for Othmane while he abducted me. I needed somebody just to feel warm.

"It's over, it's over,"[8] she repeated, while she stroked Neïla's hair.

"He hasn't been able to control himself since he got back from Syria,"[9] Karim commented in a low voice.

"It changed him," Hadja conceded. I looked up at Hadja with all sorts of questions running through my mind and started to speak but fear stifled my voice. She looked at me long and hard. *"That's right, you can't remember. He went on a jihad. We don't know*

what happened to him, but he's no longer the same man."[10]

"He's more violent,"[11] Karim agreed.

I shivered; maybe he had tried to kill Neïla. Hadja seemed to read my thoughts and said in a scolding voice, *"You mustn't go back to acting like you did before the accident. It'll end badly. We thought you had changed, and now this."*[12]

Neïla hadn't been a perfect Muslim girl, clearly the family hadn't liked that, and if I hadn't been so dazed I would have gotten angry. What right did they have to tell Neïla what she could do?

Karim nodded his head in agreement while he stared at me. *"Don't act like you did before, Neïla, or the results will be the same."*[13]

I didn't know if that was a threat or a warning, but I did understand that I was alone and that somebody wanted me dead.

* * *

I was sick the next day and wouldn't have left Neïla's room if Othmane hadn't forced me to pray in the living room. Although my head stayed bowed, I felt him watching me out of the corner of my eye. Around six o'clock there was a knock on the bedroom door and when I whispered *"oui,"* a pretty black girl peeked in, but her huge smile turned to worry as soon as she spied me. Did she expect me to rush over to her and hug her?

"Hello, how are you?"[14] she asked after a few seconds.

"Ça va (Fine)," I answered a little too dryly, because I was disconcerted by her flashy makeup and suggestive clothing.

"You don't know me?"[15]

I wanted to say "of course not" but checked my answer and shook my head instead. She puzzled over me for a minute then came to sit next to me on the bed and her hand began stroking my hair. *"My poor darling,"* she whispered in a singsong voice. *"We've known each other forever, you know my name?"*[16]

I felt like an idiot and no longer had the courage to speak, so

I just shrugged.

"What have they done to you, Neïla? I'm Bertrane,"[17] she cooed. Her eyes stayed on me for a second searching for a reaction that I couldn't give.

She sighed. *"Look, I've brought you your class work."* She took out a folder of photocopies and notes that I took with smile of relief; I had been afraid of falling behind and Neïla's high school classes weren't easy. *"I didn't think that would make you happy,"*[18] she laughed.

Her smile helped me relax so that a sigh of laughter escaped me and she gave me a hug. I returned it hoping that it would make her feel better, although there was no way I could tell her that I had taken her friend's life.

In the end, I didn't have to speak much because Bertrane was a real chatterbox and gave me all the school gossip; that Deborah had a new boyfriend, that Ryan broke his leg, how they had made fun of the history teacher who had hair growing out of his nose . . . I actually found myself laughing at her description of Mr. Drument.

Hadja opened the door. *"You have to go,"*[19] she told Bertrane, with a hard stare that looked just like Mother's. Bertrane seemed to jump, then gave me two quick kisses and scurried out.

Mother was working so Hadja had cooked dinner: grilled *merguez* sausages and oven French fries. With Josh's appetite, I would have devoured everything, but Neïla's stomach didn't want any food and I was hardly able to swallow a bite. Afterward, we went through the evening prayer in the living room. I now knew it well enough that Djahida didn't correct me, but it felt like all their eyes were scrutinizing me.

After dinner, Hadja kept her big-sister distance while Djahida put on some rap music and began dancing. I had never been keen on hip-hop so I sat in the corner watching just like I had in high school when I had to keep my musical tastes to myself if I wanted to avoid trouble. Djahida just scoffed and reached out her hand for me to join in. I would have refused if Mustapha hadn't bounced over to pull on my arm with his bright eyes and beg me to do "my moves."

At first I just stood confused, lost in the syncopated beat, but slowly my eyes closed while I let the bass beat move through Neïla's stomach and down to her feet. Suddenly, as if by magic, her arms began to gyrate and she made a spin on her heels. There was such a deep primal pleasure in undulating to the rhythm, and Neïla moved so gracefully, that I even began to laugh.

Then Mother came home. She remained silent when she saw us dancing, so Djahida switched off the music and we went to our rooms. Mother came to comb out my hair while she hummed in Arabic and somehow managed to make me feel as if I had betrayed her by enjoying myself. I knew it was silly but it made my belly ache.

1 "Tu m'as désobéi."
2 "Ca suffit. Elle a été punie."
3 "Qui était ce garçon? Ne fait pas semblant de ne pas comprendre. Qui était-il?"
4 "Tu lui as parlé."
5 "Tu lui as donné ton numéro?"
6 "Non, je ne le connais pas."
7 "Donc il t'a donné le sien."
8 "C'est fini, c'est fini."
9 "Il ne se contrôle plus depuis qu'il est revenu de Syrie."
10 "Ça l'a changé. C'est vrai que tu te rappelles plus. Il a fait le jihad. On sait pas ce qui lui est arrivé mais ce n'est plus le même homme."
11 "Il est plus violent."
12 "Il ne faut pas que tu recommences comme avant l'accident. Ça finira mal. On pensait que tu avais changé et maintenant ceci."
13 "Ne refais pas comme avant, Neïla, ou ça peut finir pareil."

14 "Salut, ça va?"

15 "Tu me connais pas?"

16 "Ma pauvre chérie, nous nous connaissons depuis toujours, tu connais mon nom?"

17 "Mais qu'est-ce qu'on t'a fait, Neïla? Je suis Bertrane."

18 "Regarde, je t'ai apporté tes cours. Je ne pensais pas que ça te fasse plaisir."

19 "Faut que tu rentres."

Chapter 10

It was impossible to fall asleep so I lay with my eyes open, staring at a shaft of light that filtered through a crack in the shutters while Djahida made mousy noises through her nose. I wished I could shake her awake to tell her to be quiet.

A blink appeared in the hazy darkness that slowly transformed into Neïla standing in a pool of shadow. She looked so forlorn that I would have comforted her, but my brain stumbled when I tried to speak. In desperation, I got out of bed and reached out to touch the air in which she was standing.

"*Désolée* (sorry)," her mouth worded.

"Why?" I asked.

Djahida stirred and Neïla's head jerked toward her. *"Be careful,"* she mouthed, *"and the code's Mustapha's birthday."*[1]

I looked at her with my eyebrows raised, but she had disappeared.

"What are you doing?"[2] Djahida mumbled, in a hoarse voice.

"Toilettes," I answered.

"Next to the computer?"[3] she scoffed.

Luckily Djahida didn't wait for an answer and flipped over with her back to me. I didn't feel safe to move until her breathing slowed down, but I still headed to the toilet because I had told her I was going there.

Sitting in the dark mulling over everything that had happened, my mind got so mixed up that I almost wished I could rush back to the canal and jump in. Why couldn't Neïla help me during the day, but instead waited for me to go to bed? Why had I been able to dance and why couldn't I stop thinking about Quincy? I had once liked chewing the fat with him, but he never made my heart beat like . . . like I were Neïla. Was Josh dying?

More depressed than ever, I slipped back to Neïla's room and curled up in bed. At some point I was asleep because nightmares replaced my worries; I was Josh again but chased by myself. If Josh caught me, I would die, and I couldn't figure out why I wanted myself dead. Every time I turned around to speak to Josh, silence sliced at me like a blade until the wounds were open and my life was flowing out into a river. Then Neïla was standing over me weeping. I tried to console her, to tell her I was fine, but then I noticed that she was the one who was injured.

"Wake up, you're screaming,"[4] Djahida shouted.

I looked over at her. She was leaning on one arm looking annoyed while a wan ray of light filtered through a crack in the shutters and lit her forehead. "What happened?" I asked.

"Encore de l'anglais (English again)!" she hissed. *"What's wrong with you? Are you no longer the same person or something?"*[5]

"What time is it?"[6] I asked in French to change the subject.

"How do you want me to know? And I have a goddamn math test today!"[7]

I curled up with my back to her, but she didn't seem to think it was over.

"Why don't you go to school?"[8]

I looked over my shoulder at her and shook my head. It would be a relief to get out of the apartment, but it seemed that I had little say in the matter. I stared at the window until Othmane called us for Çobh, the dawn prayer.

At the breakfast table, I sat wondering what day it was while Djahida complained to Mother about me not having to go to school. Mother just let her speak and then served her some mint green tea. When she had talked herself out, Mother replied, *"She has an appointment today."*[9] I looked at Mother, but only received a blank stare back.

* * *

Neïla was only a teenage girl, so whatever anyone might think, she really did have to go back to school. I therefore spent the morning reviewing her history notes and forced myself to read her science textbook. It was somewhat worrisome that I could understand French so well, but I reasoned that it was Neïla who was helping me.

Othmane was in the living room, maybe only pretending to study the Koran, and I was so afraid of him that I had been holding back from going to the toilet. The bullies that had beaten up Josh were nothing compared to Neïla's brother and I couldn't stop the trembling.

I put down the history notes. If I were ever allowed to go to school, I could escape from this apartment for at least a few hours. What's more, the hijab wasn't allowed in French schools, so I would be able to dress as I wanted. But how did I want to dress? Or rather, how would I want to if I could see Quincy again?

I stared down at Neïla's slender feet, imagining what it would be like to wear pretty clothes. My eyes closed and I pictured Quincy's blue eyes staring at me, then smiling, so I quickly opened them back up. I wasn't that sort of guy! Why then couldn't I forget him? A sudden fright seized me and I trembled at the thought that he might not ever want to see me again. Did I . . . did Neïla really have a chance with him?

Othmane didn't see me rush out and quickly lock the door just in case he realized I was in the bathroom. What if I just stayed in there until Mother came back? The sound of water running helped me to relax, but I also realized how hopeless hiding in here was—Mother hadn't seemed to care that he beat me—and the need for Quincy, the hope that he might protect me, swelled in my belly.

After a few minutes sitting uselessly on the seat, I stood up and arranged the clothes I was wearing. Then, taking a deep breath, I slipped out of the toilet and into the bathroom locking the door behind me. For a few seconds, I stood facing the wall embarrassed that I should want to see Neïla in the full-length mirror. I knew she was pretty, why did I wish to prove it to myself?

Slowly I turned to face her in the mirror. She was still just as slim, if not more so, but it was her eyes, red from crying, that drew my attention. They appeared to be pleading with me for help even though there was nothing I could do. The ugly green bruises from Othmane's slaps on her cheek and neck made her look so martyred and beautiful that when a tear started rolling down her cheek, my heart broke. I was just a chickenhearted wimp to leave her in such misery, so I wiped away the tears and went back to Neïla's room to finish reading her biology notes, and pine for Quincy.

* * *

Just before lunch I heard the door close, then Othmane's slippers on the tile floor. Soon after, Mother knocked on the door and told me with tight lips to come eat. I followed her to the kitchen where she had me sit facing Othmane. His stare bore down on me until I looked away.

After Othmane had finished his couscous, he motioned me into the living room to say the Dhohr prayer. I went through the motions behind him and he then ordered me to put on my hijab. *"We're going out."*[10] I escaped to Neïla's room where I undertook the task of putting on the veil. It was difficult to get that piece of cloth on just right, but I was finally able to join him at the front door where he inspected my work and, with a grunt, pushed me out the door.

The usual group of young boys was gathered in front of the apartment, shadowboxing and laughing. They said hello to Othmane and to me, but I bowed my head refusing to speak so none of them pursued the conversation. Othmane then pointed to his old Renault and had me get in the passenger seat while he took the wheel.

The *périphérique* was jammed with stop-and-go traffic as usual, so it was lucky that we only had to take it to the Porte des Lilas. Othmane then drove around for about ten minutes looking for a parking space until we spotted a car pulling out on a one-way street. He backed down it, parked with one wheel on the sidewalk and took off walking at such a fast pace that I had to trot to keep up. I noticed he hadn't plugged the meter.

We went past a park and then down to a small hospital stuck between the apartment buildings. Othmane stopped at the front desk to ask a question that I didn't hear before he turned to walk to the elevator without looking back. I was beginning to wonder if I shouldn't turn to run when he shot me a glare and pushed the up button.

He was so silent I could hear the humming of the machinery and the people speaking in the hall as we passed the second floor. The door slid open on the third floor and he turned left down the hallway. People averted their eyes as we walked past but when I glanced back, I could see that they were staring at us. In an open space, Othmane went to the receptionist's desk and spoke softly.

I could feel the people glancing in my direction in the waiting area and wished I could hide. As the wait dragged on, I picked up a magazine but Othmane snatched it away and threw it to the far side of the table. I looked up into his scowl and he didn't need to tell me that it was because there was a photo of a girl wearing a bikini on the cover. With a sigh, I pulled the veil over Neïla's face and curled her legs under me. Josh never sat like that. Eventually, Neïla's name was called by an elderly doctor with bushy eyebrows that I hadn't seen approaching. The doctor turned down the hall with us following and then invited me to enter one of the rooms. I glanced back at Othmane who started to follow but the doctor shook his head and stood in front of Neïla's brother.

"This is a psychiatric examination," the doctor said. *"I need to see her alone."*[11]

Othmane shook his head and didn't move while I looked from one to the other. Which of the two frightened me the most? If this man learned my true identity, I would be put in an asylum. Moreover, if he ever told Neïla's family, I could fear worse than spending my life in a hospital. For once I wished that Othmane might stay with me so that I could have an excuse not to speak. Fighting all my primal reflexes, I forced myself to take Othmane's hand while I nodded to the doctor.

Othmane stared down at me as surprised as I was frightened, then at the doctor. My gesture must have convinced Othmane that I really was crazy because he smiled at me, the first time I'd seen him smile, and strode away.

The doctor watched the whole exchange with twinkling eyes and a professional smile. Once Othmane had disappeared around the corner, he invited me into an undecorated hospital room, and after glancing over my file, asked me in a very French accent, "Can you speak French now or prefer your English still?"

I took long time deciding if that wasn't a trick question. "English is easier," I finally answered. He sat back silently with his eyes on me until I felt obliged to continue. "I understand French, but I do not trust me when I speak it."

"And what are you afraid to say to me?" he asked, without looking away.

I knew he would trap me! His eyes twinkled again so I began to stutter that I wasn't afraid, but his eyes got brighter and brighter the more I denied. I finally bowed my head not knowing what to say.

"You have no reason to be afraid. I will keep all your secrets. It is my . . . how you say *sermon*?"

"Oath," I replied in a whisper, then wondered how Neïla had known the word.

He raised an eyebrow. "Ah, yes. It is my *oath*," He said, while his eyes became soft and so grandfatherly that I wanted to trust him. "You can tell me what you have on your heart."

"I can't," I replied, shaking myself back to reality. "I can't tell you."

"When you are ready, I think it would do you good to confide your troubles." He made a little cough and waited to see if I would say anything, but I remained quiet this time. "Consent you to some tests with a neuro-psychologist? Simply to see if your executive functions have been touched."

I didn't know what he meant by my executive functions, but I didn't seem to have a choice so I nodded. He smiled and led me back out of the office while I looked around to see if Othmane was still guarding me, but there was no sign of him. The doctor then left me with a portly young woman who took me to another room and had me do stupid tasks and solve brainless puzzles for more than an hour. She was nice enough so I tried to be patient and take it seriously. I then spent another half hour thumbing through a six-month-old gossip magazine before the doctor called me back into his office. His eyes still twinkled, but he seemed a little more puzzled.

"I don't want to pronounce too quickly, but your executive functions are good and your IQ would be even quite high." He looked at me as if I should be relieved or happy at the news. I was actually wondering what he had thought before I did the tests.

"I will speak to everybody concerned," he continued, "but we must consider when you return to school. Would that please you?"

My face must have lit up like a neon light as I squealed and almost jumped over the desk to hug him. Only after I had sat back down did I realize how girlish I was being.

"Don't become much too excited," the doctor cautioned. "It must take at least a few days to set up." He saw my disappointment so he tried to reassure me. "But I'm sure it will be, you just need a little patience. In the meantime, I wish you to continue your medical treatment and I shall see you next week."

I tried to look as responsible and sane as I could while I

followed him to the appointment desk.

"When the man accompanying her returns, she will need a new appointment next week,"[12] he told the secretary.

"My brother's not here?"[13] I asked the doctor. I was surprised that Othmane would leave me alone.

He shrugged. *"Sit in the waiting area. I'm sure he will arrive."*[14]

1 "Sois prudente, et le code, c'est l'anniversaire de Mustapha."
2 "Qu'est-ce tu fais?"
3 "A côté de l'ordinateur?"
4 "Réveille-toi, tu cries."
5 "Qu'est-ce qui t'arrive? Tu n'es plus la même personne ou quoi?"
6 "Quelle heure est-il?"
7 "Comment veux-tu que je sache? Putain! Et j'ai un contrôle de maths aujourd'hui.
8 Pourquoi tu vas pas au lycée, toi?"
9 "Elle a un rendez-vous aujourd'hui."
10 "On sort."
11 "C'est un examen psychiatrique. Il faut que je la vois seule."
12 "Quand son accompagnateur arrive, il me faut un nouveau rendez-vous dans une semaine."
13 "Mon frère n'est pas là?"
14 "Asseyez-vous dans la salle d'attente. Je suis sûr qu'il va arriver."

Chapter 11

People kept glancing sideways at me while I sat there in the waiting room with the veil pulled across my face. I no longer cared because I could only think about being back in a classroom and getting away from Othmane. Then Mokhtar sauntered in with his too-large-for-comfort smile and I realized I had missed my chance to escape.

"So sly bunny, were we good?"[1] he gibed.

I didn't answer. I had a feeling there was more to his banter than appeared. *"Where is Othmane?"*[2] I asked.

"Ah, you little conniver. You don't know? Your stratagem worked."[3]

"My what?"[4]

"That's it, keep acting like you forget or don't know." His smile really worried me and I would have fled if his hand hadn't remained solidly on my shoulder. *"We all know he is not a genius but this time, you really did it."*[5] He handed me a helmet and began leading me out the front door.

"What did I do?"[6] I asked, while he pulled me down the stairs and out the front door.

Mokhtar simply winked and stopped in front of one of those little motor scooters that zip in and out of traffic. I guessed immediately what was coming so I shook my head—there was no way I was getting on one of those dangerous things!

He laughed and put his helmet on. *"Normally you love it. You haven't changed that much?"* I refused to move, but I could see he was getting a little irritated. *"What, You prefer Othmane's car? You know it's mom who pays for it? At least this is mine."*[7]

His smile disappeared, letting me understand that he was giving me no choice so I put on the helmet as best I could over the hijab and pulled my long skirt in under me before I got on behind him. I was surprised at how strong he was and even if he looked wiry, his muscles were like iron. The scooter started up with a loud rumbling screech and then he pulled out—I almost fell off the back.

As he swerved through traffic, I became convinced he was trying to kill us both. Paris traffic is stop and go at the best of times, but at five-thirty or six it's more like a parking lot. He didn't slow down. If one of the cars had decided to switch lanes, we would have both been hamburger. When he exited at Bagnolet, it was immediately to take a one-way street in the wrong direction, and that's when I shut my eyes. I only opened them again when I felt him slow and stop. He was glowing with excitement and pride.

"That's a change from the car, isn't it?" he laughed. There was no arguing with that so I nodded dumbly. *"Now, you stay beside me and don't say anything."*[8]

He looked me in the eye and waited for me to rearrange my hijab, making sure that it covered most of Neïla's face, before he made me follow him through the parking lot. When we reached the group of boys that always hung out in front of the buildings, I heard the words *pute* ("whore") and *salope* ("bitch") thrown in my direction. If Mokhtar hadn't held my arm tightly, I would have certainly turned to flee. It was lucky I didn't because I would never have been able to escape with that long dress.

Mokhtar whispered, *"Don't move,"*[9] and went forward to negotiate with the group of potential lynchers. His hands gesticulated in all directions while he skipped from one foot to the other, and although the boys didn't lose their scowls, I no longer had the impression that I was going to be stoned.

Then, when Mokhtar motioned me forward, my legs—or rather Neïla's legs—refused to budge. Mokhtar was obliged to walk back and take me by the shoulders to get me to move past the boys' hostile stares and I found myself clinging to him to stay standing.

Mokhtar didn't say anything, something rather unusual, while we made our way up the four stories to the apartment. I took off my shoes and looked at my toes through the beige nylon socks. They weren't mine, they were Neïla's, and she had very pretty feet even if her toenail polish was chipped. That shouldn't have bothered me, I would never put on anything like that, so why was I hesitating to step forward? Finally, with a sigh, I hung up Neïla's jacket and tiptoed into the living room.

Djahida and Mustapha were sitting at the coffee table doing their homework but Djahida turned her head and visibly didn't want to speak to me. Mustapha's eyes were round as a cocker spaniel's and wet from tears. I started to go to him but then thought better of it.

Mokhtar sprawled himself out on a cushion and waited for me to tiptoe to the far corner. I was determined not to say anything and had just sat down when Djahida rounded on me, *"So, are you proud of yourself?"*[10]

I was alone, in the void without any identity, and literally at a loss for words. While Djahida's eyes continued to bore into me, I tried to look for Josh's words but got muddled. In the end I simply gave a bewildered shrug.

"Don't try and make me think you didn't know or that you don't understand," Djahida barked. *"I've had enough of you acting like a screwball!"*[11]

I could see Mustapha was crying and I felt anger rise up from my gut. *"Savoir quoi* (Know what)?" Neïla screamed. My raised voice surprised everybody, even me, and although the flames didn't leave Djahida's eyes, she did observe me in silence for a few breaths.

Mokhtar put on his large smile as if he enjoyed it and simpered. *"I think she really doesn't know."*[12]

"You don't know where Othmane is?" She spat the words out. *"Well, the police took him if you want to know."*[13]

Mokhtar intervened, even though he was clearly enjoying the scene. *"Show her the video."*[14]

Djahida stood up to go to our bedroom but turned back

around to order Mustapha to stay in the living room. He looked like a punished dog. I tried to imagine how terrible this must be for him because he loved Othmane like he loved almost everyone.

In the bedroom, Mokhtar had me stand in front of him while Djahida sat at the computer and clicked on a link. I saw a picture of Neïla come up, as pallid as an icon of the Virgin Mary, and my heart broke seeing such melancholic beauty. A text began running underneath Neïla's image.

> *—She was seconds from dying when he came to her rescue. All she wanted to do was thank the parents of the boy who was murdered saving her life.—*

"Maybe you can translate for us now that you speak English,"[15] Djahida commented sardonically.

I was too intent on the video to react to her spite. The image then faded into a video of Neïla—no, I was there hugging Daddy with tears in my eyes—and he was crying too. I tried to hear what was said between us, but on the video you could only hear the background noise and the chatter of the crowd.

Dad then looked up and called for Mom but the camera changed directions to catch a madman, Othmane, pushing his way through the crowd with a terrible scowl behind his Islamic beard while his eyes burned with murder. When he grabbed Neïla, she was literally lifted off her feet and the memory of the pain almost made my legs buckle under me.

Othmane shouted over the silence of the crowd, *"Je t'ai dit de ne pas venir!"* Underneath the English translation appeared, "I told you not to come."

Then he slapped Neïla, her head whipped sideways and I could feel the pain throughout my whole body—and he slapped her again. She looked so groggy I imagined she was unconscious, but when Quincy stepped forward, her eyes pleaded for him not to intervene. Quincy looked so heroic that I felt a sudden longing to be held by him again.

"Who is that guy?"[16] Djahida asked sharply.

I refused to answer and the video ended with Othmane dragging Neïla through traffic to the car. Her picture then came back onto the screen with the text: *Help Neïla. Share this video with everyone you know.*

Kim! I knew it was Kim, and she had unfortunately done an amazing job. I glanced at the number of hits but didn't have time to count the digits. It had gone viral in forty-eight hours.

"You have to admit, our brother did a number,"[17] Mokhtar stated flatly.

"But that's no reason to arrest him,"[18] Djahida whined. She then looked at me severely as if I had been one of the policemen.

"You'll see. They won't keep him long. They just jumped on the occasion." Mokhtar gave a laugh. *"That'll teach him a lesson."*[19]

Djahida turned to me and glowered. *"Well, you should do something about your nail polish. Look at it!"*[20]

I looked down at the chipped polish. I had felt like a weirdo looking through Neïla's beauty supplies and only necessity had forced me go through her underwear. Why then had I let Kim put makeup on her face in order to seduce a former buddy? Maybe I really was a creep and Othmane had been right to beat me.

Then the door opened and Othmane's voice rumbled through the thin plasterboard walls. My legs gave way and I collapsed on the bed while Neïla's two siblings stared at me. Mokhtar smirked and they both left the room. I could barely breathe.

* * *

I sat at the floor beside the bed so that I couldn't be seen by somebody entering the room and listened to the laughing in the living room. No one had called me for dinner but my stomach was in such a knot I wasn't sure I could have eaten anyway.

I heard prayers being mumbled, no one had come to fetch me

for those either, and when the door opened, I huddled farther back into the corner until Mother's eyes found me. She was holding a sandwich and wearing a blank face.

My eyes closed while she crossed the room because I had this sudden fear that she was going to start pummeling me. Instead, I heard the plate clunk onto Neïla's desk and felt hands lift me and guide me to the chair. Mother pushed the sandwich in front of me and waited for me to start eating. It was turkey with a lot of mayonnaise.

"What did the doctor say?"[21] she asked, after I had swallowed a few bites.

I didn't want to speak but Mother stared at me until I lost my nerve. *"That I can go back to high school,"*[22] I finally whispered.

"Really?" Mother replied in a flat tone of voice. Her expression didn't change while she said, *"We go to the market tomorrow."*[23]

In the other room Othmane's voice rose, Neïla's body recoiled and a smile flickered across Mother's lips. While I was staring at her, she reached out to touch the bruise on Neïla's face and it took all of my willpower not to flinch or push her away. I couldn't help thinking that not only did she condone Othmane's violence, but that it pleased her. When she finally left the room, I went back to sit behind the bed leaving the sandwich where it was.

I fell asleep on the floor, I suppose, because the lights were off and Djahida was making her mousey sounds when I realized where I was. I stood up to get undressed and my eyes caught a ripple in the darkness. It was Neïla and her waves of hair looked like those invisible currents beneath the surface as she shook her head and mouthed, "I'm sorry—*désolée.*"

I shook my head and yelled with a soundless inner voice, "No, it's my fault. This is your body."

She shook her head and mouthed, *"It's your life."* Then she put her hand on her breast. *"Don't fight your heart."*[24]

"What do you mean?"[25] I whispered out loud.

"Quincy's a good man and I think he's cute too." I was sure I

turned red—or was that Neïla blushing? How did she know I was troubled by my former friend? *"Don't fight your heart,"*[26] she repeated.

"But it's not normal for a guy . . ."[27] I let my whisper trail off. Was I still a man?

She gave me a sympathetic smile. *"As I said, it's your life and I'm sorry."* Suddenly her eyes turned to Djahida, then back to me. *"Remember, Mustapha's birthday is . . ."*[28] She blinked out before she had finished.

"Do you want to shut up?"[29] Djahida barked, making me jump.

I began to answer but realized I was crying in little hiccups. I felt alone, like an idiot.

"I had to be the one to be stuck with a completely mental sister!"[30] Djahida spat, and rolled over.

I sat on the bed wondering what Neïla had meant, but then I heard her crying. I was sure it was her because Josh never cried like that. I was still Josh, wasn't I? I curled up into a ball and wished I could sleep.

1 "Alors pinpin futé, on est sage?"

2 "Où est Othmane?"

3 "Ah, la petite rusée. Tu ne sais pas? Ton stratagème a marché."

4 "Mon quoi?"

5 "Va, fais celle qui oublie ou qui ne sais pas. On sait qu'il n'est pas toujours futé mais là, tu as fait fort."

6 "Qu'est-ce que j'ai fait?"

7 "D'habitude tu l'adores. Tu n'as pas changé à ce point? Quoi, tu préfères la voiture d'Othmane. Tu sais que c'est maman qui la paie? Au moins, ça, c'est à moi."

8 "Ca change de la voiture, non? Maintenant, tu restes à côté de moi et ne dis rien."

9 "Bouge pas."

10 "Alors, tu es fière de toi?"

11 "Ne cherche pas à me faire croire que tu ne savais pas ou que tu comprends pas. J'en ai marre que tu joues la folle!"

12 "Je crois qu'elle ne sait vraiment pas."

13 "Tu sais pas où Othmane se trouve? Bah, la police l'a embarqué si tu veux savoir."

14 "Montre-lui la vidéo."

15 "Peut-être tu peux nous traduire maintenant que tu parles anglais."

16 "Qui c'est ce mec?"

17 "Faut dire qu'il a fait fort, notre frère."

18 "Mais c'est pas une raison pour l'arrêter."

19 "Ah, tu vas voir. Ils vont pas le garder longtemps. Ils ont juste saisi l'occasion. Cela lui servira de leçon."

20 "Et toi, tu devrais t'occuper de ton vernis. Regarde-le!"

21 "Le médecin dit quoi?"

22 "Que je peux retourner au lycée."

23 "Ah bon? On va au marché demain."

24 "Ne lutte pas contre ton cœur."

25 "Qu'est-ce que tu veux dire?"

26 "Quincy est un bon garçon et moi aussi je le trouve mignon. Ne lutte pas contre ton cœur."

27 "Mais ce n'est pas normal pour un garçon…"

28 "Comme je t'ai dit, c'est ta vie maintenant et je suis désolée. Souviens-toi, l'anniversaire de Mustapha est le…"

29 "Tu ne veux pas te taire?"

30 "Il fallait que ça tombe sur moi, une sœur complètement ouf!"

Part 3

Dieu vaincu deviendra Satan, Satan vainqueur deviendra Dieu. "God beaten will become Satan, Satan a victor will become God."

—Anatole France

Chapter 12

I didn't have time to ask Mustapha about his birthday that morning because Mother had him packed off to his transport right after he had been dressed. She didn't give me much time either, as it seemed that we had to get to the market with the early risers. When I asked her why, she just gave me a blank stare.

The stairwell was empty because it was too early for the gang of boys who had wanted to lynch me and I let out a little sigh of relief but still stayed close to Mother. She pulled a wheeled cart while I carried a basket down the littered street between the graffiti-tagged buildings. I felt tiny and fragile, nothing like Josh.

We turned west along a meandering urban street that was first lined with bankrupt businesses but then, as we neared Paris, the buildings became cleaner and the open shops more numerous. Fewer women were wearing the hijab, too. Some heads turned as we walked past and I guessed they didn't like seeing veiled women. Though I might once have been tolerant, now I couldn't blame them; it wasn't right to force Neïla to cover herself like that.

We passed a café as we neared the market and I glanced in at the men standing at the counter drinking espressos or glasses of white wine. A few weeks ago, I might have walked up to the counter and ordered a coffee in my poor French, but today I was carrying a basket so that Neïla's mother could show me how to do the shopping. Did she plan on Neïla becoming a housewife? I might never be a history professor now but I didn't want Neïla to be stuck at home with children. Mother glanced over at me as if she could read my thoughts, so I turned away. This was Neïla's life and I had to give it back to her as she would have wanted it.

People swarmed around the market while vendors vaunted their wares at the top of their lungs. There were so many stands and planks supported by trestles displaying fruit, vegetables, clothes, hardware and other items that little room was left for the crowd to circulate.

Mother clearly knew her way about, so I guessed that she shopped here often. She left me for a minute at the back of a stall while she bought some olives, then beckoned me to follow to another one owned by an Arab woman displaying underwear and perfume. The lady smiled and I whispered, *"bonjour,"* while Mother held out a bottle of perfume for me to sniff. It had a flowery citrus smell that made Neïla's senses tingle. Mother looked me in the eye, nodded and handed it to the lady along with some large underwear for herself.

The next stop was a halal butcher's refrigerated van. Mother explained to me the importance of buying meat only from a halal butcher in whom you could have faith and since this man was a friend of her uncle's son-in-law, he was fully trustworthy. I listened carefully not wanting to appear disinterested while she bought a shank of mutton to show me how to make tajine.

After that, Mother headed for a vegetable stand and pushed her way between two other ladies to grab a bunch of carrots before she waved me over. I heard one of the elderly women grumble as I excused my way through. Mother stuck the carrots in my basket along with a few lemons and told me to pay.

"Je n'ai pas d'argent (I have no money)," I stuttered.

She gave a wry smile, pointed behind me and I found myself face-to-face with Mokhtar.

"So are we teaching sly bunny to do her shopping?"[1] he said with his big smile and turned to serve the grumbling French lady who gave me a wicked look before she huffed away.

"You work here?"[2] I asked, when he turned back around. The words had come out without my thinking.

"She's capable of speaking again!"[3] His smile made me a little uncomfortable, but it then flashed in the direction of a young black mother holding a head of cabbage. He walked over to take

her money while I looked around for Mother. She had disappeared.

Mokhtar suddenly yelled out that he had the best vegetables in all of Bagnolet and I almost collapsed in fright. He gave me his smile when he noticed I was trembling and sidled back over.

"Did Othmane beat you last night?"[4] he asked. Although he looked me in the eye, something in his attitude made me think he didn't want an answer. I shook my head anyway.

"Of course he didn't."[5] Mokhtar sneered. I looked at him surprised. He had clearly meant something by that but he wasn't going to elaborate.

"Where does Othmane work?"[6] I asked in a soft voice. If I were to ever figure out who had tried to kill Neïla, I needed to know more.

Mokhtar's faced screwed up momentarily before the smile stretched his lips out again. *"Othmane work? You're kidding! He wants to be an Imam. He lives off of our mother and welfare."*[7]

His answer seemed in contradiction with everything I had seen. *"But he's so respected,"*[8] I blurted out.

"Not everyone has done the jihad by the sword." His smile was now severe and his eyes darted from right to left before they focused on me. *"Nobody respects the little guy who starts work in the market at five in the morning,"*[9] he hissed.

I watched him while he took change from a pretty young French woman with whom I would have liked to chat but, unfortunately, she avoided looking at me. Mokhtar then came back to where I was standing and started rearranging the tomatoes. I had a feeling that the young woman hadn't liked me. *"And what was I like before?"*[10] I asked, when he had finished.

"You spoke a lot more." He gave a wry smile. *"You've always been a sly bunny; the smartest and the only one of us not to go to trade school."* He seemed melancholic for a second. *"Djahida won't do any studies. It's okay if you don't either now."* His smile became mocking again. *"And you were always the best dancer."*[11]

I looked at him trying to find a reply, but he didn't wait and turned to serve some overweight bleached-blonde woman just before Mother appeared beside me. She put some bread in my basket and took my arm to leave. I started to speak, but she cut me off.

"He'll take care of the bill,"[12] she said, pointing at Mokhtar who blew me a kiss.

* * *

The day was spent cleaning, cooking and preparing North African pastries. *"You are going to have a husband,"*[13] Mother explained, while I dusted off the living room lamp.

I looked at her with my eyebrow raised; Neïla was only sixteen, why would Mother talk to her about that? She, however, continued without paying attention to my frown.

"A woman must make her man happy. The first thing is cooking. When a man doesn't eat well, he gets mean. You must also keep things clean. Men have to worry about more important matters than tidiness. And afterward, you must be prepared when he needs you. You must make yourself pretty and smell nice, that's why perfume is important, and you mustn't deny any of his desires. If you have pleasure, that's fine, but if you don't, he mustn't know."[14]

She was quite serious, and I felt obliged to nod, but what were her reasons for making this speech? I sort of doubted Othmane would have looked kindly on Neïla having a boyfriend and I certainly didn't want one, except for—

The door opened and I heard several male voices. Mother shook her head when I started to go out into the living room to see who it was and instead shooed me back to Neïla's room where she pulled out a hijab and a jilbāb. The long robe was like the one Mother wore and I looked at her hoping she wasn't serious.

"It's your job to serve," she said, by way of explanation. *"But*

first, put on some perfume."[15]

I was on the verge of refusing when I heard Othmane's low rumbling voice echo above the others and my whole body began to quake. Mother took advantage of my silence to dab a rather large quantity of perfume on my neck and arms before she slipped the large fabric over my head. She then scowled at me until I put on the hijab as best I could. With a snort, she readjusted it and handed me a pair of gloves.

"Pourquoi les gants (Why the gloves)?" I asked, as I put them on.

Mother simply sighed, led me to the kitchen and indicated for me to take the tray with green tea out into the living room.

The men's stares made me flinch and I was about to retreat when I caught Othmane's blank face out of the side of my vision. Fear forced me to keep my head down and put up with their condescending smiles while I served the tea and went to stand in the corner. There were four of them. One was older and spoke more Arabic than French. The others were younger, about Othmane's age, and preferred French. They spoke about the uprising in Gaza, with insults directed at the Jews and Americans, and about a demonstration in Paris. When I went back to the kitchen to refill the pot, Mother handed me the tajine.

"You serve the oldest person first, then the other guests,"[16] she instructed.

They ate slowly, the older Arab with his fingers, and talked. There was tension in Paris between the Jews and Muslims and the recent Israeli bombing of Gaza had sparked open conflict here. None spoke of illegal violence, but I guessed that they hadn't excluded the option.

I cleared the dirty plates and was preparing to take out the pastries when Mother put her hand on my arm and signaled for me to sit down for a few minutes. I could hear their muffled voices but couldn't catch what they were saying although Mother went to stand near the door.

After what seemed like an hour, she pointed at the pastries and hurried me out with them. The men's smiles were still condescending and their eyes made me feel that I was just another pastry. Would I have any more say in who would partake in me than one of those little moons covered with powdered sugar?

1 "Alors pinpin futé, on t'apprend à faire des courses?"

2 "Tu travailles ici?"

3 "Elle retrouve donc l'usage de la parole!"

4 "Othmane t'a pas battue hier soir?"

5 "Bien sûr que non."

6 "Il travaille où, Othmane?"

7 "Othmane travaille? Tu plaisantes! Il veut être Imam, lui. Il vit de notre mère et du RMI."

8 "Mais il est si respecté."

9 "Pas tout le monde a fait le jihad de l'épée. Personne respecte le petit gars qui commence le boulot au marché à cinq heures du matin."

10 "Et moi, j'étais comment avant?"

11 "Tu parlais bien plus. Tu as toujours étais pinpin futé, la plus maline, la seule à faire le lycée général. Djahida ne fera pas d'études. C'est pas grave si tu n'en fais pas non plus maintenant. Et tu as toujours été la meilleure danseuse."

12 "Il s'occupera de la note."

13 "Tu vas avoir un mari."

14 "Une femme doit savoir rendre son homme heureux. La première chose est la cuisine. Quand un homme mange mal, il devient méchant. C'est aussi à toi de veiller sur la propreté. Les hommes s'occupent de choses plus importantes que le ménage. Ensuite, quand il a besoin de toi, tu dois être prête. Tu dois te faire jolie et sentir bon, c'est pour ça que les parfums sont importants, et tu ne dois pas discuter de ses envies. Si tu prends plaisir, c'est bien, mais si tu n'en prends

pas, il ne dois pas le savoir."

15 "C'est à toi de faire le service. Mais d'abord mets un peu de parfum."

16 "Tu sers la personne la plus âgée d'abord, puis les autres invités."

Chapter 13

I had just finished the dishes when Hadja brought Neïla's younger siblings back home. Mustapha gave me a big hug, Djahida openly ignored me and Hadja kissed me on the cheeks even though I wished I could refuse. I was sure that she had been part of the scheme to get Neïla married. Luckily Hadja didn't stay for long and Djahida rushed off to shower so I found myself alone with Mustapha in the living room.

"*Ton anniversaire, c'est quand* (Your birthday, when is it)?" I whispered into his ear while he was playing a video game.

Mustapha looked at me with wide eyes. "*But you know it.*"[1]

I put my finger to my lips and shushed him. "*I just want to make sure.*"[2]

He shook his head like I was crazy but answered, "*It's in January, the 19th.*"[3]

"*And you're ten years old.*"[4]

"*No, I'm eleven!*"[5] he replied with a miffed frown and resumed his game.

I was sorry that I had upset him but I was sure I had Neïla's password now. Maybe there weren't any secrets on her pages, but I would have bet she didn't want her family spying on her. A door then opened and I got back to doing the housework before anybody saw that I'd been talking to Mustapha.

The bathroom was empty when Mother finally gave me permission to shower and brush my teeth. When I had finished, Djahida was already in bed with the lights out. I slipped under the covers and quickly fell asleep. Neïla didn't come to me that night. Maybe she never would again. She had said this was my life, but I still hoped that her soul hadn't been carried up the spiral of wind.

* * *

I heard Othmane in the living room the next morning, so I hid in the corner behind the bed and pretended to read. Around eleven o'clock the front door opened and closed but I wouldn't feel safe until I was certain he had really gone out. I slipped out of Neïla's room on tiptoes and peaked into the living room. It was empty, although I heard Mother humming in the kitchen. She was probably sewing or mending something and the last thing I wanted was another lesson on how to be a good wife. I quickly padded back to the girls' bedroom.

I booted up the computer wishing it didn't make so much noise—it sounded like a helicopter—but I was still lucky to have it. Even so, with the whir it made, I'd never hear the front door opening.

Neïla's kittens appeared. I had never been happier to see the fluffy little things, but I quickly went to her host's page and put in her address: phu.phu.neila@orange.fr. Next I typed Mustapha's birthday using only numbers, but a big red *X* appeared. I only had two more tries. If the password really was his birthday, Neïla had used a mix of numbers and letters. My hand trembled so much that I had difficulty typing and clicking on the button. Did the French capitalize the months or not? I typed "19janvier2006," hit enter and held my breath.

An hourglass appeared and I almost fainted when "Bonjour Neïla" appeared at the top of the page. I sat looking at the screen suddenly confused. Wasn't it impolite to go through somebody else's messages? I wished her ghost would appear and tell me it was alright but the room remained hopelessly empty. Something then clanged in the kitchen making me jump and my eyes darted back to the screen. I had to do it and just hope she would forgive me.

There were hundreds of messages and my heart began racing until I realized most of them were spam; Neïla had won the lottery, received money from Africa or could buy Viagra for cheap. I didn't find the latter amusing and junked it.

Disappointment welled up in my chest; Neïla hadn't e-mailed much. I guessed she had mostly texted but unfortunately she had lost her phone during the accident. Even If I got a new phone, I doubted I could ever recover her messages. Where had she found the money to buy one in the first place? There was no way I would ever ask Mother for the money.

I looked back at the screen and one e-mail looked out of place: *"Demain, Kiko* (Tomorrow, Kiko)." The name of the sender, Kiko, meant nothing so I looked at the date and noticed it was just before the accident. I didn't want to take too many risks, so I typed as short a message as possible. *"I can't remember. Have we met?"*[6]

I spent another half hour searching through the other messages. She liked knowing about private sales and clothing shops—where did she get the money for shopping?—but there were also lots of FB messages. When I clicked on one, it redirected me to the FB page home page and asked for the password. Hoping Neïla hadn't been too careful, I typed Mustapha's birthday again and held my breath. When the page opened, I had to sit back because my head was spinning.

Messages concerning Kim's famous video filled the screen with hundreds of people I didn't know asking how Neïla was, wishing her well or insulting Othmane for being a brute. What could I answer? I glanced up at her picture and my heart sank; she had large doe eyes and a wistful smile.

I then saw she had hundreds of friend requests and it appeared they had all seen the video. Should I have been pleased? On the one hand, it did make me feel a little less alone, but on the other it made me fear Othmane twice as much. Would he just sit back and do nothing or would he want to get his revenge on me, or on Kim.

I was about to switch off the computer and go back to hide in the corner when I noticed Kimberly Wasser wanted to be Neïla's friend. I looked carefully and saw it really was Kim! I clicked "yes" and wrote "thank you for the video" in spite of my mixed feelings.

"Neïla, poor Neïla, how are you?" Kim wrote back almost immediately.

The contact was so sudden that I almost felt like I was caught in the spiral again. I sat back trying to collect my thoughts and decide if it were wise to answer. "I wish I could say okay," I finally typed, while a tear ran down my cheek.

"Everybody asks about you. Quincy is almost sick with worry. What can we do to help?" the words seemed to flash on the screen in warning—did I really want to get Kim involved? I had hoped the Internet would give me solutions but now, I just couldn't see how.

It took me a long time to type the answer as I couldn't find the right keys on the French "azerty" keyboard. When I had finished, I reread it twice hoping to rid myself of the fear.

"The police have questioned my brother but he was released just after a few hours. He did not beat me since but I'm so afraid I tremble. If the police have done nothing yet, I don't think they will ever. Now I'm even afraid that my mother wants that I get married."

I had already written too much. Would I put Kim in danger? In spite of my misgivings, I hit "enter."

"My poor Neïla, you can't stay like that! Isn't there someplace you can go?"

Neïla's head shook, things weren't so simple, and I had already tried leaving twice without success. Neïla's life was in danger and somebody had really tried to kill her. "I'm not sure running away is safe," I wrote.

The noises from the street got louder and I knew that Mother would probably call me to do some chores soon. "Will he hurt you?" appeared on the screen in the little bubble.

This was unreal. I had heard about girls being beaten but had never paid much attention when I had been Josh. Now my hands were trembling. "Somebody already has," I typed, "and Josh was killed. I don't understand about what's going on."

The response was long in arriving. "We'll find a solution. I'll try to work out a way for you to live elsewhere. Just hang in there. I also created a fan page for you if you want to visit it. "

"I will," I wrote, "and thank you. It helps so much to know I'm not forgotten."

The last statement felt like a lie but she answered with a large-sized smiley face and switched off her connection. I was alone again. Someone yelled below. There must have been a fight going on. Neïla's legs curled up under me in a contortion that Josh never could have made.

I looked back at the screen to scroll through the friend requests and Quincy Torp was one of the first. I stared at his picture, longing to see him so badly that it felt shameful. How could my heart beat like that for a guy? My finger clicked "yes" and a rectangle came up for me to send a message. I sat for a minute until I turned the computer off and went to sit in the corner. I was too ashamed of those desires and too afraid of what Neïla might make me say if I started pouring out my heart.

* * *

Mother called Neïla's name so I stood up from the corner behind the bed, and when she called a second time, hurried out to find her beside Othmane. His expression was unreadable and I had to hold on to the wall to keep from falling.

Mother's scanned me with squinted eyes before she said evenly, *"I'm going out. It's your job to cook for your brother. I also want you to clean the living room, the toilet and the bathroom. If I don't come back before this evening, you'll have to make dinner for the children. Alright?"*[7]

I nodded and glanced at Othmane who didn't look interested. Mother put her hijab on and took her purse before I gave her two kisses as was expected. Then she shut the door and I turned to find Othmane staring at me while his hand lifted as if he wanted to strike me or give me a caress on the cheek. I recoiled and bowed my head.

He looked at me a second and turned away letting me scurry past into the kitchen. He never seemed to spend much time in there, but Mother had warned me that men got mean when they were hungry so I quickly started lunch.

I was beginning to learn how she cooked with the coriander, cardamom, and *ras el hanout*. I found some chicken that I began grilling while I put on bulgur to boil and washed lettuce for a salad which was eaten with "sauce blanche," a sort of yoghurt sauce. Then, while the meal cooked, I slipped past the living room on my way to the toilet. Othmane was sitting hunched over his book with his back to me and he hadn't heard me leave the kitchen. I was about to continue through to the bathroom when I noticed his shoulders were shaking. He was crying.

* * *

Mother came back looking exhausted while I was serving dinner to Neïla's siblings, vegetables cooked into a sort of couscous. Djahida made a face. "*This isn't how you make it, Mom.*"[8]

Mother sat down, let me serve her and looked at Djahida severely. "*In Islam, you never criticize what you're served. If you don't like it, you don't eat it, but you keep your mouth closed.*"[9]

Djahida bent her head with an annoyed snort and ate in silence, while Mustapha stared at her. I had the impression he didn't much care for my cooking either. I couldn't really blame him.

It was already Mustapha's bedtime when I finished tidying up the kitchen and the living room was empty. Where had Othmane gone off to? I hurried through to the girls' bedroom and found Djahida sitting on her bed looking exasperated albeit a little less irate.

"Why are you letting yourself go?"[10] she asked.

I looked down at Neïla's feet and at the toenail polish that had almost disappeared. They did need trimming. I looked back up at Djahida who was shaking her head.

"You know we have remover?"[11] she sighed.

I nodded not wanting to appear ignorant or admit that I hadn't looked through the beauty products. With a frown, Djahida led me to the bathroom, opened a cupboard and took out nail clippers, a bottle and some cotton.

"Cut your nails and remove that. Take a shower."[12]

I took my time in the shower because I still had trouble touching Neïla's breasts, but I did wash her long hair and tried rolling it up like the nurse had done. I then sat on the edge of the bath tub to trim her nails and remove the polish. The smell was so horrible I hoped Neïla didn't die of liver failure before she took her body back. When I had finished, I wrapped a towel around her thin torso and opened the door.

Mustapha was waiting in the hall, but he only half-heartedly returned my smile. I was about to rub my hand through his curly hair when I heard a door open and found myself face-to-face with Othmane. I felt naked and hurried away.

Djahida was on the computer laughing at some video with rap music, so I sat on my bed watching her and said nothing. When the music stopped, she looked over at me. *"Get up,"* she ordered grabbing my hand, dragging me over to the dresser and opening the drawer with all the beauty supplies. *"Look at all you've got."* She picked up a bottle. *"And look, you have body lotion and face cream for after the shower."*[13]

I took the lotion and dipped my finger in ashamed at my ignorance.

She shook her head and began explaining what each was for. *"Are you listening?"* she barked, grabbing my chin and making me look in the mirror. *"Look, that's my sister. You were always the most intelligent and the prettiest. Why did you want to die?"*[14]

Tears were streaming down Djahida's face now and I realized how selfish I had been. She was just a young girl and she missed her older sister so I took her into my arms and began to rock her until she pushed me away. Djahida didn't say another word to me that evening, but she did come over to kiss me on both cheeks before we went to bed.

1 "Mais tu le sais."

2 "Je veux juste être sure."

3 "C'est en janvier, le 19."

4 "Et tu as 10 ans."

5 "Non, j'en ai 11!"

6 "Je ne me souviens plus. Est-ce que nous nous sommes rencontrés?"

7 "Je m'en vais, C'est à toi de cuisiner pour ton frère. Je veux aussi que tu nettoies la salle de séjour, le WC et la salle de bain. Si je ne reviens pas avant ce soir, tu t'occupes de faire manger les enfants. D'accord?"

8 "C'est pas comme ça que tu fais, maman."

9 "En Islam, on ne critique jamais ce qu'on te sert. Si tu ne l'aimes pas, tu ne le manges pas, mais tu ne dis rien."

10 "Pourquoi tu te laisses aller?"

11 "Tu sais qu'on a du dissolvant."

12 "Coupe-toi les ongles et enlève ça. Prends une douche."

13 "Lève-toi. Regarde tout ce que tu as. Et regarde, tu as de la crème pour le corps et pour le visage."

14 "Tu écoutes? Regarde, ça c'est ma sœur. Tu as toujours été la plus intelligente et la plus belle. Pourquoi tu as voulu mourir?"

Chapter 14

I couldn't ignore the pains in my belly the next morning as I put on my nightgown and shuffled to the kitchen for breakfast. Had Othmane's punches caused some internal damage that would send me back to that hospital room? Mother served me tea and put out bread and olive oil with honey but I didn't feel like eating and only sipped at the tea.

Mother stared at me. *"You must get ready with the others,"*[1] she said.

I lifted a questioning eyebrow, but no other words were spoken until Mustapha came in and sat beside me. I put my arm around him while he recited his personal pronouns in English and corrected him on the first person plural. When I asked if he had a test, he nodded very seriously and began drinking his tea. Djahida then came in with her hair put up on top of her head and makeup that made her eyes look like a doe's. I smiled at how pretty she looked while she batted her lids.

"I found how to do it on the Internet," she giggled. *"If you want, we'll give you the same tomorrow."*[2] Even though I knew Neïla's eyes were already unnaturally beautiful, I nodded my agreement.

"Go get ready,"[3] Mother told me.

I did my best to make Neïla presentable, but her hair was nearly unmanageable, and with my back to the mirror, almost impossible to roll up onto my head. I got so frustrated that I turned around to look at her but her eyes staring into mine made me so uncomfortable that I had to admit defeat.

Feeling inept and worrying about what Djahida would say, I began to take off her nightgown only to discover blood on my leg—I really was injured and bleeding! Should I tell somebody or let myself die and be rid of this whole family? I collapsed onto the bed.

"But aren't you going to get ready?" Djahida barked from the

hall. *"Maman said . . . and what's the problem now?"*[4] She sighed and stepped into the bedroom.

My body curled up, a big sob escaped and I admitted, *"I have internal bleeding."*[5]

"You have what?" Djahida asked surprised, but then her brow knitted with skepticism. *"What makes you say that?"*[6]

"I have blood"—could I really tell where the blood was coming from? It seemed indecent but if Neïla was injured, she had to see a doctor—*"blood running down my leg from . . ."*[7]

"From your what?" Djahida scoffed and grabbed my arm. *"You really are spaced out! Come with me."*[8]

I was dragged past a wide-eyed Mustapha to the toilet and handed a pink box. *"Here, use these. The instructions are on the back,"* Djahida sneered. *"And you're not allowed to pray until your period is over."*[9]

"How come?"[10] I asked, feeling stupid.

"It's a corruption," she explained, as if she were talking to a child. *"And you must wash yourself before you start praying again."* Then, just before she closed the door, she hissed, *"and your underwear, you wash yourself."*[11]

I took off the underwear and put them in the washbasin to clean. Neïla was of course a girl, how could I be such an idiot? At least I wouldn't have to get down on all fours several times a day, I mused, while I scrubbed the pink panties.

When I had finished, I inspected the box but the operating instructions made me so uneasy that I felt like staying locked in there until the bleeding stopped. Djahida then yelled for me to hurry up, other people needed to use the toilet, so I whispered my apologies to Neïla's ghost and continued on to step three.

When I had successfully completed the procedure, and washed off Neïla's thighs, I hurried back to the bedroom to get dressed. Djahida sat at the desk and I could tell she was assessing each of my choices in clothing. The pair of pink jeans got a nod but when I grabbed beige blouse, she jumped up and sighed,

"Not that one. Here put on this."[12]

I inspected the lacy pale-blue blouse before I pulled it over my head. Her choice was obviously better than mine so I put on my socks and was about to go into the living when she snapped, *"Not yet. Sit down,"*[13] and began redoing Neïla's hair and applying makeup to my eyes. I felt like a klutz.

Djahida was quite proud of her work and presented me to Mother like a piece of art when she had finished. Mother simply gave her tight-lipped smile and told us we had to be going while I put on Neïla's pink sneakers.

We went down the stairs together with Mother and Djahida on either side of Mustapha so that he wouldn't fall. The entranceway was empty so I concluded that our local dealer hadn't opened shop yet, but there were a number of boys horsing about outside. The boy with light brown eyes smiled at me and I felt Neïla smile back until embarrassment began prickling my cheeks and I looked away. I had no wish to be attracted to him, or to Quincy, I wasn't . . . what was I?

Mustapha's transport was waiting and the driver didn't seem pleased about us being so late. He began gesticulating to Mother who stared back blankly until, with a loud grunt, he loaded Mustapha into the backseat of the van next to a girl in a wheelchair who was smiling out the back window at me. I waved to her and she waved back joyfully as the van pulled away.

Djahida then headed off in the direction of her junior high while Mother led me down the same street we had taken to the market. We walked in silence past the 1960s public funded apartments, which slowly gave way to two- or three-story cement rendered buildings, before Mother turned to me and said, *"Luckily your father isn't here or all this would have made him sick."*[14]

"Where is he?"[15] I asked.

Mother looked at me with a raised eyebrow, then shook her head. *"That's right, you don't remember. He was killed a year ago. They think a thief did it. It happened in our home country."*[16]

My jaw dropped. Somebody had tried to kill Neïla too and that person was still roaming free. *"How did it happen?"*[17] I asked in a whisper.

"You were there, too. We went to visit my parents in Algiers. He was found with his throat cut in the alley behind the house. His billfold was missing. I don't know anything else." We turned onto a street that I didn't know and walked for another minute in silence. Then, at a stoplight, Mother turned to me and said, *"If you have other questions, you must ask the man we're going to see."*[18]

I waited for more information, but Mother simply stared at where we were headed, a large businesslike structure with a mall and middle-class shoppers pushing carts full of food and clothing. It looked inviting and comfortable but Mother took me down a flight of stairs into the metro and gave me a pink ticket that I inserted before I pushed my way through the turnstile. We went down more stairs into the immense tunnel system through which we walked for another minute until we arrived beside the long, well-lit train track.

Mother sat down while I stared at the billboards. It felt odd wearing my hijab in front of an ad featuring a nude woman rubbing her legs. A few weeks ago it would have been the focus of my, or rather Josh's attention, but today it did nothing but make me uncomfortable.

The metro train eventually hummed to a stop and we had to push our way onto it while the other passengers made their displeasure at having to stand next to me felt. I knew it was because of my headscarf and found myself getting angry; I wasn't dressed like this to annoy them!

We remained standing for two stops while more people pushed their way on and off. The commuters read, or tapped on their phones, but most observed the other passengers silently while keeping their expressions neutral. At the third stop, Mother grabbed two seats when a group of four women got up to leave and a black-African man and his pregnant wife pushed their way to the seats in front of us. She gave me a smile, which I returned, while I looked at her cumbersome belly. Was that Neïla's future?

"It's a boy. He's due at the end of December,"[19] the woman said to me. She must have seen me staring.

"A Christmas present,"[20] I replied, hoping to hide my embarrassment.

"True, God loves me a lot,"[21] she answered with her bouncy African accent while she squeezed her husband's hand.

I looked over at Mother, who was frowning, so I gathered she didn't like me talking about Christmas to a Christian. I lowered my gaze until Mother tapped my arm indicating we had to get off. She headed toward the number eight metro with me following, then up a long flight of stairs, and finally down a long corridor to a track in the direction of Balard. A train stopped on the other side of the tracks and then hummed away.

I looked at Mother and asked, *"Where are my other grandparents?"*[22]

At first I wasn't sure she had heard me, but eventually she replied, *"They are in Marseille."*[23]

"Will I meet them one day?"[24] I asked.

A scowl seemed to flitter across her features, but it was quickly replaced by her blank expression. She shook her head while her eyes continued to examine me. *"You already know them. You just don't remember."*[25]

The train arrived and although it wasn't very crowded, Mother remained standing while I gripped the rail beside her. We exited after less than a minute, walked up some stairs, down a corridor, through a turnstile and up more stairs into the hazy Parisian daylight, Haussmann-style buildings and well-dressed businessmen heading off to work.

I stared wide-eyed at the expensive apartments, the Roman-looking building across the street, and although I shouldn't have been awed by the show of wealth, feelings of inferiority still welled up from inside me. It was silly because I had often been in higher class places than this—my hometown of Evanston was not poor—so why did Neïla pull my shoulders in and make me bow my head?

Mother examined a sheet of paper and stared around while I tried to control my breathing and relax. People kept pushing past us and frowning at our attire until I realized Mother barely knew how to read. I reached out to take the paper to read it to her, but her hand jerked back and the scowl she gave me looked so much like Othmane's that I recoiled in fright.

We then spent the next twenty minutes walking around comparing the paper with the brass plates professionals in France put outside their offices until Mother got lucky and rang a buzzer next to a large green door. I glanced at the plate before going up: Maître Lombard, lawyer at the bar of Paris, third floor.

The entranceway was decorated in the Art Nouveau style with forged railings and a marble floor. The outside of the elevator was from the same period, but the machinery had clearly been replaced so that, with a *ding,* the door opened smoothly.

We stepped out at the third floor into a carpeted hallway with brass ornamentation and gilded plaster along the ceiling. On the door was another brass plate with "Maître Laurent Lombard, avocat au Barreau de Paris," written on it. Mother rang the bell and pushed the door open.

The reception area was fairly large and carpeted in red. Pictures were hung all over the off-white walls and small modern sculptures decorated the corners. A good-looking middle-aged woman greeted us and asked if we had an appointment. Mother gave Neïla's name, the woman nodded, and then asked us to wait in the first room on the right.

The waiting room was as richly furnished as the reception area and made Neïla feel like hiding. I looked at one of the paintings and recognized it as a Fernand Leger. He might have been a communist, but his paintings are worth a bundle today. A man with a graying beard was already waiting there and he nodded to us with an angry frown. I knew the reasons and shifted my hijab so it covered my face. His scowl intensified and he looked back down at the magazine he was reading.

After a few minutes the secretary came to call the man so I looked over at the magazine he had been reading. It was in English and when I picked it up to read, I saw that it spoke of the conflict in the Middle East. Mother glanced at the magazine with hostility in her eyes, so I put it back on the pile and took an art review in French instead.

When the secretary called me some twenty minutes later, I put down the article on the 1970s French movement "support/surface" with some regret. Mother stood up with me, but the woman indicated she should wait where she was. Mother sat back down stoically without comment.

The secretary led me down a hallway that was just as luxurious as the rest of the office and opened a heavy forest-green door. The lawyer's office was decorated entirely with second empire furniture and paintings which contrasted to the starker modern decoration of the waiting area. I remained in the doorway with my mouth open; Neïla had rarely been in such a richly decorated place.

A fiftyish-year-old man in need of a haircut, the lawyer I guessed, sat writing at the desk. When he had finished and read over what he had written, he handed the paper to the secretary who walked past me and shut the door. The lawyer hadn't looked up yet.

My breathing accelerated again while my hands clasped each other as if I were praying. I realized Mother often stood like that and become even more uncomfortable. The lawyer's gaze suddenly fixed me. My legs became rubber. He looked me over carefully with raised eyebrows and I hated myself for trembling like a scared rabbit.

"Miss Saadallah, please come in and sit down," he said, with only the hint of a French accent. When I didn't move, he stood up and strode over to me extending his hand. I tried to give a strong grip but my hand felt tiny and limp in his.

"There's no reason to be nervous." He put his hand on my elbow and guided me to a chair. "You do prefer English? That's what I've heard at least."

I felt obliged to say something now, but my voice seemed stuck in my throat and I only managed to squeak, "That's correct."

He smiled. "Intriguing. Have any memories from before the accident come back to you?"

"Sorry, they have not," I whispered apologetically.

"Your English does seem to be quite good. You're in premier L in high school so I suppose that could explain it. Do you have good grades?"

I had never been a good liar and it was even worse now with my face getting hot. Neïla just couldn't hide her emotions. "I don't know. I have no memory before I wake . . . woke up."

"Good, but please tell me if you don't understand. I will repeat in French. It is important. Are you sure you don't want me to speak French?"

I hesitated. Was my French really better than my English? Even if I stumbled over my words from time to time, or if I didn't catch what somebody said, English was still my mother tongue. Losing my language would be like losing what little of Josh I still had. Not only was Neïla making me like boys, now she was wanting to take my language from me! "No, I prefer English," I said, as resolutely as possible.

"Uh-huh," He muttered, keeping his gaze on me. "First of all, you are still a minor so you don't have the final say in the decisions made concerning you."

He waited for me to make some sign that I had understood so I looked up, nodded and looked away again. "I understand."

"Now there is some belief that you were intentionally thrown in the water. Others think you attempted suicide." His eyes were scanning me for a reaction again.

"I don't remember," I whispered.

"And then there was that incident with your brother that made you a small celebrity on the Web."

I lifted my eyes and saw he was still observing me. "I did not want that."

"Do you mean being slapped or having it on the Internet?"

A jaded smile trembled on my lips. "Both," I replied. "My life is not easier because of it." I realized I had said the life was mine. This life I had been given seemed more and more to be a poisoned chalice and tears began to blur my vision.

His face became very serious and he formed a triangle with his fingers. "Well, as you have probably noticed, I'm a lawyer. You see, the courts insist you be represented. Your mother hasn't got sufficient resources to pay my fees, however, under French law, we are required to represent a certain number of low-paying cases such as yours. I found your situation rather unique and have volunteered my services rather than having one of my associates take it."

He stopped speaking for a second and I looked back up at him. "Thank you for your help," I answered, "but there is nothing you can do, is there not?"

He gave a short laugh. "First I can make sure your interests are taken into account and keep you updated on the investigation and—"

"—did they found . . . find anything?" I interrupted.

"Not to my knowledge. They don't tell me everything, you know? Concerning your brother, it seems the acts aren't of sufficient gravity to merit prosecution. As it stands, we can't have him removed from the domicile. However if things continue, we could have you put in a boarding school for your protection."

He was watching me closely again for a reaction. The idea shocked me at first but the more I thought about it, the more I liked it. "Why can't I leave from the home now?" I asked.

"It would seem your mother is against it and she does have some good medical arguments on her side."

It hit me like a stone. Mother was blocking my escape and freedom. I felt betrayed. "And I have not got . . ." I began forgetting my words. "I have no . . ."

He smiled solicitously. "Your point of view is taken into consideration," he said in a conciliatory tone of voice. "However, you are still a minor."

So I was being treated like a child in spite of an attempted murder and beatings. I decided to put the question to him. "The murderer . . ." My breath caught in my throat and I had to start again. "He is looking for me?"

The lawyer sat back before answering. "There seems to be no evidence that anybody close to you is involved." His eyes showed that he was hoping that would reassure me. I had no idea who had thrown Neïla into the water but somebody as violent as Othmane would be perfectly capable of such a crime.

"Is there evidence that the family aren't?"

His smile now looked forced. "I'm afraid I can't go into any details of the investigation. I just know the police don't believe you to be in any immediate danger."

I began to shake a little thinking about the hooded man who followed me the night I escaped. I hadn't told the police, but then, they hadn't asked me. "*Etes-vous certain* . . ." I began to say in French before I caught myself. "Are you certain they are truly investigating?" I asked more for reassurance than for information.

His eyebrow raised but he frowned before answering. "There is some talk that it was an attempted suicide, you realize?"

I felt my face and head go numb as the blood rushed out of it. I didn't want to faint so I tried to breathe slowly and stop my heart from pounding. "The night I escaped . . . *euh* . . . I was followed, chased by man in a sweat . . . sweatshirt. A shirt like the night of my accident," I stammered.

"And you haven't told this to anybody?" He looked surprised and a little annoyed. Then he seemed to realize the irrelevance of his question and shook his head. "No, of course you wouldn't."

"I'm scared," I suddenly admitted.

His frown became tender and he shook his head again. "I can try to push for a boarding school, if you like, but there are many parties involved in the decision."

"You want say . . . you mean I must wait until I'm eighteen?" I added dejectedly.

He studied me for what seemed like forever, his face showing no expression even when he began to speak. "It hasn't been done yet, but there is a good chance your mother might ask to have her guardianship prolonged."

My fear suddenly flared to anger. "She can't!" I shouted. Then the anger turned back to fear. "It's because of my mental . . ." Again I was at a loss for words.

"You mental health? I'm afraid so." He said soothingly.

It seemed the die had been cast. "So I need prove my intelligence," I said, as much to myself as to him.

He shook his head. "It's not that simple but that does play a role."

"So I must go back to school." I looked him straight in the eye. If he could do something, maybe he should start with that.

"We're working on that, but you realize that you fall into the category of handicapped students now." He again examined me closely for a reaction but I refused to look away. "The commission must meet and decide what is in your best interest." he added flatly.

"And I decide nothing?" I wanted to remain calm now and look sane but it wasn't easy. I felt that my body, Neïla's body, was about to go to pieces.

"You have a say but not the decision, no." His tone was final and the doors to the prison had just clanged shut. Instead of crying out loud, I stood to make my way to the door.

"There is another problem that you must not forget," he added, with a sigh. When I turned back to face him, wrinkles creased his forehead as he said, "the problem with your father in Algeria hasn't been resolved."

"What problem? My mother said me a thief killed him."

"Truly, truly," He let his voice trail off. "It's simply that the investigation hasn't been closed. You should know that the Algerian police have asked to have you sent back for the investigation."

I sat back down. "Did Neï . . . did I do something illegal?"

He studied me for a long moment. "I'm sure you didn't." He stood up and walked around the desk. "I will do my best to look after your interests; that's my job." His hand took mine and lifted me to my feet although I could feel my legs shaking. "Here, don't fret, everything will turn out fine. The secretary will call to make another appointment if necessary. Why don't you go sit in the waiting area for a few minutes while I speak to your mother?" He escorted me to the door and pushed it open.

The secretary appeared beside me as if out of thin air and I followed her to the waiting room where met Mother's gaze. Maybe she thought she was doing what was the best thing but at that moment, I hated her. Tears were about to flow down my cheek so I went to sit in the corner while Mother left with the secretary.

1 "Il faut que tu te prépares avec les autres."

2 "J'ai trouvé comment faire sur internet. Si tu veux, on te fera les mêmes demain."

3 "Vas te préparer."

4 "Mais tu n'es pas encore prête? Maman a dit… Quel est le problème maintenant?"

5 "Je pense que j'ai un saignement interne."

6 "Tu as quoi? Qu'est-ce qui te fait dire ça?"

7 "J'ai du sang…du sang qui coule sur ma jambe de…"

8 "D'où? Tu es vraiment space! Viens avec moi."

9 "Tiens, utilise ça. Les instructions sont au dos. Et tu n'as pas le droit de prier jusqu'à la fin de tes règles."

10 "Pourquoi?"

11 "C'est une salissure. Et tu dois te laver avant de prier à nouveau. Et ta culotte, tu la laves toute seule."

12 "Pas celle-là. Tiens, mets celle-ci."

13 "Pas encore. Assieds-toi."

14 "Heureux que ton père n'est plus là, il en aurait été malade."

15 "Où est-il?"

16 "Tu te rappelles pas, c'est vrai. Il a été tué il y a un an. On pense que c'est un voleur qui l'a fait. Ça s'est passé au pays."

17 "Comment est-ce que ça s'est passé?"

18 "Tu y étais aussi. On est allé visiter mes parents à Alger. On l'a trouvé égorgé dans la ruelle derrière la maison. Il était malade, il n'a pas pu se battre. Son portefeuille n'y était plus. On n'en sait pas plus. Si tu as des questions, tu demandes à l'homme qu'on va voir."

19 "C'est un garçon. Il va arriver à la fin de décembre."

20 "Un cadeau de Noël."

21 "C'est vrai, dieu m'aime beaucoup."

22 "Où sont mes autres grands-parents?"

23 "Ils sont à Marseille."

24 "Je vais les rencontrer un jour?"

25 "Tu les connais déjà. Tu t'en souviens pas, c'est tout."

Chapter 15

Mother bought me a chicken Tikka sandwich on the way home from the lawyer's office at one of those greasy-spoon sandwich shops you find on any busy street around Paris. She let me understand that it was Neïla's favorite and, while I wolfed down the pocket bread with spicy chicken, I really did have a terrible time convincing myself that it contained too many lipids to be healthy.

When I had finished, I glanced sideways at a group of girls Neïla's age sitting near us. They were wearing skirts or tight blue jeans, pretty makeup and mocking smiles. I cursed them although I couldn't blame them. I was certain I looked like a clown with this cloth covering my head.

"I want to go back to high school,"[1] I stated flatly to Mother.

She didn't blink while she stared into my eyes and forced me to look away. The girls broke out laughing in shrill voices and I glanced over; they were all looking scornfully in my direction. My chest contracted—I hated this family!—so I got up to go to the water closet.

As I walked by the group of girls, there was a hush that broke out in giggling before the door had closed and I almost turned around to shout at them that I didn't want to dress like this! Instead, I shut myself in the dirty stall.

It smelled horrible and, in spite of the tears that refused to stop flowing, I didn't want to spend any more time in there than necessary. The procedure I had read on the box, albeit embarrassing, was quickly over but then I was faced with a quandary I hadn't foreseen; where could I dispose of that bloody thing? My only two choices were throwing it into the toilet or directly into the trash. I chose the latter. As I exited, one of those pretty girls was waiting to get in and I was sure she would see it. She gave me a snarly smile so I covered my face with my hijab before I hurried out.

Mother didn't ask me why I was so sullen on the walk home. I'm not sure she even cared. The boys outside our apartment watched us in silence and then went back to their joking and antics. I wished I could hide. When the door to the apartment had shut, I ran to isolate myself in Neïla's room.

I felt like a freak so I turned to glance at Neïla in the mirror. Her large dark eyes were swollen but instead of turning my head, I let her fuss with that unruly mass of hair for a second and she turned it up nicely in a few twists. I could never have managed that!

I shook my head and strands of her hair tickled my cheeks. This was crazy! I couldn't really be Neïla, could I? Tears were running down her cheeks and I would have like to have comforted her but it didn't make sense. Had I ever been Josh?

I turned away from the mirror and went to the computer where things were more anonymous. There were a couple of messages of condolence on Josh's FB page but otherwise it remained abandoned. The boy in the picture was distant and it felt as though I were visiting a cemetery.

I changed identities. Neïla's page looked less abandoned with numerous videos of animals and hip-hop singers. Would I ever be able to call it "my" page? There were also ads for makeup and clothing aimed at a young girl, shallow yet alluring, but what interested me were the messages and— my heart jumped up into my throat—Quincy had written. Right under it were new messages from Kim and Bertrane. I was about to click on Quincy's when I clicked on Bertrane's instead.

Her message didn't say much. *"How are things? When are you coming back?"*[2] I still mixed up the *A* and the *Q* on the French keyboard but managed to type off a quick answer that was so superficial I found it embarrassing. My male pride should have been nonplused.

When I looked back at Quincy's message, Neïla took control; my heart began racing and my hand trembled so much that I had trouble clicking on the right spot. I was forgetting myself. How could Quincy, a handsome guy like that, fall for . . . ? I opened my eyes, scanned the first few lines and let out a groan because it wasn't a declaration of love. He asked how I was and said how pleased he had been to meet me. He finished by writing, "if you ever need anything, please don't hesitate to ask."

What I needed was for him to tell me I wasn't a freak, that he might like me. No, I couldn't write that or tell him that I quivered every time I thought of him. That wasn't natural, or normal. Was I normal?

In the end, my message was as flat as his. I thanked him and told him I hoped to see him again. I also apologized for what Neïla's brother had done. It really looked inane but I couldn't think of anything truthful to write.

Kim's message hit closer to home. "I hope you are holding up there. You can't be forced to stay locked up as you are! When I get you out of there, I'm going to take you shopping in some of the most immoral places in Paris and you'll knock Quincy's eyes out. Luv Kim."

I had to smile at the thought of shopping with Kim. Still, it was as unrealistic as this whole situation. I shook my head and wrote back, "Kim, your message gives me hope but I think it will be impossible. The lawyer I have seen today said that my mother's guardianship (I was forced to look that word up on the Internet) may be prolonged (this one too) because of my amnesia. If this is the case, I may never be released from their surveillance."

As for the other hundred well-wishers, I opted for a short post on Neïla's fan page thanking them and saying I was hoping to return to class soon. I was about to close the computer when my eyes fell on a reply from Kiko Just. I opened it and read.

"But I remember you well. We even had more than a drink together. You must be careful. I'll get in touch with you. Best wishes Kiko."[3]

Kiko was clearly the man at the café who had sat down next to

Neïla and he seemed to know more than he wanted to communicate by Internet. I looked around the room hoping to see her ghost but maybe she had already gone up the spiral. I leaned back with my eyes shut, wishing I had died instead of her.

* * *

I was curled up on my bed when I heard Othmane's chesty voice in the living room and Mother call my name. I knew she would want me to do the cooking and cleaning because she was working the night shift so I forced myself to stand up and put on Neïla's flowered slippers. I then opened the door as quietly possible hoping to make it to the kitchen before Othmane noticed me. Unfortunately, he was standing in the doorway and I was about to turn back to hide in Neïla's bedroom when he stepped aside and Mother looked at me with a raised eyebrow. *"I want you to go get dressed properly,"*[4] she told me, while she put on her coat.

"And dinner?"[5] I asked.

"Hadja is coming tonight. She'll take care of it,"[6] she stated and gave me two kisses before leaving me to face Neïla's jihadist brother alone.

Othmane was looking at me quizzically, maybe wondering why I was backed up against the wall, while his hand reached out toward my face. I flinched. He started to pull it away but stroked my hair instead making all my muscles go as taut as violin strings ready to snap. His cheek twitched and then, without a word, he turned to walk away to his room.

A long, deep breath escaped my lungs and I made the few steps that separated me from the living room before I sagged onto one of the cushions while my heart beat as if I had just swum a 200-meter butterfly. I was helpless and I didn't see an end to it.

The door opened and Hadja entered holding Mustapha's hand. They both stared at me lying balled up on a cushion, and as soon as Hadja removed her shoes, she came to sit beside me while Mustapha made himself discrete on the other side of the room.

"What's wrong?"[7] Hadja's asked, with a knitted brow.

I shook my head. Could I trust Hadja any more than the others? Every time I opened my mouth, I feared being discovered. What would she do to me if she discovered a half-Jewish American had taken over her sister's body?

"Don't be like that. Come here and sit next to me." Hadja pulled me to her and began rocking me while I tried without success to relax. *"Some friends are coming over. We ordered out a couscous. That'll help you relax, you'll see."* She pushed the stray lock of hair back. *"You did up your hair just like you used to before the accident. It's pretty but you might want to put on your hijab and a little makeup."*[8]

I wasn't unhappy to go back to my room, and I would have stayed all evening if I could have, but that didn't seem to be an option. I went to the closet to choose a blue-and-pink scarf before I sat down in front of the mirror and forced myself to look at her, at Neïla, the girl whose body I had taken. She was so beautiful that she didn't need any makeup. Why did she have to be dead?

I wiped the tear away and opened her drawer to stare at all her jars, tubes and brushes. It looked daunting but Hadja had told me to put on some makeup and that was what Neïla would have done. I just hoped she had bequeathed as many reflexes with eyeliner as she had with the hair. I took a deep breath and attempted to look at her image in the mirror again but I couldn't bear the pain and had to look away. That girl who was no longer here.

"Are you watching me? Will you help me if I try to put some of this on your magnificent face?"

I heard the mirror rattle so I glanced back at her eyes that were so forlorn I could have sworn she was pleading with me. After that, all I could think to do was reach into the drawer and grab the first tube of lipstick I found. It was an orange-red. I tried to look in the mirror while I put it on but it seemed lewd to stare at her rubbing that color over her full lips so I did the best I could with my back turned. I then took some mascara, it was purple, and dabbed on her eyelids without daring to look back at those sad eyes.

When I turned back to the mirror, it was clear that I had botched everything; the left eye was all purple while the orange lipstick looked funny and was smeared around in the wrong places. It all had to come off, that much was clear, but I had no idea what girls used to remove the stuff. I took a Kleenex and wiped it across my eyes but that smudged it even more. I then fumbled through the drawer looking for something that was marked "makeup remover," wondering if it had been with all those bottles in the bathroom.

"Neïla, are you ready? They'll be here soon."[9] Hadja called from the living room.

I didn't reply and quickly took another Kleenex to wipe the lipstick off but . . . Hadja stuck her head in the door. *"Oh, Neïla, what have you done to yourself?"* She looked aghast. *"Don't move. I'll call Djahida."*[10]

Neïla's little sister appeared a moment later and broke out laughing hysterically while she pulled out her phone to take a picture. Luckily, Hadja stopped her.

"But haven't you seen her?"[11] Djahida guffawed, making me feel like a circus attraction.

Hadja stepped up to her little sister looking just like Mother with her hard stare and black hijab. *"Stop it! Just help her get cleaned up."*[12]

Djahida bowed her head and led me by the hand to the bathroom while Hadja went to open the door for the guests. As soon as the bathroom door was closed Djahida broke out in a hiccupping laugh. *"Purple with orange lipstick,"*[13] she kept repeating between snickers.

I took the bottle she was pointing at with the cotton pads beside it and began to swipe at my face without looking in the mirror. When I had finished, I glanced at Neïla who was as beautiful as ever although Djahida continued to giggle while she led me back to our room. Between sarcastic comments, Djahida then applied some of the same mascara and handed me a purple pencil.

"Draw the outline of your lips," she instructed. I looked down at Neïla's hands. *"Look at yourself in the mirror, good God!"*[14]

I tried to but couldn't keep my eyes focused on Neïla's lips. They were so sensuous I got embarrassed and Djahida ended up grabbing the pencil from my hand and doing it for me. She then added the lipstick and told me to turn around and admire her work.

The girl in the mirror was magnificent; her eyes turned up like a doe's and her lips would have made Josh sink to his knees. I looked away.

"What have you got against mirrors? And why are you blubbering?" Djahida crossed her arms and gave me an exasperated huff. *"You'll make your mascara run like diarrhea down your face."*[15]

My head dropped in shame and embarrassment.

"Okay, we'll put on your hijab and go see the others,"[16] she sighed.

Under Djahida's scrutiny I covered Neïla's hair and, after a few minor adjustments, she took me by the hand and led me out into the living room. There was a young couple and two teenage boys sitting on the cushions. All four got up to kiss me on the cheeks. The woman also gave me a big hug which I returned timidly. She wasn't wearing a hijab.

"Neïla, you don't recognize your cousins?" Djahida laughed. A silence followed but Djahida took no notice. *"Since the accident you have to explain everything to her,"* she explained and then turned to me with a large smile. *"These are your first cousins, Sofiane, Hamid and Zaria. Momo is Zaria's husband."*[17]

Zaria gave me a friendly smile that I wished I could return and Momo was smiling too. *"Where is our Imam?"*[18] he chuckled.

"We haven't seen him. He must be in his room,"[19] Hadja replied.

"Wasn't he the one wanting to organize this?"[20] There was a hint of sarcasm in Momo's voice.

The door then opened and Mokhtar burst in with two bags of takeout. I was happy for an excuse to escape so I hurried over to help him while he took off his shoes. He gave me the two obligatory kisses and, while he went into the living room to greet the others, I disappeared into the kitchen with the bags.

Hadja came to help me, or more probably to make sure I didn't do anything stupid. She put the couscous into the microwave while I got out the dishes and put them on a tray. When I walked out with the glasses, the men were in earnest discussion and Djahida was sitting in the corner looking disgruntled. I got the feeling she was being left out.

"This must be done peacefully,"[21] Momo was saying.

"Who cares about peace? Our voices need to be heard,"[22] Mokhtar retorted with his grin. He was more boisterous than usual.

"Do you want the kids from around here to get arrested?"[23] Momo shook his head.

"So what?"[24] Mokhtar shrugged.

"Imagine things go to hell and Neïla is there?" Momo looked at me with a tender smile. *"Do you feel up to going?"*[25] he asked me.

I looked away. I was afraid to tell him I didn't know what they were talking about.

"Of course she wants to go,"[26] Othmane's voice cut in behind me. I hadn't seen him come in and recoiled, almost dropping the tray.

Zaria was beside me holding me around the waist. *"Sit down,"*[27] she whispered.

I glanced over at Othmane who was giving me a hard stare. *"She will do her utmost to help our brothers in Gaza,"*[28] Othmane declared. Momo shook his head and Zaria looked exasperated while Neïla's other two cousins seemed indifferent.

"Do what?"[29] I whispered in Zaria's ear.

"Sit down," she repeated and took the tray before Momo grabbed my hand and made me sit beside him. Zaria set the tray down and came to sit on the other side of me. *"It's just a demonstration against Israel's Zionist policies,"* she said. *"Your brothers will insist you go."*[30]

"I think she should carry a sign, and in English since she has decided to speak that language,"[31] Mokhtar quipped.

"Why don't you leave her alone? Can't you see how scared she is?"[32] Zaria shot back at him.

Irritated, Mokhtar hissed, *"She can invite her American boyfriend. What's his name? Quint?"*[33] He then snickered and gave me a wink.

Nobody laughed.

"Don't pay him any attention. He's always been a bad-mouth,"[34] Zaria said.

I couldn't ignore him. How had he known about Quincy? Had he intercepted my FB messages? Hadja then came in with the couscous and everybody dug in. I tried to eat but the food got stuck in my throat and the thought of going to a demonstration against Israel made me more and more nervous.

The evening dragged on with everybody cursing Jews, Israel, the USA and even France. If Zaria had not remained beside me, I think I would have broken down in hysterics. Finally, when she was leaving, I whispered to her, *"Can I stay close to you during the demonstration."*[35]

"You can ask anything of me, little cousin,"[36] she answered, and I gave her a hug.

"I told you you'd like them,"[37] Djahida remarked, after they had left. I didn't remember her saying that, but I smiled and gave her two kisses before we went to bed.

1 "Je veux retourner au lycée."

2 "Comment ça va? Quand est-ce que tu reviens?..."

3 "Mais je me souviens de toi. On a même pris plus qu'un verre ensemble. Il faut que tu sois prudente. Je te recontacte. Amicalement Kiko."

4 "Je veux que tu ailles t'habiller correctement."

5 "Et le dîner?"

6 "Hadja vient ce soir, elle va s'en occuper."

7 "Qu'est-ce que tu as?"

8 "Faut pas que tu sois comme ça. Tiens, viens te mettre à côté de moi. On a des amis qui vont venir. On va commander un couscous. Tu vas voir, ça va te détendre. Je vois que tu t'es coiffée. C'est joli, comme tu faisais avant l'accident, mais tu veux peut-être mettre ton hijab et un peu de maquillage."

9 "Neïla, tu es prête? Ils vont arriver."

10 "Oh, Neïla. Qu'est-ce que tu t'es fait? Bouge pas, j'appelle Djahida."

11 "Mais tu l'as pas vu?"

12 "Arrête! Aide-la à se nettoyer."

13 "Violet avec un rouge à lèvres orange."

14 "Dessine le contour de tes lèvre. Mais regarde-toi dans le miroir, bon sang!"

15 " Mais qu'est-ce que tu as contre les miroirs? Et pourquoi tu chiales? Tu va faire dégueuler ton mascara."

16 "Bon, on va te mettre ton hijab et aller voir les autres."

17 "Neïla, tu reconnais pas tes cousins? Depuis l'accident il faut tout lui expliquer. Ce sont tes cousins germains, Sofiane, Hamid et Zaria. Momo est l'époux de Zaria."

18 "Où est notre Iman?"

19 "On ne l'a pas vu. Il doit être dans sa chambre."

20 "C'était pas lui qui voulait organiser cette chose?"

21 "Il faut que ça se passe dans le calme."

22 "On s'en fout du calme, il faut qu'on se fasse entendre."

23 "Tu veux que les jeunes d'ici se fasse arrêter?"

24 "Eh alors?"

25 "Imagine qu'il y ait du grabuge et que Neïla est là? Tu te sens d'y aller?"

26 "Bien sûr qu'elle veut y aller."

27 "Assieds-toi."

28 "Elle fera tout ce qu'elle peut pour aider nos frères à Gaza."

29 "Faire quoi?"

30 "Assieds-toi. C'est juste une manif contre la politique sioniste d'Israël. Tes frères vont vouloir que tu y ailles."

31 "Je pense qu'elle devrait porter un panneau. Et en anglais puis qu'elle a décidé de parler cette langue."

32 "Tu peux pas lâcher un peu? Tu vois pas qu'elle est terrifiée?"

33 "Sinon, elle peut inviter son copain américain. Comment s'appelle-t-il ? Quint?"

34 "Ne lui prête pas attention. Il a toujours été railleur."

35 "Je peux rester à côté de toi pendant la manif?"

36 "Ma petite cousine, tu peux tout me demander."

37 "Je t'ai dit que tu allais les aimer."

Chapter 16

I had no desire to participate in their asinine demonstration, but at least I might not have to freeze to death. I rolled on my back to watch the sun shine through the shutters onto my bed. With a little luck, the weather would continue to be this nice all afternoon.

I had come to understand that the demonstration had been prohibited by the prefect but, whatever the authorities might say, Othmane was dead set on us going. According to him, the government was controlled by the Jews so what they said had no relevance. When I spoke to Djahida about it, I realized she was even more radical than our jihadist.

Mokhtar arrived before I had dressed with a load of cardboard, paint and wooden rods. "Go Neïla, write English thing," he demanded in English, with a chuckle and a horrible accent while I shook my head resolutely. I would have preferred to stay out of the whole thing completely so I wasn't about to start writing anti-Semitic slogans on a sign. My Jewish cousins had also been militantly pro-Israel and supporting Palestine would have made me a traitor.

When I refused a second time, Mokhtar snarled and lifted his hand. For a moment I thought he was going to hit me but then he smiled and simpered, *"Are you telling me you don't want to help Palestine?"*[1]

Behind me Djahida let out a long, exasperated sigh and it appeared that I had no other option, if I wanted to live in peace or stay alive, than to find a nice pro-Palestinian slogan. Unfortunately, I had no idea where to begin and I didn't want to say anything that I couldn't believe in. I sat down to watch Djahida paint "Israël assassin" with a picture of a knife in the back of what must have been a Bedouin but which actually looked like a turtle.

"Why don't you draw something since you're so good at it,"[2] Djahida barked at me. She seemed more frustrated than angry.

Josh didn't know how to draw so I just shrugged and leaned back to think. The only thing that would come mind was my life back in the States with my family, my cousins arguing when they came over for dinner, and finally my mother crying. Neïla's instincts then took over and in a few minutes she had drawn a crying mother carrying a dying baby. The slogan "Babies aren't terrorists," seemed like something I could believe, so with Neïla's elegant hand, I wrote it underneath the picture.

Djahida looked over my shoulder and gave a squeal of delight. She then dragged me to the bedroom to make me up like she had last evening, although insisting that I wear both a hijab and a jilbab. When Mokhtar came back, he gave a big smile and said to me, *"You see that you can do it."*[3]

While we finished getting ready, Mokhtar stapled the cardboard to the rods and told us that we should get going if we wanted him to buy us Turkish sandwiches. That put Djahida in such a frenzy that we were out the door in five minutes.

Djahida displayed her sign proudly as we walked down the street and continued to yell slogans even when the encouragements changed to circumspect stares after we had left the neighborhood. On the metro station platform I noticed other signs, tens of fellow demonstrators and more girls in jilbabs and hijabs. Even though I hated the costume, being just one of the crowd did make me feel a little less like a freak.

The metro slid to a stop and the demonstrators pushed into the car. I noticed a French couple in a corner seat trying to go unseen as the demonstrators began to chant and yell slogans in French and Arabic. I had the impression we were going to a football game rather than a protest. When the metro jerked to a stop at République, Djahida dragged me out onto the platform and up the stairs.

"With this crowd, we had better go for the sandwiches right now,"[4]

Mokhtar yelled above the hubbub.

It was barely half past eleven but I nodded my agreement because I had discovered that Neïla loved Turkish sandwiches. Mokhtar led us up Rue du Faubourg du Temple to one of those hole-in-the-wall sandwich shops and left us in line while he stepped away to make a phone call. I covered my face and tried not to look anyone in the eye.

"A friend is going to come eat with us,"[5] Mokhtar declared a minute later.

Djahida frowned and turned to face him. *"Is it your deejay friend who pretends to be a beatbox?"*[6]

"So what?" Mokhtar spun on his heels to look her in the eye. *"And his name is Romain."*[7]

"It's just that he won't stop making those noises with his mouth. Does he think he's making music or fart sounds?"[8] Djahida snorted and sputtered a few times rhythmically as she moved her butt like a duck dancing hip-hop.

Mokhtar shrugged her off and started ordering sandwiches with cokes and mayonnaise on the fries from a bearded man behind the counter.

Djahida turned to me. *"You remember him?"* She then continued without waiting for an answer. *"Before Othmane came back, before we started wearing the hijab, he was always hitting on you."*[9]

"*Quoi* (*What*)?" I exclaimed, staring at her.

She gave me a coquettish wink. *"He then converted to Islam, maybe just to see you."*[10]

"We haven't always worn the hijab?"[11] I asked, a little too naively.

Both Djahida and Mokhtar broke out laughing. *"Of course we haven't always worn it. Othmane advised us to do it,"*[12] Djahida answered.

"And you do everything Othmane says?"[13] Mokhtar gibed at Djahida.

Djahida turned away with a miffed look. *"It was after the death of Daddy. Normally you should know more about it than me,"*[14] she hissed, and I noticed Mokhtar was watching me intently.

The bearded man behind the counter came back with the sandwiches and Mokhtar took out his credit card to pay. That was when the rhythmic mouth noises approached me from behind and I turned to find myself face-to-face with the Human Beatbox, the son of the family that had boarded me. It was strange seeing him smile. In the month and a half I had spent at his house, the most amiable thing I had heard was a burp and now he was nothing but courtesy. He gave me a kiss on either cheek and pushed past me to carry the tray with my sandwich. I found myself sitting opposite him while he watched my every bite. I set my sandwich down and looked away.

"Are you going to let her eat?"[15] Djahida barked at him.

He turned to Djahida. *"But I'm not bothering her."* He then looked back at me. *"Am I?"*[16]

The last thing I wanted to do was open my mouth so I pulled the veil over my face.

"Don't you know that she hardly speaks since her accident? The doctor says we mustn't push her."[17] Djahida's smile was full of care and pride.

Beatbox nodded and then looked back at me. *"And she remembers nothing?"*[18]

"You can be sure she won't forget what a jerk you are!"[19] Djahida shot back at him.

Mokhtar's smile remained just as wide while Beatbox made a few woofer sounds and rolled his shoulders. I looked down at my French fries covered with mayonnaise wondering if I could really eat them.

It was Djahida who broke the silence. "So *how is this demonstration going to work?"*[20]

Beatbox looked away and shrugged while Mokhtar's smile became even more mocking. *"First we show our signs cheerfully and then we start yelling at the police. At some point, people will begin throwing things at them and they'll charge. That's when you girls hightail it."*[21]

Djahida looked at Mokhtar confused. *"But I thought everything was supposed to remain calm."*[22]

"Because Othmane said so?"[23] Mokhtar's smile was now close to a sneer.

Djahida nodded with wide eyes. *"He's on the organizing team, isn't he?"*[24]

"Othmane says lots of things . . ."[25] Mokhtar finished his sentence with a few circular hand movements and a mocking grunt.

Djahida's mouth remained open and Beatbox started staring at me again, so I excused myself and slid off to take my precautions. This time I hadn't forgotten the plastic bag, but the toilets were so dirty that I could have left it on the floor and nobody would have noticed. As a boy, I might have made-do, but now I was sick to my stomach with all that filth. I tried in vain to avoid contact with any object but I still felt like I needed a thorough scrubbing when I had finished.

The three were standing outside waiting and Djahida was skipping from foot to foot with excitement. *"You see there? That's where the heroes killed those blasphemers."*[26] She pointed at a building around which a group of people were chanting. She then grabbed my arm and practically dragged me toward the square while the two boys followed behind chatting and gesturing. Djahida held up her sign and began chanting, *"Palestine libre."*

The traffic around the large square had been blocked off by the protestors, but on the far side I could make out a line of policemen in their riot gear. There were others on the avenue that went down toward Bastille. Place de la République looked like it had been turned into a battlefield.

"Where is Zaria?"[27] I asked Djahida over the tumult. She

glanced at me blankly and shrugged. Then her face broke into a huge smile and she pointed at a group of women wearing hijabs, jilbab or niqabs and all chanting anti-Semitic slogans. She pulled me in their direction and took up their chants. When I looked around, I had lost sight of Mokhtar and Beatbox.

Many of the girls in the group were no older than us and as excited and vocal as Djahida. Whenever a person with a camera ventured by, all the girls screamed and took poses while Djahida jerked me around to get me in the picture with her. Then suddenly Djahida squealed and pointed at a black Islamic State flag. *"That's too awesome,"*[28] she exclaimed, before darting over to the boys carrying the flag. I stayed where I was preferring to keep my distance from those future jihadists.

Shrieks erupted from the group of girls and I spun around fearing the worst—it was just a camera crew for the television—however, all the girls started pushing and screaming to get filmed. When I looked around for Djahida, she had been lost in the pandemonium.

I made my way toward the place I had seen her last, but there were too many people and too many girls dressed in jilbabs. Suddenly the crowd began moving and I was swept toward Boulevard Magenta. I felt tiny and totally helpless while boys pushed and rushed past. One knocked me down as he forced his way through the crowd and before I could get up, feet stumbled over me kicking me in the back and ripping the sign from my hands.

Then strong hands, a man's hands, grabbed me, pulled me to my feet and turned me around. It was Beatbox's and he was incredibly strong, a lot stronger than Josh had ever imagined. *"You remember nothing? Not even us?"*[29]

He was speaking to me, his eyes focused on my face, and yet I had the impression he was addressing somebody else. I tried pulling away but I couldn't break free and his grip became more and more painful. I didn't know what he was talking about.

"I'll have to explain it to you,"[30] he shouted sternly, and began dragging me through the crowd toward one of the adjacent streets.

Fear began to well up into my belly. I tried fighting, but he didn't seem to feel my blows. He whipped around and lifted his hand as if he were about to hit me, then lowered it.

"You're trying to act innocent with your robes. Come on, you want me to believe you've changed? I think it'll all come back to you."[31]

A boy running from the police bowled into him just then and I pulled free. It was hard running with my Jilbab but I didn't stop until I was in the middle of the square with more women. I saw him watching me and then he seemed to disappear into the crowd. I was shaking so badly I could hardly stand.

* * *

The crowd ebbed and flowed with the movements of the police when they charged to drag away some protestor. Mokhtar had been right, things didn't stay calm, and I even thought I saw him throwing something in the direction of the police. I had moved over behind a bench to avoid being kicked in the back again, or worse. Should I tell anybody about what Beatbox had tried to do? Neïla's body began to shiver. What had he tried to do?

A hand touched my back and Othmane was staring down at me with melancholic defeat in his eyes. Although he was wearing one of those yellow jerseys identifying the organizers, those who were supposed to be keeping order, he did nothing to stop a fight that broke out in front of us. A boy's head was smashed into the pavement, there was blood all over, and Othmane just sat down beside me with his arm around my shoulder.

After a few minutes, Othmane removed his jersey and took out his telephone to write a quick text. He then helped me up because my legs were quivering so badly that I could barely stand. Othmane's hint of a smile was sympathetic so I let him keep his arm around me as he led me through the crowd. It was the first time I hadn't shrunk from his touch.

Djahida met us at the metro station ten minutes later, growling oaths under her breath at Othmane, and then openly at me when he told her to take me home. I tried to say something to her, or tell Othman that I could find my way, but no words would come out, only tears, as if I had never known how to speak any language. I hated myself for being weak and helpless.

"Don't cry," Djahida barked. She then looked at me more closely and raised an eyebrow. *"What happened?"*[32]

"Beatbox," I answered, with an American accent.

She nodded. *"So it was Romain. I should have known."*[33]

"What did he do to me?" I asked in English, without thinking or even knowing why I might ask that question.

Her eyes darted in my direction. She had understood. *"Qu'est-ce qu'il t'a fait?"* she repeated in French. "I don't know."

1 "Tu me dis que tu ne veux pas aider la Palestine?"

2 "T'as qu'à faire un dessin, toi qui es si forte."

3 "Tu vois que tu peux le faire."

4 "Avec tout ce monde, on a intérêt à trouver nos sandwichs tout de suite."

5 "Un ami va venir manger avec nous."

6 "C'est ton copain D.J. qui fait semblant d'être un beatbox?"

7 "Eh alors? Et il s'appelle Romain."

8 "C'est qu'il n'arrête pas de faire ces bruits avec sa bouche. Il pense faire de la musique ou des pets?"

9 "Tu te rappelles de lui? Avant qu'Othmane revient, et avant qu'on porte le hijab, il te draguait."

10 "C'est alors qu'il s'est converti à Islam, peut-être juste pour te voir."

11 "On n'a pas toujours porté le hijab?"

12 "Bien sûr qu'on ne l'a pas toujours porté. C'est Othmane qui nous l'a conseillé."

13 "Et tu écoutes tout ce que dit Othmane?"

14 "C'était après la mort de papa. Normalement tu devrais en savoir plus que moi."

15 "Tu va la laisser tranquille pour qu'elle mange?"

16 "Mais je l'embête pas. Pas vrai?"

17 "Tu sais pas qu'elle ne parle presque plus depuis l'accident? Le médecin a dit qu'il ne faut pas la brusquer."

18 "Et elle se rappelle de rien?"

19 "Je peux te dire qu'elle va se rappeler de ta connerie!"

20 "Alors, cette manif, ça va se passer comment?"

21 "D'abord, on montre gaiement nos panneau et ensuite on se met à crier contre la police. A un moment donné, il y en a qui vont se mettre à lancer des choses et la police va charger. C'est là que vous les meufs déguerpissez."

22 "Mais je pensais que ça devait se passer dans le calme."

23 "Parce qu'Othmane l'a dit?"

24 "Il fait partie des organisateurs, non?"

25 "Othmane dit beaucoup de choses..."

26 "Tu vois là? C'est là où les héros ont tué ces blasphémateurs."

27 "Où est Zaria?"

28 "C'est trop fort."

29 "Tu te rappelle de rien? Même pas de nous?"

30 "Il faut que je t'explique."

31 "Tu fais l'innocente avec tes habits. Maintenant tu veux me faire croire que tu as changé? Je pense que tu va t'en souvenir."

32 "Pleure pas. Que s'est-il passé?"

33 "Romain donc. J'aurais du savoir."

Part 4

Il n'y a pas de lumière sans ombre. "There is no light without shadow."

—Louis Aragon

Chapter 17

Mother turned on the TV news after breakfast. The violence had continued on into the night and a synagogue had been attacked. Mother's impassive expression made me want to do Neïla's homework on life in the trenches during WWI; it might cheer me up.

Djahida suddenly squealed for me to come see, so I put on Neïla's slippers and flip-flopped to the bedroom. She was pointing at a picture on the computer of her holding up her sign and shouting while Neïla stared at the sky. It illustrated a newspaper article entitled, *"Why are teenage girls attracted to radical Islam?"*[1]

I didn't even pretend to be excited, because I had no wish to make Neïla famous again. Djahida ignored my exasperated sighs and immediately posted it on Neïla's FB page as a favor. I didn't thank her.

Luckily, Mother called to ask if she was doing her homework and I was able to wrest the computer from her grasp and remove the picture from Neïla's page. Then, with a glance over my shoulder to make sure Djahida was busy, I looked to see if Kim or Quincy had written.

Kim was a regular writer of short messages about boys, homework and dancing. Quincy wrote less often and never said much. I had made an attempt to steer the messages toward his interests and had asked if he still thought Caravaggio announced modern European culture more than any other cinquecento artist. He had taken his time answering and I was afraid I had scared him.

But there was his name on the list of messages. I held my breath, clicked on his reply and when I opened them, I realized how stupid I had been. "How did you know?" was all that was written. I had bungled everything. I let out a groan, sat back and stared at the little picture he used in his profile.

"It's a message from who?"[2] Djahida simpered from across the room with a sickly-sweet smile.

My scowl only excited her nosiness and so she tried to look over at the screen before I closed the page. She hit back with another question. *"Is it your American sweetheart?"*[3]

I turned around startled. *"How do you know?"*[4] The question had escaped me.

A smile then spread across her lips. *"I was told."*[5]

"Who told you?"[6] I almost shouted, but lowered my voice at the last second.

"You speak a lot more when it's about your American."[7] Her smirk was like a barrier.

"Who's spying on me?"[8]

Her smirk didn't budge. *"I promised not to tell."*[9]

"But you told me."[10]

She shook her head and zipped her lips closed. With a last scowl in her direction, I went to sit on my bed and took out one of Neïla's schoolbooks to bury my nose in it. Now I was sure somebody was spying on me.

* * *

Othmane stayed silent while he drove me to my appointment the next morning and I turned my head away to look at the people in the other cars. Among all the hundreds of faces staring straight ahead, I spied a little blue-eyed girl staring at me. When I smiled at her, she quickly looked away giving me the feeling that I frightened her. Did she think I was a terrorist?

Othmane parked in a loading zone not far from the hospital and put his hand on my shoulder as we walked down the sidewalk. I wished he would take it off, but I couldn't figure out how to tell him so I continued on obediently.

I was left in the waiting area while Othmane ran to find a safer place to park. People avoided looking at me so I pulled the scarf over Neïla's face until the doctor called my name. I stood up to shake his hand but he only touched the tips of my fingers as if I were fragile.

"So, how have you been since our last meeting?"[11] he asked, inviting me into his office and motioning toward a chair.

"Ça va (I'm fine)," I answered. It didn't seem right for me to sit down before he did so I remained standing until he shook his head and sat in his swivel chair. *"Your French has improved,"*[12] he stated, after I had taken the chair opposite him.

"Oui," I admitted weakly, *"but can we speak English like the last time?"*[13] My French was probably better than English but I was sick and tired of pretending to be somebody I wasn't. This appointment gave me the chance to be a little more myself although I had to be extra careful with the psychiatrists for fear they might discover the truth.

"Certainly, but why prefer you English when your French is better?" he asked with his crooked smile.

"I don't trust myself," I answered truthfully, and immediately regretted having said it.

"And what are you afraid of?"

I just shook my head. I had said too much already.

He looked at me thoughtfully. "How are relations with your family?"

I didn't know whether I should lie this time or not. "Better. Othmane hasn't beaten me lately." That was at least true.

His eye twitched slightly. "Are you afraid of him?" he asked.

I couldn't deny that so I nodded. "Except that . . ." could I tell him about what happened at the demonstration. I looked him in the eyes and then away. He had blue eyes under those bushy eyebrows.

"Except what? Who frightens you?" he asked in a soft voice.

My head turned away before I spoke. "They all do. They make me . . . like wearing this . . ." I grabbed the veil wanting to pull it off, but paused and I looked into his blue eyes. "It's just that I don't believe Neï . . . that I ever—" I cut myself off and stared down at her slender fingers. I had to shut up.

When I glanced back at him, his smile looked truly sympathetic. "I know you don't believe you are the same person."

My head jerked back up in surprise. I wanted to deny it but my mouth refused to obey. His eyes looked so tender that I wished he would hug me like Daddy.

"We all change," he continued softly, "but people expect you to be the same."

I had to wipe the tears from my eyes. "They will hurt me. Somebody wants me dead. I was attacked by a boy at the demonstration."

He knotted his brow and silently rubbed his hands together before asking, "Have you told the police?"

I shook my head. "I'm afraid of what her . . . my family might say. They don't like the police. I don't even know if anybody would believe me." I glanced back at his serious expression. "And you probably think I'm just paranoid."

He didn't move for a second and his smile was forced when he answered. "You went through a great trauma; I shall see that your treatment is continued."

So he did think I was getting paranoid on him! Could I trust anyone?

He closed his notepad. "Now, we spoke about you returning to school. Are you still motivated for that?"

"Oh, yes!" I squealed in an embarrassingly girlish way. "Do you really think it can happen soon?"

His smile became more genuine. "We shall see." He looked at his watch. "Please wait here for a minute." He left me sitting in the sparse hospital office and I could feel myself fidgeting. He came back a minute later with a woman in her early thirties, reddish-brown hair and carrying a few pounds too many. She frowned when she saw my hijab but then sat down facing me.

"Madam Jacquet is your referral teacher,"[14] the doctor explained.

I didn't offer to shake hands and neither did she. I knew that Mustapha had a teacher like Mme Jacquet because he was handicapped. Did I fall in that category?

"Tomorrow you will see the principal of your school," she explained. *"He's been told about your difficulties."*[15]

I nodded even though it bothered me that Neïla was thought to have mental problems. When she asked me if I had any questions, I shook my head. She smiled for the first time and added, *"The veil however is forbidden."*[16]

I tried not to show my joy when I thanked her. I was as fed up with the veil as with the prayers. The doctor escorted me to the door and shook my hand so lightly it seemed he was afraid he'd break my hand.

1 "Pourquoi les jeunes filles tournent-elles vers l'Islam radical?"

2 "C'est un message de qui?"

3 "C'est de ton chéri américain?"

4 "Comment tu sais?"

5 "On me l'a dit."

6 "Qui te l'a dit?"

7 "Tu parles plus quand il s'agit de ton américain."

8 "Qui m'espionne?"

9 "J'ai promis de ne pas le dire."

10 "Mais tu me l'as dit."

11 "Alors, comment allez-vous depuis notre dernière rendez-vous?"

12 "Votre français s'améliore."

13 "Peut-on parler anglais comme la dernière fois?"

14 "Mme Jacquet est votre professeur référant."

15 "Demain tu vas voir le proviseur de ton lycée. Il est au courant de tes difficultés."

16 "Le voile par contre n'est pas permis."

Chapter 18

I noticed that Mother's cheek twitched when she found me preparing pens, notebooks and fumbling though Neïla's school supplies. Maybe she would have preferred Neïla at home with kids rather than working to get an education and a job. Before I was able to justify myself, she had turned her back and gone off to the kitchen.

I had actually spent most of the afternoon browsing Quincy's profile, looking at where he lived, staring at his pictures and I hadn't resisted downloading the one in which he was wearing a musketeer hat and smiling like a movie star from the 1930s. His message, however, I only read once. "Yes, the horrible realism of our century, its shadows and light, makes me think humans haven't changed. Will our lust for pleasure lead us to decadence? Caravaggio certainly flirted with it. Since you ask, in which direction does your heart lean?"

He sounded too much like the Quincy who debated with Josh over an espresso, so I quickly wrote a message to Kim asking if he was angry with me. She probably wouldn't know but I hoped she would make me feel better. I then pulled his picture back up and my heart raced while I inspected the lines of his chin. Why had he become so important to me?

Djahida and Mustapha came home a little later and Djahida cracked a huge smile when she learned that justice had been served; she would no longer be the only one plagued with homework and report cards. Mustapha took the news that I was going back to school with a smile and a kiss on my cheek.

I helped Mother cook the chorba that evening, a soup with chicken, chick peas, celery, cumin and coriander. I was getting better at anticipating what she needed done and doing it before she asked. She even smiled at me once. Did she really expect me—or rather Neïla—to stay at home making chorba to feed the kids?

At dinner Djahida continued to gloat that tomorrow I wouldn't be able to spend the day having fun cooking and I made no effort to correct her. It wasn't that I didn't like cooking, it was that I just didn't want to condemn Neïla to the miserable future of being a housewife. Most especially, the presentiment that I might have to marry a man made me sick.

After dinner, Djahida insisted on helping me decide what to wear to school as if I didn't know how to do it myself. She first explained that the hijab and jilbab were forbidden, but that there were still enough clothes on Neïla's side of the closet for us to find something suitable. I also noticed that there were more clothes on Djahida's side and glanced at her wondering if she hadn't appropriated a certain number of Neïla's favorite outfits.

I kept my mouth shut however, because there was no way for me to prove she had taken anything. Still, being a little miffed, I pushed in front of her and grabbed some jeans and a sweat shirt but Djahida let out a snort. She insisted I look feminine—nobody was going to laugh at her sister if she could help it—and chose a skirt that she had me put over some tight jeans with a long sleeved pink blouse. Although it didn't show any bare skin, it was very cute and Josh would have had trouble keeping his eyes off of Neïla if he saw her.

I didn't sleep well that night and lay awake after Fajr prayer hoping that Neïla would come to give me advice before I was thrown a little further into her world. Unfortunately, the darkness remained unnervingly empty. When the rumble of cars in the parking lot below let me know it was nearly time to get up, I slipped out of bed and went into the kitchen to put on mint tea and set out the toast and honey.

Mother arrived a few minutes later and raised an eyebrow at my eagerness to be off to class. Djahida then came shuffling in followed by Mustapha. I didn't say anything during breakfast in spite of my exhilaration while Neïla's two siblings kept looking at me as if I had gone nuts. After breakfast, Djahida insisted on redoing my hair and putting a little makeup on my eyes, but I was still ready ten minutes before the others and had to wait next to the door for Djahida who was taking care of her own hair and face.

Djahida finally sashayed out of the bedroom with Mother following. I realized with a pang of shame that she was going to accompany me. I tried to tell myself that Mother's presence was only temporary but I still dreaded what all of Neïla's friends would say about me being led to school by her.

* * *

The high school was a large glass, steel and blackened cement structure with hundreds of high schoolers milling about the gate. A number of them waved at me so I waved back not knowing what else to do. None approached, however, and it didn't take a genius to figure out that it was because Mother was holding my arm. I felt like a sideshow attraction with everyone watching and commenting until Bertrane trotted up, kissed me on either cheek and shook Mother's hand. *"See you later,"*[1] she chimed and headed off into the school.

Mother first stopped at a glassed-in cubicle to speak with a harassed-looking lady who stared at me as if I were a hardened criminal. *"The principal's office, please?"*[2] Mother asked. The bell then rang and the lady watched the last of the stragglers evacuate the open area before she pointed at the far end of the lobby. We followed her directions through a door and down a little hall whose walls were covered with posters condemning racism or warning of AIDS. Mother stuck her head in the first open office and I glanced over her shoulder at the gruff-looking middle-aged secretary who wordlessly waved us to a chair.

I heard a few latecomers making their way to class and stared down at my book bag nervously, wondering if I could really make people believe that I was Neïla. Would I even be able to keep up with her French classes? I knew they weren't simple because I had been through Bertrane's notes and had hardly understood anything.

Mother simply stared into space until a middle-aged woman in a tight dress sauntered up, spoke to the secretary and sat opposite us. The lady looked over at me and a smile stretched her red lips to either side of her hooked nose. She crossed her legs and I noticed she was wearing stockings with a black line down the back. Josh might have found them appealing but Neïla just thought they were vulgar. Mother seemed to have come to the same conclusion seeing as she had turned her head away with a frown.

The secretary in the office started barking at somebody over the phone and I felt Neïla's body jerk with fright. Would the teacher shout at me like that if I missed the first hour of class? Even if I had been a college sophomore just a few weeks ago, my ingrained fear of teachers made my chest contract and my head spin. What's more, Neïla needed a good education if she were ever to get away from the family.

A short doughy man then hurried past, said something to the secretary and disappeared into the principal's office. Again the wait became excruciating although Mother didn't move or lose her frown whenever the lipstick lady smiled.

The door opened and the doughy man stepped out presenting what would have been a calm smile if he hadn't had a stressed twitch of the eye. *"Come in, come in,"* he mumbled, while beckoning us into his office. *"And you too, Mme Jalbert."*[3]

He shook Mother's hand and then the hand of the lady with the lipstick before going around his desk to sit. Mother and the lady took the two chairs, which left me standing.

The principal turned to address Mother. *"I received the commission's report and it would seem that your daughter is fit to return to class. They indicated, however, that some cognitive difficulties may persist without affecting her intellectual capacities. They have therefore required that she be accompanied, at least at the beginning, by an assistant to make sure her integration goes well. Have you got any questions?"*[4]

Mother nodded but I was sure she hadn't registered everything because I certainly hadn't. One point came through clearly, however; this glossy-lipped lady was to follow me around school. I looked over at her and she gave me a sticky smile. If I had had any hopes of making new friends, they were now dashed.

"Fine, I will leave you with Mme. *Jalbert."*[5] The principal was speaking to me but he handed the timetable to the lady before he shook Mother's hand and escorted us out.

When the door shut behind me, *Mme* Jalbert held out her hand for me to shake. I took it timidly and nodded in greeting.

"Pleased to meet you. I am Pauline and your name is Neïla,"[6] Mme. Jalbert said, with a suave chuckle.

I could only nod but Mother came to my rescue. *"She doesn't speak much, only in English, ever since her accident. We don't know why because she does speak French."*[7]

Pauline turned back to me, "My English no good. We speak French?" I didn't answer which made Pauline break into a larger smile as she reached out to caress my cheek. *"Elle est si mignonne*—oh sorry, in English—she is so cute." I turned my head and Mother frowned, but Pauline seemed quite pleased with herself. "And she become red!" she exclaimed in a high-pitched singsong. *"She is really delightful."*[8]

Mother had heard enough and turned to leave without kissing me goodbye so I was left alone with the lipstick lady who was pushing the strand of hair from my eyes.

"Tu ne m'en veux pas? . . . Sorry, in English, You not angry?" Mme. Jalbert simpered while a man, probably a teacher, walked by. He looked at me briefly, then at Pauline's hosiery and I shook my head. I didn't like being cooed at in public, especially with a teacher walking by.

"*C'est quand, ton anniversaire?* When your birthday?" She asked, putting her hands on my shoulders.

The question surprised me and I almost gave Josh's birthday in August. When I stopped to think about it, however, I didn't know Neïla's birthday so I looked at her and shrugged.

Pauline gave me a skeptical smile. "*Come now, why don't you want to tell me?*"[9]

I had to shrug again and shake my head before comprehension dawned on her and she lost her smile for the first time. "*You really don't know,*" she whispered, shaking her head while I stared down at Neïla's sneakers. Her hand touched my cheek softly again and then stroked my hair. "*Look in your grade book. It's written.*"[10]

I didn't know what she was talking about so she took my school bag and removed a small notebook that seemed to have all my official information. "*It's your passport to school,*" Pauline explained, as she leafed through it. "*31 of October, Scorpio!*"[11] she suddenly trilled.

I shrugged while she took a step back to inspect me from top to bottom as if I were a sculpture in an art museum. "*I'll have to calculate your ascendant,*" she said thoughtfully, "*but I wouldn't have said Scorpio.*"[12]

I gathered my courage and asked in a whisper, "*Quel signe, alors* (What sign then)?" I hoped I wasn't as transparent as I felt.

The sticky smile spread across her face. "You not prefer English?"

"What sign would you have said?" I repeated. My English took her back because Pauline hadn't been expecting me to speak so fast and I realized that Neïla was making progress.

"*Ton signe* (Your sign)?" she mumbled shaking her head. "*Sagittarius . . . or Virgo. Yes, I'd say Virgo.*"[13]

"Pourquoi (Why)?" I asked, surprised because Josh had been a Virgo.

"*You must be creative and sensitive . . . and shy. I think you like making people happy."*[14]

I had to mull over that a second, doubting the description corresponded to Neïla and certain it didn't fit my self-image. But what was I really like? Or rather, who was I?

Pauline gave a chuckle and stroked my shoulder. *"I am Aries. I go straight to the point."*[15]

Doubts still swept over me—had Josh really died?—and wouldn't people here expect me to act like Neïla even though I was incapable of doing so. I was suddenly terrified of facing her old friends and teachers.

"What's the matter?"[16] Pauline asked, while she dried a tear from my face with a Kleenex she had taken from her purse.

"I don't know who I am," [17] I admitted with a hiccup.

She didn't understand my confession, but she still took me into her arms and rocked me. *"Are you sure you feel up to going to class?"*[18] she murmured.

Her perfume smelled heavily of roses and I felt like staying nestled against her soft chest but I stepped back and said *"oui"* resolutely.

Pauline took out another tissue and handed it to me to wipe my cheek, then tut-tutted, *"You can't go to class with your mascara like that. Sit down. I'll redo it."*[19]

She did more than just redo Neïla's mascara; her handbag was full of bottles and powder and I would have bet she used all of them on my face.

"My word you are pretty!"[20] She exclaimed when she had finished and held up a compact mirror for me to admire her work. Doe-like eyes gazed at me, they were magnificent, but then Neïla's red lips began to quiver and I pushed the mirror away. Could I go into the classroom with Neïla looking so made-up? I was about to tell her to take it all off when the bell rang and a rumble of stampeding feet erupted as kids rushed out of their first-hour class. The teacher who had walked by earlier came out of the office and did a double-take of me.

"You mustn't be shy; your eyes could melt a glacier. One sigh and any man would follow you."[21] Pauline said with a wink, after I had turned my head.

I knew that to be true because Josh would have melted if Neïla had so much as spoken to him. She'd had that hypnotic magnetism that no man could resist—with the exception of Quincy—and he was the only one that I wanted to notice me.

"Let's go, it's time for French,"[22] Pauline chimed. Then, without noticing my hesitation, she took my hand to pull me out into the main hall. As we made our way to class, people stepped aside and stared. Pauline held her head erect and enjoyed every second of the attention while, mortified, I tried to move away but her hand whipped out to drag me back next to her.

A woman of about sixty with unkempt hair and neurotic-looking eyes watched me enter room E12 so warily that I almost walked back out. Pauline then stepped in front of me, extended her hand and gave the French teacher a quick, brusque shake while I moved back against the wall. Although I couldn't hear what was said, I got the impression the teacher couldn't care less and was more harassed each time Pauline smiled. She finally pointed to two tables in the back of the room and went to tell the rest of the class to enter.

The other kids filed in staring at sheets of paper and cramming until the last second; I had come back the day of a test. I then remembered that Bertrane had given me a list of words a week ago which I hadn't bothered studying. Bertrane came in almost last, gave me a stressed smile and went back to studying her list. Mme. Lumière, the teacher, stood up and clapped her hands. The papers disappeared into the book bags and everyone began drawing ruled lines on double sheets of paper. I noticed that the format was completely different from anything we had in the States.

In a panic, I looked over at Pauline who smiled and began showing me how to make a box for the teacher's comments and where to put my name. She then had me write a dash with a twenty underneath which I understood that was for the grade. I looked up as the teacher set a paper in front of me with two poems and a long list of words, *"hyperbole, métonymie, oxymore . . .* (hyperbole, metonym, oxymoron . . .)" which I had to explain after having found examples in the poems and show their significance.

I was at a total loss. Pauline tried to encourage me and I did what I could with oxymoron and metaphor. I then made a guess at hyperbole but the other words were Greek to me. Mme. Lumière strolled by a few minutes into the test, saw I was stumped and scowled at my paper.

"Didn't you receive the list of words to memorize?"[23]

I began to nod that I had but the fear of opening my mouth to try uttering a French word was too great so I simply stared at my feet. Mme Lumière shook her head as if I were a complete moron and went back to the front to sit. That's when Neïla's tears began flowing down my cheek and I couldn't stop them for the last half hour of the test. Pauline put a hand on my shoulder while all the kids turned to stare. When the bell finally rang, I ran out without waiting for Pauline or gathering my things. I was sure that I'd never be able to handle the pressure of classes—Mother was right, I should go home and cook chorba.

1 "A tout à l'heure."

2 "Le bureau du proviseur, s'il vous plait."

3 "Entrez, entrez. Et vous aussi, Mme Jalbert."

4 "J'ai eu le rapport de la commission et il semblerait que votre fille est apte à retourner en cours. Ils ont marqué cependant qu'il pourrait rester quelques séquelles de l'ordre cognitif bien que cela n'affecte pas ses capacités intellectuelles. Ils ont donc mis pour condition qu'elle soit accompagnée, du moins au départ, par une AVS pour s'assurer qu'elle s'y intègre correctement. Avez-vous des questions?"

5 "Bien, je vous laisse avec Mme Jalbert."

6 "Très heureuse. Je suis Pauline et je crois que tu t'appelles Neïla."

7 "Elle ne parle pas beaucoup, ou en anglais, depuis son accident. On ne sait pas pourquoi parce qu'elle parle français."

8 "Elle est vraiment craquante."

9 "Allons, pourquoi tu ne veux pas me le dire?"

10 "Tu ne sais vraiment pas. Regarde dans ton carnet de correspondance. C'est marqué."

11 "C'est ton passeport au lycée. 31 octobre, Scorpion!"

12 "Il faut que je calcule ton ascendant. Je n'aurais pas dit Scorpion."

13 "Sagittaire... ou Vierge. Oui, on dirait Vierge."

14 "Tu dois être créative et sensible... et timide. Je pense que tu aimes rendre les gens heureux."

15 "Je suis Bélier. Je vais droit au but. Mais qu'est-ce qui t'arrive?"

16 "Qu'est-ce qui va pas?"

17 "Je ne sais pas qui je suis."

18 "Tu es sure que tu te sens d'aller en cours?"

19 "Tu ne peux pas aller en cours avec ton mascara comme ça. Assieds-toi. Je te le refais."

20 "Mais qu'est-ce que tu es belle!"

21 "Faut pas que tu sois timide, tes yeux pourrez faire fondre un glacier. Un soupir et n'importe quel homme te suivrait."

22 "Allons, il est l'heure de français, Mme. Lumière."

23 "N'avez-vous pas reçu la liste des mots à apprendre?"

Chapter 19

Bertrane found me in the corner behind the toilettes. *"Don't get upset, the hag's crazy,"*[1] she said, sitting down beside me.

Bertrane was right, and Neïla was making me act too emotional, but I couldn't help feeling that the door had just been locked and that Neïla would never get away from her family. I laid my head on her shoulder and let her warmth relax me until after the bell had rung.

"Come on," Bertrane said, pulling me to my feet. *"Mr. Hubert the English teacher is great."*[2]

She led through the empty halls to a closed door and I suddenly realized how late we were. I would have turned around and walked away if Bertrane hadn't held me tight around the shoulders and pushed the door open. A hush fell over the class and everyone, including the teacher, looked at us. He was athletic, unshaven and wore a gruff smile as he said, "Good morning Neïla, and welcome back to class." His voice came from deep in his chest and I couldn't detect even a hint of a French accent.

"Thank you. I'm glad to be back," I answered. "I'm sorry I'm late and that I have interrupted your class," I added, as politely as possible.

His gruff smile widened, the class murmured, and I realize that Neïla's English was far too good. I sputtered a second or two wondering how I could correct my lack of errors but the teacher spoke first. "No need to be sorry. Do come in and sit down. You have no reason to be worried."

I hadn't realized I looked upset and tried to act as calm as possible while I followed Bertrane to the back of the class where Pauline was gesticulating.

"I didn't know your English was so good,"[3] Bertrane whispered, when I had sat between her and Pauline.

I looked away not wanting the teacher to take any more notice of me and afraid he would yell at me if he saw me chatting. Unfortunately, he looked in my direction as if he expected me to answer the next question. The class was studying an extract from *Animal Farm*—I had seen that old animated film—and so on impulse I held up my finger.

Mr. Hubert swiftly pointed to me. My voice cracked when I tried to speak—I had to start a second time—but the answer that came out was too well worded and I heard the murmuring again.

"You're a whiz, you are,"[4] Bertrane whispered.

After that the teacher pointed at me every time the others were stumped and I might as well have sprouted whiskers and a tail with the looks I got from Neïla's classmates. I felt like fleeing back to hide in the same corner when the bell rang.

"Can I speak to you, Neïla?" Mr. Hubert said to me, before I could make my escape. I looked over at him surprised, hoping he wasn't angry.

"You seem to have made progress so may I speak to you in English rather than French?" he asked, while I watched his lips.

"I'm just as happy to speak English," I replied in the same whisper I had used in class and gazed at Neïla's feet.

"Fine." He gave me his gruff smile when I looked back up at his lips. "First I have to give you the work you missed, but that doesn't seem to be a problem as you understand the text better than the rest of the class. There are written exercises, too." His lips made Neïla breathe a little too fast.

"Thank you? I'll try to catch up on them as best as I can." I knew I sounded lame with Neïla's high-pitched whisper. Why did I wish to touch his lips?

"Good. Now I'm going to put on my other hat. I'm also your *professeur principal*. That means I'm the one who looks after all the problems that occur and I will lead the class councils when we decide who will pass into senior year."

I felt my stomach knot up; he was a lot more important than I had imagined. "You will decide if I pass?" I asked, but then felt silly and horribly ashamed that I had wanted to be snuggled by my head teacher.

"I won't be alone," he answered, without taking note of my embarrassment. "I'm afraid the French teacher has her say, too."

I felt myself tremble. "She hates me, doesn't she?"

"She can be rather caustic. If you have any problems, come to me and I'll see what I can do. I won't promise any miracles however."

A smile spread over my face and when I dared to look into his eyes, his pupils widened before he turned his head. Then he looked back up with his gruff smile and I wanted to hug him but I knew that wasn't done. Instead, I muttered a demure "thank you" and went to meet Pauline in the hall.

* * *

Bertrane pulled me away while Pauline was in the toilet. "*On cours* (Run)," she whispered and broke into a run with me following.

"*Sticky much?*"[5] Bertrane laughed, when we had slowed to a walk and we both broke into giggles which for once didn't embarrass me. People looked at us with smiles while Bertrane put her arm around my shoulders and guided me in the direction of the cafeteria where we met up with a number of other kids who all seemed to know Neïla. Everyone had a question that I could only answer in monosyllables. It was as if she, Neïla, didn't know a word of French.

"*Are you still dancing hip-hop?*"[6] A tall black boy asked and started playing some rap on his telephone. When I shrugged, they looked at me astounded. "*Well, you're really good. You even take* classes," he intoned and gesticulated.

Bertrane cut in. "*She didn't even know her name.*" Then before the others could ask more questions, she added, "*She probably doesn't know your names either."*[7] It was embarrassing, but I had to nod so they all introduced themselves with kisses on the cheek. By the time I picked up my tray, I had at least ten names to remember.

The cafeteria fare looked barely edible: a sort of spaghetti Bolognese. The lady serving saw the face I made and told me not to worry, there was no pork in it, as if I were Muslim. My father had always laughed about my Jewish grandparents who didn't eat pork, but now people were expecting the same thing of me. If I ever did, and word got back to Othmane, I was as good as dead.

There weren't many places left to sit when we came out with our trays, but a group of boys smiled and made room for us. Bertrane was more than happy to oblige and cuddled up against a muscular black guy whom she introduced as Jean-Jean. He put his arm around her and joked as if they were going out together.

I was between two dark-haired boys. When one of their thighs touched mine, my legs automatically tightened together. Luckily, a girl came up to say hello and pushed in to sit next to me. She was a beautiful mulatto who adeptly fended off the two boys. Her name was Kendra and she told me we had known each other since we were twelve.

I felt like answering, "Pleased to meet you," but murmured instead, "*Je suis désolée de ne pas m'en souvenir* (I'm sorry that I don't remember)."

She rubbed my shoulder. *"I was told that you might not even be able to speak. Don't feel bad."*[8]

Looking up into her beautiful dark eyes, I replied, *"It's sometimes easier than others."*[9] Her smile was radiant and Josh would really have fallen for her.

"Are you able to talk about the accident?"[10]

"The thing is that I don't remember,"[11] I lied.

"I saw your video on the Web. It was so awful," she whispered. *"And he makes you wear the veil, too?"* Her face screwed up compassionately. *"You'll do as you please in the future."*[12]

I had to wonder if that would be true so I shook my head. *"How long have I been wearing the hijab?"*[13] I asked.

Her brow knitted. *"Since the beginning of the school year. It was after you came back from your home country."*[14]

"My brother says that it has something to do with your father's death,"[15] the boy next to me put in. He looked Arab, too.

"What happened?"[16] I asked, trying to hide the urgency in my voice. I needed more information about Neïla if I ever hoped to figure out who had tried to kill her.

"Well, everyone knows he was stabbed. After that . . ." he looked around as if somebody might be listening in. *"Afterwards, I heard you were a suspect."*[17]

The information took a second to sink in, but then I realized what the lawyer had been insinuating. Might Neïla have killed her own father? I shook my head not wanting it to be true but unfortunately everything fit. Why else would she have given me her life? Kendra's arm was around my shoulder and she was rocking me. "*Pourquoi* (Why)?" I asked.

The boy's head shook but he continued to stare at me. *"I don't know much, only what my cousin told me. He is from the same town. Over there people just say that you did it."*[18]

A shudder ran through me and when I looked back at the smiling boy, I realized he had a crush on Neïla. I tried to smile back but failed.

* * *

The school let out at five o'clock, but it was a quarter past and most of the students had already deserted the premises. Pauline, however, insisted on waiting with me until somebody came to pick me up and continued chatting about my astrological sign while I assessed the feasibility of running off and escaping. I didn't want to go back to the apartment.

Othmane's car drove up and my twitch turned to a scowl. I

would even have preferred to listen to Pauline talking about my ascendant rather than sit in a car with that sadist. He opened the door and handed me a scarf to put over my hair that I took without saying a word.

"*Raconte-moi la mort de notre père* (I want to know about father's death)," I said, looking at the side of his face once the car had pulled into traffic.

He glanced at me with a blank expression. "*I wasn't there. You should ask Mokhtar.*"[19]

The last thing I wanted to do was ask Mokhtar—I didn't trust him any more than a snake—and Othmane was the only member of the family who hadn't been in Algeria when Neïla's father was murdered.

"*Do you think I killed him?*"[20] I asked bluntly.

He slowed the car, pulled to a stop and his dark eyes turned to stare at me. "*You were never obedient. We have been thanking Allah that you have changed since the accident. We have been thinking that you'll make a good wife. Don't start up again.*"[21]

I sputtered but couldn't find the French words to insult him for being a male chauvinist—did he really expect Neïla to be a good little wife who was knocked up by a hubby once a year? "*I won't get married,*"[22] I stated flatly.

A little bit of his jihadist smile appeared. "*And you'll kill me, too?*" His question ended in a hiss that felt like an ice bath. Maybe Neïla was able to commit a murder, but I didn't have the guts. A hint of tenderness then fluttered across his forehead. "*You are my sister. Maybe you hate me for it, but I have to protect you.*"[23]

I refused to lower my eyes in spite of the tears of anger. I then noticed that he had tears in his eyes, too. "*Protected from whom?*"[24] I asked.

He looked away, turned the key and I thought he wasn't going to answer until he whispered, "*de gens comme moi* (from people like me)."

1 “Faut pas t’en faire, la vieille est folle.”

2 “Viens, M. Hubert, le prof d’anglais, est génial.”

3 “Je ne savais pas que tu parlais si bien l’anglais.”

4 “Mais tu es un as, toi.”

5 “Quel pot de colle!”

6 “Tu danses toujours le hip-hop? Ben, tu es super forte. Tu prends même des cours.”

7 “Elle ne savait même pas son nom. Elle ne sait probablement pas vos noms non plus.”

8 “On m’a dit que tu ne saurais peut-être pas parler. Ne t’en fais pas.”

9 “Des fois, ça va, des fois, non.”

10 “Tu arrives à parler de l’accident?”

11 “C’est que je ne m’en souviens pas.”

12 “J’ai vu ta vidéo sur le net. Ça m’a fait trop mal. Et il t’oblige à mettre le voile maintenant aussi? Plus tard tu feras ce que tu voudras.”

13 “Je porte le hijab depuis combien de temps?”

14 “Depuis la rentrée. C’est après que tu es revenue du bled.”

15 “Mon frère dit que ça a à voir avec la mort de ton père.”

16 “Que s’est-il passé?”

17 “Bah, tout le monde sait qu’il a été poignardé. Après... après, on dit qu’ils t’ont soupçonnée.”

18 “Je ne sais pas beaucoup plus, juste ce que mon cousin m’a dit. Il est de la même ville. On dit là bas juste que tu l’as fait.”

19 “Je n’étais pas là. Tu devrais demander à Mokhtar.”

20 “Crois-tu que je l’ai tué?”

21 “Tu n’as jamais été obéissante. On remerciait Allah que tu aies changé depuis l’accident. On se disait que tu pourrais faire une bonne épouse. Ne recommence pas.”

22 “Je ne me marierai pas.”

23 “Et tu me tueras aussi ? Tu es ma sœur, je fais ceci pour toi. Peut-être que tu m’en veux mais il faut que je te protège.”

24 “Me Protéger de qui?”

Chapter 20

Mustapha hugged me as soon as I walked in the door and then pulled me into the living room where he had left his video game. As I walked past the kitchen, I saw Mother staring at Djahida with her grade book on the table and wondered what Mother would do when she found out I had failed the French test.

Mustapha asked if I wanted to play with him, but I shook my head as nicely as possible and hurried to my bedroom to see if Kim had written me. She often sent me messages about shopping, boys or parties and I liked her treating me like one of the girls even though I knew it wasn't true. Djahida would occupy the computer if I dallied, however, and I'd have to wait all evening before I could read my messages.

My heart started beating wildly because it was Quincy who had written but then I read the first line and it felt like an ice cube had gone down my back. "Kim is in the hospital. She was attacked early this morning while she was jogging in the Butte Chaumont. She is in reanimation at the hospital Lariboisière in the 10th arrondissement. I'm sorry, I have no other details. I really hope you are well and that we can see each other at the hospital for another selfie with Kim. I'll tell you when they start allowing visitors. Your friend, Quincy."

When there was a crime, I was always in the middle, and it was generally my fault. My head was spinning and—

"What does all that mean?" Djahida asked over my shoulder. *"Is it from your American sweetheart?"*[1]

I nearly jumped out of my skin, I hadn't heard her enter, and turned to scowl at Neïla's little pest of a sister. She just sat on her bed and scowled back.

"Where was Othmane this morning?" I asked. He was angry at Kim because of the video and he was certainly capable of violence. *"And who told you about Quincy?"*[2]

Djahida shrugged, puckered up her lips, and then smiled. *"So his name is Quincy?"*[3]

"Who told you about him?" I repeated loudly, while she continued to give me her hypocritical smirk. *"Was it Othmane?"*[4]

She shook her head and I got the impression she was telling the truth. *"Is he cute?"*[5] she simpered.

"Mokhtar, was it Mokhtar?" I shouted and her lip twitched. *"So it was Mokhtar!"*[6] I insisted.

She stood up and hissed *"No! It wasn't him."*[7]

I wasn't going to back down this time and so I didn't look away in spite of her snarls. *"Who then?"*[8]

She made the gesture of zipping her lips closed but it was clear that I was getting close. It had to be somebody Mokhtar knew and that only left Beatbox. What's more, he had tried to attack me. Had he attacked Kim, too? *"It was Beatbox! Or Romain, whatever you want to call him."*[9]

Her lip twitched again and I knew I was right. *"Did he pirate my accounts?"*[10] I asked standing up in front of her.

She shook her head. *"I don't know, he just told me that you had American friends. But you know he's really good with computers?"*[11]

I sat on the bed to mull over the situation. *"What happened between us?"*[12] I asked as much to myself as to Djahida.

"I don't really know," she said, when I looked back up at her. *"You never really liked him but after you came back from Algeria, after daddy died, you started to spend more time with him."* She turned her head away. *"Don't tell them that I told you!"*[13]

I nodded, said *"oui"* and laid back with a pillow over my face. I hoped to never see Beatbox again.

"But what happened to this girl?" Djahida asked in a low voice. I took the pillow off my face and saw that she was reading my FB page. *"That's the girl who did the video?"*[14] Her eyes were wide, and for a moment, she looked just like Neïla.

"Je ne sais pas (I don't know)," I replied, and covered my face with the pillow again.

"You don't think it was Romain?"[15] Her voice cracked.

"Je ne sais pas," I repeated through the pillow. I didn't want her to see that I had started crying.

"So why all the questions?"[16] she shrieked in a voice that was becoming hysterical and jerked the pillow off my face.

I stared and her and sniffled until she sat on the edge of the bed. *"I think somebody tried to kill me, too,"*[17] I whispered.

Her mouth dropped open. *"But who tried to kill you? I mean didn't you try to commit suicide?"*[18] she murmured.

"Je ne sais pas."

* * *

All the other students avoided us while we crossed the school courtyard, but I knew what they were whispering before they disappeared into the building. It was bad enough having a chaperone, why did Othmane have to keep his hand on my shoulder? I glanced up at his blank expression. It was worse than a scowl.

Pauline bounced up a few minutes before the bell rang wearing her makeup, long nose and sticky smile. Othmane observed for less than a second before turning his head away in disgust and leaving without shaking her hand.

I was about to apologize for his bad manners when she grabbed me by the arm and steered me inside to the toilets. *"We absolutely must redo your makeup,"*[19] she explained with urgency and pushed me into the girls' room.

I was a little put off at her criticizing Djahida's efforts, and I never felt comfortable in the girls' restroom, but she was holding my hand too tightly for me to pull away. *"We'll be late,"*[20] I argued while she pulled me in front of the mirrors.

"I brought a color especially for you. You'll see,"[21] she tut-tutted and began rummaging through her handbag.

I had no desire for Neïla to be painted like a Hollywood

Indian, especially with French being my first class that morning. *"It's not necessary,"*[22] I replied and tried to head for the door.

She laughed and blocked me next to the mirror. *"With your black-diamond eyes, you need a bronze eye shadow highlighted with iridescent white,"*[23] she explained, while she began powdering my face and humming.

"What is the powder for?"[24] Things were getting out of control so I needed more pertinent arguments.

"Oh, you hardly need any with your beautiful skin," she cooed as began to apply her bronze eye shadow. *"Hold it, don't move and keep your eyes shut."*[25]

I did as I was told to avoid getting poked in the eye. *"But I don't need makeup to get through my classes. What's the point?"*[26]

She stopped painting and when I opened my eyes, she was staring at me as if I were a ghost. It took her a few tries to stutter, *"Well . . . to feel pretty."*[27]

There was something about being a girl that I was missing. Josh had never been handsome and now I was forced to wear hijabs and jilbabs. Only Quincy had made me want to be attractive and I felt horrible about that. My brow knitted and my lips puckered.

"Don't you want to feel pretty?"[28] she asked.

My head shook and mumbled, *"I don't know what it's like to feel pretty."*[29]

All sorts of different expressions crossed her face as I looked at her vain efforts to make herself attractive. Finally something akin to compassion eased onto her features. *"My poor little thing, you are so pretty . . ."* She didn't finish her sentence as tears appeared in her eyes. *"I see now that you need help. Don't worry, I will help you."*[30]

She took me in her arms and suddenly I was crying on her shoulder. Maybe I did really want to be pretty, or at least not the freak that I was. *"But I don't have the right to be pretty,"*[31] I blurted out.

"But of course you do, and you are." She said softly, holding my face in her hands. *"Tell me what you're afraid of."*[32]

"Mostly of being late to Mme Lumière's class. Please, can't we go?"[33]

"Not now that you've rubbed your mascara all over your face," she said sternly. *"And don't you worry; I tell her it's my fault."*[34]

I had trouble believing that the wicked witch who taught French would care what Pauline said, but I was already late so I let her do her worst. She hummed and painted while I shut my eyes and tried to contain the tears. Finally, she told me to look in the mirror at the face of an Arabian princess. Neïla was stunning, so I turned away.

"What's the matter?"[35] Pauline asked.

"Nothing," I answered. *"She . . . I mean, I am too beautiful."*[36]

Pauline was a little put off and we got to class more than ten minutes late. Mme Lumière listened to Pauline's excuses with a tick in her eyes before she marked something in the attendance book and went back to making her speech about artists. We went to sit at the back next to Bertrane who had been keeping two seats for us and when the teacher's wasn't looking, she rubbed her knuckles against her chin to mean *barbant* (boring). She then handed me a note. *"The old hag wrote a book last year and now she thinks she's an artist."*[37]

Pauline glanced over my shoulder to read the note and let out a giggle. I started to shush her when Bertrane nudged me, but too late; the "hag" was already scowling at the scrap of paper with her hand held out. Josh would have given the note over but Neïla had more character and, so as not to get Bertrane in trouble, I wadded it into my pocket.

It looked like the hag's hair frizzled even more while her glower turned to Pauline. *"Take this young lady to the office. She'll make up the time in detention tomorrow afternoon."*[38]

Bertrane looked abashed as I was escorted to the door, but the other faces presented a potpourri of expressions ranging from amusement to indifference. Neïla wasn't friends with everybody, it would seem.

I had never been kicked out of class before and the halls rang empty save for Pauline's heels clicking against the floor tiles. When we arrived at the counselor's office, Pauline left me in the outer room next to a young man with a thick mass of hair falling about his shoulders and brown eyes that kept glancing in my direction. I had no idea what was expected of me so I looked away, then back when I felt the tingle of his stare on the side of my face. Our eyes met and I was sure Neïla's cheeks turned as red as beets.

Luckily Pauline came back out before I had to say anything and the young man disappeared into the counselor's office. She poked me. "*Il est beau, n'est-ce pas* (He's cute, isn't he)?"

I looked away and whispered, "*Who is he?*"[39]

"*Un pion.*" When my brow knitted in confusion, she explained, "*He's a college student paid to supervise the high schoolers, and I think he likes you.*"[40] She nudged me again.

I refused to reply even though Pauline might have been right. How could I think about things like that when Kim was in hospital? Then the councilor stepped out. He was an ugly man with horrible teeth and I had to look away when he gave me a smile inviting me into his office. For once I regretted not having Pauline at my side for support but she had decided to wait in the outer office with the "*pion.*"

The counselor looked at me with his yellow-toothed smile. "*So mademoiselle Saadallah, you're back at it like before, I see.*" His comment was followed by a shake of the head and I didn't know what to answer, so I averted my eyes. "*Would you like to explain?*"[41]

I looked up but could only concentrate on those ugly teeth. Even If I had been able to find the words, I don't know what I would have said. It seemed that Neïla hadn't been unknown to him.

"Did you insult Mme Lumière again?" I nodded, shook my head and finally held the paper up for him to see. *"Can I see it?"*[42] he asked.

I shook my head and wadded it back into my pocket. There was no way I was going to put my only friend in a difficult situation.

He sighed and rolled his eyes. *"And I imagine that you didn't write it."* When I nodded, his lips pulled back into his yellow-toothed smile. *"So Bertrane gave you a note and you refused to show it to the teacher."*[43] I looked up surprised that he had guessed everything, but he simply sent me back out into the care of the *pion.*

* * *

The *pion* seemed to think my tears were from my being kicked out of class and he tried to reassure me while Pauline stroked my hair. I wished I was alone, until I looked back up into his brown eyes.

"What's your name?"[44] I asked, or maybe it was Neïla that spoke for me.

"Franck," he answered, with a smile that made Neïla's breath catch in her chest. I didn't want to be attracted to him so I turned my head toward the wall hoping to control those emotions. My heart, however, wouldn't listen and I couldn't resist just one more peek—and he was still looking at me with such tenderness that my mouth opened slightly as if I wanted to say something while his eyes widened.

Pauline left me with Franck until the ten o'clock recess. He was doing his master's in archaeology and I was fascinated to listen to him tell me about his summer spent on a Gallo-Roman site in the south of France. He talked to me about his plans to write his thesis on the Visigoths and what evidence of their passage remained in France. My heart sank when the bell rang and he had to go watch the front exit.

As soon as Pauline came back to fetch me, she began to joke about how I hadn't wanted to wear makeup and about how I didn't want to be pretty while I did everything I could to shut her up. Bertrane then came to join us and squealed about how cute Franck was while Pauline embellished the whole story and took credit for the bronze eye shadow. Kendra showed up next and Pauline performed the whole show a second time, followed by the prediction that I'd be dating him in a week. I refrained from mentioning that my brother would sooner have me dead than going out with a non-Muslim.

Relief came with the bell and biology class. Science had never been my best subject, but at least I could have some peace and try to reflect on everything that was happening without being the object of cooing and squealing. My mind kept going back to Kim and how she had comforted me the day of the memorial service. How could I have forgotten her while Neïla had been making me flirt with Franck? And Quincy? Wasn't I being unfaithful to Quincy? Maybe Othmane was right when he called me a slut.

At lunch, Bertrane had Pauline sit with us and talk about horoscopes and makeup while I inspected the piece of breaded poultry named "cordon bleu." Maybe it was science class that inspired me to carry out a dissection whose results confirmed a complete lack of nutritional interest. Bertrane and Pauline had meanwhile become the best of friends.

The afternoon was highlighted with an hour of history class followed by English with Mr. Hubert. My mind was elsewhere though and I couldn't stop dwelling on Kim and how it must have been my fault. Mr. Hubert asked me if I was all right before I left and I gave him what I knew to be a wan smile. Pauline then escorted me to the front desk where she waited for a "responsible" person to come pick me up. Unfortunately, it was Mokhtar who sidled up with his big smile.

"So sly bunny, have we learned anything today?"[45]

I didn't answer, but Pauline gave him her stickiest smile. *"Oh, she's adorable."*[46]

Mokhtar took immediate interest in Pauline. *"That's normal, she's my sister. Has she done something exceptional again?"*[47]

Pauline seemed to realize she was making an error and waved her hands as if it weren't of interest. Mokhtar looked me over and reached out to touch my face. He held it a second inspecting the makeup before he flashed a wide grin that made me become even more wary. Then, when I made an attempt to smile back, he bowed to Pauline and took me by the hand to lead me to his scooter.

"So you have a boyfriend,"[48] he stated, when we were far enough away from Pauline.

"Non," was all I answered.

"You don't know how to lie,"[49] he replied with his back turned. He then pivoted back with his smile and a twitch of his lip before he handed me my helmet. As he spun the scooter out of the parking lot, he made a gesture with his hand to somebody across the street. My breath caught in my throat; Beatbox was leaning against a wall watching us with his typical glower.

1 "Qu'est-ce que ça veut dire? C'est de ton chéri américain?"
2 "Othmane était où ce matin?"
3 "Donc son nom est Quincy?"
4 "Qui t'a parlé de lui? C'était Othmane?"
5 "Il est beau?"
6 "C'était Mokhtar, donc!"
7 "Non! C'était pas lui."
8 "Qui alors?"
9 "C'était Beatbox! Ou Romain, tu l'appelles comme tu veux."
10 "Il m'a piraté mes comptes?"
11 "Je sais pas, il m'a juste dit que tu avais des amis américains. Mais tu sais qu'il est très fort en informatique?"
12 "Qu'est-ce qui s'est passé entre nous?"

13 "Je sais pas, vraiment. Tu ne l'as jamais aimé mais ensuite, après le retour d'Algérie, après la mort de papa, tu as commencé à passer du temps avec lui et Mokhtar. Tu ne leur dis pas que je te l'ai dit!"

14 "Mais qu'est-ce qui est arrivé à cette fille? C'est la fille de la vidéo?"

15 "Tu ne crois pas que ce soit Romain?"

16 "Alors, pourquoi les questions?"

17 "Je crois qu'on a essayé de me tuer aussi."

18 "Mais qui a voulu te tuer? Je veux dire, tu n'as pas essayé de te suicider?"

19 "Il faut absolument te refaire ce maquillage."

20 "On sera en retard."

21 "J'ai apporté une couleur pour toi. Tu verras."

22 "Ce n'est pas nécessaire."

23 "Avec tes yeux de diamants noirs, il te faut un fard à paupière bronzé rehaussé avec un peu de blanc irisé."

24 "Et la poudre c'est pourquoi?"

25 "Oh, tu n'en as pas besoin de beaucoup avec ta peau d'ange. Tiens, bouge pas et garde tes yeux fermés."

26 "Mais je n'ai pas besoin de maquillage pour réussir mes cours. A quoi ça sert?"

27 "Mais… pour se sentir belle."

28 "Tu ne veux pas te sentir belle?"

29 "Je ne sais pas ce que c'est de se sentir belle."

30 "Ma pauvre petite. Mais tu es si belle et… Je comprends maintenant que tu aies besoin d'aide. T'inquiète pas, je vais t'aider."

31 "Mais j'ai pas le droit d'être belle."

32 "Mais bien sûr que tu l'as. Et tu l'es. Dis-moi de quoi tu as peur."

33 "Surtout d'être en retard au cours de Mme Lumière. S'il te plait, on peut y aller?"

34 "Maintenant que tu as mis du mascara partout, non. Et

t’inquiète pas, je lui dirai que c’’est de ma faute.”

35 “Qu’est-ce qui va pas?”

36 “Rien. Elle… Je veux dire je suis trop belle.”

37 “La vieille a pondu un bouquin l’année dernière et elle se prend pour un artiste maintenant.”

38 “Amène cette jeune fille au CPE. Elle rattrapera en heures de colle demain après midi.”

39 “Qui c’est?”

40 “Un pion. C’est un étudiant payé pour superviser. Je crois qu’il t’aime bien.”

41 “Alors Mlle Saadallah, tu recommences comme avant, je vois. Tu peux expliquer?”

42 “Est-ce que tu as encore insulté Mme Lumière? Je peux le voir?”

43 “Et je suppose que tu ne l’as pas écrit. Donc Bertrane t’a passé un petit mot et tu as refusé de le montrer au professeur.”

44 “Vous vous appelez comment?”

45 “Alors, pinpin futé, on a appris quelque chose aujourd’hui?”

46 “Oh, elle est adorable.”

47 “C’est ma sœur, c’est normal. Elle a encore fait un truc exceptionnel?”

48 “Alors, tu as un petit ami.”

49 “Tu sais pas mentir.”

Chapter 21

We were lucky to be alive—Mokhtar could have killed us a dozen times on that motor scooter!—and he just chuckled at my fear with that his sarcastic twist of the lip. I tried to push him away, but he took me by the arm and forced me toward a group of boys gathered outside the building.

There were hand slaps and greetings while I searched unsuccessfully for the boy with light brown eyes. Although I tried to slip away several times, Mokhtar kept his arm tightly around my shoulder and I had to witness what seemed like endless swaggers and tasteless jokes. His grip finally loosened just before I went hysterical and I took off toward the apartment.

Mokhtar caught up with me before I made ten yards. *"You see, you don't need a crusader for a boyfriend. You can go out with any of those guys. Just give me the word,"*[1] he commented behind me.

I stopped in my tracks. He continued walking past me and then turned around with his hand held out. I stayed where I was and Neïla shouted, *"What's it to you?"*[2]

He gave me the sweetest smile his hypocrisy could muster. *"You're my sister,"* he intoned, while he spread his hands in an offering gesture. *"And you accepted my help in the past."*[3]

I didn't know what he was talking about, and didn't want to know! *"Accepted it to do what?"*[4] I spat.

His nose flared with his smile. *"You don't remember? All the better."*[5]

He was playing games with me. *"Remember what?"*[6] I asked holding my ground. *"Only that you must be careful."*[7] He said, with no pretension of smiling.

With that he turned around and started walking toward the apartment. I waited for a second and then followed at a distance. The information he was keeping from me had to be important so I ran to catch up with him and he turned to stare straight into my eyes. I hesitated a second, but then stood fast and threw the question out. *"What happened with our father?"*[8]

His face showed no sign of emotion. He studied me for a long moment before putting his smile back on. *"You stuck a knife in his throat."*[9]

It took a second for the information to register but when it did, I felt the ground sway under me. *"Why would I do that?"*[10] I whispered more to myself than to him.

He gave me his hyena laugh. *"Maybe you had the same reasons to want to kill him as me. You, however, went through with it."*[11]

I shook my head. I was shaking. I didn't want to believe it. *"But how could you know it was me?"*[12]

"Because I helped you cover up the murder by making it look like a burglary and then I arranged for you to flee the country." His eyes locked onto me while his smile hardened. *"And you promised to return the favor."*[13]

If what he said was true, Neïla had sealed a pact with the devil, and I was the one who would have to pay up. I couldn't look at him but I had to ask, *"Did I ever return it?"*[14]

"Come on, sly bunny, we'll talk about it another day."[15] He turned and walked to the entranceway where he began joking with our building's drug dealer.

Neïla's body continued to shake uncontrollably. Only when he had disappeared up the stairs did I find the strength to walk the last fifty feet, my eyes on my feet as I passed the boy selling hashish, while I cursed Mokhtar. I hated this apartment, this life, and I wished Neïla had let me die.

* * *

"You got detention, you got detention . . ."[16] Djahida laughed in a singsong from her usual spot in front of the computer.

I threw my book bag on the floor and sat on the bed. Detention was the least of my worries but it bothered me that one of Neïla's so-called friends had told her. When she got no reaction from me, she slumped over her chair to stare with a puzzled look on her face.

"You have changed. It's like you aren't the same person,"[17] she mumbled.

I didn't hear any hostility in her voice, but I felt the danger and knew what they would do to me if they ever discovered my true identity. *"I don't know who I am,"*[18] I replied hoping to dodge the conversation.

"Even Mokhtar says you are different."[19]

They thought I was ill, and it had to stay like that, so I turned to face the wall and Djahida went back to exchanging jokes on the computer about some person in her class. If Neïla hadn't been a murderer, I would have told her to stop harassing people but as it stood, I no longer had the right to tell anybody what was right or wrong.

The front door opened, Othmane's voice slithered through the apartment and Djahida quickly took out her math homework, abandoning the computer. In a flash, I grabbed her place and went straight to Neïla's mailbox hoping Quincy had left a message.

> Dear Neïla, the good news is that Kim is doing better. She has been moved out of intensive care. If I understand right, she was stabbed several times and was found in the bushes by a man walking his dog. She is still very injured and very tired. They only allow visits between two and four in the afternoon.
>
> I think of you often and have put your picture on my desktop. I would also really like to talk about renaissance art with you. Tomorrow I'll be at the hospital around two-thirty. If by any chance you can come, I promise your brother that I'll be a gentleman.
>
> Your friend,
>
> Quincy

For the first time in my life, I felt like I might swoon and began writing the reply in spite of Djahida's observant eye.

> You cannot know how relieved I am learning that Kim has become better. I feel somehow it was my fault she was attacked and that it had to do with the video. I don't know what I shall be able to do to help her if not come offer her support. I will do everything possible to be there tomorrow.
>
> I wish I was able put your picture on the computer here but that should not be wise. Waiting to see you. I will secretly listen to Monteverdi's *Orpheus* and think of you.
>
> Yours,
>
> Neïla

As I reread my reply, I realized Djahida had been right; I had changed. Josh would never have written a letter like that and, whether I liked it or not, I just couldn't get Quincy out of my mind. With a sigh, I clicked on send and sat back to breathe.

"Are you writing to your American sweetheart?" Djahida bleated. *"I thought you liked the college student at your high school now."*[20]

Her singsong laughter grated on my ears so I glared at her. *"Who told you all that?"*[21] Neïla barked for me.

"It's all over FB with your hours of detention. They say that you got detention on purpose to spend time with him."[22]

She looked at me defiantly and I scowled back. As much as I wanted to rip into her, there was no good retort so I turned back to the computer and huffed while my stomach knotted up. Only Bertrane and Kendra had known about me and Franck; had they betrayed me? I wanted someone I could trust—I wanted to see Quincy—but what could I do about the detention tomorrow?

"What's the matter?"[23] Djahida asked.

I looked up at her and wiped the tears from my eyes. *"Shut up and do your math!"*[24] I shouted at Djahida who just smiled hypocritically. Now that I had told Quincy I would meet him, I had to go whatever the consequences might be.

* * *

My mind was still so wrapped around Kim and Quincy that I couldn't even begin to listen to Othmane and Mokhtar go on about Islam. At least the lamb couscous Mother had made was excellent. With the exception of Hadja, the whole family was at the dinner table. *"Neïla, are you listening?"* Mustapha chirped gleefully. *"We're going home."*[25]

I looked at him, and then at Mother who was explaining how she had managed to find cut-rate tickets for us to Algeria. We were going for two weeks over the end of the year holidays and Djahida looked almost as excited as Mustapha. Mokhtar's smile, however, was too large to trust while Mother's and Othmane's faces remained so straight they might have been playing poker.

"*Pourquoi* (Why)?" I asked and all the eyes focused on me.

Mokhtar was the only one to smile. *"See the family,"*[26] he answered with a shrug.

"And the doctors I see here?"[27] I tried objecting.

Mother and Othmane let Mokhtar do the talking while they sat straight in their chairs making no effort to smile. *"They can't force you to stay,"*[28] Mokhtar laughed.

"You don't remember grandma?"[29] Mustapha asked, while he bounced around in his chair.

I shook my head. Of course I didn't know her. Moreover, I had no desire to go to Algeria to do so. The last time Neïla had been there, she had killed somebody, and I only had a month to find a way to get out of the trip. I didn't feel like eating anymore so I pushed my couscous aside.

1 "Tu vois que t'as pas besoin d'un croisé pour copain. Tu peux sortir avec n'importe lequel de ces mecs. T'as qu'à me dire."

2 "De quoi je me mêle?"

3 "Mais tu es ma sœur. Et tu as accepté mon aide par le passé."

4 "Accepté pour faire quoi?"

5 "Tu te rappelles pas? Tant mieux."

6 "Me rappeler de quoi?"

7 "Juste qu'il faut que tu fasses attention."

8 "Que s'est-il passé avec notre père?"

9 "Tu lui as planté un couteau dans la gorge."

10 "Mais pourquoi j'ai fait ça?"

11 "Peut-être tu avais les mêmes raisons que moi de vouloir le tuer. Toi par contre, tu l'as fait."

12 "Mais comment tu le sais?"

13 "Parce que je t'ai aidé à fuir le pays après avoir maquillé le meurtre en cambriolage. Et tu as promis de me rendre un service."

14 "Et je te l'ai rendu?"

15 "Va, pinpin futé, on en reparlera un autre jour."

16 "Tu t'es faite coller, tu t'es faite coller…"

17 "Tu as changé. On dirait que tu n'es plus la même personne."

18 "Je ne sais pas qui je suis."

19 "Même Mokhtar dit que tu es différente."

20 "Tu écris à ton chéri américain? Je croyais que tu aimais le pion du lycée maintenant."

21 "Qui te raconte tout ça?"

22 "C'est partout sur FB, avec tes heures de colle demain. On dit que tu as fait exprès de te faire coller pour le voir."

23 "Mais qu'est-ce qui t'arrive?"

24 "Tais-toi et fais tes maths!"

25 "Neïla, tu écoutes? On retourne chez nous."

26 "Voir la famille."

27 "Et les médecins que je vois ici?"

28 "Ils ne peuvent pas t'obliger à rester."

29 "Tu te rappelles pas de mamie?"

Chapter 22

High schoolers in France have class Wednesday morning but the afternoon free. That old hag of a French teacher, however, had decided I would be kept prisoner here until somebody came to pick me up at five. Did I really have what it takes to run off? I watched Bertrane joking with Pauline as if they were old friends while I curled my knees up to my chest. Would Othmane really kill me when he found out?

"You shouldn't be like that, it's only going to be one afternoon of detention,"[1] Bertrane said, sitting next to me after Pauline had scurried off to the WC.

"Why did you tell everyone what happened with Franck?"[2] I asked, trying not to look at her dark eyes.

"But I didn't tell anyone."[3]

I glanced at her and saw she was looking at my forehead, not at me, so I stared back down at Neïla's pink shoes. Maybe it was better not to know why she was lying. *"You know we have tickets to Algeria?"*[4] I asked.

"They want you to go back?"[5] I heard the concern in Bertrane's voice and I got this feeling that she knew more than she was saying.

"What happened the last time?"[6] I questioned her in a whisper.

"All you said was that they wanted to marry you off."[7]

"Who wanted to?" I asked, even though I was convinced I knew the answer; it had to have been Neïla's father and that was why she had stabbed him. Maybe now they were trying to carry out her father's wishes by taking me there. *"Who wanted to?"*[8] I repeated.

Bertrane simply shrugged. *"You didn't want to talk about it. That's all I know."*[9]

Pauline came sauntering back not long before the end of recess and I jumped up to drag her back into the girl's room. *"Can you do my makeup again, please?"*[10] I asked with more authority than I expected.

"But quickly, you mustn't be late,"[11] she answered, while she prepared her materials. I closed my eyes and followed her instruction trying not to shiver at the touch of the pad against my cheek or the brush on my eyelids. If I did manage to meet up with Quincy, I wanted to be ready.

Pauline was putting on the final touches when the bell rang and I ran to class arriving just before the door shut. Mme. Lumière's eyes stayed glued to me as I sat down at the back but when I looked at her, her stare fumbled before it turned to irritation. She signaled for me to come to the front. *"With your bag!"*[12] she hissed.

I picked up my bag and Bertrane gave a shrug. Then Pauline made her entrance humming a *désolée* (sorry) that put Mme Lumière in an even worse mood. I looked away while the two girls who were made to move to the back scowled and sat next to Bertrane.

I felt like crawling into a hole and I wanted nothing more to do with that witch. I tried to listen to her drone on, but she made Zola so boring that I never wanted to read him again. I tried to take notes to stay awake but by the time I got a sentence down, the teacher had gone onto something else. At the end of the hour, I understood the book less than before class.

When the bell finally rang, my only desire was to escape. I put my notepad in my bag and was about to stand up when I felt her presence in front of me and saw the paper she was holding out for me. My hand shook as I took the assignment and read it under her scrutiny. *"Is the novel a reflection of society? 500 words using the dialectical method."*[13]

I didn't want to look at her self-satisfied sneer—I had no idea what the dialectical method was!—so I looked imploringly at Pauline who was preparing to leave but she only gave me a wave as she headed for the door; she had finished her day and didn't have to stay with me while I did detention. I picked up my school bag defeated and shuffled out.

I knew I was supposed to go to the office but hatred boiled from my gut all the way up to my throat. Here I was to write about the conditions of life more than a hundred years ago while Neïla's brother was preparing to marry her—no me!—to somebody I didn't even know and Kim was lying in a hospital bed. She had only wanted to help. I sobbed with anger as I stood there in the empty hall feeling strangely alone.

Franck was watching the front gate so I dried my tears hoping he wouldn't notice while I followed the stragglers to the front entrance. I felt like a traitor, but I still let Neïla flash him her sweetest smile and he seemed to forget all about his instructions to keep me in school when I gave him a kiss on either cheek. The stubble scratched a little and a tingle ran down my belly making me wish I could stay with him. That was impossible.

"*Ça va* (How are you)?" he asked.

I put my hand on his arm and my bag at his feet. "*Je suis désolée* (I'm sorry)," I murmured, and fled.

I ran as fast as Neïla could but soon had to slow to a jog because it felt like I had taken a swig of hydric acid. She had once been in good shape but since the accident, I had done no exercise. Beyond dancing, I didn't even know what sort of exercise Neïla ever did. Running certainly wasn't one of them.

A few people were staring at me so I continued at a walk as quickly as my shaking legs would take me. From time to time I looked over my shoulder to see if a gray-hooded figure was following but the people on the street all ended up looking the same and just as menacing. Then, while I was glancing around a corner, I realized I didn't know where I was.

Some men were doing street repairs at the next intersection and their eyes followed me so impolitely, making me feel so naked, that I turned on them angrily. Their grins quickly made it obvious that I had done the wrong thing.

"What can we do for you, honey?"[14] a guy with weight-built muscles brayed.

I stood with my feet apart as if I were still a man but that only got chuckles from the group and my courage started slipping. *"I'm looking for the metro,"*[15] I finally answered in a quivering voice.

Mr. Muscle started rolling his shoulders and his muzzle puckered. *"But we can take you where you want,"*[16] he said, and took two steps forward.

"Leave her, she's just a kid."[17] A black guy stepped in and put his hand on Mr. Muscles' shoulder.

Muscles snorted and backed up. The black guy then turned to me with a sympathetic smile. *"Turn right at the next street and it's straight ahead. And sorry for my co-worker."*[18]

I thanked him and hurried away with my heart beating faster than it should have. Although I disliked the hijab, I understood it now; it deflected the stares of all those people who were now looking at my face and body. Having been a boy, I could guess what they were thinking. I turned down the street the black guy had indicated wishing I could be invisible.

The metro sign appeared above a newspaper kiosk and I sped up my pace while each of my steps echoed against the metro tunnel's graffiti-tagged walls. I still had trouble breathing so I stood behind one of the ticket vending machines to calm my heart. A few people rushed past, swiping their monthly pass over the sensor and pushing through the double doors. I had no money to buy a ticket and the barriers were too high to jump over but I had once seen a young man crowd his way through behind another person. It seemed very impolite, yet I didn't know what else to do.

I peered around the vending machine at an elderly lady shuffling by. She would think I was a savage if I ever pushed through behind her. A younger man in torn blue jeans then ambled up and began rummaging through his billfold for his pass giving me just enough time to scurry out and push in behind him. He turned to look at me wide-eyed before bowing with a smile. I whispered an almost silent "merci" knowing that Neïla's cheeks had blushed red. He looked like he was about to answer when his eyes turned to something behind me and he hurried off.

"Mademoiselle," someone called in back of me.

I began to walk down the corridor hoping the person wasn't speaking to me. "Mademoiselle!" I heard again and turned to find a casually dressed man and a woman with a square jaw jogging toward me. The woman then flashed a card in my face. "Police," she said flatly. *"May I see a piece of identification?"*[19]

I felt my throat drop down to my gut while my head shook. When I tried to speak, no sounds would come out.

"Vous parlez français (Do you speak French)?" the woman asked while the man circled behind me and all my fears came to the surface. It seemed that if I uttered a single sound, they would discover who I really was. I looked away, down, while my body began to tremble so badly that I thought I might collapse.

Her voice punched at me again. *"You understand what I'm saying?"*[20]

I was clear that I had failed. The police would now take me home to that stifling apartment. Mme Lumière would make me write an essay every Wednesday afternoon while Othmane slapped and punched me every evening until I was sent off to Algeria and—

"Miss, it's no good crying," the policewoman's voice snapped. Her hand then grabbed my arm and began dragging me back toward a door near the entrance with the man following. He rang a bell behind the cashier's booth, a door opened and I was pulled to a small room with a table and two chairs. The woman pushed me into one and sat facing me. *"Do you have a name?"*[21]

It took me a second to register, and then it was as if Neïla no longer spoke French. "Jo . . ." I began to murmur but I knew that wasn't right. My brain wasn't working properly. "Neïla, Neïla

Saadallah," I finally managed to whisper.

"You see, that wasn't hard." Her aggressive smile made me feel like a real wimp while she noted the name on a sheet of paper spelling out each letter. *"And do you have an address and telephone number?"*[22]

The question took me off guard so I stuttered for a second before admitting, *"I don't know them."*[23]

She looked at me long and hard as if I were lying. *"But you do live somewhere?"*[24]

I nodded and whispered, *"But I don't remember the address."*[25]

She glanced at her colleague who shrugged. *"I think you have some explaining to do,"*[26] she enunciated, with her eyes staring straight into mine.

I tried not to look away. *"Je ne peux pas* (I can't)," I replied.

Her stare turned to a glare. *"You think I'm stupid?"*[27]

I looked away knowing there was no easy way to get out of this. *"I just wanted to visit a friend at the hospital,"*[28] I admitted, with a little involuntary choke.

"And has this friend got a name?"[29]

"Kimberly Wasser," I murmured, with an American accent. The woman shook her head as if she hadn't heard. *"Kimberly Wasser,"* Neïla repeated with her French accent.

The man then whispered something in the policewoman's ear and she looked back at me. *"The girl who was attacked?"*[30] she asked cautiously.

When I nodded, the man took the sheet of paper and disappeared through the door while the woman sat back examining me as if I were a jigsaw puzzle. A few minutes later, the policeman stuck his head through the door and the woman gave me one last glare before she stepped outside.

They spoke for a minute and then the policewoman came back in to ask me if I wanted something to drink while I waited. I was wary of her calm and lack of hostility but nodded because I really was thirsty. She studied me for a short moment and walked out leaving the door open. I thought briefly about trying to flee but before I could act, she had come back with a bottle of water. While I drank, I heard her joking with her colleague just outside the door.

Two uniformed cops strode in before I could finish the bottle and I was escorted out of the metro station, up the stairs and to a police car. There were people all around watching and commenting. I felt like a hardened criminal and I would have covered Neïla's face if I had been wearing the hijab. The crowd must have thought I had done something much worse than not paying my train fare.

As the policeman opened the door, I noticed a teenage boy of Arabic origin watching us and it seemed I knew his face. He turned to leave just as the policeman put his hand on my head to guide me into the car. The doors clicked shut and the car made a U-turn while I put on my seat belt. The policeman next to me hadn't put on his.

I looked out the windows at the people in their cars on the *périférique* until the traffic slowed and the policeman put on the siren to speed between the lanes. Each time I tried to focus on a person, he or she turned into a blur and another face appeared. My head began spinning and so I covered my eyes with my hands until the car turned off the *périférique* at Bercy to take the Berges along the Seine River. The flashing blue lights forced the other cars to give way as we sped through a stop light but I kept my eyes on Îsle Saint Louis which seemed to float calmly on the other side of the river as if it were sleeping.

The car turned up around the Hôtel de Ville (City Hall) where I saw tourists milling happily about or heading to the Pompidou museum a little farther down. Not so long ago, I had been one of them and believed that Paris was romantic. Unless you count my high-school crush on Lisa, I had never been in love. Would I ever be able to fall in love now that Neïla was messing with my mind?

The car took Notre Dame Bridge across the north branch of the Seine to the Îsle de la Cité where it turned right. We sped past little flower shops in green wooden cabins and then the Conciergerie, the place where Marie Antoinette had been beheaded, so I preferred to keep my eyes on the trembling water of the Seine.

We finally stopped in front of police headquarters on Quai des Orfèvres and a policeman put his hand on my head before he pulled me out. A few words were said to another policeman holding a machine gun, the iron barrier was opened and I was taken up a large winding stairway whose steps were almost black from use and in which sounds echoed against the plaster walls. At each floor, a net was placed over the stairwell to keep people from jumping. Was that something I might have tried?

On the fourth floor, I was taken into a hall with an olive green linoleum tile floor, beige walls and laughter behind the first door. Behind the second door, somebody was yelling angrily.

I didn't have time to listen because the policeman pulled me to the fifth door to the left and knocked. I heard a grunt from inside the office and the policeman opened the door a crack, peered in and announced "Mademoiselle Saadallah." There was another grunt from inside and the policeman opened the door wider. My heart jumped and I had to look twice to confirm what I saw. "Kiko!" I exclaimed, recognizing him as the man from the café.

"I'm happy that you know me,"[31] he said with a smile and I noticed he used "tu", the familiar form. *"Sit down,"* he said, indicating a chair.

As I examined his face, I realized something wasn't right because my body reacted to his broad shoulders and well-combed blond hair. I couldn't deny that he was handsome but that didn't explain the wobbles in my belly.

"Do we know each other well?"[32] I asked and sat down.

He gave a long hearty laugh. *"Work can be a pleasure, too."*[33]

My gut told me I should be angry so I glared at him until he stopped smiling.

"You're not going to get into a huff because I didn't contact you sooner?"[34]

"I'm a job?"[35] Neïla spat.

He chuckled again. *"More than you know. So it seems that you don't pay your fare on the metro and that you don't have any papers. That's worth a fine, you know?"*[36]

I let Neïla glare at him, that much I had gathered, but this had nothing to do with me not paying my fare. *"How am I mixed up with the police?"*[37] I asked more calmly.

His smile turned hard. *"Beyond killing your father, nothing."*[38]

I wanted to deny it. I didn't care what everyone said. After all, Neïla gave her life to me so she couldn't have done something like that. *"Je le crois pas* (I don't believe it)," I heard Neïla enunciate.

His smile gave way to a penetrating squint before he shook his head. *"In any case, extraditing you will be difficult. And in France you're a minor. You'll get attenuating circumstances. Hasn't your lawyer explained all this?"*[39]

I shook my head that he hadn't, but then it struck me. *"My family wants me to go back!"*[40] I exclaimed.

"Don't do it,"[41] he replied sharply.

"Why would I have killed him?"[42] I blurted out a little too quickly.

He shrugged. *"That's not my problem. Maybe it had something to do with him abusing you or he wanted to marry you off. Why don't you tell me?"*[43]

I felt myself slump into the chair. Neïla may have had a good reason for fighting back, but I didn't think the justice in Algeria would be very understanding. It seemed odd that Neïla's family wanted to take me back to a country where I'd be thrown in jail. I noticed he was studying my face so I looked him in the eyes. *"Does my family know all this?"*[44] I asked.

He knitted his brow before answering. *"Your mother does. As for the others, it depends on what you've told them."*[45]

"How do the police know it was me?" I asked. He smiled, but said nothing. *"So what does this story have to do with you?"*[46]

"You're being formal with me now?"[47] he replied and flashed a very dashing smile that made my belly flutter again. I had said "vous," as you would with somebody you didn't know well, and it would seem that wasn't the case.

"Why wasn't I charged?"[48] I asked, hoping I could get my belly to forget that he had very strong arms.

"We made a little agreement with your lawyer," he said, and then winked. *"With my insistence. After all, how do you think you got such a good lawyer?"*[49]

So Neïla had a secret agreement both with the police and with Mokhtar. I could see why she had been upset. *"What was this agreement?"*[50] I asked hesitantly.

His smile turned to satisfaction. *"Officially? Only that you watch that jihadist brother of yours and his friends."*[51]

"And unofficially?" I asked, but only got what was supposed to be a charming smile in return. *"And the fact that he beats me, doesn't that change anything?"*[52]

Kiko waved his hand in circles and puckered his lips like the French do when they don't care about something. *"We need more than that."*[53]

"He does nothing but pray," I answered while Kiko raised an eyebrow. *"You think he tells me everything?"*[54] I hissed using the informal "tu."

He smiled again and leaned back in his chair as if my answer satisfied him. *"Fine, but you're going to have to dig a little deeper. That was the agreement."*[55]

"*Quoi* (What)?" I shouted and stood up.

He held his hands up feigning fear. *"Ask your lawyer."* He then suddenly stopped smiling. *"They say you've had problems with your memory. In the police, we take that sort of thing with a grain of salt."*[56]

He watched me for a long moment waiting for me to argue. I

thought about my psychology class and how psychoanalysts always believe the opposite of what is said. I could believe the same thing of the police.

His stare became softer. *"Your brother was implicated in war crimes in Syria. We haven't got proof, but we don't think he's changed since he got back. Find out what he's plotting, okay?"*[57]

I couldn't argue with the principles. If Othmane was preparing a terrorist attack, I wouldn't hesitate to tell the police. That didn't make me like this guy's methods—or him—in spite of what my belly seemed to think. I nodded my agreement and he clapped his hands together like that was a closed and forgotten matter.

"It seems you want to see your friend at the hospital. Let's go, I'll drive."[58]

He tossed his keys in the air, caught them and offered me his hand. I didn't take it. He shot me a disappointed look before opening the door and bowing me through. I walked out with my head high, feeling insulted at his hypocritical gallantry. Still, while I stood there watching him close the door, turn the key in the lock, the ripple of his muscles in his forearm made my belly go all flimsy again.

1 "Faut pas que tu sois comme ça, ce ne sera qu'une après-midi de colle."

2 "Pourquoi tu as dit à tout le monde ce qui s'est passé avec Franck?"

3 "Mais je ne l'ai dit à personne."

4 "Tu sais qu'on a des billets pour l'Algérie?"

5 "Ils veulent que tu retournes?"

6 "Que s'est-il passé la dernière fois?"

7 "Tout ce que tu m'as dit c'est qu'ils voulaient te marier de force."

8 "Qui voulait?"

9 "Tu ne voulais pas en parler. C'est tout ce que je sais."

10 "Peux-tu me refaire ce maquillage, s'il te plait?"
11 "Mais rapidement, faut pas que tu sois en retard."
12 "Avec ton sac!"
13 "Le roman est il le reflet de la société? 500 mots selon la méthode dialectique."
14 "Que peut-on faire pour toi, chérie?"
15 "Je cherche le métro."
16 "Mais on peut t'emmener où tu veux."
17 "Laisse-la, ce n'est qu'une gamine."
18 "Tu tournes à droite à la prochaine rue et c'est tout droit. Et désolé pour mon collègue."
19 "Puis-je avoir une pièce d'identité?"
20 "Vous comprenez ce que je dis?"
21 "Mademoiselle, ça ne sert à rien de pleurer; Vous avez un nom?"
22 "Mais vous voyez, c'est pas si difficile. Et vous avez une adresse et un numéro de téléphone?"
23 "Je ne les sais pas."
24 "Mais vous habitez bien quelque part?"
25 "Mais je ne me souviens pas de l'adresse."
26 "Je crois qu'il me faut des explications."
27 "Vous me prenez pour une idiote?"
28 "Je voulais juste rendre visite à une amie à l'hôpital."
29 "Et elle a un nom, cette amie?"
30 "Celle qui a été agressée?"
31 "Heureux que tu me connaisses. Assieds-toi."
32 "On se connaît bien?"
33 "Le travail peut être du plaisir aussi."
34 "Tu ne vas pas te mettre en boule parce que je ne t'ai pas contactée plus tôt?"
35 "Je suis du travail?"
36 "Plus que tu n'imagines. Alors Il parait que tu ne paies pas tes tickets de métro et que tu n'as pas tes papiers. Ça vaut une amende, tu sais?"

37 "Qu'est-ce que j'ai à voir avec la police?"

38 "Mise à part que tu as tué ton père, rien."

39 "De toute manière pour t'extrader, ce sera difficile. Et en France, tu es mineure. Tu auras des circonstances atténuantes. Ton avocat ne t'a pas expliqué tout ça?"

40 "On veut que j'y retourne!"

41 "Faut pas."

42 "Pourquoi je l'aurais tué?"

43 "C'est pas mon problème. Peut-être ça à voir avec des sévices ou il voulait que tu épouses quelqu'un et tu as refusé. C'est à toi de me le dire."

44 "Ma famille, ils savent tout ça?"

45 "Ta mère, oui. Pour les autres, ça dépend de ce que tu leur as dit."

46 "Comment la police sait-elle que c'était moi? Alors qu'est-ce que cette histoire a à voir avec vous?"

47 "Tu me vouvoies maintenant?"

48 "C'est pour ça qu'on ne m'a pas poursuivie?"

49 "On a négocié un petit accord avec ton avocat. Avec mon insistance. Après tout, comment tu penses que tu as trouvé un avocat de ce calibre?"

50 "C'était quoi l'accord?"

51 "Officiellement? Simplement que tu surveilles ton grand frère jihadist et ses amis."

52 "Et non officiellement? Et le fait qu'il me bat, ça ne change rien?"

53 "Il nous faut plus que ça."

54 "Il ne fait que prier. Tu crois qu'il me dit tout?"

55 "Bon, mais il faut creuser un peu plus. C'était l'accord."

56 "Demande à ton avocat. On dit que tu as des soucis de mémoire. Dans la police on prend ce genre de chose avec des pincettes."

57 "Ton frère a été impliqué dans des crimes de guerre en Syrie. On n'a pas de preuves mais on voit mal qu'il ait changé

comme ça. Trouve ce qu'il prépare et avec qui, d'accord?"

58 "Il parait que tu veux voir ton amie à l'hôpital. Allons-y, je conduis."

Part 5

Tout homme est un criminel qui s'ignore. "Every man is a criminal without knowing it."

—Albert Camus

Chapter 23

Neïla was the object of smirks as Kiko led me out of the police headquarters. The urge to turn around and scream that she wasn't some sort of tart almost got the better of me, but I remembered what had happened when I had confronted the workmen so I bowed my head and followed.

The policeman at the entrance told us to have fun while he lifted the barrier and winked at Kiko who slapped him on the shoulder with a smile. The locks on a Peugeot 308 then clicked open and Kiko held the passenger door for me. I would have refused to get in if I'd had money for a metro ticket but after a short hesitation, I sat down while my knees pressed together.

The door slammed closed beside me and Kiko hopped into the driver's seat. "*You don't trust me?*"[1] he laughed, as he pulled out of his parking place with a screech of tires, ignoring the right-of-way of an on-coming bicycle, and into traffic. I buckled my seat belt.

"*What are you in the mood for? Chinese? Turkish? Gaulish?*"[2] He said, the last with an ironic twist of the lip.

I frowned at him. "*You can say French rather than Gaulish. I'm not anti-French.*"[3]

He squinted at me and then snorted. "*If you say so, but it wasn't clear at the demonstration.*" He then gave me a big smile. "*So what do you want to eat?*"[4]

I turned my back to him and he gave a horselike laugh. "*Stop acting like a child. Of course you're hungry. I'll take you to a brasserie.*"[5]

He switched on some French pop song and sped along the quayside road while I watched the *bateaux mouches* (sightseeing boats) floating serenely down the Seine River. My difficulties, and tears, had begun beside a canal that flowed into the Seine.

Kiko soon turned away from the Seine and parked in a

loading zone near the Place de la Bastille. My head was spinning when he opened the door for me—I no longer knew to whom I could turn—so I followed him wordlessly into the brasserie.

He slapped a man on the shoulders, yelled out hello to the manager and the waiter was beside us with the menus before we sat down. They made small talk so I turned my head to watch a family of American tourists sitting at a table and smiling.

"Do you like octopus in tomato sauce. It's their specialty."[6] Kiko asked me.

I didn't want to tell him that I had never tasted octopus, he would probably laugh at me, so I looked back at him and nodded. He raised an eyebrow, ordered two, and asked me if I wanted wine.

"De l'eau, s'il vous plait (Water, please)," I whispered.

"You can have a coke or sparkling water, if you want."[7]

I shook my head and looked back at the Americans who had a girl about Neïla's age. She glanced over at me and I realized I had been staring, so I looked back at Kiko's seductive smile. I hated Neïla's fuzzy feelings for him and stared down at her pink fingernails instead hoping that he wouldn't see his effect on me.

A fifty-something-year-old man sidled up and shook Kiko's hand. His shirt was open down his chest and he obviously wanted to impress me by how manly he was. Kiko made the introductions, he was the owner of several restaurants, and it felt as if Neïla were being shown off like a trophy.

"I'm going to the restroom,"[8] I said, standing up.

Kiko gave a wry smile and fished in his pocket. "*Tiens* (Here)," he chuckled handing me a 50-cent coin.

I gathered that this was one of those restaurants where you have to pay to use the toilet—and that made me feel all the more vulnerable—I couldn't even go to the bathroom without his intervening.

The American family watched me as I walked past them on my way to the back of the brasserie. They looked so comfortingly familiar that I almost stopped to speak to them, to beg them to help me, but after a few seconds standing idiotically in front of them while my mouth refused to work, I raced off to the restrooms.

The toilets were in a vaulted basement that might have dated back to the Middle Ages and the place was so damp that I wouldn't have been surprised if rats crawled up into them from the catacombs. I clunked the coin into the slot on the stall marked *"Femmes,"* opened the door and found a toilet that was so smelly I almost walked back upstairs to ask for my coin back.

Luckily I was getting used to Neïla's restroom protocol and I was able to finish rather quickly. When I climbed back out of the basement, the Americans had left and Kiko was watching with what looked like *gourmandise.* I was alone and glanced at the door, wondering if I should run.

It was an error not to leave but I really was hungry. I trudged back to his table where he motioned to the plates of food. *"I was waiting for you,"*[9] he said, picking up his fork.

The food was excellent and Kiko took his time before he asked if I wanted dessert or coffee. I had no room left so I shook my head and did my best not to smile at his jokes while he ate a crème brûlée.

Before we left, he spent five minutes going around saying goodbye to different people and shaking hands. A few of the men kissed me on either cheek, some four times, and invited me to come back. I made no reply.

"Did you have a nice meal?"[10] he asked, while he held the car door open for me.

"*Oui* (yes)," I replied a little too contentedly and got in.

"Where should we go?"[11] he asked, smiling at me after he jumped into the driver's seat.

His question surprised me—weren't we going to the hospital?—and there was a malicious twinkle in his eyes. I was about to say something when his hand began sliding up my thigh. Neïla's body froze, although her belly quivered, and I realized she liked it! His hand then reached her crotch and I had to force myself to push it away while his arm slithered around my back. With his strength, I was as helpless as when I used to wrestle my uncle when I was ten.

Tingles began to run up my back as his other hand touched Neïla's breast and I was about to surrender to that wobbly feeling so I let go a slap that hit him on his neck. His grip loosened and he studied Neïla for a second.

"Okay, you don't want to." He sighed. *"But the last time you didn't say anything, and it was part of the agreement, whether you remember or not."*[12]

Neïla's shout came out almost like a scream. *"I just want to see my friend in the hospital."*[13] I tried to open the door but it was locked from the inside so I turned back to him ready to fight.

"No, stay. I'll take you."[14] He answered in a clipped voice while he turned the key and pulled out into traffic. It then dawned on me that if we hadn't been on a busy street, he might not have given me any choice and I started shaking like a scared rabbit.

From time to time he looked in my direction but I refused to give him the satisfaction of glancing back. I watched the pedestrians and parked cars as he sped down the large Parisian boulevards wishing I could lose myself in the safety of the crowd. Would Josh have acted like that if he had found himself alone with Neïla? I remembered sitting in the café ogling Neïla and was all the more upset because I had been incapable of controlling my behavior.

As soon as we arrived at the hospital lot, I jumped out and backed away from the car. My instincts told me to run, but my priority was Kim so I forced myself to stay where I was and not let Kiko out of my sight. He got out nonchalantly and stepped toward me. I backed up. Only after he shrugged and started walking toward the elevator did I follow at a distance.

There was an elderly couple waiting at the parking lot elevator so I put them between me and Kiko as we got on. The lady kept looking from him to me until the bell dinged. I slipped out before the couple and hurried into the lobby.

There were hallways leading in every direction, and people swarming about, so I stood for a moment turning in circles wondering where to go. Behind me, Kiko laughed, *"third floor. Room A323,"*[15] and strode over toward the main elevators.

I decided on the stairs and took them two at a time hoping to get there before Kiko. Unfortunately the elevators were faster and he was leaning against the wall with a mocking smile when I pushed the stairwell door open. I didn't wait for him to make any snide remarks and stamped down the hall in the direction of Kim's room. When I heard him chuckling behind me, I had to restrain myself from turning around and screaming at him.

My head was so wrapped up with that jerk that I almost walked right past Quincy who was reading in a chair. My breath caught in my throat and before he looked up, I had thrown myself into his lap. I wanted him to hug me so badly.

I put my head against his chest and his whole body embraced me gently as I listened to the beating of his heart. One of his hands began stroking my hair and so I looked up into his blue eyes. I don't know if it was me or Neïla, it no longer mattered, but my lips approached his and we softly, passionately, kissed. I only realized how fiercely, intensely, I needed him when our tongues touched, mingled and my soul seemed to float as if I had left my body again.

Somebody cleared his throat behind me and Quincy pulled away. I had forgotten about the jerk! He was standing with his hand out presenting himself to Quincy, "Capitaine Jacques Justin, police national."

We stood up and Quincy shook the jerk's hand while I buried my face in his jacket like that time my father had saved me from a bully.

"What's wrong?" Quincy asked.

"Nothing," I lied.

He squeezed me in close and led me down the hall with Kiko following behind. Quincy stopped in front of a door, knocked and pushed it open. I looked up and saw him nod so I slipped inside before the door shut quietly behind me.

With her blond tangled hair spilled out over the pillow, Kim was still so beautiful that I almost ran to her. I then noticed how chalky her skin looked and was about to step back out into the hall when her eyes opened and she smiled. I rushed over and kissed her on both cheeks.

Tears were welling up in Neïla's eyes. "Kim, my poor, beautiful Kim," I stuttered. "How could anybody do this to you?"

"I guess I was stupid to go jogging alone," she sighed, with a wan smile.

"It's not your fault it's mine," I whispered. "I can't help thinking this had to do with the video."

Kim shook her head, but I could see the doubt in her eyes. "I like your makeup," she whispered, in a hoarse voice.

"Somebody helped me with it," I admitted and then blurted out, "would you like me to help you do yours before Quincy comes in?"

"You're an angel," she replied, and I immediately regretted having opened my mouth because I didn't know a thing about makeup.

"Only you might want to give me some pointers," I cautioned.

"I'll do that," she said, with a weak laugh.

I found a comb in Kim's personal items and began teasing the knots out of her hair while I told her about my first days at school. Josh would never have had enough patience, but Neïla enjoyed chatting and pampering so much that Quincy was forced to wait outside for nearly half an hour. It was a lot easier putting makeup on Kim than on Neïla and in the end, I didn't do such a bad job. When I held up her hand mirror for her to see my work, Kim said with a laugh, "You should quit high school and become a beautician."

I smiled at her and went to the door to call Quincy who was chatting with Kiko in the waiting area. His eyes squinted when he looked over at me and an irrational fear gripped my heart; what if Kiko had told Quincy that Neïla was a murderer? The tempo of Quincy's footfalls dragged out like a requiem while my head turned as if I were about to receive a blow to the face. His finger lifted my chin. "You are the most delicate girl I have ever met," he whispered and took me in his arms. "I'll never hurt you."

I buried my face against his chest so he couldn't see my tears. "Thank you," I breathed while he rocked me.

Kiko coughed and Quincy, pushing himself away, suggested, "Maybe we should go in to see Kim, don't you think?"

It suddenly felt cold without his arms around me so Neïla stood me on my tiptoes to give him a kiss on the cheek. He smiled and pushed the door open.

Kim's eyes sparkled when Quincy took her hand. Then Kiko stepped in. "Sorry I bother you," he intoned, with his French accent. "I accompany this young girl."

I scowled—if it had been me, I would have sent him packing—but Kim smiled back. "Come in, please," she replied, in a hoarse voice.

His arms muscled like a boxer's, Kiko smiled at Kim and sat on the table. Her eyes shone and I glanced uneasily at Quincy who seemed as oblivious as Kim to what sort of man Kiko was.

"I'm very sorry our police forces were not there to stop the villain," Kiko was saying, with that seductive twist of the lip I hated.

"And how do you know Neïla?" Quincy asked.

He gave a chuckle. "We know each other for a long time, *n'est-ce pas* Neïla?"

I looked him straight in the eyes and replied, "Luckily, I don't remember."

Creases of amusement appeared in the corners of Kiko's eyes. "I learn in my job that memory is an unfaithful mistress. *Ah, les maitresses infidèles* (Oh, for unfaithful mistresses)!" he sighed loudly.

I squeezed in closer to Quincy. I didn't want to know what Kiko was hiding behind his chummy smile, but if he thought Neïla was some sort of perk, he would be terribly disappointed.

Kiko turned to Kim and asked in a bantering tone, "And you know Neïla from where?"

"The memorial service for our friend, Josh," she replied softly.

"Yes, the one of the video. Did you not do it?" he asked, with an appreciative nod. "Very well done video."

"Thank you," Kim whispered.

"Very effective. Mr. Saadallah must be very angry, no?" Kiko's eyes went from me to Kim.

"He was, but he didn't beat me again," I answered, looking straight at Kiko.

Kiko didn't turn away. "He is violent, is he? Might he attack a young girl doing jogging?" It was more a statement than a question.

"He can be very violent, but I don't know what he is capable of," I replied, and looked over at Kim although tears had started to form in Neïla's eyes. "I'm sorry, I really am sorry I got you into this."

She reached out her hand and I took it. "It's not your fault," she said.

Kiko coughed. "But you did not see your attacker?" From Kiko's tone, I could hear that he already knew the answer.

"I only saw he was wearing a gray sweatshirt," she murmured.

"A gray sweatshirt?" I stammered. My heart began racing and I glared at Kiko; he had been preparing this. "He had his hood on?" I asked. "Like the man who killed . . . Josh?"

Kim's eyes opened wide and her forehead trembled. "Yes, he

had a large hood over his head."

A smile eased onto Kiko's face while I pushed in closer to Quincy. "And Quincy? Is Quincy in danger?" I asked fearfully.

Kiko shrugged nonchalantly while Quincy's arms held me tighter and Kim looked at us alarmed. "Quince, maybe you should go home, back to the States, where it's safe," she said.

My body went numb; I had just lost my family in the States and was about to lose my only friends here in France. But Kim was right, so I held back my tears and looked him in the eyes. "You must go. We will keep in contact on FB and—"

"Neïla, I can't leave you. Not in your situation." He gave me a daring smile that made Neïla's heart flutter and I almost gave in. I should have known that Quincy would want to be a hero, a sort of musketeer, but it was too dangerous so I pulled away and shook my head. I wanted him to live happily to an old age, remembering that strange girl he left behind in France.

"The girls are right," Kiko broke in authoritatively. "You should not stay here. You are in the video and you become a target now."

Quincy looked over at Kiko and squeezed me. "I'll have to think about it. For the moment, the priority is the girls." His chin stuck out like Errol Flynn's.

"You have no police protection," Kiko replied with a sigh. "It is wise you return to your country." He then flashed his grin in my direction. "No worry concerning Neïla, I shall look after her."

I felt like saying, *I bet you will*, but kept my mouth shut; I didn't want to give Quincy any more reasons to stay. Quincy looked down at me with his blue eyes. "Will you come to the United States if I get you a ticket?" he asked.

"Of course," I answered, almost choking.

"You know that if you don't come, I'll be back here in a day."

"I will follow you anywhere," Neïla whispered in his ear.

1 "Tu me fais pas confiance?"

2 "Qu'est-ce que tu veux manger? Chinois? Turc? Gaulois?"

3 "Tu peux dire français, pas Gaulois. Je suis pas anti-français."

4 "Si tu le dis mais ça ne se voyait pas à la manif. Alors qu'est-ce que tu veux manger?"

5 "Arrête de faire la gamine. Bien sûr que tu as faim. Je t'amène dans une brasserie."

6 "Tu aimes le poulpe à la provençale? C'est leur spécialité."

7 "Tu peux avoir un coca ou une eau pétillante, si tu veux."

8 "Je vais aux toilettes."

9 "Je t'attendais."

10 "Tu as bien mangé?"

11 "Où est-ce qu'on va?"

12 "D'accord, tu veux pas. Pourtant, la dernière fois tu n'as rien dit, et que tu te rappelles ou non, ça faisait bien partie de l'accord."

13 "Je veux juste voir mon amie à l'hôpital."

14 "Non, reste. Je t'y amène."

15 "Quatrième étage. Chambre A323."

Chapter 24

Kiko shot a leering smile over his shoulder at me in the backseat, as if he were admiring a pastry he no longer had to share. Well, if he thought he'd get a piece of Neïla just because Quincy was going to the other side of the Atlantic, he was kidding himself. I put my hand on Quincy's shoulder wishing I could hold him for eternity.

It was dangerous to be seen in a car with two men, especially a policeman, so I made Kiko pull over four blocks from Neïla's apartment complex. Contorting himself to reach me, Quincy gave me a kiss from the front seat and then promised to see me again before he left.

Neïla was on the verge of tears, so I jumped out and covered her hair and breasts with her scarf before I walked away from the car. It wasn't dark yet and Djahida would be finishing her Arabic class while Mustapha would be back from his specialized school in an hour. I crossed my fingers in hope that Mother was working this evening and that Othmane had gone off to wherever.

My mind kept going back to Quincy while I walked down the wet street and I found myself humming songs from *West Side Story* in a high treble—I could sing Maria's part!—so I began to dance a waltz until I remembered that he would be headed back to the States soon. Would he really come back for me or buy me a ticket so that I could escape this place?

The apartment complex came into view with the usual crowd milling about. One boy waved hello, it was that boy with light brown eyes, so I waved back. Maybe they weren't really as dangerous as I believed, but I still considered it wise to keep my berth and hurry past.

In the entranceway I came face-to-face with a young Caucasian man wearing a suit. The boy who did his business there was counting money while the man inspected a plastic bag.

I whispered, "*salut* (hi)," to the boy.

"*Wesh, Neïla* (wassup, Neïla)," he answered.

I felt the Caucasian man's eyes running over Neïla's body as if he thought she was for sale too, so I gave the boy a smile and the man a scowl before rushing up the graffiti-lined stairs. The last thing I needed was some drugged-out businessman making a pass at me.

I had hit the timer for the hall lights and walked down to the door before it came to me that I didn't have a key. After the first knock, nothing happened, and I wondered whether to be relieved or not. I knocked again but this time I could hear footsteps, so I backed away from the door before Othmane appeared. My head dropped, my shoulders hunched and he stepped back while I entered and removed the pink sneakers. His hand fell on my shoulder. The door then slammed. His hand forced me into the living room where I stood in the middle of the carpet waiting for the blows.

"*Sit down,*"[1] he barked, behind me.

I sat on a cushion next to the wall. "*I don't have a key,*"[2] I whispered.

He stood over me with his shadow falling across Neïla's slender feet. I looked up into his eyes. There was that despair that I had sometimes noticed, but his sigh was more like a hiss. "*Why do you make me hit you?*"[3]

I almost denied everything but instead whispered, "*Je suis désolée* (I'm sorry)."

He raised an eyebrow. "*We've changed, both of us. Me, I have a demon, a djinn, inside. I can't control it. You used to have a djinn too, but today it isn't the same.*"[4]

A chill ran through me. Did he know I wasn't Neïla? I waited for him to continue, but he only stared at me. "*I don't know who I was,*"[5] I replied cautiously.

"*You were a demon.*" His eye began to twitch. "*I thought I was guided by angels . . . and everything changed. I cause pain. It's not me, it's the demon. I pray but he won't let me be."*[6]

Othmane's brow contorted with so much rage and sorrow that I began to fear for Neïla's life. I had to keep him talking. "*Et moi* (And me)?" I asked in a whisper.

"*You knew how to cause pain,*" he uttered, with a suddenly blank face, "*But you have become a good person.*" His face screwed up again in agony. "*And that hurts me.*"[7]

"*So you must hit me?*"[8] I asked in a voice that quivered.

His head nodded, then shook, and finally he looked at me impassively. "*You left the high school. You went to see your crusader boyfriend.*"[9]

I couldn't deny it and I wasn't going to. "*A friend was attacked. She is in the hospital. I had to go see her.*"[10]

His expressionless eyes observed me for maybe a minute. "*Did she deserve the punishment?*"[11] he asked, in short clipped syllables.

I defied his stare even though his eyes looked as compassionless as a serpent's. "*Nobody deserves that,*"[12] I stated resolutely.

"*It's Allah who decides what we deserve.*" His features then began to tremble. "*But I deserve hell.*"[13]

He sat beside me, took me in his arms and began to weep. Instinctively, I rocked him in spite of the possibility that he might be the one who had tried to kill me and Kim. Between sobs, he kept asking, "*How do you do it? Why are you so nice?*"[14]

He curled up with his head on my lap and I stroked his unkempt hair while I whispered, "*Ça va aller* (It will be fine)." I thought he had gone to sleep when his eyes flew open.

"*You must go to your room. Mom's going to come home. If she asks, tell her that I beat you, okay?*" I looked at him, shaking my head trying to understand the urgency. "*Okay?*"[15] he repeated.

"*D'accord* (okay)," I replied as he pulled me to Neïla's room. The door shut behind me and I sat down on the bed. I couldn't understand why he was so afraid of Mother, it had always seemed like he was head of the household, but for the moment he was letting me off easy for having skipped out of school.

School! Tomorrow I would be in big trouble with the administration. Neïla's homework had to be done and I had Mme Lumière's assignment. Just thinking about it made me nauseated. I sat staring at the screen trying to decide if I shouldn't take Kim's joke more seriously; quit high school and go to beauty school.

The front door opened so I left the computer and put my ear to the door. Othmane was explaining that I had been punished. Then Mother spoke but her voice was too soft and I only caught two words: "*obéissante* (obedient)" and "Algérie." They stopped speaking and I rushed back to my desk just before the door opened and mother stuck her head in.

"The high school called. Tomorrow I have to go see your principal." I looked at her but refused to speak. *"Are you going to start acting like you did before?"*[16]

I brooded on the question a second. *"How did I act before?"* Mother studied me for a good minute and I held her stare. There was something hard in her eyes that sent a chill down my back. *"You know I can't remember,"*[17] I mumbled.

"You'll make a good wife if you learn to obey. I'll go tell Othmane that I've spoken to you."[18]

The door shut and, enraged, I waited until the sound of her shuffle reached the living room before I threw myself on the bed. Be a good wife? Never! I would slip away to the U.S. with Quincy even if that meant living as a fugitive. I stared at the computer wishing I could talk to Quincy. Why not put his picture on my desktop?

I jumped up and switched on the computer. There was the little warble and the desktop picture appeared—only it wasn't Neïla's picture of kittens—I was staring at the black Islamic State's flag. There was no way Djahida was going to get away with that! She must have changed it in the afternoon before going to her Arabic lessons.

I first pasted a picture I had copied off FB on the desktop but then thought better of it; Neïla's picture of kittens was safer and

Djahida might make fun of me if she saw Quincy's picture on the computer. I put the kittens back up and began writing a letter to Quincy. The note gushed out and I didn't try to stop it even though I knew it sounded as if it were written by a love-sick teenage girl. I no longer cared. Writing made his absence a little less painful.

I had just finished and was about to reread it when Djahida rushed in greeting me in guttural Arabic tones and a big smile. The last thing I wanted was to have to deal with her caprices so I gave a "*salut*" before turning my back.

"*What are you doing?*"[19] she asked, as she craned over my shoulder to see what I was writing.

I pushed her away and quickly posted the message before she grabbed for the mouse. "*Laisse-moi* (leave me alone)," I shrilled and gave her a big shove that sent her falling onto my bed. She giggled, but when I closed the browser and the desktop picture of kittens appeared, her giggle turned into a scream. "*But where is my flag?*"[20]

I swiveled around. "*This isn't your computer and I don't want that flag.*"[21]

She looked at me both horrified and puzzled. "*You're turning too much into a French frog.*"[22]

I didn't care what she thought and I had had enough of pretending to be a good Muslim girl. "*I couldn't give a whack! Those people are barbaric.*"[23]

She was standing over me scowling. "*But Othmane is one of those people. What have you got against Othmane?*"[24] she growled.

I put on the most hypocritical smile I could manage. "*You don't think he regrets what he did?*"[25]

"*You're totally nuts!*"[26] she yelled and lunged for the mouse. I pushed her back and held it out of her reach—I was fed up with being pushed around—but she screamed and punched at my face. My head spun sideways. Then Neïla reacted and I shoved Djahida flat onto the floor.

Rage spread across Djahida's face as she jumped toward me, but Neïla was faster and Djahida was slapped hard knocking her back to the floor. She began wailing, and I was about to cry victory, when strong hands suddenly threw me down next to her and my eyes met those scary, impassive eyes of Othmane's.

"She removed my flag of Islam!"[27] Djahida whined.

Othmane paid no attention to her, but spoke to me. *"If you want to fight, fight with me."*[28] He grabbed me by my arm and dragged me to my feet. His hand came down on my face knocking me to my knees.

"Go ahead, hit me,"[29] he said, as I knelt there. I glanced up. For a second his face showed sorrow, but the demon quickly reappeared and he grabbed me by the hair lifting me and—the wind whooshed out of my lungs. I lay curled in a ball trying to breathe.

I heard Djahida giggling until there was a loud smack and she was lying on the floor next to me with her face contorted in pain and anger. I stayed where I was until she sat up.

"Leave her picture of cats," Othmane said calmly, as if nothing had happened. *"Girls shouldn't get involved in politics."*[30]

I turned over to watch him push past Mother who was standing at the door.

1 "Assieds-toi."

2 "J'ai pas de clé."

3 "Pourquoi tu m'obliges à te frapper?"

4 "Nous avons changé tous les deux. Moi, j'ai un démon en moi, un djinn maléfique. Je ne le contrôle pas. Toi, tu avais un djinn avant mais aujourd'hui, il n'est pas le même."

5 "Je ne sais pas qui j'étais."

6 "Tu étais un démon. Je me croyais guidé par des anges, moi... et tout a changé. Je fais du mal. C'est pas moi, c'est le djinn. Je prie mais il ne me laisse pas tranquille."

7 "Tu savais faire mal. Mais tu es devenue quelqu'un de bien.

Ça me fait mal, ça."

8 "Donc tu dois me frapper?"

9 "Tu as quitté le lycée. Tu es allée voir ton *gouère* de copain."

0 "Une amie s'est faite agresser. Elle est à l'hôpital. Il fallait que je la voie."

1 "Méritait-elle la punition?"

2 "Personne ne mérite ça."

3 "C'est Allah qui décide ce qu'on mérite. Mais moi, je mérite l'enfer."

4 "Mais comment tu fais? Pourquoi tu es si gentille?"

5 "Il faut que tu ailles à ta chambre. Maman va arriver. Si elle te demande, tu lui dis que je t'ai frappée, d'accord. D'accord?"

6 "Le lycée a téléphoné. Demain, je dois aller voir ton proviseur. Est-ce que tu vas recommencer comme avant?"

7 "Qu'est-ce que je faisais avant ? Tu sais que je ne me rappelle pas."

8 "Tu feras une bonne épouse mais il faut que tu apprennes à obéir. Je vais dire à Othmane que je t'ai parlé."

9 "Tu fais quoi?"

20 "Mais où est mon drapeau?"

2 "Ce n'est pas ton ordinateur et je ne veux pas de ce drapeau."

22 "Tu deviens trop une céfrane, toi."

23 "Je m'en fous! Ces gens là sont des barbares."

24 "Mais Othmane est un de ceux-là, tu as quoi contre Othmane?"

25 "Tu ne penses pas qu'il regrette ce qu'il a fait?"

26 "Mais t'es complètement ouf!"

27 "Elle a enlevé mon drapeau d'Islam!"

28 "Si tu veux te battre, c'est avec moi."

29 "Vas-y, frappe-moi."

30 "Tu lui laisses sa photo de chats. Les filles ne devraient pas s'occuper de politique."

Chapter 25

Djahida answered my *bonne nuit* (*good night*) with a snort, threw herself into bed and turned off the light. In the dark, I could make out a ray of moonlight slipping through the shutters, then disappearing, and Djahida whistling through her nose like she always did when she slept. I hated the sound. I hated this apartment. I felt Neïla's breasts pushing into the mattress and Josh slipping away, fading into obscurity. Why wouldn't Neïla take her life back?

"It's for you to decide," Daddy said. "Do you want to go or not?"

I looked at the waves, the dark water in the lake, and hesitated. What month was it, November? Wasn't Lake Michigan too cold in this season?

"Don't be afraid, just jump," Daddy shouted encouragingly. "You remember how to swim, don't you?"

Of course I did, but the waves looked so large that it seemed they would swallow me. Was I a coward to fear walking to the edge of the rocks where the lake showered me in cold drops like rain? If I'd had a choice, I wouldn't have come to the lakeside at all. However now that I was here, I had no choice but to jump so I prepared to dive and—

An alarm sounded, a girl groaned not far from me and I found myself shivering in bed with no covers. The groan came again and Djahida slammed her hand down on the alarm clock, then buried her head in her pillow. Silence fell over the bedroom while I stared at the rays of morning light that streamed through the shutters. I was Neïla again.

My body was trembling from the cold because the heating hadn't kicked in yet and I had pushed the covers off during my sleep. I sat up and put my . . . her small and delicate feet on the carpet beside the bed. In the half-light I stared at them for a second wondering how long this masquerade could continue.

Djahida hadn't moved and was making sounds through her nose again. I slipped over to the closet to get dressed before she woke up and tried to dictate what I wore. I wanted to make my own decisions, and I was fed up with her bossiness, so I chose some baggy pants and a sweatshirt that would hide Neïla's frail body.

While I was dressing, I realized that my body and face hurt. In the mirror, I caught a glimpse of Neïla alight in the wan sunlight. She was beautiful in spite of her eye and cheek that were turning black. Othmane had hit me hard.

I found Othmane in the living room and went through the prayer ritual without him having to order me to do so. When I had finished, Mother gave me a cup of tea in the kitchen, told me to hurry so that we wouldn't be late and disappeared into her room. I sipped the mint tea until she came back to sit across from me and I began dipping pieces of bread into honey mixed with olive oil to avoid her stare.

Djahida arrived soon after looking like a marmot woken from hibernation. Mother put a cup of tea in front of her and told her to hurry. She simply grunted and bit into a brioche. It was wise to keep my distance from Djahida just in case she remembered to be angry so I gave the pretext of having to get ready and slipped away.

Neïla's hair felt like a mass of tangles and it wasn't easy to tease them out without looking in the mirror. Djahida would certainly have things to say about the results. I then brushed my teeth and washed Neïla's face. My cheek hurt. Djahida would also want me to hide the bruises under some makeup but I shook my head and left the bathroom. Everybody would see what Othmane did to Neïla even if Djahida had a hissy fit.

I began looking for a new book bag because mine had stayed at Franck's feet. I only needed something big enough to carry my biology book and Neïla's swimsuit and cap; I had been told we were going to the pool for P.E. The other morning classes were science and English. It wasn't until the afternoon that I would have to face Mme Lumière without my homework. I sat on the edge of the bed for a minute with my stomach knotting up while I forced myself to breathe slowly.

Djahida stood at the door, but I was unable to look up into her glare. *"Stop acting like you're crazy and get ready,"*[1] she barked, before closing the door.

I wiped a tear from my eye and went to rummage through Neïla's drawer. At the back I found a bathing cap, a pink one-piece swimsuit and I felt Neïla's amber skin turn red. Should I be embarrassed about letting her be seen in it? With a sigh, I stuffed it into a plastic bag.

I went to sit in the kitchen while Mother took Mustapha downstairs to his transport and Djahida, who was late, finished getting ready. The front door shut and I had to look away while Mother sat down opposite me. Djahida huffed in and sat beside me to write out a letter excusing her tardiness. I glanced at it but refrained from pointing out all the spelling mistakes. Mother calmly signed it, stood up to leave and shot me a terrifyingly blank stare as she closed the door. My legs wobbled so badly as I followed Djahida down the stairs that I had to hold on to the rail.

I sighed with relief when I saw that there were fewer boys milling about outside than usual. Djahida turned in the direction of her junior high school while I followed Mother toward the high school. I hated being treated like a child and so I held the hijab across Neïla's face in the hope that no one would recognize her.

The front gates were closed so Mother rang the buzzer while I took off my head scarf. There came a click and Mother pushed the gate open. Her jilbāb blew in the wind as I followed her across the courtyard to the main building where Pauline was waiting with a scolding look on her face. I averted my eyes but waved while Mother spoke to the lady in the cubicle beside the entrance.

She then grabbed my arm and led me toward the CPE's office.

Mother left me waiting in the hall while she spoke to Franck and although his voice made my heart skip a beat, he was the person I least wanted to see. I had lied to him. After mumbling some more, Mother stuck her head out and waved me in. Franck first smiled but then a frown knitted his forehead when he noticed my black eye, so I covered Neïla's face as I followed Mother into the counselor's office.

The CPE stood and stretched out his hand to shake Mother's. *"Mme Saadallah, I'm Mr. Bernadot, the head counselor. Please sit down."*[2] He gave her a gray-toothed smile.

Mother didn't seem to be looking at him. *"Hello,"*[3] she mumbled after she sat down.

Mr. Bernadot looked at me then back at her. *"Your daughter had an hour of detention yesterday that she refused to do."* He waited for a reaction from mother that didn't come. *"You know that we can't tolerate this sort of behavior, all the more so since she is under our responsibility?"*[4]

"She's been punished,"[5] *Mother* replied laconically.

Mr. Bernadot looked at me and my eye. *"You know we can't allow you to beat your daughter either?"*[6]

"I didn't beat her,"[7] Mother said, with a sideways glare at me.

"I fell,"[8] I whispered, while my eyes stared down at Neïla's pink sneakers. The last thing I needed was another investigation from the police that led nowhere. They knew all about Othmane and didn't care if he used me as a punching bag. What was the use?

Mr. Bernadot shook his head. *"Whatever the case, she will be detained until the Christmas holidays. That makes five Wednesdays."*[9]

"She'll be there,"[10] Mother replied dryly, then stood up.

Mr. Bernadot looked me in the eyes but I turned away. With a sigh he also stood to show us out of his office. When his door closed, Mother gave me a kiss on both cheeks and left without looking back.

"What happened to you?"[11] Franck asked, with his eyes running over my face.

I felt like hiding until the bruises had disappeared. *"Rien* (nothing)," I mumbled.

"Nothing?"[12] Pauline neighed behind me. *"You look horrible."*

I wished I could control Neïla's tears, but Pauline already had her arms around me and was making cooing sounds. *"Tell us what happened,"*[13] she said.

I glanced up into Franck's distressed eyes and shook my head. *"I can't."*[14]

"Who beat you? Was it your brother again?"[15] Franck asked in soft, determined syllables.

"It was just a fall," I whispered. Franck stared at me with a furrowed brow while Pauline fussed with Neïla's hair. *"I have to get to* class,"[16] I said pulling away.

Franck shook his head and reached behind the desk for my school bag and a shiver ran down my back when his hand brushed against mine. *"Merci,"* I mumbled in a voice that sounded horribly fluty.

His lips turned up at the corners in a half-smile. *"Forget it, okay?"*[17] he said, and handed me a late slip.

Pauline jumped up. *"You can't go to class like that. Let me put some blush over it."*[18]

I tried to smile because she was doing what she thought best. *"It's not necessary,"*[19] I replied and strode away down the hall with Pauline's heels clicking behind me. What use was there in hiding my misery behind makeup? I was a stranger to everyone. They saw my features but never who I was inside.

The whole class looked up at me as I opened the door and muttering followed me to the back where I sat next to Bertrane. The teacher continued talking about optics without even asking me for my late slip. I couldn't listen. What would happen when Neïla's family found out everything? There was no way I could keep this masquerade up much longer. From time to time Pauline tried to bring me back to reality with a nudge or a whisper but I ignored her.

The bell rang and Bertrane put her arm around my shoulder as we walked to English class through the boisterous hallways. Monsieur Hubert looked at me gravely, he had the knack for making me feel guilty, so I turned away and went to sit at the back. His eyes kept turning to me as he went about his lesson, and even though I could have answered the questions, I kept quiet. It wouldn't have been fair. I was a fraud.

The bell rang the end of class and I rushed to get out.

"Just a minute, Neïla," Mr. Hubert called. His hands were clasped in front of his belt. "Would you like to explain why you ran off yesterday?"

The last of the students rumbled out and Pauline waved goodbye because she didn't have to accompany me to P.E. I turned around but was unable to look him in the eyes. "I had to see a friend at the hospital," I explained. There was a long silence so I added, "She was mugged and beaten. I had no choice." I wished my cheek would stop twitching.

"You should have said something and we could have postponed your detention." His voice was a mixture of bureaucratic authority and compassion.

"I'm sorry, I didn't think about doing that." I didn't want to tell him that Othmane would never have let me go if he had known.

"You know that the administration isn't happy at all. They were hesitant to accept you back in the first place." It was the bureaucrat who was speaking.

"I didn't know that," I admitted. A tear escaped and trickled down my cheek.

The bureaucrat disappeared as his brow creased. "I'm sorry if I frighten you."

"It's not you," I stammered. "It's complicated."

"What is complicated?" he asked, raising an eyebrow.

I felt like telling him everything but answered instead, "It's better you don't know."

He stared at me and was about to speak when the bell rang again. He waited for it to stop before speaking. "The next time you have a difficulty like that, come to me. I'll see what I can do. You have a lot of potential and I don't want you to throw it out the window on a whim. Now hurry off to gym or you'll be late."

1 "Arrête de faire la folle et prépare-toi."

2 "Mme Saadallah, je suis M. Bernadot, le conseiller principal d'éducation. Asseyez-vous."

3 "Bonjour."

4 "Votre fille avait une heure de détention hier qu'elle a refusé de faire. Vous savez qu'on ne peut pas tolérer ce genre de comportement, d'autant plus qu'elle est sous notre responsabilité?"

5 "Elle a été punie."

6 "Vous savez qu'on ne peut pas vous permettre de battre votre fille non plus?"

7 "Je ne l'ai pas battue."

8 "Je suis tombée."

9 "Quoi qu'il en soit, elle sera collée jusqu'aux vacances de Noël. Cela fait six mercredis."

10 "Elle viendra."

11 "Mais qu'est-ce qui t'est arrivée?"

12 "Rien? Tu as l'air horrible."

13 "Raconte ce qui s'est passé."

14 "Je peux pas."

15 "Qui t'a battue? C'est encore ton frère?"

16 "C'est juste une chute. Il faut que j'aille en cours."

17 "Oublie, d'accord?"

18 "Tu ne peux pas aller en cours comme ça. Laisse-moi te mettre un peu de fond de teint."

19 "Ce n'est pas la peine."

Chapter 26

I slipped into the back of the line beside a gangly black guy whose face lit up when our shoulders rubbed. *"Am I very late?"*[1] I whispered to him.

"Non," he answered just as the gym teacher, a fit, brown-haired woman with over-worked eyes, began calling out names. I thought it was a shame that her hair was cropped so short because she could have been attractive.

"Mlle Saadallah?" the teacher called.

"Présente," Neïla's high-pitched voice chimed.

Would Quincy have preferred an athletic woman like that? Not that it made any difference with him headed back to the States. I kept my eyes down so that nobody could see the tear forming in my eye.

The teacher finished calling role and the line started moving out into the chill wind and drizzle which plastered Neïla's wet hair against my forehead. I put the scarf over my head, pulled her jacket around my shoulders, and wished I had Josh's resistance to cold weather while another tear, or drop of rain, began rolling down my cheek.

We walked through streets for about five minutes and climbed a flight of concrete stairs with graffiti-tagged walls before we crossed a large square closed in by low-income apartment buildings. The pool was hidden on the other side and we filed through the glass doors with the girls going off to the left. Then, almost to my surprise, I found myself in a cramped room with girls undressing. Bertrane chanted a hip-hop song, the others laughed, and soon they were all nude or in swimsuits. I dared not take my sweatshirt off.

"The teacher doesn't like it when we take too much time changing,"[2] Bertrane said, while she put her swim cap on and the girls started heading out. I slipped off my sweatshirt but felt Neïla's face go

red so I covered her bra with my arms. Bertrane raised her eyebrows, sighed and disappeared with the last of the girls.

Once I was alone, I stripped with an eye on the door just in case any of the girls should come back. I had been worried about fitting into that tiny swimsuit but it was so stretchy that Neïla's lithe body slipped into it much more easily than expected. The fact that she probably looked quite sexy didn't comfort me. All I had to do then was get her mass of hair under the swim cap, which took some time, while I shivered in spite of the warm air. Shouldn't Josh have been excited about being in the girls' dressing room?

I decided to stop by the showers even if I was late. The water was tepid, which made me shiver even more, so I kept my arms tight around Neïla's breasts as I waded through the cold footbath. Yells resonated off the tiled walls and I could see Bertrane in the shallow end taking instructions on how to put her face into the water with a few other non-swimmers.

The better swimmers formed four lines along the deep end and were practicing how to dive into the water and make it to the other side without breathing. It was something I had done a thousand times, so while the teacher was busy correcting a boy's jump with her arms stretched out in front of her, I slipped into the back of a line.

Her whistle blew, four kids jumped and it seemed she hadn't spotted me. The whistle blew again, but the boy in front of me came up sputtering halfway across while I stood at the edge of the water. The teacher pulled him aside after he had climbed out of the water and, without looking, blew her whistle.

I jumped as far as I could but in midair, I had the impression I was about to fall into the cold waves of the lake. My body contracted and I lost control just before hard water slapped my belly knocking the wind out of me—and Neïla didn't know how to swim! My arms flailed. I gasped for air, swallowed liquid, choked. The lights dimmed and— I was floating face down in the murky canal watching the almost imperceptible glow of the street lamps penetrating the charcoal gray water around my body. Neïla's whispers then trickled to my ears and I saw her take form among the rays of light that were splintering into viridian kaleidoscopic patterns. I imagined that she had finally come back for her body but when I gestured to her, she just smiled—her smile like a sunrise—and when I tried to argue with her, only gurgles and sputters came from my mouth. Her head shook. My body racked with unbearable pain. My stomach spasmed. I choked.

Voices reverberated, but were they in English or in French? I vomited while a roar imploded in my ears, softened, and was slowly replaced by the buzz of whispers. Hadn't this happened to me before? Maybe it was better for me to keep my eyes closed. Maybe my dead body was lying beside me with its head caved in. Why couldn't I just—

A slap jolted my head painfully and a voice was directed at me. For fear that the person might slap me again, I squinted my eyes open and they fell on the P.E. teacher who was bent over me with her mouth moving. I watched her lips but the sounds had no meaning. My eyes shut and—

I was shaken awake. A man, maybe a lifeguard, was holding me in his strong arms. I stared at the crumbling concrete ceiling while the rumble of the water pump echoed in my belly rather than in my ears. There was no other sound. My classmates had all left.

The man's strong arms laid my head on the tile floor and a flurry of paramedics swarmed around me asking questions that I did not understand. When I tried to speak, only garbled sounds came out and they looked at me with furrowed brows while my vital signs were read. I knew what was going to happen and on three, they picked me up to put me on a gurney. I watched the ceiling roll by until a cold wind whipped raindrops against my face and onto my now closed eyelids. When I opened them again, the gray mist had been replaced by the roof of an ambulance.

* * *

The hum of the ventilation was just loud enough to keep me from dozing off while I lay in Neïla's damp swimsuit with my eyes shut. I had been through this before and was therefore all the more distressed knowing they would lock me up in an insane asylum this time around.

The curtains were pulled aside and a young man stepped in, glanced at my chart, said something that I didn't understand, looked into my eyes, flashed his penlight toward my pupils and away, then mumbled incomprehensible sounds.

His eyebrows rose when I didn't react. He repeated the sounds, waited, pulled the survival blanket off of me and put his warm hands on my shoulders to help me sit up. His cold stethoscope then skipped from place to place on my back and when he spoke, I knew to breathe deeply. He finally walked back in front of me and emitted a long string of garbled French sounds but I could only shake my head feeling like an idiot.

His lips curled and he said something I recognized as being English but I couldn't understand it either. I wished he would repeat it, and he did, but the meaning still remained elusive. I understood nothing, neither French nor English, and it felt like a door had just clanged shut. The little that had been left of Josh was washed away leaving me with nothing but this rag of a body which had begun to tremble.

His hand touched my shoulder again and he made calm noises while he had me lie back down. My eyes shut but for a second I imagined I was floating again in that cold canal so I opened them hastily, just as a nurse entered with my clothing. She too made strange noises and all I could do was watch her lips move, they were thin and painted some color of lavender, but then they pulled back in irritation and she started to help me out of the swimsuit.

I shook my head—I could undress Neïla myself—but then my

hands began to shake. The nurse stepped back over to help me, but I pushed her away and struggled out of the damp swimsuit alone.

I wished I had a towel yet the nurse only handed me Neïla's underwear and brassiere which, in spite of my knees wobbling, I managed to get on. I then pulled the sweatshirt over my head and the jeans up to my waist but my legs gave out and I would have crumpled to the floor if the nurse hadn't helped me to a chair. I was no longer anybody, neither Josh nor Neïla, and could make no more sound than a ghost.

I dared not look at the nurse's lavender lips while she spoke a soft string of words to another person who had entered, Dr. Moulin, the psychiatrist, with her ponytail and penetrating gaze. She said something to me which I knew to be "bonjour," even though the sounds were garbled, so I nodded to be polite. Then she said something else and I tried to utter, "I don't understand," but my mouth fumbled and my brain fogged.

Dr. Moulin sat in front of me and her hand reached out to touch my chin lightly and direct my gaze in her direction. Her brow knitted while she ran her index finger across my cheek where there was another bruise. I was ashamed to be so weak but when I glanced up into the psychiatrist's eyes, I understood she wanted to help me. To keep my tears back, I looked away and shook my head.

Her hand touched my hair and pushed it out of my eyes while she whispered sounds that made me want to hold on to her while I cried. I was at the psychiatrist's mercy, and although I would be as good as lost if she ever learned the truth about me, I still wanted to trust her. She gave me an encouraging smile and started to stand up but my hand reached out for her automatically. For the first time, I regretted her leaving. Her smile was tender while she patted my hand and turned to stride out past the curtain.

* * *

Ever since they had put me back in the cubicle, Mother did nothing but stare at me. Was she here to guard me? I wanted to run away, to flee, just like when the doctors had sent me through the scanner—noises like machine-gun fire so loud that I was unable remain still and they'd had to strap me down. Blood was also taken and a swarm of white jackets had trooped around. They were convinced I was crazy, so why not just lock me up?

The door opened and a nurse walked in, glanced over at me, then went to speak to Mother in hushed tones. I might as well have been a throw rug so I turned my back. The hushed sounds then stopped, a hand stroked my hair and I looked around at Mother who was holding out a hijab. I never wanted to put that thing on again, but after the nurse had left the room, Mother stared at me so sternly that I realized I had no choice.

When I was covered, Mother even smiled. She pulled the curtain aside and a young dark-skinned man with a wheelchair came over to help me stand. I pushed him away and got to my feet. He gave me a crooked smile but stayed close while I walked out of the cubicle.

A passing nurse rushed to take hold of my arm, then shook her finger under my nose while she pointed at the wheelchair. Smirking, the young man leaned against the wall while I sat down and Mother came over to kiss me goodbye. The wheelchair then began to move away and I turned to watch Mother disappear down the hall.

As soon as we rounded a corner, I yanked the scarf off my head and the young man pushing the wheelchair laughed out loud. I didn't care. I was sick and tired of all this. I glanced back at him, but still grinning, he kept his eyes on where we were headed.

The wheelchair attendant punched a button, the elevator door opened with a *ding* and an elderly man entered behind us with a kind smile and gentle eyes. When the door opened again, he elegantly insisted that I be pushed out first. I tried to thank him but only managed an ugly sound akin to a meow.

The young man rang a buzzer in front of a large sliding door and after it had opened, he wheeled me down a hall to what could have been the same hospital room as before. When he proceeded to help me out of the chair, I hissed at him and he stood back as if I might scratch. Then, when he chuckled, it struck me that I wasn't being very polite and in lieu of an apology, I let him help me up and over to the bed. His hands were so strong that I almost wished he would stay but unfortunately he gave a crooked smile and bowed his way out.

* * *

Was it possible to be any less bored? Mother hadn't paid for the television again and I had no magazines to read—if I was still able to make out the words. Not long after I arrived in the room, a nurse bustled in and took my vital signs, then handed me a little blue pill. I knew what it was, one of their happy pills, and hated myself for taking it.

Dinner was wilted salad and tasteless cannelloni. As I sat staring at the disappointing tray, the door opened and I heard the words "*pinpin futé* (sly bunny)"—I had understood something!—and squealed with excitement at being able to speak again. In my euphoria, I even hugged and kissed Mokhtar on either cheek.

His eyes went round with surprise for a second, but then that habitual smirk stretched his lips back across his face. Even though I didn't like or trust Mokhtar, his being there made it feel like I had been let out of solitary confinement. He laid down a small suitcase, held me at arm's length and said something while I listened intently to his sounds hoping I might understand more.

He kept talking and waiting for an answer but in the end I had to shake my head like an idiot. Then he looked at my dinner and his face screwed up in anger. All I could do was raise an eyebrow before the slap came and my head was thrown sideways. When I looked back, he had thrown my salad against the wall and I realized there had been little pieces of ham in it. No words could be found to apologize, or tell him that I had only poked at it with my fork, so I curled up into a ball waiting for more blows to fall.

Instead, he grabbed me by the arm and pulled me to the middle of the floor while he looked on his smartphone and pointed to the direction of the Mecca. I went through the whole routine of prayers as best as I could and then looked back up at him. He motioned for me to do it again.

I was halfway through the third routine when the lady came in to remove my dinner. She looked at me on the floor and then at Mokhtar before hurrying away. A moment later, a large African nurse stomped in and stood in front of him while I crawled into a corner. Soon after, a security guard appeared and Mokhtar squared his shoulders but made no resistance to being shown out. Just before he left, he shot me a wink and a wry smile.

1 "Je suis très en retard?"

2 "Le prof n'aime pas quand on prenne trop de temps pour nous changer."

Chapter 27

The more Mother's eyes followed my every movement, the more I felt like fleeing. She was showing me how to make some sort of cross-stitch so I nodded and copied her gestures afraid she might strike out like Othmane or Mokhtar. I got the feeling she was going to use my aphasia to pressure me into marriage and into being a good little wife. My only wish was that Quincy would show up and whisk me away to the United States. Alas, I had no way of telling him that I was back in the hospital.

The nurse watched me swallow my "medication" while Mother inspected my dinner for pork. She didn't need to worry about me eating anything *harem* (forbidden) because the smell of the lasagna disgusted me and I pushed it away as soon as Mother had gone home to feed Neïla's siblings. My dinner stayed on the table until the nurse's aide came back to pick it up. She gestured for me to eat, but I shook my head and turned my back. With a sigh, the woman left some cookies on the table and removed the cold food.

Lying back in bed, I stared at the street lights playing across the ceiling like ghosts until I felt my eyes get heavy. I mustn't sleep, I told myself, that's what they wanted. That's why they give me sedatives. After all that had happened, wasting my time watching reflections in this prison was out of the question so I stood up, stuffed the cookies into my jacket pocket and put on my hijab.

With a glance right and left, I slipped down the hall toward the entrance hoping to go unnoticed. I could hear the nurses' muffled voices seeping out from their office next to the sliding doors. It had a large mirrored window so that they could keep an eye on what was happening in the hall.

I stooped down to creep past the window and looked at the keypad against the wall that opened the doors—this wasn't going to be simple!—but if they wanted to keep me prisoner so that Mother could marry Neïla off, they'd have to think again. The problem was that I didn't know the code to open the doors and without it, they could do with me as they wished.

There came a sudden howl from a room down the hall that made my heart jump so badly I almost yowled. Then, while I was trying to slow my breathing, a nurse came out of the office and walked to the room, stuck her head in, huffed and shut the door. Luckily she hadn't looked in my direction and I managed to hide behind a door opposite the keypad. After she had had gone back into the nurses' office, I sat back wishing I was still as cool and collected as Josh.

A buzzer sounded and I jumped again. The nurse clomped out to the keypad and punched the numbers. From where I was hiding, I could see that there were four numbers: one at the top, the same two times at the bottom and then another at the top right. The door slid open, a man with a package came in and they both disappeared into the office.

I was about to sit back and breathe when they came back out and the nurse typed the numbers again: one in the middle on the left, two in the middle at the bottom and then at the top on the right. The man made a comment which got a smile from the nurse and then walked away while she returned to the office.

I sat with my eyes closed thinking that the code might be 4883. Would I be able to read the numbers when I couldn't understand a word anybody said? The howling started again from the room down the hall and a whimper almost escaped me just as a nurse stamped out of the office. She stuck her head into the room and then called to a second nurse. I waited for them both to disappear into the room before I hurried over to keypad.

I practically hopped with delight that I was able to read the numbers. My hands shook as I punched in the code and then, like magic, the doors slid open. There was no time to rejoice, however, because the nurses might reappear any second so I hurried off down the hall to the left. The drugs made my legs feel like lead but I forced myself to go faster. They might soon discover I was missing.

The front entrance was dangerous territory, so before I ventured out into plain sight, I glanced around the corner to observe the guard talking on his cell phone. He looked like the same one who had caught me when I first tried to escape and would certainly recognize me if he looked straight at me.

I pulled my hijab over my head, took a deep breath, and began to stride to the door although my legs wobbled. What sort of pills had the nurse given me? Luckily, the guard didn't notice or stop me from walking freely out onto the front plaza. I felt as if I were going to collapse.

The evening breeze whipped my hijab over my face while I shuffled past the same group of smokers who still milled about outside the hospital. Their smoke still gave me the urge for a cigarette but I knew not to slow down for fear that the guard might dash up behind me or that Mokhtar might be waiting somewhere out of sight.

Each step felt like I was pulling my feet out of mud and my breaths came short and fast. When I reached the street, I had to stop for a second to keep from falling. The drugs they had given me were stronger than I had imagined.

Footsteps approached me from behind and I spun around startled and ready to defend myself but it was only an elderly black man. He looked concerned and spoke in soothing sounds. When I shook my head wishing he would leave, his eyes screwed up with worry. He took a step forward so I backed away. Then his hand reached out and panic lurched through my chest.

I bolted, running, not stopping, until a car screeched to a stop with its horn blaring. The driver then jumped out to yell, to bark at me while I gaped at the black hood. I wanted to flee those hostile noises, to keep running, but when I stepped up on the sidewalk, my legs gave out and I found myself sitting on the pavement watching the angry man stare down at me. He kept moving his mouth, saying things I couldn't understand. Finally, he threw his hands up in disgust and stomped back to his car.

I knew I shouldn't just sit there, that I had to keep moving, because somebody might be following. However when I laid back and closed my eyes, it felt so good—

A young woman with a ponytail was shaking me awake. I would have jumped up and ran if there hadn't been two serious-looking men standing behind her. All three were dressed like firemen and an ambulance's flashing blue lights lit the sides of their faces. I realized they were from the SAMU Social, an emergency assistance for homeless people.

The woman began speaking to me in soft sounds that I could not understand and stayed squatting beside me while she waited for an answer that I couldn't give. She was close enough for her lavender perfume to stir luxurious and fearful recollections, Mother had bought me one similar, so I sat up and glanced around for an escape.

Her eyes continued to observe me until I began trembling and her hand reached out to touch my blackened eye where a tear was welling up. My sleeve wiped it away and I cursed myself for being a wimp. She gave me a kindhearted smile, mimed sleep and motioned to the ambulance. I had no idea where she wanted to take me but I wasn't about to risk returning to the hospital so I shook my head and scooted away against a wall.

One of the men then brought over a cup of soup and some bread that I nibbled while the woman sat beside me. She appeared kind and charitable but like all the others, she would send me back to that prison. As I swallowed, I realized how hungry I was and took another bite of bread and a sip of the soup. My muscles relaxed enough to hear that the sounds she was making weren't French. Maybe she thought I spoke Arabic.

When it became clear that I wasn't going to get into the ambulance, or answer her questions, she made gestures indicating that I should be careful and handed me a blanket. Josh had never needed to worry about aggression but my stomach now lurched at the thought of being left alone. She seemed to read my thoughts and motioned to the ambulance again.

I shook my head emphatically and her hand caressed my cheek while the men loaded their gear in the ambulance. It turned off its blinking lights and pulled away leaving me alone on the pavement with the late-night pedestrians, most of whom gave me a wide berth, although a few gawked at me as if I were a sideshow. I had no desire to attract attention so I stood up, draped the blanket around my shoulders and hurried away.

The chill whipped against my face and the people's stares were unnerving so I kept as best as I could to the shadows. Suddenly a group of boys came out of a café laughing and I stood staring at them like a rabbit caught in the headlights. The tallest one puffed his chest and stood in front of me while he spoke. I was at a complete loss, a total idiot, and when his hand reached out to touch my shoulder, I bolted, tripped and sprawled painfully on the pavement. His hands then began to lift me, to hold me tightly, and I shrieked, panicked, ran.

I only made it to the next street before I had to slow to a walk. The drugs were still making me woozy, throwing a haze over my vision, so after stumbling past bars and kebab shops, I knew I had to stop and rest. Across the street I saw a park with cloaked forms hunched against the cold. As I stood staring, it dawned on me that these were homeless people and that I had no choice but to spend the night among them.

I shuffled past sleeping men until I came to an empty park bench and sat down with my blanket pulled tightly around my shoulders. How could they sleep with this cold, damp breeze? This wasn't a place for me. I wasn't one of these derelicts, was I?

Not far away two men were drinking from a bottle and I told myself Neïla should be fleeing those drunks—this wasn't safe—so I was going to stand up and keep walking but my head bobbed, my eyes blinked closed and I let the soft numbness slip down over my forehead and face.

I was sprawled on a bench, chilled to the bone and my eyes opened onto a man sitting on the ground facing me. He may not have been more than thirty but with his weather-beaten face, he seemed much older. When he noticed I was looking at him, a smile brightened his features and he removed the stained wool cap from his matted brown hair.

I sat up wondering if I should try to run in spite of my woozy head and stiff legs. The homeless man then said something in low-pitched sounds although he clearly didn't expect me to understand; he wasn't speaking French. He just wanted to reassure me so I drew in a long breath and smiled. He beamed.

The cold breeze picked up making me shiver and, with a shake of his head, the homeless man held out a thick sleeping bag to me as if it were an offering. I no longer cared how dirty it was, or if it were infested with fleas, as I wrapped myself in its warmth and nodded my thanks. The homeless man then gestured that I should sleep and tapped his chest showing that he would keep watch. When, in spite of my fatigue, I attempted to refuse, he just laughed and rolled up a sweater for me to use as a pillow.

The street lamp flickered like my shadow while I let him put his sweater under my head and stroke Neïla's cheek. His hand tickled and he smelt of plaster and perspiration while he knelt beside me. Was he going to hold me while I lay on the bench? There was nothing I could do about it if he decided to force me so I let my eyes close.

Chapter 28

My room had always been the coldest in the house but never like this. I shivered wishing the central heating would kick in so I could lay next to the duct by the stairs with hot air blowing on my backside while mom put on breakfast. I reached for the side of the bed and touched a cold park bench. What was a dusty sweater doing under my head?

The murmur of people walking by startled my eyes open and I was on a park bench with the homeless man watching me. As soon as I looked over at him, a smile cracked his lips. He uttered something to the effect of "good morning" and I wished I could reply but my mouth only flapped idiotically. He nodded sympathetically as if he understood.

Cold and stiff, I sat up and pulled the sleeping bag around my shoulders. With a few soft sounds, and movements as slow as if he were approaching a feral cat, the man sat beside me. Neïla's body tensed and I almost darted away but then his warmth drew me to him and a shiver ran down my spine as his arm slipped around my shoulders.

My body curled up against his strong torso while his hands rubbed my shoulders to get the chill out. He was strong, reassuring, having probably worked with his hands all his life. I put my head against his chest wanting comfort but instead began to cry.

His hand stroked my head scarf while he made chesty sounds and I scolded myself for acting so childishly. When I was able to stop the tears, I pulled away and he studied me for a second, but then turned to open a pocket in his knapsack. With a nod, he handed me a piece of day-old bread that I had to tear with my teeth.

The bread had the taste of generosity so I looked up at him with one of Neïla's smiles and noticed a tear in his eye just before he turned his head away. He had surely suffered and I realized that we both needed to hold somebody tightly or our souls would wither. As my arms wrapped around his back, his shoulders tensed, then relaxed and he didn't move.

From time to time he let out a little hiccupping sound, and sniffled, but never turned to face me. People strode by, some glancing over at us, without anybody seeming to care. A fight broke out across the park between two other homeless men and he took in a long deep breath, turned back around and held out a bottle for me to drink from.

I took the bottle hesitantly and sniffed before drinking in case it contained alcohol. A huge smile spread across his face as I examined the liquid and he let out a chesty laugh because there was just water in the bottle. After a long drink, I looked back at him with an apologetic pout which made him laugh even harder.

He didn't take me in his arms again, preferring to sit on the far side of the bench observing my movements. I had trouble knowing whether to be self-conscious or not, so when a gust of wind blew at my hijab and ruffled Neïla's hair, I took off the scarf to tease the tangles out with my fingers. The man shook his head and went to rummage through his pack again. After a few seconds he held up a comb in triumph. I reached out to take it but he clucked his tongue and went to stand behind me. His calloused hands gently undid the tangles while he whistled a tune, a soft sound like the breeze off the taiga, and then braided my hair on the back of my head. With a smile, he pulled out a mirror for me to see.

I pushed it away with a shiver and tears began running down my face again. What a useless wreck I had become! His hand touched my back and I laid my cheek against his arm. He smelled of cheap soap and strong body odors but I took him into a long hug until—

He stiffened; three policemen were coming through the sparse crowd and observing the homeless people. Before he could stay me, I jumped up ready to run. If they caught me, I was a goner!

A policewoman's head turned in my direction and she began marching toward us. I was in a panic, trembling and at a loss, but the homeless man made urgent noises and pointed to the metro. He was telling me to flee while he distracted them.

I shook my head because I didn't want him to get arrested but with a smile he slapped his chest. "Kosta," he said, and then gently shoved me toward the metro.

Before I took off running, Neïla gave him a kiss on the cheek.

* * *

I pushed though the turnstile behind a young man in a gray suit without excusing myself and then hurried away down the subway tunnels. The commuters all seemed to be headed toward the platform in the direction of Mairie d'Ivry so I followed, hoping no one else would notice me while I tied the scarf over Neïla's hair. I doubted Neïla's brothers would find me but I couldn't get rid of the nagging fright that they might catch me without my hijab.

When I reached the stairs, the sound of an approaching train made the crowd accelerate to a run and I had to push my way onto the car before the doors closed with a buzz. No seats were free with the rush-hour traffic but I managed to slither my way between a man and a heavy black woman to get hold of the central pole. Then, after the first stop, the black lady pushed me against a woman wearing a pinstriped pantsuit when more people got on and the well-dressed lady jerked back as if I had the plague. Pinstripes didn't seem to want any contact with an Arab girl.

More commuters boarded at the next stop squishing me further and forcing me to let go of my handhold. I was looking for something to grab for stability when the train jolted forward and I fell against pinstripes. I wanted to say, "sorry," but no sound came out and the more I tried to speak, the more she glared at me. It was as if I were some piece of garbage—dirty, immoral, indigent—and I knew she was right. I had no home, no family, and no hope so I shuffled as best as I could to the door to get off at the next stop. I wouldn't make her suffer my presence any longer.

This was Gare du Nord, Josh had been through here many times, and after the crowd had pushed me up the stairs into the shopping area, I continued walking without thinking about where I was going. It was obvious. I just hoped Quincy hadn't already left for the United States.

Peruvian music hummed out of one of the tunnels and grew stronger with each of my steps until I found myself watching three South Americans play guitar and flutes. They took up, "El Cóndor Pasa," the tune that Simon and Garfunkel had sung as "If I Could," and smiled at me. I wondered if they were just trying to be nice but then I heard a girl singing in a high treble and saw I had attracted the crowd's attention.

The men began yelling encouragement, as people gathered around to listen—they were all looking at me!—and I realized it was Neïla who was singing. How did she know Paul Simon's lyrics and why did she sound so distant? Then a different woman in pinstripes pushed past me and the words fluttered away. I could no longer sing or speak so I turned and ran off in shame.

The crowd got denser and I was soon lost in its anonymity but the words to the song wouldn't leave my mind. What would I rather be, a swallow or old lumbering Josh? I had never been given a choice but if Neïla did ever come to take her life back, would I be disappointed?

I followed people down the next flight of stairs on to the number 4 metro platform and pushed up against a wall while I waited. There were fewer people going in this direction so when the train did finally arrive, I was able to make my way into a corner seat and be forgotten. With the hijab over my hair, people tended to look away.

After only two stations, I got off, headed up the tunnels and stepped out into the morning haze near Montmartre where Quincy lodged. While I strolled past the sundries displayed in the shops held by Africans, I blended into the multicultural crowd easily. When I began climbing the mount however, tourists and trendy Parisians quickly replaced the immigrants that populated Boulevard de Rochechouart.

Quincy's street rose off to the right and I stepped aside to let an Italian sports car roll past. I knew exactly where he boarded, a beautiful townhouse that had been turned into condos, because I had saved it on Maps. You had to have money to live near the place where Picasso painted "Les Demoiselles D'Avignon." How had Quincy managed it?

Today, unlike what I had seen on Maps, the building opposite his was hidden behind scaffolding and tarpaulin. Machines howled in the upper stories while workers shouted and my head began to spin. It felt as though I were walking through one of those dreams in which you struggle to make it somewhere only to discover that your goal has disappeared. I looked everywhere desperately hoping for a sign of Quincy but the machine-gun fire of a pneumatic hammer almost made me run and hide.

While I stood turning circles in the middle of the street, an elderly-looking Arab man stepped out from under the tarpaulin and nodded good-day to me. His smile had the rugged kindness of somebody who had worked hard his whole life, so I did my best to smile and nod back. When he spoke to me, I quickly turned my back and scurried to the large green double door behind which Quincy lived. I didn't want the man to know I couldn't speak.

My eyes scanned the twelve buzzers, but I could not tell if his name was on any of them. I felt defeated, a loser, and would have walked away if I'd had any other place to go. Instead, after a glance back at the Arab man who was watching me, I decided that the only solution was to ring all of buzzers and hope that Quincy answered.

I got no answer from the first two but the third buzzer was answered by a hoarse female voice and I was forced to speak, to make myself comprehensible, if I wanted to find Quincy. Instead, an undecipherable mewl escaped my throat. There was a silence and then the woman barked words and their anger pushed me back while anxiety made me lean against a green sports car.

It started to rain after I had collapsed on the sidewalk next to the car and I pulled my hijab over my face. Before I was completely soaked, however, the Arab worker walked over, lifted me off the sidewalk and led me under the scaffolding.

He pulled a handful of dried figs from his pocket and handed them to me while I looked into his dark eyes. I started to push them away but the bridge of his nose wrinkled with worry, so I accepted them and smiled. The man's face lit up; I had forgotten that my smile was Neïla's.

Men then started yelling at him from above, so he hurried back to his job while I hunched under the plastic tarp with rain streaming down the scaffolds and around Neïla's wet sneakers. I bit into a fig, its taste sweet and earthy, and watched the runoff flow down the street on its way to the Seine River. I was shivering more than I had all night.

I must have drifted off to sleep because when my eyes opened, the rain had lightened up enough for people to venture back out on to the street. Quincy's door opened and a giggling dishwater blonde with a lavender Montmartre umbrella appeared. Josh's tongue would have been hanging out, but Neïla immediately disliked her. Why couldn't she get a move on? She finally swung her hips out onto the sidewalk while she chatted to somebody in the entranceway.

She let out a giggle loud enough for me to hear across the street and Quincy stepped out beside her. I jumped up to wave but then the blonde gave him an unexpected kiss on the cheek—

and he did nothing! He should have pushed her away, but he just smiled and played with her umbrella. Numbness gripped my belly and chest and I was about to dash over to grab him away from her when he returned her kiss.

My only desire was to go back to the canal, jump into that cold water and let it carry me away in its spiraling current. I started to walk away, tripped and Quincy spied me. His hand pulled away from the blonde who continued giggling while I turned my back and saw the old Arab man watching me.

Quincy's hand touched my shoulder and he said something in English, but I refused to look at him. I didn't want to hear it or understand his excuses. I just wanted him to hold me, not smooch with dumb blondes, so I spun around and began pounding on his chest.

Then the Arab workman calloused hands gently pulled me away while he made soft guttural sounds and I stared back into Quincy's blue eyes. He looked so sorry that my anger turned to despair and so I buried my face in the Arab's dirty blue coveralls to cry. The workman put his arm around me and directed harsh sounds at Quincy who was trying to push past and grab me. I ran to hide under the tarpaulin.

Their argument continued while I huddled against the wall with a fig in my hand. At some point the pneumatic hammer began banging in the upper stories making me cover my ears and close my eyes. I didn't want to hear either its pounding or Quincy's pleas. Then shouts erupted next to me and I knew I was at the center of the dispute.

The old Arab worker's boss was pointing red-faced from me to the work site—this was going to cost him his job—while Quincy spoke to his blonde and made large gestures with his hands. Their anger was unbearable but I was unable to call for them to stop, to beg them to speak softly and to try to understand each other. In the end, however, who was I to be giving lessons? I was just a liar, a phony and even a murderer?

Nobody paid attention to me as I crept along the wall under the tarpaulin to the corner of the street and gazed at the fig in my hand. Guilt made me cry as I laid it on a piece of timber—maybe the old worker would find it—and stole away like a criminal without glancing back at either the old Arab or at Quincy.

Chapter 29

Only the sky's dreariness reflected off the surface of the canal as if no beauty surrounded it. Did its current carry anything other than silt and debris? In the end, what difference would it make if I sank down to the bottom rather than remain here in the cold? Both options were gray and lifeless.

I had been drifting since I had fled. My thoughts were drifting. I needed words to cry out my anger, but my mouth remained silent while Neïla's sneakers stood the edge of the canal. If she fell in, she wouldn't be able to save herself.

On my walk through Paris, hookers had looked askance at me. A car had pulled up beside me and I hadn't needed to comprehend the man's utterances to understand what he had wanted. Maybe he had thought I was simpleminded because when I ran, he followed and I was finally forced to take refuge in an African emporium where I hid until the owner chased me out.

Josh had spent a month living near this canal and he had often come to watch its ripples' unending patterns. I tried to think back to his suburban house in the United States, but the memory was so faded that I might wonder whether it had ever really happened. More ripples appeared, disappeared, all the same yet different. Now it was my turn.

Where could I get a glass of water? I was really thirsty.

Two lovers walked by on the other bank cuddled under an umbrella. I was soaking wet. Maybe Neïla would die of hunger and exposure before I came to a decision. I turned to look at the bistro and the old curmudgeon of a waiter who was standing at the window. He might recognize Neïla if I went in there now but what good would that do without any money?

I began walking away, or maybe it was Neïla who had made the decision, and the wind whipped against my face as I turned onto a small street that led toward the center of town. The bar and the canal were now behind me but I had to see one last person before this came to an end. She had said she was being sent to Pantin.

A group of people broke out in laughter as they flooded out of a doorway but they took no notice of me passing by with my hijab pulled in front of my mouth. It was wet. Neïla's hair was so wet and tangled that Djahida would have had a fit if she had seen me. My sneakers were soaked too and my feet hurt so much that if I sat down, I would never be able stand up again. Was that my goal? Keep going until the real Neïla took back what was hers so I could return to oblivion?

I reached my destination; a large modern apartment-like building with *Maison de Retraite Médicalisée Saint Jean* written on a white sign in blue lettering. The sliding glass door was set back under the upper stories with a small patio where there were wet lawn chairs for the elderly to sit. I could see them through the window. They were staring about, at nothing, or at each other. I couldn't see Espérance.

The overhang kept me out of the rain while I took off my hijab and folded it up. What would I say to her? Wouldn't I just be able to stare at her with my mouth open? I looked back through the window. Would I even be able to find her? A woman walked out and brushed past me but the sliding doors remained open and they wouldn't close until I moved out from in front of them. After a second's hesitation, I pushed myself forward.

A plump bleached-blond woman sitting behind the front desk made a noise and then lifted an eyebrow. My head shook, I hadn't understood the question, while I tried to get my mouth to say, "Espérance." The woman cocked her head so I took a pen and paper off the table hoping I could write but the symbols turned to ciphers. I wanted to scream and discovered I could only hiss.

The woman came around and held me by the shoulders while she spoke commanding words. Was she trying to comfort me or would she push me back out into the rain? I was about to struggle when I heard someone call.

"Neïla," I heard. "Neïla dear."

The voice was weak—but I understood it—and I spied her in a wheelchair in the corner away from the others looking so frail and insubstantial with the protective foam padding tucked all around her. I pointed to Espérance and the blonde receptionist took her hand off of my shoulder but watched me carefully as I shuffled over to give Espérance a kiss on either cheek. I would have hugged her if I hadn't been afraid she might break.

"It's good of you to come see an old woman. I've been waiting for your visit," Espérance said, with a hoarse chuckle.

How could I understand her?

"Oh, that? You're the only one that can. They all think I'm *gaga*, as they say here. Come now, you look tired. Take one of those chairs and sit down."

Her hand barely moved and I could see she was much weaker than she had been in the hospital. I didn't want to tell her, but she clucked her tongue as I sat down.

"Don't you worry about me, I know I look terrible, it's you we need to speak about. But first, I want you to look in this little purse beside me. I believe my children have left a few coins. I want you to take fifty cents and buy yourself a hot chocolate from that machine at the entrance."

I tried to object because I was certain the receptionist was watching me with distrust.

"Don't you worry about her; she's a nincompoop," Espérance sighed, before she turned to the receptionist and barked something. The woman's brow furrowed but she stayed behind her desk while I trudged to the machine and inserted the coin. The other residents and the receptionist warily observed me as I took the hot chocolate and went back to sit beside Espérance. I hadn't realized how cold I was until I took a sip and began shivering. Espérance waited for me to finish the drink.

"You mustn't do that to yourself, you know? How long were

you out there in the rain?"

I didn't really know and I certainly didn't want to talk about Quincy and his blonde.

She shook her head knowingly. "Finding boys will never be a problem for you." She gave a few hacking laughs that frightened me. "And if he leaves you for that bimbo, he doesn't deserve you."

I turned my head embarrassed that she knew about my feelings for Quincy. Was it really immoral? Would I ever find anybody I longed for as much? She gave a good-natured chuckle and I looked back intrigued by the serenity in her dark eyes.

"When your goal is death," she said with a sigh, "you'll never find peace. But if your goal is peace, you just might find out who you are. When you do, you won't dwell on death any longer." She pointed a weak finger in my direction. "You need to find yourself."

What did she mean?

"I can tell you these things but you won't grasp them till you feel them in your flesh," she said, tapping her chest. There followed a long moment of silence while she seemed to reflect on things that had disappeared years ago and I thought I caught a hint of blue in her eyes.

"You can't keep trying to live a life that isn't yours," she whispered. "You're in neither world. That's why you can't speak. You aren't a phony, you hear?"

I wasn't really sure I had understood, so I shook my head while her eyes became black as obsidian again.

"I told you it wouldn't mean much. We should be chatting about the awful weather and our families, not about all that serious stuff."

I had no family, not any longer.

"Don't you say that either. They're your family now even if you can't trust them any more than cobras. But don't you give up on all of them."

How did she know about Neïla's family? I was about to ask

when her eyes began to wander and a multitude of expressions crossed her wrinkled features. There seemed to be a flow of images running past her eyes which only came into focus when she looked back at me.

"I'm glad you came when you did. It's been hard waiting for you. Sometimes I got to believing that nothing ever happened like I remembered. That I was just an idiot telling tales." She had a tear in her eye. "And then you showed me it was possible. Don't you ever believe you're mad, you hear me?"

I nodded, took her hand and a shiver rippled between our fingers before it flowed deep into my belly. As I looked into her eyes they grew younger—how beautiful she had been with her dark chocolate skin and pixie smile! Suddenly she began to fade, to become fuzzy, and a young white boy was smiling and waving goodbye to me.

A nurse pushed me aside screaming for help.

I was on the floor watching Espérance dance to a rhythm I couldn't hear. Her legs were long and muscular, her neck as elegant as a gazelle's, and joy undulated out of her. Around me was a lush tropical forest filled with African women and sweaty white men in starched shirts. The spotted cat came out of nowhere.

Somebody was lifting me into a chair—I must have fallen asleep—and a woman stood over me, shaking me, saying incomprehensible things. I tried to get up but my legs gave out and I was in the forest again staring at my black skin while a white man gave me orders. I tried to tell him I was white too but received a scornful curse and a slap in return.

I opened my eyes to discover a paramedic leaning over me. Fear of being captured ran through my body and I attempted to get up to flee but my shoulders were held down firmly. Espérance's lighthearted laugh then told me to relax. Everything would be fine, peaceful, calm, and her words became a mantra that put me to sleep.

Part 6

Avouons qu'il n'y a de sens que du désespoir. "Let us acknowledge that there is no meaning aside from despair."

—Julia Kristeva

Chapter 30

"Can you read this?"

With the psychiatrist's shrewd eyes observing my every gesture, I wasn't thrilled that I could. My chest started contracting and I wanted her to go away but she stared at me until I nodded.

"Et vous lisez le français (And can you read French,") she jotted down on the paper and held up for me to read.

I never had a good poker face and her arched eyebrow told me I had failed to remain impassive. With an encouraging smile, she then handed me the pen and gestured for me to write. I knew how to hold it, but I couldn't think of a thing to say or a word to express myself.

When my hand started trembling, the psychiatrist removed the pen from my fingers and wrote a question. "Why did you run away?"

Because I was afraid of her and what she might discover, my mind screamed.

"Was it to go see the woman in the rest home?" the next question read.

My head shook, but I then nodded hoping to throw her off track. My tactics, however, didn't appear to work because she observed me with her serious smile.

"Did you know she was unable to speak coherently after her stroke?"

That wasn't true! Espérance had kept all her mental faculties. I didn't want to hear those lies so I stood up to leave but her hand touched my arm and guided me back to my chair.

"You know I want to help you?" she wrote.

A blush spread across Neïla's face, I could feel it, and I regretted not being able to trust the woman. I was sure she had good intentions.

"You didn't take your medicine. It's important, you know?"

She thought I was crazy and that if I didn't take those little pills, I'd lose all contact with reality. I refused to accept her condescension and turned to face the window. The psychiatrist's breathing continued rhythmically behind me until I turned back around to face another note.

"What are you afraid of?"

Nothing! Josh is dead but he should have saved Neïla from drowning, not stolen her life. I had failed, that's all. Spasms of guilt shot through me and Neïla headed for the door. I was going back to the canal. Her bare feet slapped against the linoleum floor as I ran for the exit. 4883 was the code, I was sure, but the sliding doors remained closed.

Hands grabbed me from behind and Neïla screamed. Her words were incomprehensible, but she fought until the nurse gave me a shot. My chest relaxed. Geometric patterns played across my vision. Then I was asleep and Neïla was swimming across the zigzags of a maze, trying to drag me to the other side, but I was too heavy so she disappeared into a spiral leaving me alone without any way out. I began to panic—if I didn't get free, I would drown—and took off running but only turned in circles. When I cried for help, it was like screaming in water and I was going to be lost in this emptiness if—

I rolled over to face Mother's unnervingly detached expression and sat up wishing I could get away from her horrible scrutiny. Mother just went back to her sewing. It seemed like she could sit there for hours without looking at me while her needle went in and out. She was making a jilbab, I gathered, and from time to time she bit off the thread, shook out the fabric, before she began again.

The nurse arrived with a tray of food an hour later but I pushed it away. Mother then looked back in my direction, dropped her sewing and put the fork in my hand. It seemed I didn't have a choice so I nibbled at the spaghetti and ate the salad.

They would never let me out of here—I would be sent to a mental institution, or back to the apartment—and I screamed before I sent the plate flying across the room. Then Mother slapped me. I stared at her, ready to fight, but her eyes were like those of Othmane so I collapsed onto the bed.

Was it Josh or Neïla who was being a crybaby? The nurse stroked my hair, gave me a Kleenex, pointed to the little pill on the tray and waited for me to swallow it. Mother kept her eyes on me until the lights dimmed.

* * *

The psychiatrist's voice was calm and steady. Although she had preferred to speak to Mother in the hall I could hear enough to know that there was a difference of opinion. Then a tap on the door made me jump. Hadja peered in and said something that I took to be friendly. Mother's voice rose in the hall and Hadja hurried into the room closing the door behind her.

I noticed that Hadja's smile trembled while she opened a tote bag, took out a jilbab and held it out for me to put on. The buzz from the drugs made my movements slow and my head spun when I sat up. Mother entered and strode over to pull me to my feet while I stared at the jilbab. Enough was enough! I pushed it away.

The slap took a second to register before pain pierced the numbness from the drugs. Mother's hand had grabbed my arm and was shaking me while she raised her hand again. I sank down on the bed and let them dress me. What difference did it make?

People turned their heads as Mother pushed me out into the drizzle and past the smokers. I would never get used to the hostility, but Hadja seemed pleased by the onlookers' reactions. I pulled the veil over my face with my gloved hand, not wanting anybody to see Neïla cry.

Hadja drove and spoke to Mother in a hushed voice. It was clear they were talking about me, but they could have spoken as loudly as they wanted and I wouldn't have understood a word. Their backward glances only made me feel more like a freak.

Hadja turned the car down the entrance ramp onto the *périférique* as cars zigzagged around us, as the traffic came to a stop, nausea crept up my throat. The woman in the car next to us made a face and turned to the man beside her who shot me a sarcastic sneer. I wondered if they had noticed Neïla was crying.

We exited at Bagnolet near the unfinished mosque. On the main street people milled about the kebab sandwich shops and glanced disinterestedly at our car. This was where I would have to live now and there was no way back. I was trapped in the maze.

The boys in front of the apartment came to greet us, but I turned my head wishing they would go away. The only one that caught my attention was the boy with the amber eyes who gave me a timid, joyless smile. He then turned away to speak with a friend and Hadja gave me a wink. Did she think I might want one of those prison guards touching me? Neïla's head shook in denial.

Hadja continued to smirk while she led me up the graffiti-tagged stairs and I waited behind her until she opened the door. Mustapha then rushed up to greet me with a big hug and led me into the living room where I zonked out on a pillow. Even though I was surprised he wasn't at school, I couldn't ask him why so he sat and watched me until my eyes closed.

When I awoke, Mustapha had disappeared and Mother was with Hadja cooking dinner. I lifted myself, trudged to Neïla's room and observed it from the door because for once, Djahida clothes weren't strewn all over. Out of curiosity, I went to open the closet door. It was half-empty.

"*Elle est partie* (She's left)," I heard Mustapha say behind me, as I looked in her dresser drawer. I had understood and turned my head in surprise. Then I noticed Mustapha was crying so I knelt down to hold him, but he pushed me away and ran to his room.

Hadja appeared at the door and made some noises that sounded like running water while tears filled her eyes, too. Finally she tapped her right wrist to indicate that Djahida had really left and I collapsed onto the bed.

Something had gone wrong. Was it my fault? Hadja rocked me in her arms and made humming sounds until she stopped crying. When I looked at her, she said something, and then repeated it, while her dark eyes stared pleadingly into mine. I shook my head and took out a paper and pen.

"Djahida has gone off to wage the jihad,"[1] Hadja wrote.

I stared at the paper wishing I didn't know how to read. Djahida was only a child! Neïla's head began shaking and a word escaped, *"Comment* (How)?"

Hadja continued to stare me in the eyes but if she knew, she wasn't going to tell. How could a fifteen-year-old girl find the money to go off to the Middle East? Had Othmane prepared this? Mother then called us for dinner and Hadja held me as if I needed to be led to the table.

Dinner was strange without Djahida and nobody seemed to have anything to say. I wished I could ask why Othmane wasn't there, but I doubted I would have received an answer. After the plates had been removed, Mother laid some pills in front of me and waited for me to take them before I was allowed to stand up.

Mustapha came to me with his English lessons while I sat in the living room, but even if I understood the sentences, I was unable to pronounce them. He looked at me quizzically with sad eyes so we ended up watching an American crime series that I couldn't follow. Before going to bed, I glanced at Neïla's forlorn image in the mirror and saw she had tears in her eyes.

* * *

Othmane had come home during the night and now sat on the other side of the breakfast table watching me with his reptilian eyes. Mother was working the morning shift while Mustapha was at school, so I was left alone with a dangerous criminal. When I got up to go to Neïla's room, Othmane followed and I spun around him to push him back out. Although one of his eyebrows lifted, he made no argument as I shut the door in his face. My nerves then gave out and I fell to the floor.

This was my new life. I was to be shut up and held in captivity. If Neïla had been ugly, would they have left me alone? I turned to gaze at the mirror but the image was swimming like in a dream while Neïla's eyes judged me severely. I was the same loser that I had always been and she knew it. Maybe Othmane really should beat and maim me.

I marched to the boys' room and Neïla's hand punched the door open before I stormed in. Othmane was standing beside the closet with his shirt off while his muscles rippled down through his stomach and his wiry biceps bulged. My eye caught what he was holding in his hand—a gray sweatshirt with a hood. I then noticed the stains that looked like blood on the sleeves and realized he was the one who had killed Josh and attacked Kim.

I stood petrified for only a second. Neïla then rushed at him wanting to scratch out his eyes but before I could get in even one blow, he had spun me around in a bear hug. I struggled, trying to bite his arms, until I was no longer able to stand and he let me collapse onto the floor. He then sat down in front of me and reached out to stroke my cheek. I slapped it away. With a growl, he grabbed the other arm, pulled me up and dragged me into Neïla's room before slamming the door.

The adrenaline subsided leaving my legs trembling so badly I had to crawl. My breathing came in short bursts making my head turn and little black dots appear in front of my eyes. I had to do something even if I was a useless idiot.

The computer came into focus and I realized it was my only connection with the outside so I switched it on. Djahida's black Islamic flag appeared, but I didn't have the time to change it. I had to get onto Neïla's page to warn somebody.

I knew her password although I couldn't remember how to write it. I sat staring at the keys and trembling until I decided to open document after document to find the right symbols and painstakingly paste each into the box before I clicked "enter."

Neïla's face came up followed by events and likes that were from another existence. I kept my eyes away from Quincy's picture and the numerous messages he had sent while I searched for Kiko. His smile sickened me, but he was the only one who could help so I clicked on his icon.

I was afraid that Othmane would burst in at any moment to beat me senseless and it seemed to take forever to paste the right words in the message box. When *"Othmane has the gray sweatshirt in his room"*[2] was finally written in the little rectangle, I hit "enter" and sat petrified staring at the screen.

"Is he there?"[3] came up a few minutes later.

I found the letters to type, "yes."

"We're coming," appeared in the rectangle. *"Hide."*[4]

1 "Djahida est partie faire le jihad."

2 "Othmane a le sweat gris dans sa chambre."

3 "Est-il là?"

4 "On arrive. Cache-toi."

Chapter 31

I heard the pounding, then the yelling. My heart raced uncontrollably after the loud cracking smash and I huddled back farther into the clothing when heavy feet pounded in and all about. Shouts echoed like mortar shells and then there was a moment of silence.

The closet door banged open. Cold metal touched my forehead. Unintelligible words like a dog's angry barks made me open my eyes onto a masked face with paranoid eyes. The man barked again and I was taken by my hair, pulled out of the closet and pushed onto the tile floor. A gun barrel stayed against my ear while my hands were cuffed behind my back.

Two masked policemen carried me into the living room by my shoulders while my legs pedaled between them and Othmane stared at me placidly from the floor where he was kneeling. Why wasn't he angry? After I was thrown onto the couch, I turned my head toward the wall not wanting to look at him.

A hand touched my shoulder and I looked up into Kiko's smug face. He murmured some marmalade sounds and pointed to the plastic bag with the sweatshirt inside. I looked away. I didn't want to see him. I hated myself. I doubted Neïla would have ever ratted on her brother.

Kiko grumbled something to a uniformed policewoman who sneered as she looked me up and down. She then disappeared into Neïla's bedroom and a minute later came back with one of Djahida's coats. A uniformed policeman jerked me up and she put it around my shoulders. A hand then slapped against my back and pushed me out the front door. It had been broken off the hinges.

The stairwell was empty and the policewoman's boots squeaked against the tile floor as she pulled me along next to her. My head began spinning and I would have fallen if hands hadn't caught me. They clamped roughly onto my arms and carried me down the flights of stairs.

It wasn't a surprise that our local dealer had abandoned the entranceway. The door was pulled open and wind blew Neïla's hair across my face catching a strand in my mouth. I was unable to brush it aside with my hands cuffed together and it felt as if I were going to swallow it. A crowd was kept at a distance and they were pointing and screaming at me as I was dragged to the parking lot. I almost choked.

The policewoman held my head and I was pushed into a car between her and a young policeman. Kiko got into the driver's seat, revved the motor and the car did a U-turn making me fall sideways against the young man. He gave a laughing comment as I tried to struggle away and laughed even more when Kiko turned to say something and I averted my eyes.

The car pulled over at a bus stop and Kiko said something to the policeman who unlocked my handcuffs. I pulled the hair from my mouth and put my seatbelt on without taking my eye off of Kiko. He gave me his self-satisfied smile before screeching back into traffic.

The car pulled up at 36 Quai des Orfèvres and the young policeman assisted me out with his hand on my head before he escorted me into the building. I was practically carried up to the third floor where I was led into an office and made to sit down.

An older man huffed in, shut the door and grumped a few sounds while he stared me in the eyes. I knew he had asked a question but my mouth only flapped when I attempted to speak. He grumped louder but I felt humiliated by my aphasia and was unable to look up at him. Kiko then sat on the side of the desk, observed me and made more sounds. I shook my head until the older man slammed his hand onto the table.

Kiko shrugged and escorted me to a room that reminded me of an animal cage. The door clanged shut. There were no cushions so I curled up on a hard bench and shut my eyes. Kiko came back a minute later with a pillow, a blanket and a cup of bitter coffee. He smiled crookedly as if he were regretful. I couldn't believe he was ever sorry for his actions so I hissed at him. He just laughed and left me alone in the cell.

* * *

I sat counting dried drips of paint left on the wall when the room had last seen a paintbrush. My eyes grew heavy and I laid back wishing they would turn up the heat. I couldn't stop shivering. Why hold me in jail when I had given Othmane over?

The sound of keys made me turn my head and a uniformed policeman marched up to clank the door open. His eyes followed me as I had stood up and exited the cell, but then his hand clamped onto my arm and pulled me down the hall to an office.

Mother, her cheek twitching, sat facing the older policeman. The policeman said something and she grunted without so much as a glance in my direction. When she stood up and walked to the door, the policeman indicated I should follow. As soon as Mother saw me step out of the office, she took to her heels and I had to trot to catch up.

I stayed a pace behind until we exited the building and her menacing eyes met mine. She pulled a scarf from her bag, waited for me to hide my hair and with a snort headed off again. She didn't glance back at me again until we reached the metro when she handed me a ticket.

The ride was tedious with Mother glaring everywhere but at me. A gypsy got on and played a tune for thirty seconds before his daughter came around with a hat asking for money. When she reached me, she cocked her head and took a step back. The train then stopped and the girl hurried to exit with her father.

As we crossed the parking lot, some of the boys said hello but the majority ignored us. Mother's scowls must have frightened them. I noticed that the boy with yellowish-brown eyes gave me a wan smile and I had an urge to smile back, but he looked away when Mother spied him.

Our building's drug dealer stepped aside as Mother stormed by. I kept my eyes on her slippers squishing against the stairs' tile floor while we climbed the four stories and walked down the hall. She threw the broken apartment door aside, turned to look at me and the slap that followed should never have taken me off guard. The second one hurt even more. I wanted to say something, to justify my actions, but no words came. That was probably just as well.

I saw the third blow coming and winced. Her eyes stayed on me until I looked away and she pounded off to her room. When I looked up, I saw Mustapha watching me with a tear in his eye. I couldn't bear it so I hurried to Neïla's room.

My breaths came in short gasps and I collapsed into the chair. When I leaned forward onto the desk, my hand brushed the mouse and the computer hummed. I hated the thing and was about to turn it off when I noticed that my dialogue with Kiko was displayed on the screen. How could I have been so stupid? I hadn't closed the page and Mother had surely seen it and discovered I called the police on Othmane.

When my anger subsided enough for me to breathe, I looked at the other messages that she could have read. At the top was the string with Quincy and I got embarrassed that she might have read how I felt about him—or rather how I had felt—did I ever want to talk to him again? Since I had discovered him with his blonde, he had written a dozen times, and I couldn't resist seeing if he were sorry.

I clicked on his latest message, a reply to one of mine, and fear shot through my chest—"Very important. Must meet you at 19 o'clock outside of Chez Maurice next to the Quai du Canal de l'Ourque, in Pantin. Big kisses, Neïla."—I hadn't written that!

"I'll be there," Quincy had written in the bubble underneath.

Chez Maurice was where Josh had been killed and I felt like

screaming but could only cry like a sick cat. Would it now be Quincy? I wished I couldn't care what happened to that two-timer—let him walk into danger!—but my heart throbbed. Why hadn't he left France like he said he would? I looked at the clock and realized I only had one hour before he'd be there.

My hands trembled too much to even think about writing a reply, so I grabbed my hijab and I stepped into the hall. Mother was still in the shower but Mustapha looked up as I crossed the living room. I shushed him. The water stopped running, Mustapha pointed to the door and I hurried to put Neïla's shoes on. The bathroom door creaked open. I slipped on my coat and then tried to pull the door aside as gently as possible. It grated. Panic gripped me. Neïla ran.

The dealer and his client both looked up and called after me as I darted past. I was afraid that the boys outside would want to drag me back but luckily the lookout at the corner only watched me sprint by. After several blocks I slowed to a walk, shivering and out of breath, forcing Neïla to put one foot in front of the other. Both Josh and Neïla knew the way to Chez Maurice.

My sneakers continued to slap on the pavement and I began to breathe more easily as the neighborhood changed. I was no longer in the public housing projects with their imposed *charia* but I still avoided eye contact.

A shoulder knocked me aside. How could I have missed the tall boy on the sidewalk? I tried to apologize, shook my head and a chortle behind me made me spin around. Two other boys, both wearing kippahs, were staring at me with a smirk. I was back among Jews and let out a sigh of relief but their faces screwed up into frowns. A hand then grabbed my hijab from behind and ripped it off my head. I turned and was pushed down. Neïla curled into a ball expecting blows and kicks. They simply left me lying there.

I lay on the wet pavement until an elderly man put his hand on my shoulder. His eyes were tender and I wished he would hold me but instead I leaped to my feet and ran until my legs nearly gave out. I then began walking, shuffling, out of sight. I was shivering again.

Sudden laughter made me jump into the shadows. It was a couple walking past me arm in arm. As the boy gave the pretty young girl a kiss, I stepped out of the doorway to jealously watch them hold each other. Why was I jealous?

A white utility van rumbled toward me and I stood staring into the lights like a rabbit until I jumped between the parked cars at the last second. It slowed, then accelerated past making me feel exposed and fragile. Should I turn back and accept that marriage Mother had planned for me? Go out covered with a jilbab so that no one would ever see me again?

Neïla decided otherwise, and I kept walking until the canal appeared through the drizzle with lights reflecting and shimmering off its dark surface. It had a deceptively peaceful appearance that made me wish to sink into it and let it embrace me. What other choice did I have?

The white van drove by again, but this time I jumped into a doorway. There weren't many people about, just that white van, and a jogger who ambled by without noticing me. I stepped back out and hurried along the canal in the direction of the bistro.

The main entrance to Chez Maurice was above at street level, so people only strolled down here when the weather was nice. At this lower level, a bridge ran over the canal and the bay windows made looking at the bar like watching a theater. The waiter hadn't changed and neither had the owner who stayed posted behind the cash register. I saw no sign of Quincy.

I slipped under the bridge, pulled back into the shadows and waited. The white van passed again but no one could see me. The smell of stale urine, however, made me gag. How could people be so filthy? I stared at Neïla's dirty hands in the dark. Would this be her future? I too was indigent.

A man appeared walking up the canal and it took me less than a second to recognize Quincy's stride. I stepped out, Quincy's head turned, and I wondered whether he would come to me or leave me there in the dark. I felt like hiding again. His stride slowed and he stopped in front of me while my head turned away, but then I sobbed against his chest.

A motor rumbled over the soft sounds of the drizzle and I looked up to see that the van had stopped near us. A sense of danger choked me and I grabbed Quincy's hand pulling him toward the bridge. He resisted. I tried to scream but nothing would come out. Then Beatbox stepped out of the white van and shot me his crooked smile.

I ran for the bridge but my legs wobbled and I tripped. Quincy lifted me. I wanted him to save himself, not me; I was already dead. I screamed, tried to push him away but he held me tight as we began to jog for the underpass.

The smell of urine wafted out and Quincy stopped. I hadn't seen the figure in front of us or the shadow of the handgun. Quincy took me by the shoulders and held me firmly behind him but I knew it made no difference because I heard Beatbox's syncopated mouth noises.

Then a voice made me shiver. *"So, sly bunny, it's not good to go out without your hijab."*[1]

1 "Alors, pinpin futé, c'est pas bien de sortir sans hijab."

Chapter 32

"Just like the good old days."[1]

I was able to understand Mokhtar and would have answered with an insult if Beatbox's hand hadn't been clamped over my mouth. When I tried to yell, only whining slipped between his fingers. With a laugh, Mokhtar whistled a tune Mother often hummed and began tying Quincy's hands behind his back before he duct-taped his mouth.

Mokhtar turned to me and hissed, *"Slowly, dumb bunny,"*[2] then rounded a blow to Quincy's stomach. Quincy's eyes opened wide while his mouth tugged helplessly against the tape that covered it. It looked as though he were going to choke so I began squirming and screaming, but a blow to my stomach made black dots swirl behind my eyelids and Neïla's body go limp.

A slap jolted me back to consciousness and Mokhtar's snarling leer was inches from my face—he hadn't brushed his teeth—and his hand was rubbing through Neïla's hair. The gesture felt dirty. I felt dirty.

"You're a pretty girl. That could have brought us a lot more plump pigeons to pluck."[3]

He gave my hair a tug while Beatbox syncopated in my ear. I tried to shake my head, to deny that Neïla had ever so much as spoken to that monster, but Beatbox's arms were too powerful for me to move.

"Okay, you can't remember anything, but that was our deal." Mokhtar turned to pick up his handgun. *"Too bad you refused to trap that Jew and I had to kill him. I had even promised to get rid of that policeman for you. You shouldn't have spent so much time pouring over the Jew's Facebook account, or Beatbox shouldn't have given you his password, it made you go all soft on that jerk."*[4]

Beatbox gave a bass beat chuckle. *"Hey, I'm an ace computer hack. I knew everything about you and your messages to that cop. Did you really think I couldn't get to you?"*[5]

Mokhtar gave an exaggerated bow and turned back to Quincy who was on his knees. There was a click and Mokhtar pointed his gun at Quincy's head. My eyes closed while images of Quincy's brains spraying out sent spasms down my back.

"Bang" Beatbox shouted in my ear and Neïla's body went limp. He then broke into his syncopated laugh while Quincy shook convulsively. Mokhtar looked at his companion with feigned anger that quickly turned into a large smile. While Beatbox's syncopations were becoming joyous, and Mokhtar's eyes more and more compassionless, I could see that neither one of them would have any qualms about killing us.

"All this is your fault." Mokhtar uttered the words, while he examined his pistol. *"You went to talk to that policeman! I know you wanted to tell him everything. If you hadn't lost your memory, I would have taken care of you sooner."*[6]

Neïla had been supposed to lure Josh into a trap! My head was shaking, or was that Neïla shaking my head? I felt horrible and tried to scream again but received a punch to the . . . everything spun black. Beatbox's hand was sliding down my abdomen toward Neïla's crotch. Quincy grunted angrily while Mokhtar played with the gun.

"That's right, you dress like a whore and you get treated like one," Mokhtar tut-tutted while he watched Beatbox stroke Neïla's . . . no, *my* body! *"You're not wearing your hijab; it's all your fault."*[7]

I looked to Quincy wishing he didn't have to see this, but his eyes seemed to say that he understood I was a criminal. He probably thought that I had entrapped him as well. I was trembling too badly to fight back, to push away Beatbox's hand that was now fondling my breast, and I would have jumped back into the dark canal if that had been possible.

Mokhtar stepped over and grabbed my chin. *"We couldn't understand your interest in that Jew. I didn't think you liked people of their dirty race."*[8]

I made an attempt at cursing but Mokhtar slapped duct tape over my mouth and stood back while Beatbox tied my arms behind my back. Mokhtar then stepped out from under the bridge and indicated that all was clear before I was dragged like a ragdoll to the van and thrown into the back. The door slammed shut. I wished I were dead.

The door opened again and Quincy was thrown in beside me. He had been beaten some more and blood poured from his scalp onto his face. The motor rumbled to a start, the van began moving and I scooted over next to Quincy, but his muscles tensed so I moved back away.

We were bounced and shaken as the van bumped over every pothole on the road. The only moments of relief were the seconds spent idling at stoplights. I tried not to touch Quincy but was sent skidding over next to him at every turn and longed to cuddle up against his warmth. I had no right to even think about it. This really was my fault.

The van stopped again and it sounded like a large door was opened. I braced myself for an acceleration but the van moved slowly forward and lights came on outside allowing me to catch a glimpse of Quincy's face. He was staring at the side of the van. I started to roll over next to him but Beatbox opened the back door, grabbed me, threw me over his shoulder and tossed me down among cartons of cabbages. The look of evil joy on his face sickened me.

A moment later, Quincy was heaved to the floor facing me and Mokhtar slapped his hands together as if he had just finished a job well done. "Mr. Quincy, we must ask you a favor," Mokhtar announced with a heavy French accent and a businesslike smile. *"You didn't know I could speak English,"*[9] he said, turning to me with a wink while Beatbox stepped over and ripped the tape off Quincy's mouth. Mokhtar's eyes then became slits and he hissed to Quincy, "We ask you for the code number of your credit card."

Quincy didn't flinch and stared at Mokhtar with what looked

like a practiced poker face. "And you'll kill me if I don't give them to you," he stated flatly.

The words were intelligible yet so horrible I wished that I had remained a mute idiot and hadn't been able to understand them. Mokhtar, however, seemed to enjoy Quincy's statement and gave him his congenial chuckle. "Oh, we will possibly do that." His face became monstrously expressionless before he continued. "But do you want that I kill her, too?"

Quincy's eyes widened and he must have been wondering whether Mokhtar was bluffing or not. Then, squinting in my direction, he said, "She worked with you though, didn't she?"

"Oh, so you understand some of our French conversation? But you not understand that she wished help the police. She wanted that I be arrested before her accident." He looked at me with a snake-like expression. "If accident you wish to call it." He waved a dismissive hand in the air.

I tried to yell curses at Mokhtar until the tape over my mouth made me heave for air through my nose.

"You know you're not as sly as you think, bunny," Mokhtar said, with a chuckle. *"We both had gray sweatshirts. I put Beatbox's in Othmane's closet to test you. We wanted to see if you would sell out your family again."*[10]

"What do you mean?" Quincy interrupted. "Test her with a sweatshirt?"

Mokhtar's eyes drifted toward Beatbox who was in the shadows, grinning. "You see, Romain, or Beatbox like Neïla named him, he has a little *faiblesse*. He likes to hurt girls." Mokhtar picked up his handgun and examined it before turning his eyes toward me. "Othmane is an idiot but we could not allow that video. How you say in English, 'family pride'? I no need even pay Romain," Mokhtar chuckled. "He loved hurting your friend and he made certain she sees the sweatshirt."

The blood rushed out of my head leaving me dizzy. I dared not glance at Quincy because it had truly been my fault that Kim was attacked. I glared over at Beatbox with all the rage that was building in my chest, but he leered at me and made a self-satisfied bass beat.

"Don't encourage him, little sister, he loves that,"[11] Mokhtar said amiably, before he turned back to Quincy and shook his head. "You see, he always dreams to hurt Neïla. I protect her a little, she is my sister, but I have not the code . . ." His hideous smile explained the consequences.

Quincy examined me with his poker face while Mokhtar rifled through his wallet. I wanted him to refuse and just let me die. but Neïla's body had begun trembling uncontrollably.

"Alright," Quincy sighed. "Three-five-six-eight."

"Ah, an intelligent boy," Mokhtar smirked while he noted the pin number on a Post-it. "But you have three cards, *n'est-ce pas*?"

"You take that one," Quincy spat. "It's a black card. You won't reach the spending limit."

This time I stared at Quincy; Josh was not from a poor family but my parents would never have given me a black card. Mokhtar, however, didn't seem the least surprised and handed the card to Beatbox who disappeared behind the boxes of vegetables. A door slammed a few seconds later.

1 "C'est comme dans le bon vieux temps."

2 "Doucement Pinpin tébé."

3 "T'es jolie fille. Ca aurait pu nous ramener plus de pigeons dodus à plumer."

4 "D'accord, tu te rappelles de rien, mais c'était notre marché. Dommage que tu aies refusé de piéger ce juif et que j'ai dû le tuer. J'avais même promis de te débarrasser de ce policier. Tu n'aurais jamais dû passer autant de temps sur la page FB de ce juif, ou bien Beatbox n'aurait jamais dû te donner son mot de passe, ça t'a donné un faible pour ce con."

5 "Eh ouais, je suis un as du piratage. Je savais tout de tes échanges avec le flic. Tu pensais vraiment que je ne pouvais

pas te coincer?"

6 "Tout ça, c'est de ta faute. Tu es allée discuter avec ce policier! Je sais que tu voulais tout lui dire. Tu as de la chance d'avoir perdu la mémoire ou je me serais occupé de toi avant."

7 "Et oui, tu t'habilles comme une pute, on te traite comme une pute. Tu portes pas ton hijab, c'est de ta faute."

8 "On ne comprenait pas ton intérêt pour ce juif. Je ne croyais pas que tu aimais les gens de leur sale race."

9 "Tu ne savais pas que je parlais anglais."

10 "Tu sais tu n'es pas aussi futée que tu crois, Pinpin. Nous avions tous les deux des sweats gris. Le sweat de Beatbox, Je l'ai mis dans la penderie d'Othmane pour te tester. On voulait savoir si tu trahirais toujours ta famille."

11 "Ne l'encourage pas, petite sœur. Il adore ça."

Chapter 33

Mokhtar went over to a stack of cartons of broccoli, removed the first eight or nine and pulled out a large assault rifle from underneath. "You want buy it?" he laughed. "I have many arms to sell. And my sister thinks I have just salads." He pointed it at Quincy who did not look away. "She is a rabbit, but she think she is sly like a cat. You not afraid?"

"Why ever should I be?" Quincy replied flatly.

Mokhtar chuckled and pulled the trigger.

Quincy flinched and then let out a long breath. Mokhtar observed him for a few seconds before he continued speaking in a matter-of-fact tone. "I know that is not good for the *méchanisme* but I have ten of Kalashnikov. I have pistols and grenades, too. Everything a good *jihadist* want." He then turned to me. *"It's our brother who helped me get started in the business. He's convinced I'm doing it in the name of Allah."*[1]

Mokhtar paused as if he were expecting me to answer and then screwed his finger against his temple. *"I think he's had the jitters ever since he came back from the jihad. He was supposed to be the one running this organization but he gave it to me. It's a good deal. I put aside my cut and send them a few recruits for their war."*[2]

His lip then curled in disgust as he looked at Quincy. "Maybe I even organize a terrorist attack; kill the French who invaded Algeria." He looked down the rifle's sights. "Or maybe that synagogue you visited." His eyes were on me again.

"So my money will go to terrorism?" Quincy asked bitterly, while Mokhtar loaded bullets into the cartridge.

This elicited a huge guffaw. "Some, yes, but one must look after one's necessities." He turned to me. *"And you thought I earned my money working at the market for Romain's vegetable of a father!"* Mokhtar huffed after the last statement, pushed the loaded cartridge into the rifle and spat onto the floor. He then gave me a large, brotherly smile. "*Where do you think Djahida got the money to go to the Middle East?*"[3]

I wished I could scream at him that he had no right to send a child into a war zone, but I had a gag over my mouth and he seemed to enjoy my anger.

"You could at least take the tape off her mouth," Quincy suggested loudly.

Mokhtar turned to him. "But she can't speak. Not since she had that accident *stupide* at the pool."

Quincy looked at me surprised. "You had another accident and you didn't tell me."

"Idiot, she can't speak or write. The doctor say she can't understand even."

Quincy looked into my eyes. "Can you understand me now?" His voice cracked at the end of his question.

I nodded. He seemed to be relieved but Mokhtar's biting laugh made his cheek twitch. "Reason more for not remove the tape," Mokhtar laughed snidely. "We don't want that a woman breaks our ears with her chatting." He made an exaggerated wink in Quincy's direction.

Quincy, however, looked profoundly remorseful and I couldn't help feeling that he should be. "What will you do with her when you're done with me?" He asked, in a near whisper.

Mokhtar looked up from his gun and reflected on the question. "Mama want that she return to Algeria and after maybe to Libya. The Algerian police is not easy but a marriage is arranged. I prefer send her to rejoin her sister and be married and have children in the caliphate. I must see what is most . . ." He waved his hands irritated, "How say you *pratique*?"

"Practical is the word," Quincy responded dryly.

Mokhtar gave him a large smile. "Yes, practical. You understand, the Middle East is not practical. Djahida was motivated but our Neïla will not wish to go. She likes fleeing. It is easier drive a car to Marseille and go in a boat. *Bien sûr*, she is locked in . . . what is the word for *coffre*?"

Quincy looked him straight in the eye which seemed to amuse Mokhtar. "The trunk of the car," Quincy answered. "You would do that to your own sister?" he added, with a snort.

"Oh, she is sister in blood but she is my true sister no more. I make certain our blood continues and her children be good Muslims. That is my job. That is all."

With a shrug Mokhtar then set his rifle against a stack of boxed squash and began to load cartons of vegetables into the back of the van. Quincy looked at me with the first signs of desperation; his head shook and I could see he was having trouble holding back his anger or his tears.

Hatred boiled in me and I started pulling at the cords that held my hands till they cut into my flesh. That monster wouldn't harm Quincy! Neither the pain nor the lack of air would stop me. I would prefer to die here and now rather than let him decide what Neïla did with her life.

The harder it was to breathe, the more I struggled. I didn't care that my chest sucked so hard for air that dots, spinning into blackness, covered my vision. Suddenly they coalesced into images and I was in a small apartment with children that I didn't want, clothing I hated and an ugly man who gave me a slap.

The blackness spiraled and the dots turned into mist through which both Espérance and Neïla approached me. The old lady shushed me with her finger to her mouth and pointed to a stack of boxed mangos. Neïla's eyes widened with fear but Espérance tut-tutted, nodded to me calmly and mouthed, "There is no other way."

A slap made the scene come back into focus. It was Mokhtar. He had pulled the tape from my mouth and was cursing me and everything else. I would have answered but Quincy had already begun yelling insults in English. Mokhtar let go of me with a sneer, stepped over to Quincy and kicked him in the stomach. He then laughed and gave him a blow to the head. Quincy spasmed.

Neïla—or was it me?—let out a high-pitched scream while I pulled frantically at the rope. I wanted to jump on Mokhtar and hurt him just as badly. The cord tore into my wrist as my left hand slipped out to my thumb. I bit back on the pain and ripped my hand out completely.

His back to me, Mokhtar didn't see me move. I hopped over to the mango boxes with my feet trussed together, fell onto them, found what Espérance wanted me to find—a crate of grenades—and scrambled to my feet with a grenade held high.

Mokhtar could have rushed me, he was standing just ten paces away, but instead he laughed as if it were a joke. My finger then slid through the pin like I had seen in movies and Mokhtar ingratiated me with his most charming smile. "*You aren't going to—*"[4] I pulled the pin out. His smile faltered and his hands clinched into fists while he took an angry step in my direction.

"You stop where you are, pork." Whether that had been Neïla or Josh screaming, the insult infuriated him and he took another step. "I'd rather die than have you dirty me, step back," I shrieked. The lever's spring was pushing against my grip telling me to let it go.

He stopped inching forward. "*Come now, sly bunny, you're not going to blow us all up, not with your sweetheart here.*"[5] He put back on his horrible smile.

Hatred for him flared up into my nostrils. "He'll be dead anyway. You were the one who killed Jo . . . the Jewish boy." My head began spinning at the realization I was the person shrieking. "Did you try to kill N . . . me too?"

"*Hey, I wasn't there when you fell into the water. It was Beatbox who—*"[6]

A door slammed. Mokhtar lunged. I stiffened. The grenade dropped. I looked down at it between the boxes of mangoes, over at Quincy who was rolling his way out of danger and back up at Mokhtar who was rushing to retrieve it.

I refused to let him defuse the grenade. If he did, no one

would stop him, so I grabbed his arm and began biting, clawing, until his hand connected with my jaw and I found myself thrown across the floor. Then, when my vision cleared, he was diving away so I rolled into a ball and—the searing pain, pounding against my back and through my guts, let me know I was dead even before the wind floated me in a spiral above the fuzzy surroundings. I needed no help this time to step out, look around and find Quincy lying stunned, gasping for breath, among the splinters and purėed mangoes. I longed to rush to him and hold him but my body—Neïla's body—lay crumpled on the blood-covered cement floor.

This was what I had wanted, wasn't it? Now Mother would not be able to do with me as she pleased. Then I remembered Mokhtar, and that he would kill Quincy, so in a panic I searched the scene until I spotted another spiral lifting Mokhtar's ghostly presence.

At least I had taken that bastard with me! I could see he was dead because his spirit was leaving and his body lay covered in blood. But why did he look so calm? Would he get away with his crimes? Nauseating hatred made me want to inflict suffering on him but something deep in my soul told me to wait, his punishment would come.

Then the spiral changed directions and began pulling Mokhtar back to his body while his legs jerked. If I didn't move, he was going to survive, and there was no way I would give him another chance to kill Quincy. With the speed of a thought, I reappeared next to him and wrenched him out of the wind.

His eyes opened in surprise. "Pinpin?" he mouthed, although I shook my head. *"Who then?"*[7] he seemed to ask.

I would have said "Josh" if my hands hadn't been slender with long nails and my arms hairless? How could it be that I was still Neïla? Had my spirit changed or had I been her all along?

Mokhtar began to struggle and at first I had no more difficulty holding him in place than a veil in the breeze. As the wind picked up however, he became heavier and heavier. Then she appeared standing beside me, Neïla, with a smile as beautiful as an angel's. Mokhtar looked from her to me while confusion knitted his brow.

"I'm proud of you, my sister,"[8] Neïla mouthed and stroked my long black hair.

It was like looking into a mirror with my mouth stretched into a smile. I knew it was radiantly beautiful, because it was Neïla's, but this time it felt good and comfortable. "You are magnificent," I mouthed back.

"No, that is you,"[9] her lips articulated.

I was about to shake my head and say it was her life when my grip on Mokhtar's arm began slipping and the wind pulled at me like the tide. I tried to call to her for help, for Neïla to hurry back to her body, but with a last smile she caressed my cheek, shook her head and jumped into the spiral going down into Mokhtar's body.

My hold on Mokhtar slipped and I yelled in the silence as Mokhtar rushed toward the spiral to pull Neïla's spirit out. My battle with the wind was lost; it had grown to hurricane force and was dragging me backward.

I had failed. Mokhtar would grab Neïla's spirit and send her back into the mist. I'd never be able to stop him. Then, just before his hand reached Neïla, Espérance coalesced and seized his arm. Tall and beautiful with her playful grin, she waved and mouthed, *"Adieu,"* as the wind ripped me away.

* * *

Numbness and pain held me to the ground. My back felt like it had been burned away and I heard a whispering behind the drone in my ears. It became louder and I heard my name, "Neïla." My name was Neïla. I opened my eyes and they fell into the blue of Quincy's.

"My God, Neïla! Are you alright?" He was lying next to me,

trussed and tied.

"Quincy . . ." I whispered. "Quincy, I'm so sorry. I almost killed you."

"No, you saved us. Now quickly, untie my hands before the other guy comes back."

I tried to move. Everything hurt, my head started spinning and when I tried to reach out, my left arm wouldn't move.

"Can you do it?" Quincy said urgently.

"I have but one hand," I answered above the buzzing in my ears.

"But–" His eyes widened with urgency and suddenly I was jerked backward in screaming pain.

"Hello sweetie. Looks like you've been up to some mischief," Beatbox laughed. *"Was it you who blew this place up?"* He then made syncopated beats to punctuate my shrieks. *"But this is an industrial zone so if you think the explosion will bring the police, you'll be disappointed"*—a knife clicked open—*"or not."*[10]

The blade touched my throat and my voice froze, my body trembled while I nearly passed out.

"Don't touch her," Quincy screamed.

Beatbox just laughed, a real laugh, and ignored him. *"Ever since you started avoiding me, I knew one day it would be just the two of us."*[11] He grabbed my chin and turned my head to face him while my eyes shut tight.

"Don't you want to look at me with your pretty eyes?" Beatbox said, in a cadenced chuckle. *"Too bad! Did your friend tell you what I did to her?"*[12]

"What the hell did you do to Kim?" Quincy bellowed.

Beatbox's boots stepped away and I heard a thud and a grunt. "I not answer if you not say 'please.' What did your mother teach you?" Quincy had curled into a ball and was struggling against the cords while Beatbox made happy mouth noises.

"You see, I'm an artist. I like cutting pretty things," Beatbox announced with a grin. *"Unfortunately, you escaped me the last*

time."[13]

I didn't need to ask what he was talking about so I tried to wriggle away but he caught me by my hair, ripped my blouse open and sliced my bra right between the breasts. The pain from the cut came a second later and it was worse than any of the injuries from the grenade.

"You know, I always wanted to make you into a piece of art. You're so beautiful that you have to be mine."[14] He made a few bass beats and sliced across my stomach. The hurt cut into me deeply. I was screaming. He began laughing and—

Beatbox was thrown back like he'd been kicked by a horse. The clap wasn't loud, it only registered after Beatbox sprawled to the floor, and I looked up to see Mokhtar shoot the assault rifle four or five more times into the body. The gun then dropped with thud and a shudder ran down his whole body.

Quincy's eyes were wide with anger and fright while he tried to wriggle away from Mokhtar who was approaching with a limp. I noticed my brother's eyes had a new intensity and there wasn't a trace of a smile on his lips. He grabbed Quincy by the shoulder and asked with urgency, *"Où est votre téléphone* (Where is your telephone)?"

"Please, help her. She's injured." Quincy pleaded.

Mokhtar only frowned and repeated, *"Où est votre téléphone?"*

"In my pocket here," Quincy stuttered after a hesitation.

"Désolé, en français, s'il vous plait (Sorry, in French, please)," Mokhtar replied with a hint of embarrassment.

Quincy looked at him as if it were a joke, and then repeated in a funny American accent, *"dans ma poche, là."*

Mokhtar bent down and began undoing Quincy hands. *"What's the code?"*[15] he asked in a soft voice, after Quincy had handed him his phone.

Quincy turned and looked at Mokhtar in amazement. "Four-five-seven-seven," he said in French while he rubbed his wrists.

"Thank you. Now you take care of her while I telephone."[16]

I must have blacked out. The next thing I remember was being cradled in Quincy's arms while he whispered things to me that I hardly understood. I wanted to answer but only managed to blink. The world disappeared for a second and my eyes were looking into Mokhtar's—only they weren't Mokhtar's—they were Neïla's. She had melded into his body and left him in the void.

"My little sister, they are going to heal you,"[17] Neïla murmured while sirens whined.

"They mustn't arrest you,"[18] I whispered.

Her stare was soft, I was not sure she had heard me, but then Neïla's hand touched my forehead. *"Don't worry about me,"* she said, as the doors crashed open. *"I'll only get what I deserve."*[19] Mokhtar then slumped onto the floor.

1 "C'était notre frère qui m'a aidé à me lancer dans les affaires. Il est convaincu que je fais ça au nom d'Allah."

2 "Je pense qu'il a la frousse depuis qu'il est revenu du jihad. Normalement, c'était lui qui devait mettre en place cette organisation mais Il me l'a laissée. C'est une bonne affaire. Je mets de côté mon petit bénéfice et je leur envoie quelques recrus pour leur guerre."

3 "Et tu pensais que je gagnais mon fric en travaillant au marché pour ce légume qui est le père de Romain! Où est-ce que tu penses que Djahida a trouvé le fric pour partir au Moyen Orient?"

4 "Tu ne vas pas..."

5 "Allons pinpin futé, tu ne vas pas nous faire sauter, pas avec ton chéri ici."

6 "Eh ho, j'étais pas là quand tu es tombée à l'eau. C'était Beatbox qui ..."

7 "Alors qui?"

8 "Je suis fière de toi, ma sœur."

9 "Non, c'est pour toi."

10 "Salut chérie. Il parait que tu as fait des bêtises. C'est toi qui

as tout fait sauter? Mais c'est une zone industrielle ici donc si tu penses que l'explosion fera venir la police, tu seras déçue. Ou pas."

11 "Depuis que tu m'évites, j'étais sûr que ça allait finir qu'avec nous deux."

12 "Tu ne veux pas me regarder avec tes jolis yeux? Dommage! Ton amie t'a dit ce que je lui ai fait?"

13 "Vous voyez, je suis un artiste. J'aime découper les jolies choses. Malheureusement, tu m'as échappé la dernière fois."

14 "Tu sais, j'ai toujours voulu faire de toi une œuvre d'art. Tu es si belle qu'Il faut que tu sois à moi."

15 "C'est quoi le code?"

16 "Merci, maintenant tu t'occupes d'elle pendant que je téléphone."

17 "Ma petite sœur, on va te soigner."

18 "Il ne faut pas qu'on t'arrête."

19 "T'occupe pas de moi. Je n'aurais que ce que je mérite."

Chapter 34

My long black hair whipped against my back and my Jilbab swathed my thin body as I stood facing the headwind. Why wasn't I wearing my hijab? I took a step forward and the wind turned into a swirling gray mist that literally lifted me up and set me down gently onto an oiled hardwood floor.

I pushed my long hair from in front of my eyes and took another step. Wouldn't Neïla's family want me to cover it and punish me if they caught me? I searched in vain for a veil and was about to panic when it came to me that I was dead and that they could no longer order me around. I was at last able to do as I wanted, so I danced.

The feeling of freedom was intoxicating while I did pirouettes and entrechats equal to the best ballerinas. Wanting to hear music, I began to sing the "Libiamo ne' lieti calici" from *La Traviata* in a high lyric soprano voice because I had no wish to hear Josh's dark baritone rumble up from my chest.

Then a hand came down hard on my shoulder and I was spun around to face Mokhtar, the real Mokhtar, and his hateful smile. I slipped away with a laugh—he couldn't kill me a second time, could he?—however his large hand grabbed me by my neck, squeezed and I realized that I wasn't dead, that I was just between the two realms. I tried struggling against his grip, but it was like an iron bar and while I squirmed and twisted, his laugh blasted in my ears. I was suffocating, fading, dying, while a spiral opened next to me and the squall doubled in force.

A force pushed me free into the haze and I turned around to see Othmane's hard stare. I was about to scream when his forehead wrinkled in compassion and I remembered that he had been innocent when I had sent him to jail. I attempted to ask for forgiveness but my mumbles were lost in the emptiness.

Mokhtar appeared next to him, his face contorted in anger,

and rushed for me but Othmane's arm reached out and caught his brother. The mist echoed with Mokhtar's rage while they grappled, fought, until I could see that Othmane was weakening. His melancholic eyes turned to me, and just before yielding, he shouted, *"I knew you were an angel. I forgive you. Now run!"*[1]

* * *

My body felt like it was burning and when I swallowed, I choked on a tube running down my throat. Somebody was speaking so I opened my eyes to a blurry white room with a black form hunched over me.

"How are you?" Hadja's voice whispered. I listened carefully wanting to make sure this wasn't a trick. *"Can you hear me?"*[2]

"Yes, I'm fine,"[3] I lied and gagged on the tube.

"I've called the nurse. She wanted to know when you woke up."[4]

I was back in the hospital. "Mokhtar? Quincy?" I asked. The question came out with a choke.

She stared at me quizzically for a moment. *"I don't know about your friend, but our brother's liver was badly hurt in the explosion."*[5] Her nose curled up as she spoke.

"Is Mokhtar dying?"[6] I asked in a voice that petered out.

"No, they say he'll make it." She raised an eyebrow at my sigh of relief. *"You're worried about him?"*[7]

I couldn't tell her that the Mokhtar in the hospital and the one in my dream weren't the same person. *"He's my brother,"*[8] I whispered to avoid the subject.

She studied me quizzically as if she had just discovered something unique. *"He'll spend his life in prison, you know?"*[9]

Tears welled up for Neïla's spirit who would pay for Mokhtar's crimes and I began to cough with the tube down my throat. Hadja stared at me for a second and then hurried off to call for help. An African woman bustled in and made me sit up. "*Ça va* (You okay)?" she asked calmly.

"Why aren't I dead?"[10] The question escaped me before I had time to think.

The nurse's face softened. *"Honey, you'll get better. You mostly lost blood and they had to remove two pieces of shrapnel. You'll be fine. Now let's take out your feeding tube and bring you something solid."*[11] She patted my hand and shuffled out of the room leaving the door open.

Hadja, who stood by the side of my bed studying me, was now my sister though I hardly knew her. *"Do we have any news of Djahida or Othmane?"*[12] I asked.

Her soft oval face crumpled up in sorrow. *"Othmane's dead,"*[13] she cried.

"How?"[14] I choked.

She looked at me with the first signs of accusation. *"He killed himself in prison."*[15]

Fear ran up my chest as I remembered my dream. Had it been real? Was Mokhtar's ghost out to kill me? I began to tremble. The floor nurse then entered the room pushing a cart loaded with medical supplies. She brushed a strand of hair away from my face and said, *"Don't worry,"* in a singsong as she put on some latex gloves, *"I'm going to take the feeding tube out but it won't hurt."*[16]

I felt like vomiting when the nurse began to pull on the disgusting tube and it came slithering out. She then handed me a tissue but my left arm was held in a cast so I had to blow my nose with just one hand.

"Don't move and we'll bring you something to eat in a few minutes,"[17] the nurse said over her shoulder before leaving.

I looked back at Hadja's quiet stare. *"You know why I told the police?"*[18] I asked her, in a voice that wouldn't go above a whisper.

"I know that Mom has lost her two sons. She only has Mustapha left and we both know he won't ever be worth the two others."[19]

I almost yelled that Mustapha was worth more than both combined but then I remembered that Othmane had saved me from Mokhtar in my dream. Maybe there was some good in him.

"She'll forgive you but for the moment she's rather upset," Hadja sighed and gave me a kiss on the cheek. *"I have to go. I'll tell Mom that you're awake."*[20]

She whisked out of the room, shut the door quietly and I was left with nothing but the white ceiling to stare at. My shoulder and leg throbbed and my back itched. Finally a woman aide bustled in and set a food tray in front of me. *"Be careful eating and swallow slowly,"*[21] she said, while I inspected the bowl of what looked like dishwater. I nodded and sipped. It tasted worse than it looked.

* * *

I spent the next day staring at the paint chipping in the corner of the ceiling while Mother observed me out of the corner of her eye and sewed. A medical aide came to put the bed in a sitting position before the cup of lukewarm tea was served for breakfast and I was able to count the number of stitches. Mother made no effort to utter a word, probably thinking I couldn't speak. The nurse came by from time to time to give me a shot and inspect my bandages. That was all the excitement I was going to get.

I wasn't allowed out of the bed, even to use the toilet. As far as I understood, a tendon had been damaged in my shoulder and shrapnel had lodged itself in the femur. Both were immobilized and the doctor hedged when speaking about the long-term sequelae to Mother. I looked at her and wondered if the situation was not to her liking.

Mother left early in the afternoon and I had to go back to observing the chipping paint before confronting the hospital soup alone. Luckily a spider started building its web on the opposite wall after dinner and I could watch her swinging back and forth until I got drowsy and—

Mokhtar was standing at the foot of my bed with a snarling

smile. My muscles contracted wanting to flee. Pain shot up from my leg making me scream and fall to the floor. I caught a glimpse of Mokhtar laughing just before the nurse came running in.

They put it down to PTSD. A psychiatrist, a young man I didn't know, spent a good half hour asking if I wanted to talk. Just for argument's sake, I told him that it had been Mokhtar's ghost who had frightened me. His straight-faced nod was meant to humor me but I could see he thought I was off my rocker. When I asked to talk to Dr. Moulin, the young woman psychiatrist, he said she was out of town and upped my dosage of anxiolytics.

* * *

When a knock woke me up the next afternoon and Kim peeked around the door, I let out an embarrassing squeal while she rushed over to kiss me on both cheeks. Quincy followed patiently and shook my hand. My heart sank. "He can't stay here in France, you know that," Kim said, as the tears began flowing and Quincy sat in a chair looking miserable.

Thankful for the heavy doses of happy pills, I did my best to act cheerful while Kim told me about getting out of the hospital and her afternoon shopping, but my eyes kept going back to Quincy. I tried not to look accusing. If he wanted to go back to that bimbo in the States, who was I to stop him?

"Neïla, it wouldn't be fair to you," Quincy said, looking me in the eyes. His were so blue I felt twice as miserable. "We both know I have to go back home one of these days."

"But there's no more danger now that Mokhtar is in prison," I argued, wishing he would take me into his arms.

Quincy looked away and shook his head. "My life is back there . . . I mean, you know how much I feel about you but . . . I never wanted you to think that—"

"Quince, why don't you go see the nurse about the TV?" Kim

suggested, with a glare in his direction.

Quincy stood up and was about to head for the door but at the last second he turned around and came to give me a kiss on the cheek. The laceration between my breasts and on my stomach began to itch while Quincy slipped out the door.

Kim stroked my hair until I stopped sobbing. "Don't be too angry at him," she said soothingly. "He's almost as miserable as you. It's his parents who insisted he go home and . . ." her eyes darted away.

"He talked to his parents about me?" I asked surprised.

"I've known Quincy since high school," Kim held my hand and added, "but don't worry; we've always been just friends. His parents would have liked us to get together, and his father can be very persuasive, but it just wouldn't work out."

"What does his father do?" I asked, out of curiosity.

"Different things. His passion is antique cars." Her hand brushed my hair back tenderly and she whispered, "But he found out you're only sixteen and . . ." Her voice faltered as she looked me in the eyes. "They don't want him dating an Arab girl."

My stomach and solar plexus began to burn where Beatbox had cut me. "And especially not one whose brother . . ." I was unable to finish my sentence because it seemed like I heard a bass beat surrounding me. I then noticed Kim's face screw up in pain. "It still hurts you too?" I stated more than asked.

Kim looked at me surprised. "It burned last night where he sliced me. It burns now." She shook her head with a sob. "The doctor says it's psychological and . . ."

She didn't finish her sentence but I understood what she meant. "Does it burn more now that he's dead?" I asked, as calmly as possible, even though I could have sworn I heard syncopated laughter.

"It was horrible that night and I didn't even know he had died."

I closed my eyes wishing the pain away while mist swirled up around me. I could clearly make out the bass beat. *"Beat it, you bastard!"*[22] I screamed.

The bass beat got louder and suddenly Mokhtar lunged for me but . . . My eyes met Kim's worried stare. "What happened? Are you all right?"

My heart was beating too fast to stay calm. "He was here. They were here," I stuttered.

"Who do you mean 'they'? You can't mean 'he' . . ."

I took hold of her hand and held it as tight as I could. "They are dead, both of them. Their ghosts are still here though. I can sometimes see them."

She looked at me as if I had gone off the deep end. "That's not possible. Your brother's in jail."

"I don't think the person they arrested is the real Mokhtar."

Kim smiled solicitously. "Neïla, honey, the doctors are right. You've just been through too much."

I lay back in bed defeated while Kim glanced at her watch and made an excuse to leave. The slash no longer throbbed so I knew that Beatbox had left. God forbid that he should ever find another body.

1 "Je savais que tu étais un ange. Je te pardonne. Maintenant, fuis!"
2 "Comment vas-tu? Est-ce que tu m'entends?"
3 "Oui, ça va."
4 "J'ai appelé l'infirmière. Elle voulait savoir quand tu te réveillerais."
5 "Je sais pas pour ton ami mais notre frère a été salement touché au foie."
6 "Il se meurt?"
7 "Non, Ils disent qu'il va s'en sortir. Tu t'inquiètes pour lui?"
8 "C'est mon frère."
9 "Il va passer sa vie en prison, tu sais?"
10 "Pourquoi j'suis pas morte?"

11 "Chérie, vous allez récupérer. Vous aviez surtout perdu du sang et Ils ont dû vous enlever deux éclats de grenade. Tu iras mieux. Maintenant on va vous enlever la sonde et vous apporter à manger."

12 "On a des nouvelles de Djahida où Othmane?"

13 "Othmane, Il est mort."

14 "Comment?"

15 "Il s'est tué en prison."

16 "Ne vous inquiétez pas, chérie. Ca ne fait pas mal."

17 "Ne bougez pas et je vous amène à manger dans quelque minutes."

18 "Tu sais pourquoi je l'ai dit à la police?"

19 "Je sais que maman a perdu ses deux fils. Il ne lui reste plus que Mustapha et on sait qu'il ne vaudra jamais les deux autres."

20 "Elle te pardonnera mais pour l'instant, elle est plutôt bouleversée. Je me sauve. Je dirai à maman que tu es réveillée."

21 "Attention en mangeant et avalez lentement."

22 "Casse-toi connard!"

Chapter 35

I was so afraid of Mokhtar's ghost that I avoided sleeping. With the heavy doses of medication, however, it was nearly impossible and I would wake up with a start before my eyes closed again as I drifted off.

The psychiatrist was intrigued by this new sleep dread, that he called hypnophobia, and sat there straight-faced while I did everything possible not to close my eyes. Why wouldn't Dr. Moulin come back? At least she didn't make me feel like I had lost all contact with reality.

I discovered during my attempts to stay awake that Quincy had paid for the TV and I soon became an addict. No soap opera was too idiotic for me to watch. I rationalized that it was better crying over fictional characters than over getting jilted by Quincy. Tears ran down my cheeks anyway.

The police came by to question me twice but they seemed only vaguely interested in what I had to say. I asked if I would be able to talk to Mokhtar and got a definitive "no." I looked up at their hard faces. They didn't seem to think that I was as innocent as I had hoped.

None of Neïla's friends paid me a visit and Pauline was the only person from school to come to see me. She was still just as eccentric, voluble, yet kind-hearted and I found myself warming to her while she gave me a facial and "a kiss from Franck." I also received a card that all the teachers had signed, including Mme. Lumière. Her hypocrisy made me sick and I never wanted to go back to that school if she were still there.

Mother arrived the next day with a wheelchair. She handed me a hijab and observed me while I struggled to put up my hair with only one hand. She finally grunted and came over to help. There was a knock and the doctor entered. *"We must let you go home. Your mother will take care of you,"*[1] he said, with a tentative smile.

I shook my head—I was helpless if she decided to beat me like Othmane had done—but the doctor was already leaving and with Mother's hard eyes glaring at my back, I kept quiet. This time I wouldn't be able to run.

A nurse came to help me into the wheelchair while Mother stuffed my clothes into a bag. The nurse was very gentle but every movement sent pain shooting through my shoulder. Mother then hung my bag on the back of the wheelchair and pushed me down the hall without giving me time to say goodbye to any of the medical staff.

I got a friendly smile from a bald man in the elevator, but mother frowned when I nodded to him. With a *ding*, the door slid open and she pushed me straight past the people drinking coffee at the kiosk, through the automatic door and outside into a cold drizzle. I stared at a man and a woman standing arm in arm, laughing at a shared intimacy, and got raised eyebrows. Mother turned left along the narrow sidewalk when we reached the street and barely slowed down at the corner. The wheelchair fell over the curb.

Pain shot through my arm and into my head while black dots began swirling in front of me and I heard Mokhtar's hyena laugh. I opened my eyes quickly. A nicely dressed man in his sixties was standing in front of me offering to help. It came to me that I had been screaming.

"Why didn't you use a medical transporter?"[2] the man asked, as he pulled me up the opposite curb.

He didn't get a reply from Mother who simply pointed at Othmane's car halfway down the street. It was parked with its back wheel on the sidewalk. The man pushed me up beside it and looked at the cast on my leg.

"She'll never fit in the front seat,"[3] he said, with a shake of his head.

An impassive nod was Mother's only reaction before she

pushed past him to open the back door. The man raised an eyebrow and I would have apologized if it weren't for mother's icy stare against my back.

With a sympathetic smile, the man helped me stand on one leg and hop to the car. His arm felt comforting around my shoulders and I held myself tightly against him as I sat down backward in the car with mother pulling me in from behind. I was as clumsy as a tortoise but the man smiled at me compassionately while I lay with my head against the door. Even though he wasn't very handsome, I wished he would hold me again.

"Merci," I said quietly, before I blushed and looked away.

"De rien (It was nothing)," he answered and went to help mother fold the wheelchair and heave it into the trunk.

I had never seen mother drive and had always assumed she didn't have her license. When she stalled the car pulling out, I knew I'd been right. I kept my comments to myself, however, seeing as Neïla didn't have a license either. When horns honked, or when she braked suddenly, I would brace myself for a shock because from my prone position, I couldn't see what was happening.

My shoulder ached, my leg throbbed and I was certain we were going to end up getting pulverized by one of those trucks on the *périférique* so I stared at the dome light, wishing my mind wasn't so muddled by those drugs, that my eyelids weren't so heavy that they closed. Just for a second, the calm felt so good that . . . a grenade exploded throwing burning metal through my arms and chest. I was screaming in pain.

"Neïla, calm down, easy," a boy was saying though the open car door. *"We didn't want to scare you."*[4] I recognized the boy with the melancholic smile.

Another boy came up behind him. *"Dumb ass, don't you know she nearly snuffed her brother?"*[5] He then looked at me and his eyes were Mokhtar's with that mocking smile. I heard Neïla scream—no, I was screaming—until a sunray filtered through the ghost and worried faces reappeared.

"Seriously Neïla, we're not going to hurt you. Your mother just wanted us to help you out of the car."[6] The first boy's melancholic smile had screwed up into worried compassion.

I wasn't well at all. *"Désolée* (Sorry)," Neïla's fluty voice uttered. Was this her life or mine? I was floating again while the two boys stared at me.

"Don't be afraid,"[7] the first boy murmured.

My heart was beating too fast. *"I don't even know your names."*[8] I stuttered. They stared at me as if I were a specter, and with their eyes wide, they looked so funny that I smiled. Neïla smiled.

"I'm Hachem." The first boy's melancholic smile was now genuine. *"And he's Momo."*[9]

Momo pushed in front. *"I'm really sorry to scare you. Why did you scream like that?"*[10]

My smile faded. *"It wasn't you,"*[11] was all I could mutter.

"So can we help you or do you want to keep lying there in that jalopy?"[12] Momo asked, without approaching farther.

I felt bad about having frightened them. *"No, I'm sorry Momo. It's me. I'm truly grateful for the help."*[13]

The two boys lifted me gently from the car and sat me in the wheelchair they had taken from the trunk. Although the drizzle had stopped and a weak sun had pushed through the chill, Hachem put his jacket over me before he shut the car door. Momo continued his dialogue and jokes.

"Is it true what they say?"[14] Momo asked, while Hachem pushed the wheelchair.

"Can't you see you shouldn't ask her questions?"[15] Hachem shot back in a loud whisper. I turned my eyes up to Hachem in gratitude. He squared his shoulders and pushed me to the entranceway.

Our local dealer stowed his bills away when the door opened and gave me his crooked macho smile as he swaggered over to exchange hand slaps with Hachem and Momo. They whispered a few words that I couldn't hear before coming over to stand in front of me. Their serious looks were frightening.

"*Écoute* (Listen)," the dealer began. "*We're not going to blame you for what you did. You couldn't let that guy touch you, converted or not. It's just a shame for your brother.*"[16]

I tried not to think about what would happen if they ever discovered that I had turned Neïla's brother in to the police. I whispered "*merci*" to the dealer and then dared the embarrassing question. "*What is your name, sir?*"[17]

He gave me a wink and a smile. "*Karim, and no need to be formal; we went out together in eighth grade.*"[18]

Momo's honking laugh earned him a disapproving snort from Hachem. "*Come on Neïla, I'll take you upstairs,*"[19] Hachem whispered as he pushed me toward the elevator with the other two chuckling at our back. I looked over my shoulder at Hachem in gratitude and his light brown skin turned dark red.

"*Merci,*" I whispered and touched his hand. It was rough but sent a tingle through my belly and neither one of us moved until the elevator door opened with a *ting*. The odors that wafted out, however, immediately spoiled the atmosphere and the grating noises from the machinery did nothing to reassure me.

"*We don't take it often,*"[20] Hachem said curling up his nose.

I remained quiet with my good hand holding his while the elevator door opened and Arabic music whined out of the second apartment on the right. Hachem began pushing me down the hall and I glanced up at his yellowish-brown eyes realizing that Neïla must have liked him. Unfortunately, she was in prison now. "*Are you alright, Neïla?*"[21] Hachem asked.

I wanted to tell him I was fine but my mouth replied, "*I'm scared.*"[22]

There was a moment of hesitation. "*You shouldn't be angry at Momo, he's always like that,*"[23] Hachem replied.

I had to shake my head; Momo had never done anything to me. He simply reminded me of Mokhtar. "*No, I'm scared of coming back here."*[24]

Hachem stared at me for a second and then finished pushing me to Neïla's door. *"Come on, your mother won't hurt you,"*[25] he whispered. I grabbed his hand again and squeezed while he walked around my wheelchair to knock. The sound was hollow against the new plywood door.

"Come in,"[26] was yelled from inside.

Hachem pushed the door open and Mother stepped out of the kitchen, her face blank, unreadable. I looked over my shoulder at Hachem, who was backing away, and almost called to him but coughed instead. Mother then padded out of the apartment in her silver slippers and wordlessly pushed me through the door.

Mustapha was seated in the living room looking alone and scared but Mother didn't give us time to speak and immediately pushed me into Neïla's room. It was spotless but the cleanliness only highlighted Djahida's absence. Then I noticed the desk and that the computer had disappeared.

"Who do you think paid for it?"[27] Mother sneered.

I looked up at her surprised. *"You knew that Mokhtar was trafficking arms?"*[28]

She scoffed. *"We may have social housing but do you really think we can survive on my salary alone? You wanted makeup and clothes and didn't complain when Mokhtar gave you money. If you had wanted a new cell phone, you should have asked your brother."*[29]

Neïla had known about his activities, but unfortunately Mokhtar had never given anything freely; she had paid with her life. *"What did you do with the computer?"*[30] I asked, pointing to the empty place on the desk.

"I gave it to your cousins,"[31] Mother snorted.

"And how am I going to do my homework?"[32] I asked, with a whine that slipped in unbidden.

Mother stared straight at me without blinking. *"You're not going back,"*[33] she replied flatly. Then very slowly a smile, Mokhtar's smile spread across her lips and my body began trembling.

"You don't have the right,"[34] I protested weakly.

*"You're the one who no longer has any rights. Mokhtar is in prison and it's going to be the same for you. I had hoped that after your accident—"*she snorted after saying 'accident'*"—we hoped that you would make a good wife. Now, we're not going to give you the choice. We're leaving for Algeria tomorrow."*[35]

Surprise and anger boiled up from my gut. *"You can't. I refuse—"*[36]

A slap across my face shut me up. *"How do you think you're going to stop me? You're completely handicapped. Worse than Mustapha, that poor little thing. Sometimes I'm ashamed to say he's mine."*[37] Her face contorted with suppressed anger.

I wished I could stay calm but my breathing was getting shallow. She looked at me and her face resumed its usual impassive mask. *"You're afraid of the prison there, aren't you? You know they're looking for you?"*[38]

"Because I killed my father?"[39] I stated naively.

She broke out laughing like Mokhtar. *"You really believe that?"* Her head shook and her expression became blank again. *"You were always his favorite, his little girl. You'd have never killed your daddy."* She sat down facing me while her hand reached out to stroke my cheek. *"I couldn't stand it. With your cute little smile, you had him around your little finger."*[40]

The slap startled me and when I opened my eyes again, Mother was pacing around the room. *"There was no arguing with him,"* she growled. *"He always took your side. You didn't want to wear the hijab; fine! You wanted to do your sluttish dancing; your father just smiled foolishly. You didn't want to marry my uncle's friend; he said you should be able to choose your husband."*[41]

After having spit out the last word, she sat on the bed to observe me in silence. I now understood why she had been angry when she found me dancing that one evening. Had she been forced into marriage and was that what made her so bitter? I began to utter the question but at the sound of my voice, she turned to me with so much hatred in her eyes that I held my tongue.

"No, you never wanted to do as you were told," she said quietly. *"So you see, I had to kill him—there was no other way—and everything worked out so well. They blamed you. You then had that accident and couldn't even remember your name. Mokhtar couldn't care and Othmane was too wrapped up in his prayers to see the truth. It should have turned out so well, if only—"*[42]

A sob ended her sentence. She turned away for a second, then looked back into my eyes and her face had become completely impassive. *"But now you'll take the blame and go to jail,"* she stated flatly. *"Unless of course you marry the man I've chosen."*[43]

My head was shaking. I began shaking. Never would I choose between prisons.

Mother grabbed my hair and forced me to look at her. *"Your father's mother was Moroccan—I knew I shouldn't have married a Moroccan—Moroccan women are all sluts."*[44]

Her eyes drifted before she looked back at me accusingly and hissed, *"Your father didn't like Mokhtar's trafficking either. You arrived and found your father just in time to try and stop the bleeding. Mokhtar knew you weren't involved, but he was too thrilled at being able to corner you. You got scared and put yourself in a bind."*[45]

"But what about all you said concerning the duties of a wife?"[46] I stammered.

"Your father was no longer good for anything: unemployed and sick. Look at the last son he gave me. That isn't a son!" Her face screwed up with anger and pain. *"And you took the two that I loved."*[47]

I saw the blow coming but with my casts, there was no way to avoid it. The second one made my vision blink out. When I came back to my senses, she was standing in front of me holding one of Djahida's belts.

"You are so pretty." The belt whipped across my face with a sting and it felt like blood was running down my cheek. *"They say*

you look more Moroccan than Algerian." The belt came at me again and caught me across the neck. *"A real slut. I can't believe I was the one who gave birth to you?"*[48]

She had changed into Mokhtar—her grin cocked sideways engagingly, but her eyes remained empty—and I began screaming, *"You're not my mother."*[49]

She stared at me open-mouthed but then her eyes turned to snakelike slits. *"So who is your mother?"*[50]

"I don't know any longer,"[51] I replied hoping she would drop the subject.

"Well I think that you're not my daughter. My daughter would never have done what you did."[52] She grabbed my chin and her eyes bore into mine until I closed them. So she slapped me, and slapped me again, and again, until my head was spinning and Mokhtar was standing in front of me.

"You aren't Neïla," Mokhtar was saying. *"I don't know who you are but you're not one of the family."*[53]

I swung at him with my good arm but his grin shot back at me and anger fogged my brain.

"You're just a murderer, a monster," Josh hollered in English. "I'm glad I'm not one of your family. You killed me and you might as well have killed her."

The fog suddenly cleared and Mother was staring at me like at some horrible stain on her Jilbab. *"So it's true. The doctors told me that you thought you were somebody else, but I didn't believe them."*[54]

As she began unrolling the scarf from around her neck, I wanted to protest but the words came out in short shallow breaths. When I tried to scream, my head started spinning. Her smile was in every way Mokhtar's. *"I now know that you aren't my Neïla. Maybe she's dead. Maybe you killed her. I don't care. You, for one, won't survive."*[55]

I was as helpless as a rabbit in a snare while she stepped behind me, wrapped the scarf around my neck and pulled it taut. My good hand ripped at it but my body went numb and little dots began to swirl in front of my eyes until I wasn't struggling any longer. I was too heavy. Among the dots Mokhtar's grinning face appeared. Then Espérence's calm smile drew my attention. I tried to call to her but she put her finger to her lips just before all went black.

* * *

My body buzzed while my mind fumbled. I had to do something. I couldn't just lie here. I heard talking and crying. The sounds echoed down a long tunnel and the swarm of dots converged into Mustapha who was petting my forehead.

Then Mother's voice stabbed at me and my body recoiled in pain while Mustapha held my good hand with force. He was stronger than I would have imagined. "No problem, calm, calm Neïla," he said, with his soft French accent.

I went limp, trembling and he pulled me gently against his chest saying, "*Ça va aller, ça va aller* (Everything's going to be fine)."

"Where am I?" My question came out fogged and muddled.

"Home," he replied. There was tenderness, pride and misery in his voice.

The shouting was interrupted by a loud smack. My eyes turned toward Hachem who was pushing mother back into the corner. Another voice sounded; Momo was standing at the door to my room and looking over at me with a crooked smiled. I smiled back but my lips quivered and a rush of pain—Neïla's pain, my pain, Mustapha's pain, all the pain—burned through me and I cried for real.

"*The cops are on their way,*" I heard a boy announce and looked over to see Karim standing next to Momo. "*You okay, Neïla?*"[56] His voice cracked in spite of his smile.

I fumbled for words through my muffled thoughts, but in the end, simply nodded while Mustapha pulled me in protectively.

"She's a murderer. She killed her father,"[57] Mother's voice screamed.

Mustapha's body tensed and he jerked to his feet, letting my head drop back against the rug. *"You were the one who killed him, you said so, you were the one . . ."*[58] he screamed while he pounded Mother with his good hand.

It took all of Karim's strength to pull Mustapha away while Mother scowled in silence and my head began to spin again. I imagined I heard Espérence's soft contralto voice say, "I told you they weren't all bad."

Hachem's hand touched my shoulder. *"Are you okay, Neïla?"*[59] he asked.

I nodded and he helped me sit against the wall.

"It was your brother who came to get us. I would never have believed it. I should have listened to you."[60]

I noticed a tear appear in the corner of his eye and run down his cheek before another one appeared. My hand reached out and wiped it away. I felt him shiver and his head turned slightly.

"Merci," I whispered. *"Thank you, really thank you. You saved me . . ."*[61] My words faltered.

"Hey bud, the cops are here,"[62] Karim said, with his hand on Hachem's shoulder.

Hachem stood up slowly and then police seemed to be everywhere. One was asking me questions while others handcuffed Mother. Voices from the living room echoed and paramedics appeared. I was carried to Mustapha's room and my pulse and blood pressure were taken. More questions were asked though I could barely whisper my answers. A gurney was unfolded and my limp body was lifted onto it. The elevator smelled horrible but once outside, a fresh breeze carried the smell of leaves and I heard the boys yell to me, *"Bonne chance, Neïla* (Good luck, Neïla)."

I waved to them before the ambulance door closed.

1 "On doit vous laisser rentrer. Votre mère va s'occuper de vous."

2 "Pourquoi n'avez-vous pas utilisé une ambulance?"

3 "Elle ne va jamais rentrer sur le siège avant."

4 "Neïla, du calme, cool. On voulait pas te faire peur."

5 "T'es con, toi. Tu sais pas qu'elle a failli buter son frère?"

6 "Neïla, sérieux, on va pas te faire du mal. Ta mère voulait juste qu'on te sorte de la voiture."

7 "Faut pas avoir peur."

8 "Je ne sais même pas vos noms."

9 "Hachem, moi. Et lui c'est Momo."

10 "Vraiment désolé de te faire peur. Pourquoi tu as crié comme ça?"

11 "Ce n'est pas vous."

12 "Alors on peut t'aider ou tu veux rester couchée dans la bagnole?"

13 "Non, je suis désolée Momo. C'est moi. Vraiment, je serais heureuse que vous m'aidiez."

14 "C'est vrai tout ce qu'on raconte?"

15 "Tu vois pas qu'il faut pas lui poser de questions?"

16 "On va pas te reprocher ce que tu as fait. Tu pouvais pas laisser ce roumi te toucher, converti ou pas. Bah, c'est dommage pour ton frère."

17 "Vous vous appelez comment?"

18 "Karim, et tu peux me tutoyer; on est sorti ensemble en quatrième."

19 "Va, je te monte, Neïla."

20 "On le prend pas souvent."

21 "Tu vas bien, Neïla."

22 "J'ai peur."

23 "Il faut pas en vouloir à Momo, il est toujours comme ça."

24 "Non, j'ai peur de revenir ici."

25 "Voyons, ta mère ne te fera pas mal."

26 "Entrez."

27 "Qui donc l'a payé?"

28 "Tu savais que Mokhtar trafiquait des armes?"

29 "On a beau avoir un logement social mais tu crois qu'on peut survivre qu'avec mon salaire? Toi tu voulais des maquillages et des vêtements et tu t'en plaignais pas quand Mokhtar te filait des sous. Si tu avais voulu un nouveau portable, il aurait fallu demander à ton frère."

30 "Tu as fait quoi de l'ordi?"

31 "Je l'ai donné à tes cousins."

32 "Et comment est-ce que je vais faire pour mes devoirs de lycée maintenant?"

33 "Tu n'y retournes plus."

34 "Tu n'as pas le droit."

35 "C'est toi qui n'as plus de droits. Mokhtar est en prison, alors avec toi, on va faire pareil. J'espérais qu'après ton accident.... On espérait que tu deviennes une bonne épouse. Maintenant, on ne va plus te donner le choix; on part en Algérie demain."

36 "Tu peux pas. Je refuse..."

37 "Tu comptes m'arrêter comment? T'es totalement handicapée. Pire que Mustapha, cette pauvre chose. Des fois j'ai honte de dire qu'il vient de moi."

38 "Tu as peur de la prison là-bas, n'est-ce pas? Tu sais qu'on te recherche?"

39 "Parce que j'ai tué mon père?"

40 "Tu crois ça? Tu étais toujours sa préférée, sa petite chérie. Tu n'aurais jamais tué ton père. Je ne le supportais pas. Avec ton petit minois, tu le tournais en bourrique."

41 "On pouvait pas discuter avec lui. Il était toujours de ton côté. Tu voulais pas porter le hijab; très bien! Tu voulais faire ta danse de pute; ton père souriait comme un idiot. Tu voulais pas épouser l'ami de mon oncle; ton père disait que tu avais le droit de choisir qui tu épousait."

42 "Non, tu ne voulais jamais faire ce qu'on te disait. Tu vois donc que je devais le tuer, il n'y avait pas d'autres moyens, et

tout a si bien marché. Il disait que c'était toi. Ensuite tu as eu cet accident et tu pouvais même pas te souvenir de ton nom. Mokhtar s'en foutait et Othmane était trop préoccupé avec ses prières de voir la vérité. Cela aurait dû marcher si bien, si seulement..."

43 "Mais maintenant c'est toi qu'on va condamner et envoyer en prison, à moins que tu épouses l'homme que je t'ai choisi."

44 "La mère de ton père était marocaine, je savais qu'il fallait pas épouser un Marocain. Les Marocaines sont toutes des putes."

45 "Ton père aussi n'aimait pas que Mokhtar fasse ses affaires. Toi, tu es arrivée juste au bon moment pour essayer d'arrêter le sang. Mokhtar se doutait que tu n'y étais pour rien mais il était trop content de te coincer. Tu as pris peur et tu t'es mise dans de sales draps."

46 "Mais tout ce que tu as dit concernant les devoirs d'une femme mariée?"

47 "Ton père n'était plus bon à rien: au chômage et malade. Tu vois le dernier fils qu'il m'a donné? C'est pas un fils ça! Et toi, tu m'as pris les deux que j'aimais."

48 "Tu es si jolie, toi. On dit que tu as l'air plus marocaine qu'algérienne. Une vraie pute. Et dire que c'est moi qui t'ai mise au monde!"

49 "Tu n'es pas ma mère."

50 "Alors, qui est ta mère?"

51 "Je sais plus."

52 "Mais je pense que tu n'es pas ma fille. Ma fille n'aurait jamais fait ce que tu as fait."

53 "Tu n'es pas Neïla. Je ne sais qui tu es mais tu n'es pas de la famille."

54 "C'est donc vrai. Les médecins m'ont dit que tu te prenais pour quelqu'un d'autre mis je ne les ai pas crus."

55 "Je sais maintenant que tu n'es pas ma Neïla. Peut-être elle est morte. Peut-être tu l'as tuée. Ça m'est égal. Toi, tu ne

vivras pas."

56 "Les keufs, ils arrivent. Ça av, Neïla?"

57 "C'est une meurtrière, elle a tué son père."

58 "C'est toi qui l'as tué, tu l'as dit, c'est toi..."

59 "Tu vas bien, Neïla?"

60 "C'est ton frère qui est venu nous chercher. On ne l'aurait pas cru. J'aurais dû t'écouter."

61 "Vraiment merci. Tu m'as sauvée."

62 "Les keufs sont là mon cheum."

Epilogue

On ne naît pas femme: on le devient. "You aren't born a woman: you become one."

—Simone de Beauvoir

Maman was on my back again about not making my bed. She still hoped to turn me into a proper young lady who didn't leave her covers in disarray and her pajamas thrown over a pillow. I listened patiently and refrained from making the excuse that my arm hurt while my two foster sisters turned their heads.

I knew they were giggling and when Maman had closed the door, I threw my pillow at them. Having to share my room with two girls was already difficult enough, but with two smart alecks, it was nearly unbearable. The pillow missed and knocked the lamp off of the bedside table. Their amusement doubled.

I had been considered an oddball ever since I arrived in the foster family. Tiffanie, the one who dyed her hair blond, was in beauty school and couldn't get over my refusal to look in the mirror while Christine was simply flabbergasted that I wanted to sing in the chorale.

"But only old people and losers sing that!"[1] she groaned.

"Stop bothering her," Maman would bark. *"You know she's still in a state of shock after what happened to her."*[2]

That just made me feel more like an oddball. My psychotherapist said I was suffering from a severe case of PTSD to avoid the word *psychotic* in my presence. "We have to speak more about reasons for you wanting to identify yourself with your aggressor," he had repeated. "You have no reason to feel any guilt for his being in prison."

"I don't feel guilty," I spat. "And I never want to go back to live with Neï . . . my family again."

"Your feelings are normal and the rejection of your pathological family is a sign of sanity," he would reply with a hint of a smile. "But you don't need to be self-destructive to the point that you assume a new personality. There are other ways to distance yourself from them."

I hated his logic and I would have stuck my tongue out if that could have gotten me anywhere. "Why do you insist on being so rational?"

"Why do you insist on speaking English? French is your mother tongue."

"So how did I learn such good English if my story isn't true?"

"You're an intelligent girl and you've had years of English classes. It doesn't surprise me."

I turned around and pouted. Josh would never have acted so childish but I no longer cared. A hand gently touched my good shoulder and Tiffanie sat down beside me. *"I'm sorry. I didn't want to make you cry. Here, would you like me to help you with your hair?"*[3]

Tiffanie loved playing with Neïla's hair and I should have been grateful, in spite of the blond streaks she had given me down either side, because it was almost impossible to comb it out with just one hand. It wasn't her fault that I was feeling in the dumps either, so I smiled and said, "merci."

Tiffanie gave a yip of delight and ran to fetch her tools while Christine made no effort to keep a straight face. She never tried to be nice and was clearly jealous that Tiffanie couldn't do anything with her crimpy hair.

"You're so pretty," Tiffanie chirped, as she began pulling at Neïla's long locks. *"Are you sure you don't want to look in the mirror while I do your hair?"*[4]

I knew I was getting myself into a bind but that was better than having to stare at the girl who went to prison to save me. *"No, I trust you,"*[5] I lied.

Tiffanie's simper turned into a squeal of joy at being able to do whatever she wanted and her hands went to pulling and twisting enthusiastically. It soon became clear, however, that things were getting out of control when Christine's sadistic chuckle turned to hysterical laughter.

"Why do you let them treat you like a dumb bunny?"[6] Mokhtar scoffed behind my back.

My whole body recoiled like it did each time he appeared. *"Screw off, you filthy bastard!"*[7] I shrieked.

His ghost evaporated just as the door opened and Maman shuffled in. *"What's going on . . . Oh, my God!"*[8] she choked, after one look at my hair.

"I haven't finished yet,"[9] Tiffanie protested.

"Yes, you have finished! Now put her hair back to normal this minute."[10] Maman spun on her heels and slammed the door

Wide-eyed, Christine stared at me. *"You saw him again, his ghost, didn't you?"*[11] she whispered.

Tiffanie snorted. *"She's just a little . . ."*[12] She was about to say *folle* (*crazy*) but she shook her head instead. I stared down at Neïla's tiny feet ashamed because I knew she was right.

* * *

The scene was so old-fashioned it was embarrassing, so I stared down at my bare knees while I concentrated on breathing slowly and Maman shooed my "sisters" out of the sitting room. Hachem, sitting on the edge of the armchair, kept his eyes glued to the Christmas tree. Why had I ever let Tiffanie convince me to wear a dress? I could smell Hachem's aftershave from where I sat on the couch but he had barely glanced at me.

"Are you angry that I'm in a family that celebrates Christmas?"[13] I asked.

The question seemed to startle him. "Non, non," he replied while his eyes met mine, widened, and he quickly looked back down at his teacup. I wished I could tell him that Josh's family had always put up a Chanukah bush and that Father would say

Christmas was a very healthy pagan holiday. I had been thrilled when Maman asked if I wanted to celebrate it with them.

"You know I don't want to be Muslim any longer?"[14] I whispered, and looked directly at him.

Hachem's fascinating yellow-brown eyes met mine and, for a moment, I didn't breathe. *"I'm Muslim but not Arab, you know. I'm Kabyle,"*[15] he mumbled. *"That doesn't make you angry either?"*

"Really, not at all,"[16] I sputtered. Josh would never have felt attracted to those eyes and I got nervous when he glanced at my dress. Tiffanie had spent the morning choosing it and dying my hair back to a shiny black. She had told me I would tear his heart out but now I just felt ridiculous so I turned my leg to hide the scar down my thigh.

"I think you're right to dress like the French girls,"[17] he stuttered.

"My brothers wouldn't have liked it,"[18] I replied, after a second's hesitation.

His eyes lifted with resolve. *"I never liked how they treated you."*[19]

I felt a tear begin to run down my nose. All that time he had been down there and if I'd stopped, just once, to talk to those boys and ask for help, maybe all of this could have been avoided.

"Merci," I whispered while my good hand reached out and touched his over the coffee table. "Merci," I repeated.

The pain, the scar between my breasts, began then and I felt like screaming at Beatbox to leave me alone. Instead I saw the worry in Hachem's eyes as he came around to the couch and I pulled him down next to me. His aftershave filled my nostrils, making the burning slowly subside, and I stayed curled against his body until Maman entered with more *petits fours* (cookies). She clucked her tongue but a smile twitched at the corner of her mouth.

* * *

"Why do you say that Josh would never have been attracted to Hachem?" my psychotherapist asked to my back.

"Because I was heterosexual," I spat over my shoulder.

"And you are afraid of those feelings?"

"No, I'm not!" I hissed spinning to face him. "It's just that Neïla—" I cut my sentence short before I got into trouble.

"Why do you always blame Neïla? You have a right to feel attracted to somebody or to be afraid without accusing her."

"But Josh wasn't . . . I mean he could control . . ." I was about to tell a lie and the psychotherapist's raised eyebrow told me he knew. I sputtered and sank back into the couch.

"Did you feel any attraction for Kim when you first felt the burning?"

"No, I didn't! I'm not—" My tongue almost slipped. I turned my back on the psychotherapist so that he couldn't see the tear forming in the corner of my eye. Still, I had to know.

"Is it true that I'm crazy?" I asked, looking back at him.

* * *

Everyone but Christine watched with good grace while Tiffanie cooed and squealed. Even though her father was still in prison, she had received the most presents. Neïla's "family" had sent nothing. All charges against me had been dropped but the judge didn't want me to have any contact with those involved. The medical corps was of the same opinion because I was thought to be too fragile.

Maman handed me a package from my two foster sisters and I ripped it open in a fury of Christmas spirit. It was a beautiful little dress not unlike the one I had worn for Hachem. Everyone got hugs and kisses on both cheeks.

Christine then opened our present with sullen joy. Tiffanie and I had picked out a portable speaker for her and she made a few happy rap beats with her mouth that sent a chill down my back. I tried to smile while she kissed me on the cheek.

Maman let Tiffanie open another gift before she handed me a small package. It was a new smartphone. I was sure that was Tiffanie's idea because she believed me to be handicapped without one.

"That way you can stay in contact with your friend, Hachem,"[20] Maman said, with a tender smile.

The thought of Hachem made me smile and I gave her a kiss on both cheeks before I sat down to inspect the little pink gadget and Tiffanie continued opening box after box. I was just coming to the conclusion that I would have to read the instruction manual when I noticed Maman was looking at me with a serious face. Even Tiffanie interrupted her spree.

"There's another gift for you. Don't open it if you don't want to," Maman said. She stood up and waddled to the buffet where lay a small box tied in a gray ribbon. *"It's from your brother,"*[21] she said in a low voice.

"Mokhtar?" I asked.

She nodded gravely.

My hands were shaking uncontrollably while I undid the ribbon and slit the tape open with Neïla's long fingernail. Inside, under the crepe paper, was a beautiful mother-of-pearl looking glass. I picked it up and stared at those beautiful eyes. They were mine, opening onto my soul, gleaming with tears.

Maman sat down beside. *"What did he do to you?"*[22] she whispered, and cradled me in her arms.

I shook my head and sniffled. *"No, I'm the happiest girl in the world."*[23]

1 "Mais il n'y a que des vieux et des nuls qui chantent ça!"

2 "Arrête de l'embêter. Tu sais qu'elle est toujours sous le choc de ce qui lui est arrivé."

3 "Je suis désolée. J'ai pas voulu te faire pleurer. Tiens, tu veux que je t'aide avec tes cheveux?"

4 "Tu es si belle. Tu es sûre que tu ne veux pas regarder dans le miroir pendant que je te coiffe?"

5 "Non, je te fais confiance."

6 "Pourquoi tu les laisses te prendre pour un bouffon?"

7 "Casse-toi sale con!"

8 "Qu'est-ce qui se passé... Oh, mon dieu!"

9 "Je n'ai pas encore fini."

10 "Si, tu as fini! Tu lui remets ses cheveux correctement tout de suite."

11 "Tu l'as encore vu, son fantôme, n'est-ce pas?"

12 "Elle est simplement un peu...."

13 "Tu es fâché que je sois dans une famille qui fête Noël?"

14 "Tu sais que je ne veux plus être musulmane?"

15 "Je suis musulman mais je ne suis pas arabe, tu sais. Je suis kabyle. Ca te fâche pas non plus?"

16 "Vraiment, pas du tout."

17 "Je trouve que c'est bien que tu t'habilles comme une française."

18 "Mes frères n'auraient pas aimé."

19 "Je n'ai jamais aimé comment ils te traitaient."

20 "Comme ça tu pourras communiquer avec ton ami, Hachem."

21 "Il y a un autre cadeau pour toi. Ne l'ouvre pas si tu n'as pas envie. C'est de ton frère,"

22 "Qu'est-ce qu'il t'a fait?"

23 "Non, je suis la fille la plus heureuse de la terre."

Roundfire

FICTION

Put simply, we publish great stories. Whether it's literary or popular, a gentle tale or a pulsating thriller, the connecting theme in all Roundfire fiction titles is that once you pick them up you won't want to put them down.

If you have enjoyed this book, why not tell other readers by posting a review on your preferred book site. Recent bestsellers from Roundfire are:

The Bookseller's Sonnets

Andi Rosenthal

The Bookseller's Sonnets intertwines three love stories with a tale of religious identity and mystery spanning five hundred years and three countries.

Paperback: 978-1-84694-342-3 ebook: 978-184694-626-4

Birds of the Nile

An Egyptian Adventure

N.E. David

Ex-diplomat Michael Blake wanted a quiet birding trip up the Nile—he wasn't expecting a revolution.

Paperback: 978-1-78279-158-4 ebook: 978-1-78279-157-7

Blood Profit$

The Lithium Conspiracy

J. Victor Tomaszek, James N. Patrick, Sr.

The blood of the many for the profits of the few… *Blood Profit$* will take you into the cigar-smoke-filled room where American policy and laws are really made.

Paperback: 978-1-78279-483-7 ebook: 978-1-78279-277-2

The Burden

A Family Saga

N.E. David

Frank will do anything to keep his mother and father apart. But he's carrying baggage—and it might just weigh him down ...

Paperback: 978-1-78279-936-8 ebook: 978-1-78279-937-5

The Cause

Roderick Vincent

The second American Revolution will be a fire lit from an internal spark.

Paperback: 978-1-78279-763-0 ebook: 978-1-78279-762-3

Don't Drink and Fly

The Story of Bernice O'Hanlon: Part One

Cathie Devitt

Bernice is a witch living in Glasgow. She loses her way in her life and wanders off the beaten track looking for the garden of enlightenment.

Paperback: 978-1-78279-016-7 ebook: 978-1-78279-015-0

Gag
Melissa Unger

One rainy afternoon in a Brooklyn diner, Peter Howland punctures an egg with his fork. Repulsed, Peter pushes the plate away and never eats again.
Paperback: 978-1-78279-564-3 ebook: 978-1-78279-563-6

The Master Yeshua
The Undiscovered Gospel of Joseph
Joyce Luck

Jesus is not who you think he is. The year is 75 CE. Joseph ben Jude is frail and ailing, but he has a prophecy to fulfil ...
Paperback: 978-1-78279-974-0 ebook: 978-1-78279-975-7

Readers of ebooks can buy or view any of these bestsellers by clicking on the live link in the title. Most titles are published in paperback and as an ebook. Paperbacks are available in traditional bookshops. Both print and ebook formats are available online.

Find more titles and sign up to our readers' newsletter at http://www.johnhuntpublishing.com/fiction

Follow us on Facebook at https://www.facebook.com/JHPfiction and Twitter at https://twitter.com/JHPFiction